MODERN CHINESE
FICTION

中國近代小說

MODERN CHINESE FICTION

*A Guide to Its Study and Appreciation
Essays and Bibliographies*

Edited by

**Winston L. Y. Yang
and
Nathan K. Mao**

With Contributions by

Howard Goldblatt
Joseph S. M. Lau
Nathan K. Mao

Michael Gotz
Peter Li
Winston L. Y. Yang

G. K. HALL & CO.

BOSTON, MASS.

HOUSTON PUBLIC LIBRARY

R0144014253
HUM

INDEXED IN *Balay*

Copyright © 1981 by Winston L.Y. Yang and Nathan K. Mao

Library of Congress Cataloging in Publication Data

Yang, Winston L. Y.
　Modern Chinese fiction.

　Includes index.
　1. Chinese fiction—20th century—Bibliography.
2. Chinese fiction—20th century—History and criticism
—Addresses, essays, lectures.　I. Mao, Nathan K.,
joint author.　II. Title.
Z3108.L5Y293　[PL2442]　　895.1′35′09　80-18322
ISBN 0-8161-8113-6

This publication is printed on permanent/durable acid-free paper
MANUFACTURED IN THE UNITED STATES OF AMERICA

Dedicated
to the Memory of
Professor Tsi-an Hsia
(1916-1965)

Contents

Preface	xv
Explanatory Notes	xvii
Chronological Table of Modern Chinese History	xix
Abbreviations of Frequently Cited Journals	xxi

ESSAYS

I. Modern Chinese Fiction: 1917-1949
   Howard Goldblatt 3
   1. The Period of Experimentation: 1917-1927 3
      The Beginnings 3
      Lu Hsün 5
      The Literary Association 7
      The Creation Society 11
      Communists and Independents 13
   2. The Period of Growth: 1928-1937 14
      Lao She 14
      Mao Tun 16
      Pa Chin 19
      Chang T'ien-i 21
      The Northeastern Writers 22
      Ting Ling and Shen Ts'ung-wen 25
   3. The War and Post-War Years: 1937-1949 27
      Fiction in the Nationalist Areas 27
      Communist Fiction 29

II. Chinese Communist Fiction Since 1949
    Michael Gotz 39
       Theoretical Principles of Literary Creation 39
       Industrial Production 42
       Land Reform and Agricultural Collectivization 47

       The People's Liberation Army in War and Peace 55
       Storyteller's Tales and Reportage 58
       Fiction and Politics in Contemporary China 62

III.   Taiwan Fiction Since 1949 67
       1. Pai Hsien-yung and Other Émigré Writers
          Winston L.Y. Yang 67
       2. Ch'en Ying-chen and Other Native Writers
          Joseph S.M. Lau 79

BIBLIOGRAPHIES

Part One: Bibliography of Sources in Chinese Literature
Peter Li and Nathan K. Mao 95

I.   Bibliographies and Other Reference Works 95

II.   Journals 107

III.   General Studies and Anthologies of Chinese Literature 113
       General Studies 113
       Anthologies 120

IV.   Chinese-Western Comparative Studies 123

Part Two: Bibliography of Modern Chinese Fiction
Nathan K. Mao and Peter Li 129

I.   General Studies and Anthologies of Modern Chinese Fiction 129
       General Studies 130
       Anthologies 150

II.   Chang Ai-ling (Eileen Chang) 155
       Translations 155
       Studies 156

III.   Chang T'ien-i 159
       Translations 159
       Studies 161

IV.   Ch'ien Chung-shu 163
       Translations 163
       Studies 164

V.   Lao She (Shu Ch'ing-ch'un) 167
       Translations 167
       Studies 171

VI.	Lu Hsün (Chou Shu-jen)	175
	Translations	176
	1. Translations of Individual Stories	176
	(1) "Ah Q cheng-chuan"	176
	(2) "Ch'ang-ming teng"	176
	(3) "Chu-fu"	176
	(4) "Fei-tsao"	177
	(5) "Feng-po"	177
	(6) "I-chien hsiao-shih"	178
	(7) "Ku-hsiang"	178
	(8) "Ku-tu che"	178
	(9) "K'uang-jen jih-chi"	179
	(10) "K'ung I-chi"	179
	(11) "Li-hun"	180
	(12) "Shang-shih"	180
	(13) "Ti-hsiung"	180
	(14) "Tsai chiu-lou shang"	180
	(15) "Yao"	181
	2. Anthologies with Translations of Lu Hsün's Works	181
	Studies	182
VII.	Mao Tun (Shen Yen-ping)	189
	Translations	189
	Studies	192
VIII.	Pa Chin (Li Fei-kan)	197
	Translations	197
	Studies	199
IX.	Shen Ts'ung-wen	201
	Translations	201
	Studies	203
X.	Ting Ling (Chiang Ping-chih)	205
	Translations	205
	Studies	206
XI.	Yü Ta-fu	209
	Translations	209
	Studies	210
XII.	Other Modern Writers	213
	1. Chiang Kuang-tz'u	213
	Translations	213
	Studies	214
	2. Hsiao Ch'ien	214
	Translations	214

3. Hsiao Chün (Liu Chün, T'ien Chün) 215
    Translations 215
    Studies 216
4. Hsiao Hung (Chang Nai-ying) 216
    Translations 216
    Studies 217
5. Jou Shih (Chao P'ing-fu) 217
    Translations 217
6. Lao Hsiang (Wang Hsiang-ch'en) 218
    Translations 218
7. Ling Shu-hua 219
    Translations 219
8. Lo Hua-sheng (Hsü Ti-shan) 219
    Translations 219
    Studies 220
9. Ping Hsin (Hsieh Wan-ying) 220
    Translations 220
    Studies 220
10. Sha T'ing (Yang T'ung-fang) 221
    Translations 221
    Studies 222
11. Shih T'o (Wang Ch'ang-ch'ien) 222
    Studies 222
12. Tuan-mu Hung-liang (Ts'ao Chia-ching) 222
    Translations 222
    Studies 223
13. Wu Tsu-hsiang 223
    Translations 224
    Studies 224
14. Yeh Sheng-t'ao (Yeh Shao-chün) 224
    Translations 225
    Studies 225
15. Other Writers 226
    (1) Cheng Nung 226
    (2) Chou Shou-chüan 226
    (3) Hsieh Ping-ying 227
    (4) Hu Yeh-p'in 227
    (5) Kuo Mo-jo 227
    (6) Shih I (Lou Chien-nan) 228
    (7) Ting Chiu (Ying Hsiu-jen) 228
    (8) Tung P'ing (Ch'iu Tung-p'ing) 228
    (9) Wang T'ung-chao 228
    (10) Yeh Tzu (Yü Ho-lin) 229

XIII. Communist Writers Since 1949 231
   General Studies 232
   Anthologies 241
   Individual Writers 243
      1. Ai Wu (T'ang Tao-keng) 243
         Translations 243
         Studies 244
      2. Chao Shu-li 244
         Translations 244
         Studies 245
      3. Chin Ching-mai 245
         Translations 246
         Studies 246
      4. Chou Li-po 246
         Translations 246
         Studies 247
      5. Hao Jan (Liang Chin-kuang) 247
         Translations 247
         Studies 248
      6. Kao Yü-pao 249
         Translations 249
         Studies 249
      7. Liu Ch'ing 249
         Translations 249
         Studies 250
      8. Liu Pai-yü 250
         Translations 250
         Studies 250
      9. Ma Feng (Ma Shu-ming) 250
         Studies 250
      10. Ou-yang Shan (Yang I) 251
         Translations 251
         Studies 251
      11. Tu P'eng-ch'eng 251
         Translations 251
         Studies 252
      12. Wu Ch'iang 252
         Translations 252
         Studies 252
      13. Yang Mo 252
         Translations 253
         Studies 253

xii/Contents

- 14. Yao Hsüeh-yin ... 253
  - Translations ... 253
  - Studies ... 254
- 15. Other Post-1949 Writers ... 254
  - (1) Ai Ming-chih ... 254
  - (2) *Annals of Revolution* ... 254
  - (3) Ch'en Teng-k'e ... 254
  - (4) Chih-hsia ... 254
  - (5) Ch'in Chao-yang ... 255
  - (6) Chou Erh-fu ... 255
  - (7) Ch'ü Po ... 255
  - (8) Hsia Chih-yen ... 255
  - (9) Hsü Kuang-yao ... 255
  - (10) Hu Wan-ch'un ... 255
  - (11) K'ang Cho ... 256
  - (12) Kao Yün-lan ... 256
  - (13) Li Chun ... 256
  - (14) Li Liu-ju ... 256
  - (15) Liang Pin ... 256
  - (16) Lin Yin-ju ... 257
  - (17) Lo Kuang-pin ... 257
  - (18) Lu Chu-kuo ... 257
  - (19) Ma Chia ... 257
  - (20) Pai Wei ... 257
  - (21) Shih Wen-chü ... 258
  - (22) Wang T'ieh ... 258
  - (23) Yang Shuo ... 258

XIV. Taiwan Writers Since 1949 ... 259
  - General Studies ... 259
  - Anthologies ... 261
  - Individual Writers ... 263
    - 1. Chang Hsi-kuo ... 263
      - Translations ... 263
    - 2. Ch'en Jo-hsi (Ch'en Hsiu-mei) ... 263
      - Translations ... 264
    - 3. Ch'en Ying-chen (Ch'en Yung-shan) ... 265
      - Translations ... 265
      - Studies ... 265
    - 4. Chiang Kuei (Wang Lin-tu) ... 265
      - Translations ... 265
      - Studies ... 266
    - 5. Ch'i-teng Sheng (Lin Wu-hsiung) ... 266
      - Translations ... 266

6. Chu Hsi-ning (Chu Ch'ing-hai)	266
Translations	266
Studies	267
7. Chung Li-ho	267
Translations	267
8. Huang Ch'un-ming	268
Translations	268
9. Li Yung-p'ing	268
Translations	268
10. Lin Hai-yin	269
Translations	269
11. Lin Huai-min	269
Translations	269
12. Nieh Hua-ling	270
Translations	270
13. Ou-yang Tzu (Hung Chih-hui)	270
Translations	270
14. Pai Hsien-yung	271
Translations	271
Studies	273
15. P'an Jen-mu	273
Translations	274
16. P'eng Ko (Yao P'eng)	274
Translations	274
Studies	274
17. Shih Sung	274
Translations	274
18. Shih Shu-ch'ing	274
Translations	275
19. Shui Ching (Yang I)	275
Translations	275
20. Ssu-ma Chung-yüan (Wu Yen-mei)	275
Translations	275
Studies	276
21. Tuan Ts'ai-hua	276
Translations	276
22. Wang Chen-ho	276
Translations	276
23. Wang Shang-i	277
Translations	277
24. Wang Ting-chün	277
Translations	277

25. Wang Wen-hsing 277
    Translations 277
    Studies 278
26. Yang Ch'ing-ch'u 278
    Translations 278
27. Yü Li-hua 279
    Translations 279

A Note on the Contributors 281

Index 283

Preface

Interest in Chinese literature, particularly modern Chinese fiction, has been growing steadily in the West in recent years. During the last twenty years, a large number of modern Chinese short stories and some novels have been translated into Western languages; many critical, theoretical, and historical studies of modern Chinese fiction have been published. This interest is evident not only among specialists in Chinese studies, but also among those of comparative and Western literatures, and, lately, even among the general public. Because of this growing interest, the need for a comprehensive guide to its study and appreciation has become evident. To fill this need and to enhance Western understanding of modern Chinese fiction, we have prepared this volume to parallel our *Classical Chinese Fiction: A Guide to Its Study and Appreciation, Essays and Bibliographies* (Boston: G. K. Hall, 1978), which has been well received and selected as an Outstanding Academic Book by the reviewing journal, *Choice*.

The present guide consists of two parts: essays and bibliographies. General in nature, the essays provide an introduction to modern Chinese fiction, and the annotated bibliographies provide further guidance to the reader. In addition, Explanatory Notes, a Chronological Table of Modern Chinese History, and an author and translator Index are provided. Limited to works that have appeared in English, all sections are designed in such a way that a knowledge of Chinese is not required to make full use of this book.

The book is intended for several types of readers, including students, teachers, scholars, and general readers interested in the study or appreciation of Chinese literature. The essays and the annotated guide to translations and studies should be very useful to them. In addition, scholars of Chinese or Asian humanities and those in comparative and Western literatures should find its listing of general and comparative studies helpful and illuminating. Librarians and bibliographers may use it as a guide in developing their world literature or Oriental studies collections or in helping their patrons locate reliable sources on modern Chinese fiction. Chinese literature specialists should also find its bibliographic section a handy reference tool because of its extensive listing of specialized studies. Nevertheless, this book is essentially designed for the general reader.

For the purpose of this book, modern Chinese fiction refers to the novels and short stories written since the Literary Revolution, which began in 1917. Though it covers Communist and Taiwan fiction produced since 1949 as well as the works written during the 1920s, 1930s, and 1940s, the emphasis is on the major novels and short stories of the last sixty years. A number of important works of fiction are not covered in the bibliographic section because few, if any, English-language translations or studies of them have been published. Some of them, however, are briefly mentioned in the essays.

Despite differing views on modern Chinese fiction, all the contributors have made great efforts to render their respective chapters as informative and helpful to the reader as possible.

Obviously, a book of this scope could not have been completed without the assistance and cooperation of many friends and colleagues. In particular, we wish to thank Professors Chi-Chen Wang and C. T. Hsia for their special encouragement and thoughtful assistance and the following for reading portions of the manuscript and offering valuable comments and suggestions: Professors Hsien-yung Pai, Timothy A. Ross, Chi-Chen Wang, C. T. Hsia, Donald Gibbs, and Victoria Cass. We should like also to thank Professors Joseph S. M. Lau, Peter Li (who did some preliminary work for the project at its early stage), Howard Goldblatt, and Michael Gotz for the chapters they have contributed to this volume.

We acknowledge the support and assistance of our respective institutions. Seton Hall University has provided one of us with a research grant, reduced teaching load, and a sabbatical leave for carrying on the project, and in particular we wish to thank Rev. Laurence Murphy, Dr. Richard Connors, Dr. Nicholas DeProspo, Dr. Bernhard Scholz, Dr. Barry Blakeley, and Professor Fred Wang for their assistance and encouragement.

We are also grateful to Mrs. Margaret Chiang for her excellent typing and to Mrs. Diana Rosen, Mr. Peter Acosta, and Mr. Alfred Sallette for their efficient help in proofreading.

Finally, our thanks go to our wives, Teresa and Melanie, and our children for their patience, understanding and encouragement.

In preparing this book for publication, Winston L. Y. Yang planned, designed, and edited the entire volume and wrote an essay on Taiwan fiction, while Nathan K. Mao, in cooperation with Peter Li, prepared the bibliographic section and edited the final version of the manuscript. Despite our divided responsibilities, we consulted each other often, worked closely together, and shared many hours of delightful and fruitful discussion. This book represents our cooperative effort, and since no book is ever perfect, we jointly share the responsibility for its deficiencies and errors. Comments and suggestions are welcome, and it is hoped that a revised edition will appear in the future.

The study of modern Chinese fiction has been strengthened in many ways by the significant contributions made by the late Professor Tsi-an Hsia. Before his untimely death in 1965, he had published a number of important studies. To his memory, therefore, we wish to dedicate this work.

Explanatory Notes

Arrangement. This guide is divided into two parts. Part I, consisting of four essays, provides an introduction to modern Chinese fiction. Part II, the bibliographic section, extensively lists translations and critical studies. In each chapter of the bibliographic section translations are listed first, followed by secondary sources. All entries are consecutively numbered.

Essays. Designed for the general reader, the essays provide background information on and some critical analysis of major works of modern Chinese fiction on the basis of recent Western scholarship. Introductory in nature, these essays are designed to enhance the reader's appreciation and understanding rather than to provide an exhaustive survey of the history of modern Chinese fiction or an extensive analysis of each work.

Principles of Selection. In general, the bibliographic section lists important and useful English-language studies and translations of modern Chinese fiction but excludes works of fiction in the original language, book reviews, and language textbooks. The emphasis of this guide is on translations and studies written in English in recent decades. Listed in this volume are books, monographs, journal articles, published and unpublished dissertations, lengthy review articles, reference books, general works on Chinese culture and literature relevant to the study of modern Chinese fiction, and comparative studies of Chinese and Western fiction. Though some items listed may not have a direct bearing on modern Chinese fiction, they are relevant to a general understanding of modern Chinese literature.

This guide lists selected publications of the last twenty-five years up to early 1979 and includes some earlier and forthcoming publications. Some important early 1979 publications are not listed because of their unavailability for examination; most items included have been examined personally by the compilers. Important items in major collections of essays and anthologies of stories are listed individually. More than 900 titles were chosen for their usefulness, quality, and availability. This does not suggest that all are equally useful, nor are all the translations and studies uniform in quality. Though efforts have been made to select good translations based on their readability and fidelity to the original, some clearly inferior selections are included because of the unavailability of better ones. In general, out-of-print titles are not listed, and whenever possible, information on reprints is given. To assist the reader in locating additional sources, such reference tools as specialized dictionaries, bibliographies, and biographical directories are extensively listed.

Form of Entry and Bibliographic Citations. The bibliographic entries include information essential to the identification of each title. With minor exceptions, author entries follow the general practice established by libraries in the West. One important exception is the listing of translations under the names of translators, but the translated work is usually identified by its author or title in the annotations. Studies or translations of unknown authorship are listed under their titles; Chinese writers better known by their pen names are so listed with references made to their original names in the index. Diacritical signs have been used only when necessary.

Abbreviations of Frequently Cited Journals. A list of abbreviations of journals frequently cited in the essays and bibliographies is given on pages xxi-xxii. For information on each journal, see Chapter II, Part One of the bibliographic section.

Annotations. Because of space limitations, annotations on studies, with some exceptions, are usually brief, descriptive, and informative rather than evaluative. The reader is urged to form his own conclusions on the strengths and weaknesses of each listed work. In an effort to provide guidance to the general reader, annotations on translations, in general, are more detailed and descriptive, often supplemented with critical comments.

Romanization of Chinese Names and Terms. Throughout this book, the Wade-Giles romanization system is used. For information about this system, see Winston L. Y. Yang, Peter Li, and Nathan K. Mao, *Classical Chinese Fiction* (Boston: G. K. Hall & Co., 1978), pp. xxiii-xxiv; or Robert Mathews, *Chinese-English Dictionary* (Cambridge: Harvard University Press, 1962), pp. ix-xvii.

Chronological Table of Modern Chinese History. The table includes only major events in modern Chinese history.

Cross References. Cross references refer the reader to additional sources. Major studies of more than one work, one writer, or one period are often listed more than once if necessary. References to additional titles are indicated by entry numbers.

Index. The index is primarily an author and translator index. In cases of unknown authorship and translators, the title is entered in the index. Writers better known by their pen names are so listed with references to their original names. Since all entries are numbered, cross references are indicated by entry numbers.

Chronological Table of Modern Chinese History

1912	Republic of China founded
1917-1919	Literary Revolution
1921	Communist Party of China founded
1925	Sun Yat-sen dies
1931	Japanese invasion and occupation of Manchuria
1937-1945	Sino-Japanese War
1942	Mao Tse-tung's "Talks at the Yenan Forum on Literature and Art" published
1949	People's Republic of China founded Nationalist government withdrawn to Taiwan
1950-1953	Korean War
1958	Hundred Flowers Campaign
1966-1976	Cultural Revolution
1975	Chiang Kai-shek dies
1976	Chou En-lai dies Mao Tse-tung dies Purge of the "Gang of Four"
1977	Modernization Program begins
1979	First Post-Mao Congress of Writers and Artists held

Abbreviations of Frequently Cited Journals

ArOr	*Archiv Orientálni*
AM	*Asia Major*
AAS	*Asian and African Studies*
BSOAS	*Bulletin of the School of Oriental and African Studies*
CQ	*China Quarterly*
CCul	*Chinese Culture*
ChL	*Chinese Literature*
CLEAR	*Chinese Literature: Essays, Articles, Reviews*
CP	*The Chinese Pen*
CHINOPERL	*CHINOPERL Papers*
EWR	*East-West Review*
HJAS	*Harvard Journal of Asiatic Studies*
JA	*Journal Asiatique*
JAOS	*Journal of the American Oriental Society*
JAS	*Journal of Asian Studies*
JCLTA	*Journal of the Chinese Language Teachers Association*
JOL	*Journal of Oriental Literature*

JOSA	*Journal of the Oriental Society of Australia*
JOS	*Journal of Oriental Studies*
JRAS	*Journal of the Royal Asiatic Society*
JRASHK	*Journal of the Royal Asiatic Society, Hong Kong Branch*
LEW	*Literature East and West*
MTB	*Memoirs of the Research Department of the Tōyō Bunko*
MAS	*Modern Asian Studies*
MC	*Modern China*
MCLN	*Modern Chinese Literature Newsletter*
MS	*Monumenta Serica*
OE	*Oriens Extremus*
RNL	*Review of National Literatures*
RBiblio	*Revue Bibliographique de Sinologie*
TR	*Tamkang Review*
THM	*Tien Hsia Monthly*
TP	*T'oung Pao*
THJ	*Tsing Hua Journal of Chinese Studies*

ESSAYS

I
Modern Chinese Fiction: 1917-1949
Howard Goldblatt

1. THE PERIOD OF EXPERIMENTATION: 1917-1927

The Beginnings

Modern Chinese fiction is a term which identifies the novels and short stories of China not only chronologically but also generically.[1] Chronologically, it covers the period from about 1917, the date generally accepted as the genesis of the so-called "Literary Revolution,"[2] to the founding of the People's Republic of China in 1949. Literature written after this period is generally referred to as contemporary rather than modern.

The "modernness" of the fiction from this period of slightly more than three decades can be seen in terms of its language, form, and content, all of which significantly broke with tradition. In terms of language, the new breed of writers set their sights on the creation of a literature which utilized the "national language" (*kuo-yü*); in other words, when read aloud, this literature ideally could be readily and unambiguously understood by anyone who spoke that dialect. It was called *pai-hua*, or "vernacular writing," and was a marked departure from the orthodox style of writing, *wen-yen*, or "literary writing," which was its predecessor.

The elegant, concise, and often highly ornate language of belles lettres had, over the centuries, remained more or less static, thereby becoming increasingly removed from the living and changing language of the people. The officially sanctioned and self-perpetuating monopoly on literacy which evolved proved to be a constant, though not wholly successful, block to the emergence of new literary forms and trends. In his 1918 article "Constructive Literary Revolution" (*Chien-she ti wen-hsüeh lun*), Hu Shih (1891-1962), philosopher, scholar, and vanguard of the literary revolution, wrote of China's literary tradition:

> I have carefully gone into the reasons why in the past 2,000 years China has had no truly valuable and living classical-style literature. My own answer is that what writers in this period have written is dead stuff, written in a dead language. A dead language can never produce a living literature....
> Why is it that a dead language cannot produce a living literature? It is

> because of the nature of literature. The function of language and literature lies in expressing ideas and showing feelings. When these are well done, we have literature. . . . If China wants to have a living literature, we must use the plain speech that is the natural speech, and we must devote ourselves to a literature of national speech. . . .[3]

As was true of many of the polemical writers of this period, all steeped in traditional learning, their zeal and commitment to new and exciting ideals led them to conclude that the only path to salvation was a total rejection of orthodox literary traditions—if the baby must be thrown out with the bath water, then so be it! There would be a number of reevaluations over the ensuing decades: some writers would consciously return to their traditional roots; others would see the products of these early years as nothing more than new wine in old bottles; while yet others would make serious and sometimes successful efforts to salvage the healthier babies from the discarded bath water.

The orthodox writings to which Hu Shih referred, however, did not constitute the only literary tradition, for from as early as Sung times (the tenth to the thirteenth centuries) a popular literature based primarily on the promptbooks of storytellers—both commercial and clerical—had evolved. The language in these works roughly approximated contemporary speech, so that the works could be understood (when read aloud) by virtually everyone. This countertradition gave rise to many literary masterpieces written by mavericks, but (and this takes us to the second aspect of our discussion) in new forms, such as drama and the novel.

The established literary corpus was composed of the classics (*ching*), which were the Confucian canon, the histories (*shih*), the philosophies (*tzu*), and belles lettres (*chi*). This latter category included but two broad types of writing, verse and essays—all else was heterodox. With the advent of fiction and drama nothing was changed officially, but the seeds for change were sown, for while the twentieth-century creators of the new literature were adopting whatever they could from the West, many simultaneously turned to China's own literary heritage for inspiration and models, specifically to works from this countertradition.

The content of modern Chinese fiction was directly related to the writers' concept of their role, which, simply stated, was as rebels and social critics. Most writers wanted to lead their generation away from the moribund Confucian traditions and into an age of national strength based on egalitarian principles. Thus, a new orthodoxy, critical realism, emerged to produce a highly politicized, often didactic, corpus of writings. The sense of mission of many writers would frequently be put to the test, and many would falter, but one thing was certain: never again would the novel be simply an intellectual exercise, a means of escapist entertainment, or an object of detached artistic beauty to be admired by a select few; it would be many things, but never those.

In 1915 the stage was set for a new age in literature when Ch'en Tu-hsiu (1879-1942), a founder of the Chinese Communist Party six years hence, published a journal called *Youth Magazine* (*Ch'ing-nien tsa-chih*), later *New Youth* (*Hsin ch'ing-nien*). In the inaugural issue (September 1915) he exhorted his readers to accept science and democracy and to turn against the "decadence" of traditional values and systems. After a prolonged and heated battle between *New Youth* and its old-school opponents, most prominently the noted translator and champion of the classical style of writing, Lin Shu (1852-1924), and the Harvard-trained professors who founded the magazine *Critical Review* (*Hsüeh-heng*), Mei Kuang-ti (1890-1945) and Wu Mi (1884-1939), Ch'en received support from Hu Shih, then a student in America. In "A Preliminary Discussion of Literary Reform" (*Wen-hsüeh kai-liang ch'u-i*),[4] Hu Shih made a number of concrete proposals for the reform of literature. In the following issue (February 1917), Ch'en responded with a strongly worded essay "On Literary Revolution" (*Wen-hsüeh ke-ming lun*), and the cultural revolution was launched. One year later (January 1918), the first literary offspring of this revolution appeared in *New Youth* in the form of nine vernacular poems, of which four were by Hu Shih.

Lu Hsün

Then in the May 1918 issue of *New Youth* three poems and a short story entitled "The Diary of a Madman" (*K'uang-jen jih-chi*) written by Lu Hsün (Chou Shu-jen, 1881-1936) were published. The poems have been forgotten, but the significance of the story, which received scant attention upon its initial publication, cannot be overstated: it launched its author on a career which would eventually establish him as the doyen of modern Chinese letters, and it must be considered the first modern Chinese story.

Indebted to the Russian writer Gogol for its inspiration, title, and, to some extent, form, "The Diary of a Madman" is nonetheless a highly original and innovative piece of writing. It is an indignant, devastating, and satirical attack on China's centuries-old cannibalistic morality, described through the fears of a "paranoiac" who believes that everyone, including his brother, is involved in a conspiracy to kill and "eat" him. In the often-quoted passage which follows, the diarist tells of his search through the cultural records of the nation to determine the source of the demon which stalks him:

> Everything requires careful consideration if one is to understand it. In ancient times, as I recollect, people often ate human beings, but I am rather hazy about it. I tried to look this up, but my history has no chronology, and scrawled all over each page are the words: "Virtue and Morality." Since I could not sleep anyway, I read intently half the night, until I began to see words between the lines, the whole book being filled with the two words—"Eat people."[5]

The story then ends with a passage which has since become nearly canonical:

> Perhaps there are children who have not eaten men? Save the children....[6]

With this plea, Lu Hsün is exhorting his readers to abandon the traditions that had blinded them to human suffering by promoting complacency and a sense of self-virtue.

A year passed before Lu Hsün's second story appeared, again in the pages of *New Youth*: "K'ung I-chi" is quite possibly the single most anthologized story from modern China. In this story Lu Hsün has written a moving tale of yet another victim of society, this one the product of an educational and civil-service examination system which has prepared him for nothing but a life of dead ends; from start to finish, however, he is incapable of facing the realities of his own degradation. K'ung I-chi, whose life epitomizes the "feudal" mentality which has taken China to the brink of annihilation, is, in the final analysis, a sacrificial victim and thus an object of pity as well as scorn. If his death symbolizes the demise of the system which produced him, it still elicits a sense of personal loss.

Lu Hsün's next story, "Medicine" (*Yao*), is one of equal emotive force, with the added dimension of symbolism. The medicine which figures in the shadowy but chilling opening scene of the story, the meaning of which is then revealed gradually and compellingly, is the warm blood of a victim of decapitation which is soaked up into a bun, then sold to the parents of a tubercular child. From this macabre and superstitious beginning the story goes on to relate the pertinent biographical details of the unwilling and unwitting donor of the "medicine," a revolutionary youth who was also the son of a village family. The medicine proves ineffective, and, in the final scene, inspiration for which came from the Russian novelist Leonid Andreyev,[7] the mothers of the two dead boys encounter each other at the graveyard where, through the use of various symbols, Lu Hsün questions the future of the revolution.[8]

In all, Lu Hsün wrote fewer than thirty short stories, twenty-five of which appeared between the years 1918 and 1925 and were collected in two volumes, *The Outcry* (*Na-han*) and *Hesitation* (*P'ang-huang*). Like the stories of the Russian realist Maxim Gorky, a writer whom he admired, Lu Hsün's stories are often peopled by the outcasts of society. Such is the case with his most highly acclaimed and popular work, "The True Story of Ah Q" (*Ah Q cheng-chuan*), a long story which began serialization as a comical piece, but soon evolved into one of the most devastating attacks on Chinese society and mentality ever written.

Ah Q is a village ne'er-do-well, the embodiment of the mental attitudes which allowed the Chinese to claim moral superiority as they stood passively by and watched one nation after another have its way with their country. A bully to those weaker than he but a sniveling coward in the face of greater strength, Ah Q is both contemptible and pitiable:

> If the idlers were still not satisfied, but continued to bait him, they would in the end come to blows. Then only after Ah Q had, to all appearances,

been defeated, had his brownish pigtail pulled and his head bumped against the wall four or five times, would the idlers walk away, satisfied at having won. Ah Q would stand there for a second, thinking to himself, "It is as if I were beaten by my son. What is the world coming to nowadays. . . ." Thereupon he too would walk away, satisfied at having won.[9]

In the final ironical sequence Ah Q first hopefully identifies himself with the revolutionaries, then is arrested on trumped-up charges and, with a final attempt at a heroic posture, is shot for a crime he did not commit. Many have debated the literary achievements of Lu Hsün, and though not all will agree on the greatness of "The True Story of Ah Q" as a piece of literature, few will deny its importance as perhaps the most influential story written in this century.

Following events of 1926-1927 Lu Hsün no longer considered himself a writer of short stories; he turned to other forms, most prominently the satirical random essay. Yet his contributions to fiction continued, both as the editor of a number of literary journals and as the patron of the new generation of novelists that emerged in the 1930s. In age, temperament, and reputation, Lu Hsün became the acknowledged spiritual leader of a generation of cultural iconoclasts, and to this day he remains the major figure in Chinese letters in the twentieth century.[10]

The Literary Association

One student of Chinese literature has written:

> There has been a marked tendency for Chinese writers to form societies and cliques, each publishing a manifesto of principles and controlling one or more magazines as an outlet for the writings of the group. The detailed history of modern Chinese literature is best organized around these societies, which include practically all of the writers of note.[11]

This statement is, in the main, accurate, though it requires elaboration. It is true that following the May Fourth Incident,[12] for reasons of economics, mutual support, security, and other considerations, groups of kindred spirits established societies under whose auspices magazines were published, translation projects undertaken, and the like. Furthermore, it is only natural to assume that there was some common bond, whether geographical, philosophical, or temperamental, among the founding members. Yet one must not be too quick to deduce that there was any unchanging sense of homogeneity among the members of these societies or that they were always successful in recruiting new members of like persuasions, for they were not only frequently beset by internal dissension, policy shifts, and changing memberships, but they were also often so loosely bound together and factionalized that pro forma membership with lip service to a particular ideal or advocacy was a common occurrence. Then too, one must not lose sight of the fact that many of these organizations were born of political realities rather than literary ideals, so that membership in one was a priori confirmation of one's nationalistic devotion and nothing more.

Yet in the period of experimentation immediately following the May Fourth Incident, literary activities tended to gravitate around three rather distinct foci: the Literary Association, the Creation Society, and a group of Peking University professors who published a magazine entitled *Contemporary Review* (*Hsien-tai p'ing-lun*).

The Literary Association (*Wen-hsüeh yen-chiu hui*) was founded in Peking in November 1921 by twelve professors, students, writers, and translators, with the modest goals of establishing contact among writers, promoting the new literature and reassessing the old, examining Western literary theories and output, and setting up literary guilds. It soon proved to be the most influential and longest-lived of similar associations, owing largely to its philosophy, which has generally been called "art for life's sake" (as opposed to "art for art's sake"), or realist (in contrast to romantic). Among the founders was a twenty-four-year-old editor and translator for the prestigious Commercial Press in Shanghai, Shen Yen-ping, who later wrote under the pseudonym of Mao Tun. At his urging, the Commercial Press relinquished editorial control of *Short Story Monthly* (*Hsiao-shuo yüeh-pao*), a magazine it had published since 1908, to the Literary Association, whose first order of business was to convert the magazine completely to *pai-hua*. Beginning with its first issue in January 1920, *Short Story Monthly* appeared continuously for eleven years, a rather phenomenal track record for a May Fourth magazine. For our purposes, it must be considered the most important publication of the decade, for although translations, scholarly articles, bibliographies, and book reviews graced its pages, fiction received its greatest attention and reached the highest standards of literary excellence. Among the Literary Association founders, Yeh Shao-chün, Wang T'ung-chao, and Hsü Ti-shan were the most important early contributors of stories to *Short Story Monthly*.

Yeh Shao-chün (1894-   ), who since the 1930s has preferred to be known as Yeh Sheng-t'ao, is one of a small group of writers whose careers spanned the entirety of the May Fourth and wartime periods. Among his large corpus of writings, the preponderant majority is in the short-story genre, nearly a hundred over a span of two decades, the first ones appearing even before the advent of *Short Story Monthly*. Like a number of his contemporaries, Yeh was an urban schoolteacher, but unlike so many of them, his choice of profession was dictated as much by temperament and dedication as by economic considerations. As a consequence, most of his stories are concerned with urban dwellers, particularly schoolteachers and other intellectuals, or children. His stories are permeated with a sense of the grayness and insecurity that best describe the quality of life of so many city dwellers in those trying times; his better works during this early period are descriptions of manners and social realities rather than of isolated incidents. Yeh Shao-chün, finding existing social conditions around him appalling, effortlessly, minutely, and sometimes ironically exposes these ills for what they are and what they do. In "A Posthumous Son" (*I-fu-tzu*) he uses the satirist's pen to attack the Chinese man's preoccupation with producing a male heir, a preoccupation for which he will sacrifice even his own wife. "Ah Feng," the all-too-common story of a girl who becomes a virtual slave in the home of her future husband, evokes not only sympathy from the reader, but also a sense of real moral outrage against a society which will allow such inhuman treatment to continue.

In 1926 the Kuomintang Party, under the leadership of Chiang Kai-shek, and with the cooperation of the Communists, launched the Northern Expedition (*pei-fa*) against the northern warlords as a means of unifying the country. In April of the following year, however, Chiang turned against his erstwhile comrades-in-arms in Shanghai in bloody retaliation for a series of strikes and political incidents, forcing the Communists underground, and at the same time driving large numbers of writers to the Left and well into the revolutionary camp. Yeh Shao-chün was one of these, and this pivotal historical period figures prominently in many of his stories: "Night" (*Yeh*), a tale of the wanton slaughter of rounded-up Communists on the execution ground; "The English Professor" (*Ying-wen chiao-shou*), in which this series of events proves to be the emotional undoing of the revolutionary protagonist; and Yeh's only full-length novel, *Ni Huan-chih*,[13] the first modern novel dealing with a revolutionary theme. *Ni Huan-chih* is about an elementary schoolteacher who travels to the countryside to implement pedagogical reforms, only to meet with resistance at every turn, until disillusionment drives him into the vortex of revolutionary activities in Shanghai. Initially buoyed by what he sees there, his enthusiasm is dealt a fatal blow by events of 1927. Ni Huan-chih's subsequent physical and psychological decline and his death keep the novel from earning the total approbation of leftist critics, while its story line and other elements keep it from being a great novel; nonetheless, as one of the earliest modern novels, it helped solidify its author's preeminence as a writer of fiction during the early May Fourth period.

Wang T'ung-chao (1898-1957), though not of Yeh Shao-chün's stature, was yet another Literary Association founder who wrote in the realist vein that characterized the Association. His earliest stories are collected in the anthology *A Night of Spring Rains* (*Ch'un-yü chih yeh*), first published in 1924. Though in the main unspectacular, his work enhanced the reputation of excellence enjoyed by *Short Story Monthly*.

Hsü Ti-shan (1893-1941), on the other hand, while outside the mainstream of realist writings, was unique in that he alone systematically wove religion into his fiction, analyzing and explaining its role in human existence. Hsü, who generally wrote under the pseudonym of Lo Hua-sheng, epitomized the experimental nature of this period; his best-known work is "The Vain Labors of a Spider" (*Ch'o-wang lao-chu*), the story of a saintly Chinese Christian woman living in the South Seas.

Among the other signal services performed by *Short Story Monthly* was the introduction of several women writers to an audience for whom the May Fourth catchword of women's liberation had immense appeal. Admittedly, the quality of writing by these pioneer women was often inferior and their themes melodramatic in the extreme, but their impact was substantial. Some, such as Lu Yin and Feng Yüan-chün, depended largely upon the emotional appeal of their soap-opera romances or the shock factor of sexual explicitness for their success; others, like Ling Shu-hua, while less daring, were far more sophisticated. For all, it was their exploration of the feminine psyche, particularly that of the young, educated woman searching for an identity and for a role in society, which insured their popularity.

Deserving of special note are Ping Hsin (Hsieh Wan-ying, 1902-) and Ting Ling (Chiang Ping-chih, 1907-). While Ping Hsin's most notable achievements were in poetry, she authored several highly popular stories that were particularly well received by adolescents and young adults. Her works are distinctive in several regards; unlike so many of her contemporaries, she was not given to verbal teeth-gnashings over the injustices of contemporary society. Because of her background as the sheltered and precocious only child of a wealthy and powerful military official, and her academic environment of missionary schools and American college, she was personally unfamiliar with the "oppressed masses" and was honest enough not to attempt to write of them. Another distinction of her work is that she had a solution for mankind's ills: she advocated a philosophy of love—love of parents, love of one's fellow man—and thus represents the sentimental tradition. The primary heroes of Ping Hsin's fiction are children and adolescents who are sometimes troubled and sometimes errant, but always salvageable. Occasionally, as in her well-known piece "The Superman" (*Ch'ao-jen*), a child is a force for simple goodness capable of converting even the most hard-boiled misanthrope.

Writing in an unpretentious style, with a repertoire of stock images (a mother's love, the stars in the sky, and flowers in the garden), and relying on a mixture of traditional Chinese virtues and teachings with imperfectly understood Western philosophies, Ping Hsin enjoyed considerable success through the decade of the 1920s, after which time she stopped writing creatively. According to reports, she is still active in children's literature.

In life-style and literary proclivities, no two women could be more dissimilar than Ping Hsin and Ting Ling, another early contributor to *Short Story Monthly*. Raised in a highly charged home environment (her mother was a political activist), Ting Ling represents the liberated, even bohemian, new woman. To her works she brought a boldness and candor which was virtually unprecedented, particularly since there is evidence that the heroines in her stories were often highly autobiographical.[14]

Fame came to Ting Ling with the publication of her second short story, "The

Diary of Miss Sophie" (*Sha-fei nü-shih ti jih-chi*), a frank confession of sexual desires, fantasies, and frustrations. Ting Ling was considered a leading subjectivist writer; her early stories generally focus on self-exploration and candidly expose personal feelings which so many of her readers had experienced but were unable to articulate. In "The Diary of Miss Sophie" the shock effect on contemporary readers was heightened by the unconventional and daring treatment of the subject of sex. The following passage, while reminiscent of the eighteenth-century European romanticists, incorporates an explicitness unheard of in that earlier age:

> Mar. 24—When he is alone with me, the sight of his face and the sound of his voice make my feelings rise. Why shouldn't I rush over to kiss his lips, his shoulder, all of him? Sometimes words like these are on my lips! "My Ling, let me caress you!" Yet reason—no, I've never been reasonable—say, self-respect—has always checked me. Ai! No matter how cheap or small his ideas, he has unquestionably turned my heart inside out. Why then do I refuse to acknowledge my love for him? And I'm sure, should he hold me firmly in his arms, should he surrender his body to my kisses and then throw me into the ocean or the fire, I'd wait for death contentedly—for it would forever preserve my love. Ai! I do love him! Only death at his hands would satisfy me![15]

As Ting Ling's political involvement increased over the next two decades her style of writing changed, though she continued to write of women—their struggles, their yearnings, and their roles in society.

The Creation Society

Thus far we have examined only the writings of the so-called realist school, authors associated with the Literary Association and *Short Story Monthly*. While it may not be inaccurate to say that they constituted the mainstream of early modern fiction, by no means did they monopolize the contemporary scene. Less than a year after the founding of the Literary Association, a small group of Chinese students in Japan established an organization with the express purpose of refuting the "art for life's sake" philosophy of the Literary Association and putting before the Chinese public its own romantic or "art for art's sake" ideal. One of the founding members stated their goals succinctly when he wrote: "I believe . . . that the single-minded pursuit of literary 'perfection' and 'beauty' is worthy of our life-long devotion."[16]

A diverse group despite its small size, the Creation Society was founded by a poet, two story writers, a playwright, and a literary theoretician, and it had an impact disproportionate to its small literary output. Unlike the Literary Association, the Creation Society did not remain static in its ideas; for three years after its founding, following the return to China of its members, the

Creation Society executed a philosophical volte-face, embracing Marxism, and the Society led the struggle for proletarian literature until it was banned in 1929. Of its original membership, neither of the short-story writers, Yü Ta-fu nor Chang Tzu-p'ing, would follow the society into its Marxist phase. And since Chang pandered to popular tastes with triangular and quadrangular romances in all their lurid details, only Yü Ta-fu will enter our discussion.

Yü Ta-fu (1895-1945) has long been considered the first practitioner of subjective writing, a story writer whose early works were filled with sentimentalism and decadence.[17] His characters are strikingly reminiscent of the Wertherian type in that they possess tortured psyches and are given to self-pity; the reader finds them rhapsodizing over the sensual pleasures of life one moment and agonizing over its cruelties the next.

Yü's first work, "Sinking" (Ch'en-lun), was a bombshell, for never before had sexual obsessions and frustrations been handled with such self-revealing frankness. Set in rural Japan, "Sinking" is the story of a lonely, melancholic, and romantically patriotic Chinese student who writes sentimental poetry and is obsessed with his own sexuality. The dual themes of personal inadequacy and national impotence touch at many points throughout the story, as in this outburst by the protagonist after an imagined rebuff at the hands of a Japanese waitress and the humiliating admission that he is in her eyes just another "Chinaman":

> "Bastards! Pigs! How dare you bully me like this? Revenge! Revenge! I'll revenge myself on you! Can there be any true-hearted girl in the world? You faithless waitress, how dare you desert me like this? Oh, let it be, let it be, for from now on I shall care nothing about women, absolutely nothing. I will love nothing but my country, and let my country be my love."[18]

The story ends as the hero releases one final *cri du coeur* to his beloved homeland before committing suicide:

> "O China, my China, you are the cause of my death! . . . I wish you could becomerich and strong soon! . . . Many, many of your children are still suffering!"[19]

The themes in "Sinking" struck a responsive chord with its younger readers, who keenly felt not only the demeaned status of their country in the eyes of the world, but also the psychological effects of his sexual acts on the hero of the story. Yü Ta-fu's stories, of which several volumes were produced in the 1920s, deal mainly with emotional states, the psychological processes experienced by his protagonists. Influenced, as were so many young people in China during those days, by Goethe's *The Sorrows of Young Werther*[20] (translated into Chinese by Yü's Creation Society colleague, Kuo Mo-jo), Yü most often employs the "I" narrator; his stories are thus highly introspective and heavily autobiographical. Even when he uses the third person narrator (as in "Sinking"), the influence of Goethe's "age of sentiment" is apparent, not to mention the evidence of autobiographical transference. Yü Ta-fu ceased writing stories after events of the late 1920s altered the political climate and the literature which mirrored it, finding his brand of fiction out of step with the changing times. He was reported to have been murdered in Sumatra in 1945 by the Japanese police.

Communists and Independents

During this early period two more writers, representing two opposite poles, appeared on the scene: Chiang Kuang-tz'u (1901-1931) and Shen Ts'ung-wen (1902-). Chiang's claim to fame rests on his early affiliation with the Communist Party and the fact that his works were the first major examples of proletarian literature. *The Youthful Tramp* (*Shao-nien p'iao-p'o-che*) is a 1926 novelette depicting social ills and revolutionary activities during a period of cooperation between the Kuomintang and Communist parties and is a prelude to his later, somewhat more ambitious examples of romantic-revolutionary fiction. The life and works of this controversial figure have been summarized by one observer thus:

> Chiang was the author of poetry, short stories, and several novels. None of his work has ever been recognized as having any enduring merit. He seems to be remembered more as a personality, an exemplar of so many of his fellows of the time, romantic, posturing, Byronic, persuaded of his own gifts but unable to write anything that would persuade anyone else, and unable in the end to reconcile the ego demands of his belief in his own genius with the superego demands of the Party and "the revolution."[21]

Of greater significance to any study of modern Chinese fiction is the independent author Shen Ts'ung-wen, whose short-story output was among the largest and most craftsmanlike of the modern period. A native of Hunan and a veteran of years of military life, Shen was a master of nature lyricism and a keen observer of life among the Miao tribespeople of Hunan and their Chinese peasant counterparts as well as of life in a military camp. Shen is commonly associated with the "Countryman," a term he himself used to describe both his background and his view of the world. One of the more widely traveled young writers within China, he had a true affinity for the people about whom he wrote. After coming to Peking in 1922 he began contributing stories to local newspapers and magazines, at first with little success. Eventually his talents were recognized by the so-called Anglo-American wing of writers, and he began to publish regularly in such literary organs as *Contemporary Review*. Inasmuch as the maturation of Shen's art would take several years with his finest work appearing in the 1930s, we shall come back to him later.

2. THE PERIOD OF GROWTH: 1928-1937

The second decade of modern Chinese fiction saw the twilight of some literary careers and the maturation of others, but it is most notable for the emergence of many new writers who brought with them the first experiments with the full-length novel and greater sophistication in all forms of writing, particularly in fiction. Many of these novelists had their works published first in *Short Story Monthly*. Most prominent among this group were three diverse talents: Lao She, Mao Tun, and Pa Chin.

Lao She

Lao She (Shu Ch'ing-ch'un, 1899-1966) was unique in several respects, including his origins (born a Manchu), his writing style (humorous, episodic, and written in pure Peking vernacular), and his political stance (decidedly independent and fiercely patriotic).

The genesis of Lao She the writer is well known thanks to his autobiographical writings and to recent research. After an impoverished youth he found employment as a schoolteacher and administrator, then journeyed to London where he taught Chinese to foreigners. It was during his stay in England, as he experienced strong feelings of homesickness, that he decided to record on paper what he saw in his mind's eye. Since he had recently read Dickens' *Nicholas Nickleby* and *The Pickwick Papers*, he consciously used them as models for his first novel, *The Philosophy of Lao Chang* (*Lao Chang ti che-hsüeh*), which was serialized in *Short Story Monthly* in 1926. Although Lao Chang, a mean and miserly schoolmaster and moneylender, is the protagonist of this frequently humorous novel, there are a number of occasionally converging story lines dealing with other characters, which lend the work the episodic style characteristic of most of Lao She's early novels. Yet with all its flaws of structure, characterization, and language (a mixture of modern, classical, and local), *The Philosophy of Lao Chang* holds the distinction of being modern China's first comic novel. What is more, its immediate and enthusiastic acceptance provided its author with the incentive to continue to write, which in turn established him as one of the most important and popular novelists of the century.

Lao She's second work, also written in England and published serially in *Short Story Monthly*, was another comic novel entitled *Chao Tzu-yüeh*. In this humorous satire the protagonist is in many respects a caricature of a segment of the Chinese population which Lao She personally detested—the students whose sole ambition was the accumulation of the trappings of officialdom with no thought to their responsibility to serve the common folk. The author's feelings come through clearly in the following passage:

> There are two great forces in the new society: soldiers and students. Except that they won't fight foreigners, soldiers give everybody three

lashes. Except that they won't fight soldiers, students beat everybody with their canes. Consequently, these two great forces march on in unison, giving people some idea of the "new militarism." If the soldiers who daren't fight foreigners did not oppress and maltreat the people, they would forfeit their title to soldiers; if the students who daren't fight soldiers did not beat the presidents, deans, and teachers, they would forfeit their right to be called righteous youth.[22]

Prior to leaving England in 1929 Lao She wrote and published *The Two Mas* (*Erh Ma*), a study of patriotism, racial prejudice, and the generation gap. The two Mas are a traditionalist father and his modernist son who have come to England to run a business; neither is the author's heroic ideal and both are subjected to sharp satirical barbs, the elder Ma for his blind acceptance of the superiority of China's tradition, the son for his inept, romantic-patriotic reaction to racial slurs against overseas Chinese.

After stopping off in Singapore for half a year, where he wrote a minor novel about the lives of Chinese school children, Lao She returned to China and, on the urging of friends, renounced his humorous writing style and turned to more trenchant attacks on Chinese society. The result was two serious works: *Lake Ta-ming* (*Ta-ming hu*, lost in manuscript form), a historical novel and tale of romance set around the time of the Tsinan Incident in 1928; and *Cat Country* (*Mao-ch'eng chi*), a thinly veiled satire set on Mars in which every unsavory aspect of contemporary China is paraded in its gross ugliness. One critic writes:

> The struggle between didacticism and creative impulse marks Lao She's works right from the beginning and one notices how the author often intrudes into his London novels to give some direct advice to his readers. *Lake Ta-ming* and *Cat City* [*Cat Country*] mark the stage when didacticism appears to have gained the upper hand in the struggle and creative imagination lost out.[23]

Lao She recognized this problem as clearly as his readers and critics, so he returned to a style with which he was more comfortable and created his finest work in the comic vein, *Divorce* (*Li-hun*), a much more tightly organized novel than any which preceded it and a penetrating study of men's and women's attitudes toward love and marriage.

Once he had returned to China Lao She began to subject his thoughts and ideals to a searching reevaluation. He had, from May Fourth on, clung to a belief in individualism, feeling that the fate of the nation rested on the personal actions of every man, woman, and child. But events of the 1930s, the general deterioration of the lives and spirits of the Chinese, and increasing Japanese encroachments began to raise doubts in his mind.

First evident in a slight novel written in 1936, *The Biography of Niu T'ien-tz'u* (*Niu T'ien-tz'u chuan*), his renouncement of his earlier beliefs and new advocacy of collectivism as China's true salvation formed the philosophical foundation of his magnum opus, *Rickshaw Boy* (*Lo-t'o Hsiang-tzu*).[24] Published serially in 1936-

1937, this work, in which Lao She reaches down into the lower classes for his hero, has given the reading public one of the most memorable fictional personae in the history of Chinese letters: Hsiang-tzu, a country lad of unwavering determination and seemingly incorruptible innocence who comes to Peking to earn his living by pulling a rickshaw. Giving unprecedented dignity to his profession, Hsiang-tzu single-mindedly strives for perfection in pursuit of his goal to own his own rickshaw. The plot of the novel is the continual frustration of his hopes, the corruption of his innocence, and his inevitable defeat as a victim not only of the times and the cruelties and greed of his fellow man, but also of a rigid, blind faith in his own strength and will. By systematically dismantling Hsiang-tzu, Lao She is telling his readers that only as a united citizenry can China hope to survive. He makes this point time and again, as in the following authorial comment:

> In this, as in any other endeavor, he saw no reason to exhaust himself: he had tried his hand at working really hard, and he knew how little reward it brought you. . . . He could go on destroying his own life, but he wasn't going to make the smallest sacrifice for anybody else. Those who will labor only for themselves also know well the way to work their own destruction: this is the great paradox of individualism.[25]

In the allegorical monologue uttered by an old rickshaw puller whose presence often serves to show the hero the future results of his actions, Lao She writes:

> "How much spring is there in one lone man? Have you ever watched a grasshpper? When he is by himself, the fact that he can jump surprisingly far only makes it more likely that some small boy will catch him and tie him with a thread, so that he won't even be able to get up off the ground.
> "But let him join with a swarm of other grasshoppers and go forth in battle array. Heng! In one sweep they will destroy an entire crop, and who can stop them? Where is the small boy with his thread? Tell me yourself, am I right or not?"[26]

The greatness of *Rickshaw Boy* does not lie in its message alone, however, for it is a finely told story in which believable characters act and speak naturally and convincingly. Lao She has also described his beloved Peking with skill and beauty and has shared with his readers his agonizing dilemma between an obvious sympathy for Hsiang-tzu the man, while repudiating Hsiang-tzu's ideals as the instruments of national salvation.

Mao Tun

The period of growth may be best represented by Mao Tun (1896-   ), one of the pioneers of May Fourth literature, who made literary contributions over the first decade of the modern period in every area *except* creative writing. In addition to his editorial work he translated, wrote introductory and critical articles, compiled bibliographies, and wrote reviews. He was, it seems, biding his time, and once the serialization of his first novel, *Disillusionment (Huan-mieh)*, began in *Short Story Monthly* in 1927-1928, he was immediately catapulted into the front ranks of modern novelists.

Mao Tun (whose name is a pun on the word "contradiction") is universally regarded as the leader of the realist-naturalist school, and the influence of his favorite authors, Tolstoy and Zola, is unmistakable in many of his works. Sharing with Lu Hsün and others the philosophy that literature is an instrument of social criticism, he was one of the first writers to openly advocate "art for life's sake." In 1921 he wrote:

> The aim of literature is the concentrated expression of human life; whether written in the realistic style or the symbolic, its unwavering aim is the expression of human life, the broadening of mankind's joys and sympathies, with the special characteristics of the age as its setting. Literature has now also become a science whose object is the study of human life, contemporary life, with the poem, the play, and the novel as its tools.[27]

In addition to his literary activities, Mao Tun was probably the most politically active of all his contemporaries. A member of the Communist Party since as early as 1921,[28] he was an active participant in the planning of such major events as the May Thirtieth Incident,[29] and it was political involvements which precipitated his dismissal as editor of *Short Story Monthly*.

Mao Tun's career as a novelist began after the 1927 purge of the Communists by the Nationalists. Retiring from active participation in the Communist Party because of illness, he turned his hand to fiction to write of events during this chaotic period. Within six months he completed his first novel, *Disillusionment*. It was quickly followed by two more, *Vacillation (Tung-yao)* and *Pursuit (Chui-ch'iu)*; all three first appeared in *Short Story Monthly* and were later collected as a trilogy under the title of *Eclipse (Shih)*. With these three novels, Mao Tun became the foremost novelist of the day, one whose works most accurately reflected the *Zeitgeist* of this age of revolution. As their titles suggest, the novels depict various stages of political involvement, from idealistic zeal to disillusionment, wavering of purpose, and ultimately to a search for personal identity and happiness. The search is futile, however; the trilogy ends on a very pessimistic note, for which the author was strongly criticized by leftists.

Since no Chinese novelist had previously examined contemporary history as penetratingly and objectively as Mao Tun had, his works have been praised as much for their historical, political, and social significance as contemporary documents of an age as they have been for their literary qualities. Like Balzac, whose novels constitute a detailed re-creation of nineteenth-century French society on a broad sociological canvas, Mao Tun was on his way to becoming not only a vigorous social critic, but also an indefatigable chronicler of his age.

In his next novel, *Rainbow (Hung)*, published in 1929, Mao Tun both broadens and narrows his approach: the story line spans a longer period of time (from the May Fourth Incident of 1919 to the May Thirtieth Incident of 1925) in its examination of the path from traditionalism to revolution; but by concentrating on the protagonist, a young woman named Mei, the story focuses on a single persona, resulting in the most revealing psychological study of a fictional character up to that time. Although contemporary historical events provide the setting, *Rainbow* is essentially a study of human psychology, of one woman's search for identity and the meaning of life in a highly charged political climate where "liberated" youths are trying to square their own personal needs with the demands of the revolution.

If the political scene during the closing years of the 1920s was chaotic, the literary scene was no less so. The two leading literary figures of the day, Lu Hsün and Mao Tun, were the objects of criticism from the Left: leading the attack were Chiang Kuang-tz'u, who headed the Sun Society (*T'ai-yang she*), and Kuo Mo-jo and the later Creationists. The dispute was settled after a fashion with the founding of the League of Leftist Writers (*Tso-i tso-chia lien-meng*) in 1930, an umbrella organization whose goal was to unite the efforts of the leftist community. The League, an organization under the titular leadership of Lu Hsün, proved to be an important literary entity until it fell into disarray and ceased to exist in 1936, when National Defense (anti-Japanese) literature became the order of the day.

Mao Tun's first works (*Eclipse* and *Rainbow*) were both written prior to the formation of the League—they were, in fact, the reasons for the criticism directed at him; the fictional works he wrote immediately after the founding of the League were much slighter. In 1933, however, he published his masterpiece, *Midnight* (*Tzu-yeh*), one of the major literary events of the period. Set primarily in Shanghai, it is at once a minute examination of the financial and industrial activities of China's most strategic metropolis, and a tale of conflict between the foreign-dominated capitalist, comprador, industrialist elements and the revolutionary forces and workers both in Shanghai and in the countryside. In the naturalist tradition to which Mao Tun acknowledged his debt, *Midnight* supplies an exhaustive re-creation of stock market activities, power politics, and intrigue in many forms. It is occasionally a ponderous work, but one of such scope and complexity as to hold a position of undeniable importance as the major political novel of the modern era.

The tone of *Midnight* is a distinct departure from that of Mao Tun's earlier works, which were pessimistic and depressing. While holding to his realist commitment to give the most objective expression of reality possible, he shows the revolution in an optimistic light and points to the inevitable defeat of the classes of people represented by the protagonist, Wu Sun-fu, a wealthy factory owner. Nonetheless, leftist critics were not completely satisfied with *Midnight*, singling out the author's preoccupation with the classes he was attacking at the expense of the workers, peasants, and revolutionaries.[30]

In addition to his many novels, Mao Tun also wrote a number of short stories (as did Lao She and other major novelists). In fact, some of his stories are among the finest examples of the genre, including his often anthologized and translated short story trilogy, "Spring Silkworms" (*Ch'un-ts'an*), "Autumn Harvest" (*Ch'iu-shou*), and "The Last Days of Winter" (*Ts'an-tung*). Called "perhaps the outstanding achievement in Chinese proletarian fiction,"[31] "Spring Silkworms" is a powerful indictment of the combined effect of foreign aggressors and Chinese moneylenders on the peasants. In the sequels to this first story the Marxist dialectic takes over: the peasants, in the wake of a disastrous harvest, rally around the revolutionary leadership of the son of the traditional, fatalistic, and ultimately defeated peasant who is the chief character in the first two stories. Mao Tun uses the oppressed peasant in other stories as well, most notably "In Front of the Pawnshop" (*Tang-p'u ch'ien*), though this story is related thematically to Mao Tun's earlier novels, in that no solutions for the social evils he depicts are given.

During the war years Mao Tun continued to write fiction, but it is his works up to the mid-1930s which have earned him his reputation as the foremost champion of critical realism.

Pa Chin

If Lu Hsün is modern China's most popular and best-known writer, Pa Chin certainly runs a close second.[32] Pa Chin (Li Fei-kan, 1904-) adopted his *nom de plume* by combining one syllable each from the names of two famous Russian anarchists, *Ba*kunin and Kropot*kin,* whose political philosophy he also adopted.[33] Unlike so many of his contemporaries whose families had fallen on hard times by the turn of the century, Pa Chin was born into a family which still enjoyed great wealth and power, and which became known to thousands of Chinese readers through his autobiographical writings. Another distinctive feature of this man who would become a flesh-and-blood hero to at least one generation of Chinese youth was his self-professed disdain for his craft; he was a generally sloppy and careless writer whose lack of concern with form, method, and technique is both well documented and well known, as shown in the two comments which follow:

> I lack the temperament of an artist; I cannot compose a novel as if it were a work of art. When I write, I forget myself and become practically an instrument: I have really neither the leisure nor the detachment to choose my subject and form. As I said in my preface to *Light*, at the time of writing I myself no longer exist . . . . Do you think I can still pay attention to form, plot, perspective, and other such trivial matters? I am almost beside myself. A power drives me on, forcing me to find satisfaction in "mass production"; I have no way of resisting it and it has become a habit with me.[34]

> What is literature? I for one do not know, nor do I care to know. I have never read a single book on the subject.[35]

This is not merely a formulaic expression of humility, as any reader of Pa Chin's novels can attest. His youthful exuberance and emotionalism, his deeply felt humanism, and his romantic-revolutionary themes appealed to a youthful audience who relished engagé literature. But they frequently resulted in works with transparently stereotyped characters and loosely organized structure, so melodramatic as to be almost sophomoric. Yet with all their flaws, his novels are still read and enjoyed by many people and continue to receive critical acclaim.

Pa Chin's first novel, *Destruction* (*Mieh-wang*, 1929), which was written in France, is a tale of political assassination, revenge, and revolutionary themes. Filled with patriotic and class-oriented slogans, elaborate theatrics, and emotionalism, its serialization in *Short Story Monthly* made its author an overnight celebrity. Over the following decade Pa Chin's output of fiction was phenomenal; by 1935 he had published nearly two dozen novels and short story collections. Regarding these works, Pa Chin wrote:

> I am not satisfied with any of the fiction I have written, but among the more tan twenty volumes of literary works I have penned, there have been those which I personally enjoy; specifically, *The Love Trilogy* [*Ai-ch'ing san-pu-ch'ü*]. I have never before admitted this to anyone.[36]

This trilogy, Pa Chin's major work up to that time, is representative of his style and, in the words of one critic, is "the most important of Pa Chin's contributions to the history of the young Chinese revolutionary intellectuals in the prewar Kuomintang period."[37] It comprises three novels: *Fog* (*Wu*, 1931), *Rain* (*Yü*, 1931), *Lightning* (*Tien*, 1934), and *Thunder* (*Lei*, 1933) a novelette which precedes *Lightning*. The central theme in the trilogy is not so much love as it is faith and its development in the lives of young revolutionary intellectuals. Following the pattern which he had begun in *Destruction* and would continue throughout his career, Pa Chin differed from the earlier writers as well as from many of his contemporaries in his positivist approach. A more prescriptive than descriptive writer, he peoples many of his novels and stories with positive characters living courageous and exemplary lives in the pursuit of high revolutionary ideals; if they tend to be overly sentimental and their actions too predictable, they invariably satisfy the author's didactic purpose, giving his young readers models for emulation. On the negative side, among the institutions most strongly attacked is the traditional extended family, a subject which plays an even more important role in a novel Pa Chin wrote at the same time he was working on *The Love Trilogy*.

It is interesting that in the passage quoted earlier Pa Chin did not include *Family* (*Chia*) among his favorites, both because of the intensely personal bond between author and work and also because it is the work which truly established his reputation. It too is part of a trilogy, *Turbulent Stream (Chi-liu san-pu-ch'ü)*, which includes *Family* (1931), *Spring* (*Ch'un*, 1938), and *Autumn* (*Ch'iu*, 1940); but *Family* alone has gained him international fame. It is a decidedly autobiographical novel in which Pa Chin attacks with vehemence the typical extended family of the upper class; the Kao family is in many respects a modern day reincarnation of the Chia family from the Ch'ing novel *Dream of the Red Chamber* (*Hung-lou meng*), with which *Family* has often been compared. The hero of *Family* is a high-school-aged boy, Kao Chüeh-hui, Pa Chin's alter ego and a budding revolutionary. Cast in the role of the dissenter in the family, it is he who perceives most keenly the disastrous effects traditional values and constraints have on his eldest brother and others who share the family compound. The picture of opposing forces is to some degree shown through three perspectives: the obedient eldest son who is forced to abandon the woman he loves, then marries another only to lose her in childbirth because of superstitious beliefs held by the family elders; the middle son, whose modern proclivities are blunted somewhat by timidity; and Chüeh-hui, who becomes not only the hero of the book, but also a hero of the times.

The two sequels to *Family*, both written after a lapse of several years, continue the story of the Kao family, introducing new characters and their relationships with the Kao brothers, and continuing the theme of the disintegration of this type of family.

Pa Chin's short stories deal with similar themes in similar ways, and many have received some acclaim. Still, it is as a novelist that he is best known.

Chang T'ien-i

Another new writer from this period, Chang T'ien-i (1907-), wrote only short stories (except for a few juvenile novels) and joined the ranks of Lu Hsün, Yü Ta-fu, Yeh Shao-chün, and Shen Ts'ung-wen as one of the foremost writers of this genre. Chang differs from the others in that he is the only one of the five to write from the Communist perspective; he is also known for the humor and satire he employed in many of his works.

The bulk of Chang's fiction was written during a period exactly conterminous with the period of growth; that is, 1928-1937. C. T. Hsia has divided his stories into three categories: agitational, ideological, and satirical, heaping unqualified scorn on the first, qualified scorn on the second, and praise on the third.[38] To be sure, politically motivated writing often tends to lack stylistic attentiveness, and from a Western critic's point of view, Chang's most successful stories are those in which the message is secondary to technique, especially when he employs his keen sense of wit and irony.

Yet there is often such raw power in some of his most openly "agitational" pieces that they make for compelling reading. Such is the case with "Hatred" (*Ch'ou-hen*), a fearful tale of the horrors of war and of the unbridled hatred of a brutalized peasantry bent on revenge. In "Hatred," which is reminiscent of some of Yukio Mishima's more vivid and starkly horrifying passages, Chang T'ien-i seems determined to shock his readers, as in the following description of a soldier's wound:

> The wound is the size of a teacup. Thousands of maggots are crawling in the red opening; they have eaten themselves white and fat, pus and blood all over them. Crimson blood and pale yellow pus have been mixed together. Once the grey cloth is off, the fat white maggots begin to burrow and scatter as if terrified. Several crawl out of the wound and working their backs crawl arc by arc onto Wu Da-lang's hand, painting it with red meandering lines. Several arc along carelessly, fall to the ground and struggle in the boiling hot dirt.[39]

Similar passages appear in other war stories such as "The Road" (*Lu*), but not so often that Chang T'ien-i should be considered a consciously macabre or grotesque writer. In fact, at his technical best he is a master of satire and a creator of fine, craftsmanlike stories. And the distinctiveness of his writing style is not limited to the tone of his writing alone, but lies in his language as well. Generally eschewing Westernisms, he is essentially a native writer who uses the Chinese language to the limits of its richness. At his best with dialogue, he employs it with the skill and nearly to the extent of a playwright. A prime example of Chang's unique ability to satisfy his literary aims of depicting class struggle and the bankruptcy of the bourgeoisie through deft characterization, lively and realistic dialogue, and a measured use of satire is "Mid-Autumn Festival" (*Chung-ch'iu*), a story of cruelty, submissiveness, and the dilemma of a person torn between divided loyalties. In this story of a "gentleman" farmer who subjects his impoverished in-law to humiliation, browbeats his wife, berates his tenant farmer, and is just generally obnoxious, Chang T'ien-i adroitly exposes the weaknesses of persecutor and victim alike in a fast-moving, rhythmical piece.

The Northeastern Writers

The impact of contemporary political events on the literary scene was overwhelming. This can be seen, for example, in the aftermath of the attack by the Japanese on the city of Mukden in Liaoning province, Northeast China (Manchuria) on 18 September 1931; the ensuing wave of patriotic protests and anti-Japanese sentiments changed the course of China's history and set the scene for a new type of literature.

The Mukden Incident, Japan's first overt act of military aggrandizement, and the subsequent formalization of Japanese hegemony over all of Manchuria with the establishment of the "puppet" state of Manchukuo created a new segment of the Chinese population—the refugees. It did not take long for these people and their brethren who, willingly or unwillingly, remained in Japanese-controlled territory to find their spokesmen in a group of young writers known collectively as the Northeastern Group of Writers.

First upon the scene was Li Hui-ying (1911-), whose story "The Final Lesson" (*Tsui-hou i-k'o*) appeared in the League of Leftist Writers' publication *The Dipper (Pei-tou)* in 1932; it and his novel *Wan Pao Shan* (a mountain near Ch'ang-ch'un, the capital of Manchukuo), also published in 1932, must be considered the first examples of anti-Japanese fiction set in Northeast China. Neither, however, was particularly successful, and it required writers of superior talent and a greater sense of involvement to lay the cause of the Northeastern Chinese patriots before the rest of the nation. The wait came to an end in 1935 when Lu Hsün personally arranged for the publication in his Slave Series of the first novels by two Northeastern refugees: Hsiao Chün's *Village in August (Pa-yüeh ti hsiang-ts'un)* and Hsiao Hung's *The Field of Life and Death (Sheng-szu ch'ang)*. Both painted grim pictures of life in Northeast China; both brought the anti-Japanese issue out into the open; and both were immediately and immensely popular.

Viewed in retrospect, these two novels, while flawed in a number of respects, belie the youth and inexperience of their authors. Hsiao Chün (Liu Chün, 1907-), a self-educated veteran of army life in and around the city of Mukden, had true proletarian roots and a highly colorful past prior to his arrival in Shanghai in late 1934:

> Besides my career in the army I have been a vagabond-tramp, a secretary, an apprentice to a professional boxer—one of those stunt-doers in open-air markets—a waiter, a millstone pusher in a bean-curd shop, and whatnot. My ambition was to become a regular in the "mounted-bandit" corps [guerrilla forces], and though I did not succeed, and am now writing novels, I still cherish that hope, and perhaps some day it will be realized.[40]

In the same autobiographical sketch Hsiao Chün, who had joined the small coterie around Lu Hsün, spelled out the purpose of his literary work—"to help liberate all oppressed people from their unhappy lot."[41]

Village in August, one of the most influential and popular novels in the 1930s,[42] tells of the anti-Japanese volunteer bands in the author's native Manchuria, and it is reminiscent of, if not on a par with, Aleksandr Fadeyev's *The Rout*.[43] Replete with many memorable incidents and characters—the peasant hero, the revolutionary, the intellectual leader, the commander, and the foreign girl, not to mention the Japanese soldier and the native landlord—*Village in August* is a highly episodic tale which glorifies the bandit-hero and minimizes the leadership role of the Communist Party. Years later this very aspect would be a factor in Hsiao Chün's fall from grace in the Party and eventual disappearance from public life. But for the time being he was a celebrity and continued to be one for more than a decade.

Hsiao Hung (Chang Nai-ying, 1911-1942), Hsiao Chün's common-law wife, whose roots were decidedly nonproletarian, also saw her first novel published in the Slave Series, five months after *Village in August;* it too met with immediate acclaim, propelling its author into the forefront of the new generation of writers.[44] Like *Village in August, The Field of Life and Death* deals with the anti-Japanese issue, but not from the Communist perspective, nor is it the main theme. By most standards, however, it is a better novel than *Village in August,* partly because the author eschews the romantic-revolutionary hero and concentrates on the lives of the peasants with their superstitions, simple honesty, and unfathomable poverty, and partly because of her remarkable talent to describe their natural surroundings.

In both of these novels, in keeping with the tenor of fiction of the times, the authors give dire portraits of contemporary Chinese society, leaving little if any room for optimism; yet, perhaps more than any which had preceded them, these novels proved to be the first works in a transition process from descriptive to prescriptive writings which took more than a decade to complete.

Following the appearance of *Village in August* and *The Field of Life and Death,* the "two Hsiaos" published several miscellaneous essays and stories, including two of the finer short stories of the period: Hsiao Chün's "Goats" *(Yang)* and Hsiao Hung's "Hands" *(Shou).* Hsiao Chün, whose repertoire included a broad range of characters, mostly from the lower classes—his "oppressed people"— describes in "Goats" the lives of inmates in a prison through the perspective of a political prisoner, a patriot. Hsiao Hung, who was not nearly as eclectic in themes and personae as Hsiao Chün, was at her best when describing her own childhood milieu or the lives of the peasants in the surrounding countryside. "Hands" is the story of a girl from a poor background who has been given the opportunity to study in a big-city school, but for whom the combined forces of prejudice, elitism, and cruelty prove overwhelming. One of the most popularly anthologized stories from the 1930s, "Hands" is representative not only of its author, but also of the prevailing literary sentiment of the years just prior to the opening of war with Japan.

Hsiao Chün's second major effort, *The Third Generation (Ti-san tai),* came hard on the heels of *Village in August.* Beginning serialization in *Writers' Monthly (Tso-chia),* it is a departure from and an improvement over his earlier work. The scope of this long novel, which has been called a "powerful, robust, and solemn epic,"[45] is broad, covering the period from the Russo-Japanese War (1904-1905) to the 18 September 1931 Mukden Incident. Hsiao Chün's later plans to make *The Third Generation* the first volume of a trilogy were not realized, unfortunately, because of his subsequent political travails.

Of the remaining Northeastern writers, only one was to become an established novelist. Tuan-mu Hung-liang (Ts'ao Chia-ching, 1912-), unlike Hsiao Hung and Hsiao Chün, did join the League of Leftist Writers (in 1932), but did not have the good fortune of meeting Lu Hsün, and was thus denied the rapid access to literary fame which came to so many of the master's protégés. The irony here is that Tuan-mu Hung-liang had completed his first novel, *The Steppe* of the Khorchin Banner (*K'o-erh-ch'in ch'i ts'ao-yüan*), in 1933, fully a year before the "two Hsiaos" had finished their first major works, and his second, *The Sea of Earth* (*Ta-ti ti hai*), in 1935, the year in which *Village in August* and *The Field of Life and Death* were published. Yet, as was so often the case with unknown writers during those days, getting a first novel published was possible under one of two sets of conditions: the aspiring novelist either could have a patron (as did Hsiao Chün and Hsiao Hung), or could contribute short stories to well-known magazines and thus gain a reputation sufficient to interest a publisher. Unable to find a publisher for his long works initially, Tuan-mu Hung-liang chose the latter course; in August of 1936 his story "Sorrows of Lake Egret" (*Tz'u-lu-hu ti yu-yü*) was published in *Literature* (*Wen-hsüeh*), a League publication, followed three months later by "Distant Wind and Sand" (*Yao-yüan ti feng-sha*) and "The Turbulent River Hun" (*Hun-ho ti chi-liu*) in the same magazine. Once he had gained the attention of Mao Tun and Wang T'ung-chao, the time was right for Tuan-mu Hung-liang to publish a novel, and so *The Sea of Earth* began serialization in the final two issues of *Literature*, in July and August 1937. The magazine ceased publication following the July Seventh attack on the Marco Polo Bridge by the Japanese, and book publication had to wait until the following year.

With the appearance of *The Sea of Earth* the Chinese reading public was given its third major anti-Japanese novel. Tuan-mu Hung-liang's novel is linked to the other two: to *The Field of Life and Death* by its preoccupation with the land and the symbiotic relationship between the "sea of earth" and its inhabitants; to *Village in August* by its manifold descriptions of the resistance activities of local patriots. Tuan-mu Hung-liang's career, now established, would blossom fully during the war years and after.

Ting Ling and Shen Ts'ung-wen

The 1930s also witnessed the peak of one career begun in the previous decade (Shen Ts'ung-wen's) and the beginnings of a radical shift in direction in yet another (Ting Ling's).

Following her early stories, which explored the plight of young, uninhibited, modern women in their search for the meaning of life, Ting Ling grew progressively more active politically, a trend which is well reflected in her fiction. She played an active role in the League of Leftist Writers and even spent time in a Kuomintang prison. In such works as her novelette *Wei Hu* and the story "Shanghai: Spring 1930" (*I-chiu-san-ling-nien ch'un Shang-hai*), both written in 1930, love and revolution are treated together, evidence that the author was in a transitional stage of her career. But in the novelette *Water* (*Shui*), written three years later, the proletarian theme has won out completely. It is a story of how the dual forces of nature gone wild (a flood) and greedy, heartless landlords and government officials wear the peasants down until they ultimately rise up in revolt. But Ting Ling does not do well with this type of story, in which faceless mobs replace individual characters; there is a lack of tension which no amount of sloganeering can remedy.

In 1936 Ting Ling went to the Communist stronghold of Yenan where she was welcomed as a major literary figure. Over the coming years, although she was kept busy with her Northwest Battlefield Dramatic Troupe and editorship of the Yenan *Liberation Daily* (*Chieh-fang jih-pao*) literary supplement, she continued to write fiction up to the time of the founding of the People's Republic.

For Shen Ts'ung-wen, the 1930s saw the appearance of his finest writings, including several exceptional stories and a novelette which was and is still one of the most popular examples of pastoral fiction from modern China. In the story "Eight Steeds" (*Pa-chün t'u*), Shen departs from his depiction of rural life to write of urban intellectuals: specifically, eight college professors who share living quarters and become the objects of intense scrutiny by one of their number; this observer writes of their sexual inhibitions, other psychological problems, and hypocrisy in a series of letters to his fiancée. After reading a number of superbly written satirical passages which describe seven of the "steeds" through the viewpoint of the eighth, the reader begins to doubt the reliability of the narrator, and it is this final ironic twist which makes "Eight Steeds" so unique.

No such elaborate structure exists in the story "Quiet" (*Ching*); instead, the author blends rich scenic portraiture with a touching tale of a family of war refugees waiting for the return of the man of the family. Focused primarily on a fourteen-year-old girl, "Quiet" depicts the daily lives of people whose destinies are ruled by a war which is only hinted at right through the final lines:

> Yo-min smiled aimlessly. Under the slanting sun a part of the wall and the laundry stand on the terrace cast their shadows on the floor of the courtyard just as elsewhere a paper flag cast its shadow on the tomb of the man the women here were expecting—Yo-min's father.[46]

The Border Town (*Pien-ch'eng*) takes us back to the countryside with a tale of romance portraying the devotion shared by an old ferryman and his granddaughter, and the lives and manners of the peasants Shen so admired. Although it is probably overrated and is certainly not the author's finest work, the scenic passages in this novelette continue to hold nostalgic appeal for a substantial readership.

Following the outbreak of war with Japan, Shen continued to write, including such fine pieces as his novelette *The Long River* (*Ch'ang-ho*). But like those of so many other independent writers, his works were largely out of step with the times and their impact was relatively slight.[47] With the nation's very survival at stake and with thousands dying on the battlefield, the role of literature was once again narrowed.

3. THE WAR AND POST-WAR YEARS: 1937-1949

The period from 1937 to 1949 witnessed a general decline in both the quantity and quality of fiction for an obvious reason: an eight-year war with Japan followed by a protracted civil war was not the sort of ambience that fostered high quality literature. In both the Communist and Nationalist areas, drama and journalistic writings were most popular, particularly since they best served the war effort and reached the most people. The majority of writers joined the Chinese Writers Anti-Aggression Association (*Chung-hua ch'üan-kuo wen-i-chieh k'ang-ti hsieh-hui*), founded in Wuhan in early 1938 and headed by Lao She. Governing their activities were the doctrines of "Let literature go into the villages" and "Let literature serve the army"; meanwhile, in Yenan a call for socialist realism was being sounded.

Fiction in the Nationalist Areas

Among the major writers from the 1930s, many continued to write fiction, spending most of their time in the Nationalist interior; we shall take a look at the output of five of them: Lao She, Mao Tun, Pa Chin, Hsiao Hung, and Tuan-mu Hung-liang.

After his success with *Rickshaw Boy*, Lao She, redirecting his energies to the duties of the Association which he headed, to the writing of patriotic plays, and to the editing of wartime literary journals, wrote very little fiction for several years. Then in 1943 he wrote *Cremation* (*Huo-tsang*), a novel which was entirely in keeping with patriotic demands, but which in literary terms was a waste of his storytelling talents. It is clearly a piece of propaganda which deals with the resistance efforts and is peopled by patriots, traitors, collaborators, and the Japanese enemy. The protagonist is the daughter of a collaborator; she defies her father's wishes and joins the resistance movement, and is thus a positive hero, a rarity in Lao She's works. Still, it is a slight work, which even Lao She admitted he would not have published under different circumstances.

Following the end of the war Lao She began his most ambitious project: a trilogy in which he depicts life in occupied Peking during the war. Known collectively as *Four Generations under One Roof* (*Szu-shih t'ung-t'ang*), the three novels are *Bewilderment* (*Huang-huo*, 1946), *Ignominy* (*T'ou-sheng*, 1946), and *Famine* (*Chi-huang*, 1950-1951), the last two of which were written during the author's three-year stay in the United States. *Four Generations under One Roof* is a work of vast scope, tracing the lives of several families who live on a residential lane in Peking, and thus incorporating a number of interwoven stories. Most of all it is about the common people of China in the midst of a national crisis— their sacrifices, their inherent goodness, and their ultimate victory. With its black and white dichotomy of good and evil, rewards and punishments, it approaches the socialist realist mode which characterizes the most highly vaunted post-1949 works. As for its author, Lao She was a reported suicide victim during the Cultural Revolution in 1966.

Mao Tun, who was also extremely active in political and publishing spheres, wrote three novels during the war years: *Story of the First Stage* (*Ti-i chieh-tuan ti ku-shih*), *Putrefaction* (*Fu-shih*), and *Maple Leaves as Red as February Flowers* (*Shuang-yeh hung szu erh-yüeh hua*). *Story of the First Stage*, set in Shanghai during the initial stages of the war, is, as its title suggests, about the first stages of an expression of national will to resist Japanese aggression. In *Putrefaction* Mao Tun's target shifts to the Kuomintang secret police in a tale of intrigue, romance, and personal sacrifice. Written in diary form, the novel traces the life of a young woman who uses her body in the service of the secret police, but who ultimately sacrifices herself to save a college girl from going down the same road. In his final novel, *Maple Leaves as Red as February Flowers*, the first of a planned trilogy which was never completed, Mao Tun returns to the critical 1926-1927 period and the political struggles which resulted in a triumph for the Left.

Mao Tun's political activities and a greatly altered social and intellectual climate forced him to curtail his creative writings after the end of the war, and especially after the establishment of the People's Republic in 1949. He eventually rose to the position of Minister of Culture, and is still an important figure in Chinese cultural and political activities.

Pa Chin also remains in China, although he suffered considerably during the Cultural Revolution in the late 1960s. He wrote very little fiction after the war, but during the war he was the most prolific of all the major writers, publishing a trilogy, three independent novels, and at least one volume of stories.

Like Mao Tun's *Story of the First Stage*, the trilogy *Fire* (*Huo*), published from 1940 to 1945, begins in the early days of the war in Shanghai, concentrating on resistance activities there. Pa Chin candidly acknowledged that the trilogy was written for its propaganda value, using positive and heroic characters to encourage active participation in wartime activities by his readers. His next novel, *Leisure Garden* (*Ch'i-yüan*, 1944), was not about the war, but rather was a double tale of moral and familial dilemmas in the lives of two sets of residents of a particular house. In *Ward No. 4* (*Ti-szu ping-shih*, 1946), the war appears indirectly, as the setting of the novel is a poorly funded and staffed wartime hospital in the interior. Once again there is at least one character of near-heroic proportions in this novel: a woman doctor whose selflessness and devotion to duty earn her the respect of all. *Cold Nights* (*Han yeh*, 1947), Pa Chin's final novel, has received critical acclaim as perhaps his most craftsmanlike work.[48] In it he explores the lives of three people in a predicament which transcends time and space: a man living with his wife and mother, both of whom he loves, but who are themselves bitter enemies. The protagonist's tragic deterioration and death, his wife's desertion and subsequent return (too late), and the oversolicitous and possessive nature of his mother are depicted with keen perception, making *Cold Nights* one of Pa Chin's most successful creative works.

During the war years the Northeastern writers remained active in the various centers of the Nationalist government, but only two wrote any fiction: Hsiao Hung and Tuan-mu Hung-liang. Hsiao Hung's career took an interesting turn following a split with Hsiao Chün in 1938.[49] After fleeing from one war-threatened area after another, she and Tuan-mu Hung-liang traveled to Hong Kong in 1940, where they remained until her death in 1942. Three of her novels were published there, the final one posthumously; all were decidedly outside the mainstream of wartime writing. *Ma Po-lo* (1940) and its sequel (1941), which deal with the war obliquely, are comic satires, a mode which no other novelist was then employing. The protagonist, a ne'er-do-well son from a wealthy Christian family in the north, is representative of the opportunist segment of Chinese society, certainly not the type of positive figure about which so many of Hsiao Hung's contemporaries were writing. Objectively appraised, the novels fall short of the standard set by Lao She for such works, but they show both the independence of their author and a heretofore unknown facet of her talent. *Tales of Hulan River* (*Hu-lan-ho chuan*, 1942) is another matter altogether, a novel which has been as highly praised for its evocativeness and rhetorical beauty (by the likes of Mao Tun) as it has been criticized for its "bourgeois escapist" content. It is a long, intensely personal and observant reminiscence of the author's youth in Heilungkiang and is at the same time a unique sociological study of rural life in the Northeast at the turn of the century.

In 1939, as Tuan-mu Hung-liang was writing a novel entitled *The Great River* (*Ta-chiang*), his first novel *The Steppe of the Khorchin Banner* was finally published, six years after its completion. This massive work, which describes in highly vivid terms the grandeur of the Manchurian steppes and the hardy people who inhabit them, is a remarkable testimony to the genius of its author (who was twenty-one at the time of its writing); it is a sophisticated work and a difficult one to read; it approaches epic proportions and is thus of greater scope than its inexperienced author could manage. The end result, as with many of Tuan-mu Hung-liang's major works, is an unevenness, with spectacular passages sandwiched between ponderous interludes. *The Great River* is yet another example, a novel whose geographical scope is nearly as vast as China itself. As Tuan-mu Hung-liang's works receive more detailed analysis, his stock continues to climb, and he may very well come to be considered one of the major literary talents of his time.

With this look at the wartime activities of the major veteran writers of the 1930s behind us, we can turn our attention to the school of writing which began to gain ascendancy immediately following the termination of hostilities with Japan and became the orthodox school upon the founding of the People's Republic in 1949: socialist realism.

Communist Fiction

Following Mao Tse-tung's "Talks at the Yenan Forum on Literature and Art" (*Yen-an wen-i tso-t'an-hui shang ti chiang-hua*) in 1942, in which the new role for literature in a socialist society was prescribed and the question of art versus content was put into a Marxist perspective, two things began to happen in the "liberated" areas: there was renewed interest in folk arts and popular literary forms such as storytelling and folk drama, and the traditional forms such as novels and poems were written in the socialist realist vein. Mao's "Talks" constitute the theoretical foundation for proletarian literature in China: he states that "Literature and art are subordinate to politics, but in their turn exert a great influence on politics.[50] He further states that "what we demand is the unity of politics and art, the unity of content and form, the unity of revolutionary political content and the highest possible perfection of artistic form."[51] This then was to be the role of literature: to serve the revolutionary masses; to praise, not to criticize, the revolution, the Party, and the people. As a consequence, the prime criterion in literary criticism was no longer artistic quality, but political orthodoxy. It should come as no surprise that once all literature is required to depict a single prescribed truth, it begins to look remarkably similar. Such is the case with the socialist realist fiction written during this period and thereafter.

Few of the veteran writers were qualified or willing to write this type of literature, partly because of their family backgrounds and educations, which set them apart from the peasants and workers to whom the new literature was directed, and partly because of a personal conviction that literature must be independent of Party control. Ting Ling is the major exception; for her the war years were not particularly productive in terms of fiction, though her collection *When I Was in Hsia Village* (*Wo tsai Hsia-ts'un ti shih-hou*) has several stories of high caliber. Ting Ling's interest in the plight of women, whether in Shanghai or in Yenan, in the city or in the countryside, had not abated, and it is a leitmotif which pervades this collection of eight stories written between the years 1937 and 1941.

The title story, among the best and most well received, is written in the first person, but it does not constitute a self-exploration, as did so many of Ting Ling's early works; the narrator is a secondary character, insofar as it is not her story, but that of a woman who has served her country as an agent behind Japanese lines, who is subsequently shunned, ridiculed, and condemned for having used her body as a means of gaining information. Befriended by the narrator, a mid-level cadre, she is given hope and determines to find a new life outside of the village. But the author's message is anything but hopeful, as it shows in poignant terms the dual standards established for the sexes, with no solution in sight. This piece and one or two others from Ting Ling's Yenan period later came back to haunt her in the antirightist campaign of 1956-1957, which resulted in the end of her public life.

Ting Ling's final creative work, for which she received a Stalin Prize for Literature, was a novel of land reform, *The Sun Shines over the Sangkan River* (*T'ai-yang chao tsai Sang-kan-ho shang*, 1949). At one time a highly acclaimed example of socialist literature, the novel presents a fairly lively description of the process of change in liberated rural areas as the landowners are divested of their lands and the peasants haltingly begin to rule their own destinies with the aid of the Party. There are several very revealing episodes and interesting characters, though the work is a bit too slow-moving and didactic for most Western readers' tastes.

For the most part, the new literature demanded new writers. Chao Shu-li (1906-1970), the son of impoverished peasants and himself a factory worker who had received little formal education, was the most heralded and successful of this group of proletarian novelists. He was a protégé of Chou Yang, the leading Communist literary theoretician. Chao's first story, "Hsiao Erh-hei's Marriage" (*Hsiao Erh-hei chieh-hun*), exposes the oppressive system of arranged marriages in "old" China and points to better days ahead in a "new" China. It and the story which followed, "The Rhymes of Li Yu-ts'ai" (*Li Yu-ts'ai pan-hua*), a tale of struggle between peasant and landlord, show Chao Shu-li to be a gifted storyteller who writes with a didactic purpose, but in a style which is generally more artistic than that of the majority of socialist novelists. In addition to realistic dialogue, he brings to his stories an occasional light, humorous touch. Not so with his first novel, however; in *Changes in Li Village* (*Li-chia-chuang ti pien-ch'ien*, 1945), the author tells not only of the struggle between peasants and landlords, but also of the peasants' resistance to the Japanese, with an ending which promises hope to those who will continue the struggle.

When reading the works of Chao Shu-li and his contemporaries one must keep in mind not only the established themes and tone, but also the audience, for in keeping with the policy of popularizing literature, the new works were to be written in a language and style which was readily understandable not only to the literate, but also to peasants and workers everywhere. Naturally this demanded a simpler, more universal language to which the masses could relate even if the works were read aloud to them. In this light, the significance of the following critique of Chao Shu-li by Chou Yang becomes apparent:

> His language is the effortless, rich language of the masses, demonstrating the author's unique ability to use the vernacular not only in dialogue but also in general narration. In his works, we can see how closely his style of writing is linked with our national literary tradition. In mode of expression, especially in his use of language, he has absorbed many of the good points in the traditional novel; he has, however, created a new, national form. His language is the living language of the masses. He is no stickler for tradition but an innovator, a truly creative writer.[52]

A popular style of language, of course, cannot be viewed in a vacuum, independent of the story it tells and the personae it portrays. In these respects Chao Shu-li's works measure up equally well on the socialist yardstick. In sum, Chao Shu-li, as an innovator and a natural storyteller, shows this type of writing at its best.

Chou Li-po (1908-1979), who was both a novelist and a critic, authored several works in both the pre- and post-1949 eras. *The Hurricane (Pao-feng tsou-yü)*, another Stalin Prize winner, which was written in 1948, is a novel about land reform, one based on the author's observations in the Northeast. His stated purpose in writing *The Hurricane* was:

> ... To use the lively and rich material I had collected in the land reform in the Northeast to describe how our Party, for more than twenty years, had been leading the people in the great and bitter struggle against imperialism and feudalism, and to depict the peasants' happiness and sorrows during this period, so as to educate and inspire the revolutionary masses as a whole.[53]

In pursuit of his objectives, in Part One Chou depicts the wretched existence of an impoverished person of high integrity, his conversion to the Communist cause, a period of devotion to the masses, and his ultimate martyr's death. Part Two is a new scenario, same message. Chou Li-po lacks Chao Shu-li's talent for creating lively dialogue, possibly because by nature he is more cerebral and less "folksy" than Chao, and his works tend to be more mechanical.

There were, of course, many other writers who were active during this period: Liu Ch'ing, whose *Sowing (Chung-ku chi,* 1947) tells of rural collectivization; Ts'ao Ming, whose *The Motive Power (Yüan-tung li,* 1949) depicts the struggles of factory workers; and Liu Pai-yü.[54] For the most part, however, it was the post-1949 era which witnessed the most notable achievements in this area, a period which will be treated in the next essay.

In his article "Change and Continuity in Chinese Fiction," Cyril Birch sees May Fourth fiction as an anomaly in China's literary tradition, a brief interlude of Westernized, predominantly realist, revolutionary writings sandwiched between the more didactic and conservative fiction of the pre- and post-1949 periods.[55] This concept in no way lessens the significant contributions of modern Chinese fiction either to world literature or to the Chinese revolutionary process, but it does help to explain the brevity of its existence and the improbability of any return of a similar literary movement, at least in the foreseeable future.

As we have seen, modern Chinese literature was born in a period of experimentation with Western concepts—political, cultural, and philosophical. Although eighteenth-century European romanticism and related schools exerted minimal influence on the early years of literary experimentation, it was nineteenth-century European realism which dominated the scene for most of the modern period. Over the years the fiction grew more and more didactic, owing partly to the growing influence of Communist writers, and partly to the war with Japan, which required a more patriotic, propagandistic corpus of literature. Many of the May Fourth writers modified their writing styles to suit the changing "requirements" for literature, though few were able to make the radical change to the socialist realist mode of the post-1949 period.

Some of the writers of the period we have examined died before the advent of socialist realism, often at the peaks of their literary careers (a few died while still in their thirties). Others simply ceased writing and entered new fields. A few, such as Hsiao Chün and Ting Ling, were purged in antirightist campaigns, thus ending their creative careers. Lu Hsün, of course, holds a special position, one of near sainthood, owing to his unique and significant contributions to China's modern cultural and political history. Mao Tse-tung has praised Lu Hsün as "the greatest and the most courageous standard-bearer of this new cultural force . . . a hero without parallel in our history."[56]

There remains a substantial group of May Fourth writers who are still alive in China (or who have recently died), and whose fortunes have risen and fallen in the nearly three decades since the founding of the People's Republic; their nadir was reached during the Cultural Revolution of the late 1960s. However, in the years following the death of Mao Tse-tung and the downfall of Chiang Ch'ing and her radical associates in 1976, many of the May Fourth writers purged during the Cultural Revolution are once again in the public eye. Some pre-1949 works, such as Mao Tun's *Midnight* and Pa Chin's *Family*, have been reissued. A relaxation of the rigid control is becoming increasingly evident under the leadership of Hua Kuo-feng and Teng Hsiao-p'ing, who obviously favor a more lively cultural life for the Chinese people. As a result, some of the long-silenced writers have now resumed their writing activity. Pa Chin, for instance, has already published poems and other short pieces in magazines and newspapers. According to recent reports, the atmosphere in China has changed to such a degree that a number of pre-1949 writers are on the verge of publishing long novels on which they have been working for the last ten years. An often cited example is Pa Chin, whose sequel to the *Turbulent Stream* trilogy entitled *The Masses (Ch'ün)* is expected to appear soon.[57] Quite a few literary organizations have been revived; even works of dissent literature have appeared. Some writers now feel free to write about love, which was condemned as a vestige of bourgeois decadence in the late 1960s and early 70s. Tragic tales and satirical plays designed to expose the dark side of Communist society have been allowed to be published. A number of recent works have broken through some of the conventions imposed on literature during the Cultural Revolution, which had not allowed the creation of romances, satires, or tragedies and eventually reduced Chinese literature of that period to a few "model revolutionary operas" and several dozens of "approved" novels and stories, in which only superhumanly good or infernally evil characters are found. Recently Chinese critics and writers have repeatedly affirmed the need for artistic and literary diversity and variety. Outlining the latest official policy at the first post-Mao congress of writers and artists in late 1979, Teng Hsiao-p'ing stressed artistic workers' freedom to choose subject matter and method of presentation as well as the need to work within the Party framework to educate the people in Communist ideology. It may still be too early to talk of a true revival of artistic and literary creativity, but recent developments indicate that a "new spring in proletarian literature and art"[58] seems in sight and that China has indeed entered a new literary era.[59]

NOTES

1. The periodization used in this essay is based largely upon that developed by C. T. Hsia in his *A History of Modern Chinese Fiction*, 2nd ed. (New Haven and London: Yale University Press, 1971). My personal indebtedness to Professor Hsia's work (hereafter referred to as *History*), however, goes far beyond the chronological divisions: his theories regarding individual works and authors and his overall approach have provided a starting point for a generation of students of modern Chinese fiction.

In a survey of this nature it is impossible to do justice to every writer mentioned, or even to mention the names of all those who played important roles in the development of modern fiction. The interested reader is encouraged to refer to *History* and to the bibliographies at the end of the present volume.

In the pages which follow, existing translations have been used wherever possible for ease of reference. For a selected listing of translations of modern Chinese fiction, see the bibliographic section of this book. For a more exhaustive listing, see Donald Gibbs and Yun-chen Li, *A Bibliography of Studies and Translations of Modern Chinese Literature: 1918-1942* (Cambridge, Mass.: Harvard University Press, 1975).

2. The origins of this revolution certainly predate 1917, especially in fiction. In the late nineteenth century the noted thinker and translator Liang Ch'i-ch'ao advocated a revolution in the novel, using this literary form for political education. Nonetheless, the first real fruits of a literary revolution did not appear until the second decade of the twentieth century.

3. Quoted in William Theodore deBary, Wing-tsit Chan, and Chester Tan, comps., *Sources of Chinese Tradition* (New York and London: Columbia University Press, 1960), II, 164.

4. The title has many different English translations; the present one is given in de Bary and others, eds., *Sources of Chinese Tradition*, to which the reader is directed for a translation of the article (which appeared in the January 1917 issue of *New Youth*), as well as other pertinent documents from this period.

5. *Selected Stories of Lu Hsun*, trans., Yang Hsien-yi and Gladys Yang, 3rd ed. (Peking: Foreign Languages Press, 1972), p. 10.

6. *Ibid.*, p. 18.

7. Lu Hsün, Preface, Chao Chia-pi, ed., *A Comprehensive Anthology of Modern Chinese Literature (Chung-kuo hsin wen-hsüeh ta-hsi)* (Shanghai, 1935-1936), IV, 2.

8. This story and its symbols are analyzed in depth in two recent articles: Patrick Hanan, "The Technique of Lu Hsün's Fiction," *Harvard Journal of Asiatic Studies*, No. 34 (1974), pp. 53-96; and Milena Dolezelová-Velingerová, "Lu Xun's 'Medicine,'" in Merle Goldman, ed., *Modern Chinese Literature in the May Fourth Era* (Cambridge, Mass. and London: Harvard University Press, 1977), pp. 221-231.

9. *Selected Stories of Lu Hsun*, pp. 71-72.

10. Lu Hsün's life and works have received far more critical attention throughout the world than those of any other modern Chinese writer. Several works in English have appeared recently; among the most significant are: Hanan; Leo Ou-fan Lee, "Literature on the Eve of Revolution: Reflections on Lu Xun's Leftist Years, 1927-1936," *Modern China*, 2, No. 3 (July 1976), 277-326; Leo Ou-fan Lee, "Genesis of a Writer: Notes on Lu Xun's Educational Experience, 1881-1909," in Goldman, pp. 161-188; Harriet C. Mills,

"Lu Xun: Literature and Revolution—from Mara to Marx," in Goldman, pp. 189-220; and William A. Lyell, Jr., *Lu Hsün's Vision of Reality* (Berkeley: University of California Press, 1976).

11. James Robert Hightower, *Topics in Chinese Literature: Outlines and Bibliographies*, Rev. ed. (Cambridge, Mass.: Harvard University Press, 1966), p. 115.

12. A coordinated series of demonstrations by students of Peking University and other schools were held on 4 May, 1919 in reaction to their government's appeasement of Japan, which had laid claims on China's territory. The May Fourth Movement refers to the resultant intense cultural movement which soon spread throughout the country.

13. Available in English under the title *Schoolmaster Ni Huan-chih*, trans. A.C. Barnes (Peking: Foreign Languages Press, 1958).

14. Ting Ling has been gaining increased critical attention in the West recently, and at this writing many studies are in progress; the recent article by Yi-tsi M. Feuerwerker, "The Changing Relationship between Literature and Life: Aspects of the Writer's Role in Ding Ling," in Goldman, pp. 281-307, is perhaps the most informative and penetrating to date.

15. Harold Isaacs, ed., *Straw Sandals* (Cambridge, Mass.: The MIT Press, 1974), pp. 162-163.

16. Ch'eng Fang-wu, "The Role of Modern Literature" (*Hsin wen-hsüeh chih shih-ming*), quoted in Wang Yao, *A Draft History of Modern Chinese Literature* (*Chung-kuo hsin wen-hsüeh shih kao*) (Shanghai: Hsin wen-i ch'u-pan she, 1953), I, 45.

17. Yü's writing has been widely regarded as being subjective. This viewpoint is given detailed treatment in Hsia, *History*, pp. 102-111. Michael Egan, "Yu Dafu and the Transition to Modern Chinese Literature," in Goldman, pp. 309-324, argues that Hsia and others have misread Yü's stories, and that they should be viewed as ironical rather than autobiographical, though his arguments are not entirely convincing.

18. C. T. Hsia, ed., *Twentieth-Century Chinese Stories* (New York and London: Columbia University Press, 1971), p. 29.

19. *Ibid.*, p. 33.

20. *See* Leo Ou-fan Lee, *The Romantic Generation of Modern Chinese Writers* (Cambridge, Mass.: Harvard University Press, 1973), pp. 283-286.

21. Isaacs, pp. lix-lx.

22. Quoted in Hsia, *History*, p. 170.

23. Ranbir Vohra, *Lao She and the Chinese Revolution* (Cambridge, Mass.: Harvard University Press, 1974), p. 61.

24. This theory, first developed by Hsia (*History*, pp. 179-188), has gained general acceptance by students of Lao She.

25. Lau Shaw [Lao She], *Rickshaw Boy*, trans., Evan King (New York: Reynal and Hitchcock, 1945), p. 334. By altering the conclusion of the novel in his translation, King greatly distorted Lao She's intent.

26. *Ibid.*, p. 372.

27. Quoted in Chang Pi-lai, *A History of the Beginnings of Modern Literature in the 1920s* (*Erh-shih-nien-tai hsin wen-hsüeh fa-jen shih*) (Peking: Tso-chia ch'u-pan she, 1936), p. 96.

28. He is mentioned (by his real name, Shen Yen-ping) as one of the earliest participants in Communist organizing activities in Chang Kuo-t'ao, *The Rise of the Communist Party 1921-1927* (Lawrence, Manhattan, and Wichita, Kansas: The University Press of Kansas, 1971), I, 108.

29. On 30 May 1925, during a demonstration in Shanghai by students and workers over the killing of a Chinese factory worker by a Japanese, police interfered, killing and wounding many of the demonstrators. The national outcry that followed took the form of mass demonstrations and boycotts, with the Communist Party reaping the greatest rewards.

30. This novel is discussed in Richard Yang, "*Midnight:* Mao Tun's Political Novel,"

in Paul K. T. Sih, ed., *China's Literary Image* (*Review of National Literatures*, VI, no. 1) (Jamaica, N.Y.: St. John's University, 1975), pp. 60-75.

31. Hsia, *History*, p. 162.

32. C. T. Hsia does not think very highly of Pa Chin's early works (*see History*, pp. 237-256). A more sympathetic study, which includes an exhaustive biographical and bibliographical examination of Pa Chin, is Olga Lang, *Pa Chin and His Writings: Chinese Youth between the Two Revolutions* (Cambridge, Mass.: Harvard University Press, 1967).

33. Hsia, *History*, p. 238, and Lang, p. 7. In the 1950s, however, Pa Chin denied the generally accepted view on the origin of his pseudonym, saying it was the name of a friend.

34. Quoted in Hsia, *History*, pp. 237-238.

35. Quoted in Szu-ma Ch'ang-feng, *A History of Modern Chinese Literature* (*Chung-kuo hsin wen-hsüeh shih*) (Hong Kong: Chiu Ming Publishing Co., 1976), II, 43.

36. Pa Chin, *The Love Trilogy* (*Ai-ch'ing san-pu-ch'ü*) (Hong Kong: Nan-kuo ch'u-pan she, 1968), p. 2.

37. Lang, p. 171.

38. Hsia, *History*, p. 214.

39. John Berninghausen and Ted Huters, eds., *Revolutionary Literature in China: An Anthology* (White Plains, N.Y.: M. E. Sharpe, 1976).

40. Quoted in Edgar Snow, ed., *Living China: Modern Chinese Short Stories*, reprint ed. (Westport, Conn.: Hyperion Press, 1973), p. 206.

41. *Ibid.*, p. 206.

42. It was also among the earliest works banned by the Nationalist government and had the distinction of being the first modern Chinese novel translated into English (1942 by Evan King), followed by Lao She's *Rickshaw Boy* (1945).

43. In his preface to the novel Lu Hsün briefly compared the two works. A detailed comparison can be found in Lee, *The Romantic Generation of Modern Chinese Writers*, pp. 231-233.

44. Hsiao Hung's life and works are treated in detail in Howard Goldblatt, *Hsiao Hung* (Boston: Twayne Publishers, 1976).

45. Ch'ang Feng, "Four Recently Published Novels" (*Chin ch'u hsiao-shuo szu-chung*) *Wen-hsüeh tsa-chih*, 1, No. 2 (June 1937), 180.

46. Hsia, *Twentieth-Century Chinese Stories*, p. 46.

47. After 1949 Shen stopped writing altogether and is now engaged in archaeological research in Peking. His stories have received detailed critical examination in Hsia, *History*, pp. 189-211, 359-366; and in Hua-Ling Nieh, *Shen Ts'ung-wen* (New York: Twayne Publishers, 1972).

48. *See* Hsia, *History*, pp. 381-386; and Lang, pp. 215-216.

49. Hsiao Chün spent most of the later war years in Yenan, then returned to Northeast China as a representative of the Communist Party. He ran afoul of the Party in 1948 and was sentenced to a period of labor reform. His third novel, *Coal Mines in May* (*Wu-yüeh ti k'uang-shan*), appeared in 1954, but it, too, proved to be unsatisfactory, and Hsiao Chün disappeared from view in the mid-1950s.

50. Mao Tse-tung, "Talks at the Yenan Forum on Literature and Art," in *Selected Works of Mao Tse-tung* (Peking: Foreign Languages Press, 1965), III, 86.

51. *Ibid.*, III, 90.

52. Chou Yang, "On the Works of Chao Shu-li," in Chao Shu-li, *The Rhymes of Li Yu-tsai and Other Stories* (Peking: Foreign Languages Press, 1950), p. 149.

53. Quoted in Ting Yi, *A Short History of Modern Chinese Literature*, reprint ed. (Port Washington, N.Y. and London: Kennikat Press, 1970), pp. 260-261.

54. All of the novelists are treated from the Communist perspective in Ting Yi, pp. 254-276.

55. Cyril Birch, "Change and Continuity in Chinese Fiction," in Goldman, pp. 385-404.

56. Mao Tse-tung, "On New Democracy," in *Selected Works of Mao Tse-tung*, II, 372.

57. Chou Huai, "The Impending Rebirth of Mainland Writers" (*Ta-lu tso-chia szu erh tai su*), *Ming Pao Monthly* (Hong Kong), 12, No. 7 (July 1977), 96. See also *Ming Pao Monthly*, 12, No. 11 (November 1977), 28.

58. *Ming Pao Monthly*, 12, No. 7, 96.

59. For a discussion of developments in Chinese literature since the death of Mao Tse-tung and the fall of the Gang of Four in 1976, *see* Winston L. Y. Yang and Nathan K. Mao, "Chinese Literature," in *1980 Britannica Book of the Year* (Chicago: Encyclopaedia Britannica, 1981), pp. 516-517; and Winston L. Y. Yang and Nathan K. Mao, eds., *Stories of Contemporary China* (New York: Paragon Book Gallery, 1979), pp. i-xi.

II

Chinese Communist Fiction Since 1949
Michael Gotz

Theoretical Principles of Literary Creation

The founding of the People's Republic in 1949 changed the course of Chinese fiction. Following the Communist revolution, Chinese social development entered a new historical period; transitions in the political and economic spheres produced a transformation in the cultural domain. A reevaluation of the nature and function of literature led to the creation of new forms and fresh content. Fiction writers arose to meet the challenge of the times, and a body of revolutionary literary theory was propounded to provide guidelines for the creation and critical evaluation of new works.

The central feature of the new fiction is its accordance with a set of theoretical principles prescribing the role of literature in the new socialist society. These principles were first laid down by Mao Tse-tung, Chairman of the Chinese Communist Party, in his "Talks at the Yenan Forum on Literature and Art (1942)," and they have the full authority of the Party and national government behind them. While significant challenges to their validity have occasionally arisen, these principles have withstood the tests of time and political conflict and remain the official standard almost to the present time. Since these principles differ from both Western and traditional Chinese concepts, it is essential to have a clear perception of them in order to achieve a genuine understanding and appreciation of contemporary Chinese fiction.

The foremost consideration in the new fiction is the audience: whom is the literature intended to serve? Mao's answer is unequivocal: ". . . all our literature and art are for the masses of the people; and in the first place for the workers, peasants, and soldiers and are for their use."[1] In short, he has designated that culture be consistent with politics and economics in serving the vast majority of the people who have made the revolution: the proletariat (i.e., the urban working class) and its allies among the nation's poor. No longer is literature to be the exclusive domain of the educated class and the rich (i.e., the bourgeoisie) who had dominated literary creation over the centuries. The victory of the Communist Party (or, as Mao perceived it in 1942, the imminent victory) meant the demise of bourgeois culture and the beginning of proletarian cultural dominance. Therefore, all literature is to be written at first *for* the working class and eventually *by* members of that class. Hence, the subject matter of contemporary Chinese fiction is nearly always a reflection of the lives of the workers, peasants, or soldiers.

The next consideration is how to serve the workers, peasants, and soldiers. Mao phrases the issue as follows: "... should we devote ourselves to raising standards, or should we devote ourselves to popularization?"[2] For Mao, "raising standards" means raising the masses' cultural understanding and appreciation. This is accomplished not by introducing bourgeois cultural values, but rather by continuing to develop proletarian culture. "Popularization" means writing works which can be read and understood by the masses, which can reach a widespread and diverse audience, and which can help the people progress toward socialism. In terms of aesthetic sophistication, there is a contradiction between writing simple and plain works for a semiliterate audience (popularization) and creating works of the highest quality and most advanced formal technique (raising standards). Mao, however, sees a dialectical unity (combination of opposites) between the two:

> The people demand popularization and, following that, higher standards; they demand higher standards month by month and year by year. Here popularization means popularizing for the people and raising standards means raising the level for the people.[3]

Another important consideration is the ideological nature of the new literature. Literary works, according to Mao, must reflect the revolutionary struggles or the political life of the people. Works of ficton must depict in an artistic manner the pressing social and political conflicts confronting the population, while at the same time pointing the way to their successful resolution. Thus, literature becomes a part of politics, a form of ideology invested with social significance. For writers of lesser abilities, this means nothing more than the creation of propaganda. Yet, Mao sought to avoid blatant sloganeering disguised as literature:

> What we demand is the unity of politics and art, the unity of content and form, the unity of revolutionary political content and the highest possible perfection of artistic form. Works of art which lack artistic quality have no force, however progressive they are politically.[4]

This principle does not specify precisely how the literature will look, what methods will bring about the desired results, nor in what manner social reality is to be depicted. Mao's most frequently quoted statement on this latter subject has been open to various interpretations because of its highly abstract expression:

> ... life as reflected in works of literature and art can and ought to be on a higher plane, more intense, more concentrated, more typical, nearer the

ideal, and therefore more universal than actual everyday life. Revolutionary literature and art should create a variety of characters out of real life and help the masses to propel history forward.[5]

Generally, this theory seems to be consistent with the Soviet concept of socialist realism. This is a mode of writing based on a new interpretation of Friedrich Engels' formulation of realism as the "reproduction of typical characters under typical circumstances."[6] A succinct statement of the tenets of socialist realism occurs in the first bylaws adopted by the Union of Soviet Writers in 1934:

> Socialist realism, being the fundamental method of Soviet artistic literature and literary criticism, demands of the artists a truthful, historico-concrete portrayal of reality in its revolutionary development. In this connection, the truthfulness and the historical concreteness of the artistic portrayal must take into account the problem of ideological transformation and the education of the workers in the spirit of socialism.[7]

These essential principles of literary creation underlie the works of every successful writer of fiction in contemporary China. To summarize: literature must be written for a readership comprised of workers, peasants, and soldiers (as well as political cadres arising from their ranks), it must popularize while raising the cultural level, and it must consist of an aesthetically high quality of form and a revolutionary political content. Literary works must depict reality in its revolutionary development, taking as their goal the raising of the socialist consciousness of the masses.

Who, then, are the stalwart writers who must master Marxist ideology, Party policies, and aesthetic principles in order to create works corresponding to the complicated guidelines outlined above? In general, fiction writers in contemporary China fall into one of two categories: professional or amateur. The professionals are of two types: veteran writers of the May Fourth and War periods who continue to write in the new society, and younger professionals nurtured by the Communist Party during and after the revolution. The amateurs, the largest bloc of writers, are workers, peasants, or soldiers who write in their spare time; they are encouraged by the Party to combine work and culture. The Party's plan for the future provides that every writer will work at another productive job as well. With the demise of the professional writer, work and culture would be integrated under the domination of the proletariat, and Chinese literature would become truly proletarian. Since the Cultural Revolution (1965-1969), great strides have been taken to realize this plan, inasmuch as a large number of professional writers have been discredited and seem to have discontinued their publishing.

Contemporary Chinese fiction assumes four major forms: novel, short story, storyteller's tale, and reportage. The storyteller's tale is derived from the old *hua-pen* stories and the oral folk tradition. Reportage is a type of fictionalized report on real people and real events and is therefore similar to semifictionalized newspaper feature stories. These four types of fiction writing present a variety of themes: the heroism of the Communist army and civilian partisans during the War of Resistance and Civil War; problems of land reform and agricultural collectivization; socialist construction and economic production; women's liberation; superstition; obstruction of progress by backward citizens; the problems of intellectuals; changes in the educational system; the value and experience of older workers; and so on. Since the themes reflect the activities of the workers, peasants, and soldiers, the stories are nearly always set in the factories, fields, or battlefields. The following discussion focuses on a few major representative works set in each of these work environments.

Industrial Production

One of the earliest novels depicting the life of the workers in accordance with Mao Tse-tung's principles is Ts'ao Ming's *The Motive Force* (*Yüan-tung li,* 1949). A professional writer and veteran of the left-wing literary circles of the 1930s, Ts'ao Ming was one of the few women writers sent by the Party to Manchuria to observe and write about industrial reconstruction. The product of her investigation, *The Motive Force,* is the story of a group of dedicated workers in a partially destroyed hydroelectric plant who overcome natural and man-made obstacles to rehabilitate the plant and bring it to full production. As the story unfolds, the plant has been ruined by both Japanese and Nationalist Party troops, and, during the winter preceding the Communist victory, the generators have frozen over. Prior to the arrival of a new Communist director, the workers take the initiative to begin thawing the ice in preparation for rebuilding the machines. This work is led by the hero of the novel, Old Sun, a veteran worker of intelligence and experience in the handling of both machines and people. Upon the arrival of the director, misunderstandings arise between the leadership and the workers, and the first running of the repaired machines results in a massive fire. Thereafter, the workers take a central role in the second rehabilitation effort, during which Old Sun and the director reach an understanding. Together they lead the workers to great success in their venture.

Ts'ao Ming's forte is not so much her structuring of the plot or her effective characterization, as it is her ability to depict the essence of the "world" of work. She does this by choosing striking images to recount a situation reflecting both the material and spiritual conditions. A passage describing the scene of the first attempt to rehabilitate the machines illustrates this point:

> The water wheel began to turn; the speed regulator, generator, and the oil hydraulic press started moving, too. The thin bending copper pipes attached to the machines also began to vibrate beautifully, and a smooth "chug, chug, chug" sound was once more heard in the machine shed.

> When the old hands around the power plant heard the sound they had not heard for over a year, they were inexpressably happy.—yes, they had heard famous folk-ballad singers and . . . Peking opera; they had heard the village girls singing folk songs with their clear voices, and the sweet hum of their own children singing; they had also heard the pure notes of the forest birds and the low gentle murmur of the spring breeze ruffling the surface of Jade Girdle Lake. But now, all of these appeared ridiculous, insignificant, in no way comparable to the wonderful sound of the machines running in the machine shed today—beautiful![8]

The description of the plant machinery is juxtaposed with cultural and natural images, and the overall mood evokes a sense of cheery well-being in the worlds of both man and nature. The vibration of the machines corresponds to the most beautiful songs of man, and the "chug, chug, chug" sound to the "pure notes of the forest birds." The author has produced a provocative comparison here between industrial production, nature, and human culture. Nature and culture are often considered the exclusive creators of beauty, but the process of effective labor, of successful production brought about collectively, is shown in this passage to be equally, if not more, beautiful. Labor can not only satisfy man's basic material needs, but it can also achieve a beauty every bit the equivalent of nature (which man has conquered) and culture (which has its roots in the productive process). The author is simply giving the beauty of collective labor its due.

Another writer interested in creating images reflecting the beauty of the "world" of industrial production is Ai Wu, whose novel *Steeled and Tempered* (*Pai-lien ch'eng-kang,* 1958) is generally considered to be one of the most successful in portraying the industrial environment. Ai Wu is a veteran professional, a short story writer from the 1930s who continued writing in the new society. *Steeled and Tempered* concerns the conflicts and contradictions arising among the workers in a steel plant, focusing on the special problems of a few characters representative of the major types found in industrial production in the 1950s. Ai Wu's strong point is his extremely detailed description of the actual process of steelmaking, which creates an aura of authenticity and provides the reader with a good deal of technical information by which to better appreciate the setting of the work environment. He presents the descriptions in a stimulating context and in an easily digestible fashion. Unlike Ts'ao Ming, he does not rely on lyrical imagery and juxtaposition; rather, his depictions are scientific and concrete, for example:

> [Yuan Ting-fa] did not go out to the platform to enjoy the soothing cool night air, knowing well that the new lining of silica bricks in the furnace roof would need careful watching once it showed signs of incipient fusion. A slightly higher temperature would soften the silica bricks and lumps would hang like stalactites from the furnace roof. This would thin the silica brick lining and subsequently shorten the life of the furnace, lengthen the time of overhaul and in turn reduce steel production. The only thing Yuan Ting-fa could do now was to stick around the furnace and

keep a vigilant watch on the roof through his goggles. When he saw that the silica bricks were white hot, he would swiftly raise his hand directing the operator to shift the incoming gas from the eastern inlet to the western. During this split second, the temperature inside would be slightly reduced, causing the silica bricks in the furnace roof to change from white to red, thus preventing them from softening.[9]

The authenticity of this description is unquestionable, and the reader gains a lesson in steel production that is necessary for a complete understanding of the world in which Yuan Ting-fa operates. More than that, the author has given us an insight into Yuan's conscientiousness, and has provided an illustration of his skills in the art of steelmaking. In works of fiction portraying contemporary Chinese workers, the workers are rarely separated from their work or work-related problems. Thus, the reader must be prepared to discover a character's personal traits through watching him at work. The above case describes in sufficient detail both the complex nature of the task and the seriousness and skill with which the character performs his duties. Yuan is a character out of everyday life, a man with whom any worker can empathize. The reality of the situation is an everyday affair to readers involved in heavy industrial production, and this is precisely the sort of realism for which the author strives.

Ai Wu, besides creating realistic depictions of life in the workaday world, has also produced a memorable socialist hero of the highest order, Ch'in Teh-kuei. Ch'in is a model worker, a young Communist from whom others are expected to learn. He is a man of dedication, skill, and daring, and the embodiment of the socialist ideal. A Party member of proletarian background, he becomes "steeled and tempered" in both revolutionary struggles and battles for production, emerging as a worker of high political principles. He aims to raise the level of consciousness of the other workers at every opportunity, and he is willing to risk his life for the sake of the factory and his fellow workers. All of these traits play an important role at the climax of the story—a massive furnace leak which spills molten steel and huge flames "enveloping half the shop in a volcano of fire and purple and yellow smoke." It becomes necessary for someone to brave the raging fire in order to reach and shut off the gas pipes. Ch'in Teh-kuei volunteers. At the high point of his heroic struggle, he is nearly overwhelmed:

The downstairs was ablaze. The molten steel splashed in all directions, hitting the wet concrete floor with a smack. . . .

His eyes narrowed down to slits, Ch'in Teh-kuei climbed up to the first platform, grabbed at a valve and jammed it shut with all his strength, then another and still another. . . . Closing the valve was a heavy job usually requiring two men. Ch'in Teh-kuei felt his head whirling, for the thick smoke made breathing extremely difficult. But he knew that if the gas pipes blew up, the whole plant would probably be destroyed, and the country would sustain a colossal loss. He mustered his courage and worked doggedly on. His whole mind was set on closing the valves at whatever cost, even at the risk of his life.[10]

Ch'in succeeds in his task, only to be knocked unconscious by a saboteur who had damaged the furnace to set off the blaze. The hero is victorious, however, and the saboteur is discovered. Ch'in has single-handedly saved the entire factory.

The character Ch'in Teh-kuei has been regarded by critics as a good example of the depiction of socialist heroes. Chou Yang, the powerful literary critic and cultural official who from 1942-1966 was one of those responsible for the official interpretation of Mao Tse-tung's literary principles, terms Ch'in a "lively and vivid picture of [a] young worker."[11] Chou was often concerned with the creation of heroic characters. In an important 1960 speech he set out his own views on the subject:

> Our literature and art should create characters which can best embody the revolutionary ideals of the proletariat. ... Their most admirable attribute is seen in the fact that they never are daunted by difficulties and shrink back, nor do they feel satisfied with the victories gained and so stop advancing. With their socialist ideals, they carried through the arduous democratic revolution; today, inspired by a still higher, Communist ideal, they are carrying out the mighty task of socialist construction. Lofty ideals and arduous struggle have cultivated and steeled their noble qualities and resolute characters.[12]

The novelist, Tu P'eng-ch'eng, has created several such characters in his major industrial work, *In Days of Peace* (*Tsai ho-p'ing ti jih-tzu li*, 1958). Tu is a younger writer than Ts'ao Ming and Ai Wu. He was a news reporter during the War of Resistance and Civil War and did not become a professional fiction writer until 1954. The setting of this novel is a railroad construction site deep in a mountain gorge, beset by horrendous rains which wash away men and material. In one episode, the floods have washed out a bridge, leaving hundreds of workers stranded on the far side of a raging river. Young Liu, a revolutionary romantic hero with many of the same qualities as Ch'in Teh-kuei, volunteers to cross the river hand over hand on a cable stretched from shore to shore in order to organize the workers and lead them to safety. The author describes his ordeal in a very idealized fashion, combining revolutionary realism with revolutionary romanticism:

> Liu slipped far away, very far away! They saw him slide to the very heart of the river and the cable sag until his body was nearly immersed in the water. He desperately grasped the cable with both hands, drawing himself up into a ball as bolt after bolt of lightning flashed down from the sky, cutting past his chest and back. Thunderclaps exploded all around him, and the dashing rain, like countless arrows, beat him with all its might. Great gusts of wind rocked him back and forth, tossed him up and cast him down. Yellow waves with silt like rising and falling mountain peaks, rose each crest higher than the last, as if the river in its anger would leap up and swallow him! Look! Young Liu is almost in the water, his feet are immersed now! See! Wave after wave is breaking over his head! Hai!

> What is happening? A jumble of pitch black objects is sweeping downstream. If these things are tree roots or timber and they crash into Liu, they will dash him to pieces! All of our hopes will also be smashed![13]

Here is the archetypical battle between nature in all her fury and those who desire to conquer her and have her obey their will. There is high adventure, drama, and suspense in the narration. Nature has concentrated her forces and man must struggle just to survive. Yet, the romantic hero literally clings to life, tenaciously grasping the man-made weapon (the cable) which is the mainstay of his defenses. This is not the only weapon he brings to the war, however, for he also fights with his physical strength, mental fortitude, and life experience.

Romantic, larger-than-life, typical situations are best described by heightened imagery and urgent tone, in much the same way as the use of stirring music is a common cinematographic technique designed to enhance the drama and suspense of an adventure episode. This passage contains dramatic images appealing to every sense and evoking a variety of emotions. The incident is representative of the manner in which "typical characters under typical circumstances" are reproduced and is an example of the successful integration of revolutionary content and literary aesthetics.

Not every contemporary writer of industrial fiction is concerned with lyrical or technical descriptions of the industrial environment or the depiction of revolutionary romantic heroes. One of the best of the younger professionals, Hu Wan-ch'un, often concentrates on the reflection of the innermost thoughts and feelings of older workers. Hu is a genuine proletarian writer, a former steelworker who for many years wrote as an amateur while working in a steel mill. One of his most sensitive portrayals of an older worker is in the short story "Aging Years" (*Wan-nien*, 1962). In this story he displays considerable skill in creating the thorough and rounded characterization of a retired master worker, Shun Fa. This man, who had been a dynamic worker and instructor in his time, now faces a lonely and comparatively inactive period of his life. As the story opens, he is alone in his apartment on New Year's Eve; his wife is at work, and he has no children. The opening passages reveal a great deal about him and the problem he confronts:

> On the eve of the lunar New Year, Instructor Shun Fa's mood underwnt a slight change. He suddenly felt that there was something lacking in his life. That morning he had not taken his usual stroll down to the factory nor had he gone to the neighbors to gossip; in the afternoon, he also had not gone to the Workers' Cultural Center to listen to readings or to look at the newspaper. In fact, he had not been interested in going anywhere; he was not in particularly high spirits. He paced back and forth and all around his apartment, as if he thought to find in some corner the thing that he lacked. The apartment, which ordinarily seemed not at all spacious, now suddenly became large, became empty.
>
> It seemed exceptionally quiet in the apartment; the tick-tock tick-tock of the clock on the grain cupboard sounded clear and sonorous. Shun Fa

paced slowly for a moment, then halted in front of the window. Outside in the dusk, standing straight and solitary, was a small pine tree. When Shun Fa's gaze fell on the pine, he involuntarily raised his hand to feel his own bald head: "Ah! I'm already sixty-six years old on this New Year's day! Already retired half a year."[14]

The old man is defined here by his relation to time and space. These two concepts play a major role in his life, and so they are central elements in the passage. It is New Year's Eve, a time when all Chinese add another year to their age, according to the old custom. For Shun Fa at sixty-six, each year becomes increasingly significant as he moves closer to the end of his life. On this particular day, in the silence of the early evening (the evening of his life as well), the clock's ticking off of each irretrievable moment probably sounds even more ominous than usual. On this day also, the juxtaposition of the aging man to the lone pine, the age-old Chinese symbol for longevity and strength, provides a stark contrast. The dusk has not detracted from what must be a lush outer appearance of the tree, but Shun Fa's hand immediately points up the damage the "dusk of life" has done to his own "foliage."

Just as the effects of time are accentuated by the fact that it is New Year's Eve, so the dimension of space is distorted by the effects of Sun Fa's "lack." What he lacks cannot be completely discovered in this passage, but its effect on his perception of his living space can be seen. In his mind, his apartment has been transformed from small to large, from full to empty. Yet, objectively, his space has become decidedly smaller. Whereas he ordinarily would walk all over the neighborhood (to the factory, the neighbors, and the cultural center), he now paces inside his small apartment—and he still feels he has room to spare.

What Shun Fa lacks is a feeling of usefulness and worth. This feeling of self-worth in a retired person comes from, among other things, a sense of progressive generations, the view that one's life forms a link between past and future. Shun Fa has no children to carry on his name or his tasks, and, hence, no future. The author does not leave him in this sorry state, however, for he provides Shun Fa with surrogate children—his apprentices and their apprentices, who visit him in a cheery, jocular group the next day. They have come to praise him, and to tell him how much they owe him for their own development as master workers. Overjoyed and proud to receive their respect and gratitude, the old man feels whole again, his sense of worth returns, and his life takes a new turn. The visit of these "children" reveals to Shun Fa the nature of his role in society and its immeasurable value.

Land Reform and Agricultural Collectivization

China is a country in which the vast majority of the population is engaged in agriculture, while only a relatively small percentage are industrial workers or soldiers. It is therefore not surprising to find that the largest category of Chinese literary works consists of fiction reflecting agricultural and village life. Agrarian reform and the development of socialist collectivization, along with their intrinsic problems, provide the subject matter for agricultural fiction. In the longer works, the central plot elements are nearly always the same: the progressive peasant forces, led by a Communist hero, overcome obstructionism on the part of the ideologically backward peasants, and pave the way for the socialization of agricultural production and other Communist goals. Often in these stories, the Communists and poor peasants must struggle against former landlords and their sons, who are bent on sabotaging local efforts to implement Party policies. In many cases, the problems in the human realm are compounded by the whims of nature: rains or drought. In the end, the progressive forces triumph, although in each story the specific circumstances vary widely, as do the methods of presentation. Within the parameters of the formulaic plot structure dictated by political guidelines, a body of diverse literary works exploring the fabric of the lives of the Chinese peasants under socialism has been created.

One of the earliest and best-known contemporary agrarian novels, regarded highly not only in China but throughout the Communist world (it won the Stalin Prize for Literature in 1951), is Ting Ling's *The Sun Shines over the Sangkan River* (*T'ai-yang chao-tsai sang-kan-ho shang*, 1949). Ting Ling is generally regarded as one of the foremost woman writers in modern China. Her works span the period from the late 1920s to the purges in 1957, during which she and her close colleagues were accused of various crimes and sent to distant communes to reform through labor. The present novel is based on her experiences as a member of a land reform team. The Party sent her to work with the team in 1946 in order to give her an opportunity to experience the political struggles in the liberated areas (i.e., those parts of China controlled by the Communist Party). The novel is generally considered to be a realistic reflection of the central problems and issues of the land reform.

Land reform was the major agrarian policy of the Communists during the Civil War and was completed in 1951. It involved primarily the confiscation of farm land from the rural landlords (leaving them only that portion which they could work with their families) for redistribution to poor peasants and hired hands. Thus, many poor farmers for the first time came to own the land that they tilled and had been working as serfs for the landlord. The movement was further designed to teach the peasants to stand up against their oppressors, the landlords, and to demand their rights (from the Communist perspective). Peasant associations were formed, women were encouraged to take part in politics nd to help till the soil, and changes occurred in the social and cultural life.

The plot of Ting Ling's novel reflects the typical process of the land reform movement through the experience of one village. The peasants successfully complete the confiscation of one landlord's property, but they are not able fully to carry out land reform. The Party sends a land reform team to help local cadres (political leaders) to mobilize the peasants, with the idea that the peasants themselves, at the instigation of the Party, are to organize, confront the chief landlord en masse, and demand the deeds to his land. The local leaders are not confident, fearing the return of the (Nationalist Chinese) enemy, and the land reform team cannot convince the masses to confront the landlord. A seasoned political worker, Comrade Pin, arrives just in time, firmly organizes the cadres, and helps sever any social relationships between them and the landlord, after which the peasants are mobilized. They fearlessly and viciously attack the villain, Schemer Chien; his land is redistributed, and the team moves on to another village.

A portion of the passage depicting the climactic confrontation between the peasants and the oppressive landlord illustrates the deep hatred felt by the peasants:

> Peasants surged up to the stage, shouting wildly: "Kill him!" "A life for our lives!"
>
> A group of villagers rushed to beat him. It was not clear who started, but one struck the first blow and others fought to get at him, while those behind who could not reach him shouted: "Throw him down! Throw him down! Let's all beat him!"
>
> One feeling animated them all—vengeance! They wanted to give vent to their hatred, the sufferings of the oppressed since their ancestors' times, the hatred of thousands of years; all this resentment they directed against him. They would have liked to tear him with their teeth.[15]

This passage is representative of the method of socialist realism which depicts the masses as a single group actor. The protagonists, unlike the antagonist, have no names and no faces; they are participants in a group action. As such, they are representative of an entire type, of all peasants everywhere who are laboring under the oppressive landlords. Their pent-up anger explodes with the force of the ages, with the violence of revenge for all of the tyrannies suffered by both themselves and their ancestors. Indeed, the description goes beyond the bounds of one group of villagers attacking one evil landlord. Each side is the representative of an entire social class, and their confrontation is a class struggle, with the particular situation as a microcosm. The author has captured the spirit of this struggle and recorded it for the education of future generations.

The policy of the Party is not to allow the enraged peasants to take the law into their own hands and murder the landlords; rather, landlords are permitted to maintain enough land to earn a living, and to serve as negative examples of behavior. Ting Ling allows her villain, Schemer Chien, to be spared death at the hands of the peasants largely through the efforts of a leading cadre, Chang Yu-min. Schemer Chien is then humiliated by the crowd, humbled to the depths of his soul, and degraded and shamed before the assembly. At one point, he is forced to write a confession. As he begins to read it aloud, the following lively exchange takes place, demonstrating the author's adroitness in shifting quickly from the mood of the previous passage to that of the following one:

Chien knelt in the middle of the stage, his lined gown hanging in shreds, shoeless, not daring to meet anyone's eyes. He read: "In the past I committed crimes in the village, oppressing good people...!"

"That won't do! Just to write 'I' won't do! Write 'local despot, Chien.'"

"Yes, write 'I, local despot, Chien.'"

"Start again!"

Schemer Chien started reading again: "I, Chien, a local despot, committed crimes in the village, oppressing good people, and I deserve to die a hundred times over; but my good friends are merciful...."

"Who the devil are you calling your good friends?" An old man rushed forward and spat at him.

"Go on reading! Just say all the people of the village."

"No, why should he call us his people."

"Say all the gentlemen."

"Say all the poor gentlemen. We don't want to be rich gentlemen! Only the rich are called gentlemen."

Chien had to continue: "Thanks to the mercy of all the poor gentlemen in the village...."

"That's no good. Don't say poor gentlemen; today we poor people have stood up. Say 'the liberated gentlemen,' and it can't be wrong."

"Yes, liberated gentlemen."

Someone chuckled. "Today we're liberated gentlemen!"[16]

After completing land reform, the Party began the next stage in the socialization of Chinese agriculture, the establishment of mutual aid teams and elementary agricultural cooperatives. This process is the subject of a majority of literary works written in the 1950s, well-represented by Chao Shu-li's novel, *Sanliwan Village (San-li-wan,* 1955). Chao Shu-li is one of the first writers recognized as a follower of Chairman Mao's theoretical guidelines on literature. He began writing in the 1940s as a propaganda worker during the War of Resistance and produced a large number of short stories and several novels during his career. His early short story, "The Rhymes of Li Yu-ts'ai" *(Li Yu-ts'ai pan-hua,* 1943) gained him widespread recognition in the Communist areas. His most salient features are a simple yet vivid style and the use of the folk language and somewhat traditional mode of writing, all of which make his works popular among the literate peasants and cadres and easily understood when read aloud to the others.

Sanliwan Village, one of his later works, represents a change in pace from his earlier stories because usage of the folk idiom and his usual humorous satire are largely absent. It tells of the efforts of a number of progressisve peasants in Sanliwan to collectivize agricultural production through the inauguration of an agricultural co-op. There are no landlords standing in their way (as in Ting Ling's novel) because land reform has been completed. The main obstruction comes from the so-called backward characters, peasants who, out of a sense of individualism and the desire for individual profit, do not support collectivization, but who are not counterrevolutionaries or class enemies. The central characters are progressive people holding socialist ideals, who, through their courage and selflessness as well as by cooperative example, eventually manage to persuade the backward to join the co-op movement. Interestingly, there is also a subplot involving love and marital relationships among the leading youthful characters, who pair up on the basis of corresponding attitudes about ideology and work.

A sample from one such relationship will illustrate the integration of political ideology and love among young Communists. Fan Ling-chih, a pretty, able, educated young Communist Youth League member and co-op bookkeeper, has always thought her logical mate to be Ma Yu-yi, also a comparatively well-educated Youth League member. However, as the story progresses, Ling-chih begins to see ideological defects in Yu-yi, which she cannot overlook and which prevent her from considering him as a potential husband. One evening she begins daydreaming of another marriage possibility, Wang Yu-sheng, whose characteristics she describes as follows: "He's straight, dependable, unselfish, intelligent, competent, and handsome! But he's had no education." In comparison to Yu-yi, Yu-sheng has the higher ideological qualifications: "Yu-sheng gave all his thought to building socialism, Yu-yi to obeying his feudal-minded mother." With some effort, she is able to overcome her intellectual snobbery, reasoning as follows:

> "Someone with education should do better work than someone without," she told herself. "But Yu-sheng has done a lot of things nobody else could do, and what has Yu-yi, for all his schooling, done? What have I done, for that matter? I've merely been a few years at junior middle school, and the little I learned there is only good for playing about with. As soon as I teach Yu-sheng anything, he can use it straight away on worthwhile jobs. That shows which of us is the better . . . . I mustn't go on underestimating him . . . ."[17]

Thus, it is the young man's native intelligence and dedication to the socialist ideal which attract the central female character. Only a positive character, one who possesses the qualities ascribed to Yu-sheng, can win the heart of a female Communist Youth League member. Her ideology and love are inextricably intertwined, and love therefore is founded on a concrete basis. It is impossible for Yu-yi, a backward yet intelligent boy, to win the love of his sweetheart, because his obedience to the feudal dictates of his obstructionist parents (despite his Youth League membership) makes him unacceptable. In the end, Ling-chih's engagement to Yu-sheng jolts Yu-yi and he revolts against parental oppression. It has taken this loss of love to convince him of the error of his backward ways. The above passage defines the positive characteristics to which every Chinese youth is expected to aspire and implies that backward ideology will lead to failure in love.

The question of backward ideology is one of the most pressing themes in contemporary Chinese fiction. It goes much deeper than a difference of opinion or success and failure at love. Those peasants with ideologically backward perceptions, or those who believe it more profitable to acquire land and build up one's own family fortunes, can, in actual fact, stall the advance of socialist economic development. This problem forms the central issue in one of the most celebrated novels in contemporary China, Liu Ch'ing's *The Builders* (*Ch'uang-yeh shih*, 1960). Liu Ch'ing has been a Party member since the mid-1930s. He worked as a newspaper editor, novelist, and political cadre during the War of Resistance. In 1952, he settled down in a small village, taking a post as a high-ranking local Party representative. He became an expert on the economic and political issues of the countryside, and he produced *The Builders* largely in an effort to present issues and offer suggestions for their resolution. The story concerns the efforts of Liang Sheng-pao, a poor peasant and Party member, to organize other poor peasants into a successful mutual aid team and then a small cooperative. He is required to struggle against every obstruction, primarily the machinations of the local rich peasant (not quite a landlord but able to hire wage laborers and possessing the highest allowable level of wealth in the countryside). Sheng-pao succeeds brilliantly in the end through hard work, correct politics (he is guided by the Party), and persuasion by positive example.

Another important opposition is the hero's father, Liang the Third. He is an old peasant beaten down by poverty and by the oppression of the local landlord. With the arrival of land reform, his lifelong hope of building up the family fortunes is boosted. However, his chances for success are destroyed when his son, Sheng-pao, decides to put his energies into the mutual aid team and cooperative movements, devoting no time to building family prosperity and individual gain. The arguments between these two stubborn men are representative of the two contradictory sides of the central issue facing all Chinese people: should they engage in individually building up their family fortunes, an opportunity provided by the Party's redistribution of land, or should they sacrifice immediate personal advantage for the sake of the development of the entire community, which in the end would result in everyone's gain? The former alternative is "taking the capitalist road," while the latter is the "path to socialism."

Liang the Third's ideology and his personal goals are reflected in his lifelong dream:

> ... he dreamed that he no longer lived in his thatched cottage but in a fine house with a tile roof, and it stood on the site of the three-room building he had razed years ago. The two shacks on either side had been converted into tile-roofed wings! Ho-ho! Liang the Third was the owner of a splendid compound. He wore winter clothes with thick padding. A strong blue sash bound his waist. He was deliciously warm, so heavily upholstered in fact that he walked a bit clumsily. Still, what could he say? The clothes had been made for him by his son and daughter-in-law. They were so devoted. He could only wear the heavy garments and parade about his splendid courtyard.[18]

This dream will not come true, for Liang Sheng-pao has his dream as well:

> It was in the idealistic spirit of the Red guerrillas that he formed one of the first mutual aid teams amid a sea of individualistic small peasant producers. Secretary Yang put it well: The shooting phase of the revolution was over; the revolution to prove the superiority of cooperative farming, to produce more grain, was just beginning. Sheng-pao was determined to model himself after the older generation of Communists. He would devote all of his ardour, intelligence, spirit, and practical work to this cause of the Party. Only in this way, he felt, would life be interesting, stimulating.[19]

The difference between these two dreams is the difference between the spirit of the old China and the new. The old man's dream may appear to be more realistic, but it is a personal one, doomed to failure in a collective society. Is Sheng-pao too idealistic, too "pure-hearted'? This becomes a moot question when he succeeds in his tasks. Moreover, Liang the Third, watching his son, seeing his honesty and determination and his ability to continue despite setbacks, is persuaded to alter his dream. Overcoming his fears and suspicions, and recognizing the limited nature of his goals, Liang the Third has a change of heart:

> ... It was as the father of Sheng-pao, chairman of the Lighthouse Agricultural Producers' Cooperative, that he trod the streets ... in brand new cotton padded clothing, nice and warm and dignified....
> "You're a good boy, son. You have a heart," Liang the Third had said. "... you go out and level the bumps in the world. Your grandpa told me it couldn't be done even if you used a shovel. I believed him and always accepted my fate. I passed his words on to you, but you didn't believe me. Go out and fight, then. I'll look after the household, sweep the courtyard, and feed the pigs...."[20]

The theme of the struggle in the countryside over the issue of agricultural collectivization is a common one in the works of one of the most prolific newer writers in contemporary China, Hao Jan. Even though he has recently been attacked for his connections with the "Gang of Four," Hao Jan has won acclaim for his two important novels, *Bright Sunny Skies* (*Yen-yang t'ien*, three volumes, 1964-1966) and *Great Golden Highway* (*Chin-kuang ta-tao*, two volumes, 1972-1974). Hao Jan is a peasant writer turned professional. He began his career with only three years of formal education by producing Party propaganda work during the Civil War. Later, he studied literary theory and began writing short stories. His works are quite popular, both for their peasant earthiness and their Party-approved ideology. He is one of only a few professional writers to have come through the Cultural Revolution unscathed, and he is currently the most favored Chinese writer.

Hao Jan's short stories cover a variety of themes, including individual heroism, learning from the older generation, and the role of women in Chinese agricultural production. One of his best stories, "Jade Spring," published in 1964, considers the latter theme. It is a vignette from the life of a young, energetic, idealistic village girl, a commune member who is embarking on a life of "building the new socialist countryside." Although she is very active in commune work, her mother plans to send her to Peking to acquire a higher education. Jade Spring has a deep sense of her rural roots and duty toward her community. She is not interested in leaving agricultural work and rural political struggles merely to pursue her own possible material gain in the city. Her strength of character is discerned through two brief dialogues about Peking in which she engages with the narrator, Comrade Liang. An excerpt from the first one:

> ... "Are people living in Peking all happy?" she asked.
> "Of course."
> "I don't think so." And she shook her head.[21]

And from the second one:

> "Jade Spring," I said, "that day when I said Peking was beautiful, you replied that it must be as beautiful as the Winding Hill Village. When I answered you that people living in Peking were all happy, you didn't agree with me. I wondered why you thought that way. Now I understand.
> ... "You should have known, Peking is beautiful because its builders are fine people. By dint of hard work people can make a place that's not so beautiful into a magnificent one. If you have no socialist consciousness, no will to devote your whole life to socialism, but only wait for other people to build Peking into a lovely place and then go there to enjoy what others have built with their labor, without lifting a finger yourself, you will never be happy."[22]

Jade Spring's comments reflect her depth of vision and her ability to understand fundamental principles. Hard work toward community goals—socialist consciousness—includes the precept that man makes of his world what he will. Only the participants in the ongoing process can find real happiness; the mere bystanders, the hangers-on, those who would profit from the labor of others, will never be truly happy. Thus, she sees little point in abiding by her mother's strong yet backward desire to send her off to the city—true happiness and purposeful work await her at home.

Hao Jan pays close attention to the craft of writing. In describing the setting he draws a portrait of a healthy and lively environment, which directly corresponds to the mood of the story and the personal traits of the young girl. He utilizes the description of lush scenery to reflect both the natural and spiritual prosperity of the commune:

> We proceeded along a path on a slope. Except for the path the whole area was green—dark green, with a few flowers here and there, like white and yellow lanterns gladdening the eye. Birds and insects were chirping, flying, or leaping about in the bushes and among the flowers, making a lively scene all round.[23]

Hao Jan employs this device throughout his various works, so that lush imagery has become symbolic of the spiritual and material wealth of the Chinese people under Communist Party leadership. In the story "The Lean Chestnut Horse" (*I-p'i shou-hung ma*, 1957), for example, he describes the natural setting of a successful cooperative:

> It was an enchanting spring morning on the farm. Wild geese flew in formation amidst white clouds in a sky of blue. Peach and pear blossoms brightened the river bank beneath swaying willows, a light breeze scattered the pink and white petals on to the blue stream, which carried them away. The fields were green, either with turf dotted with small wild flowers, or with wheat sprouts, all nodding with dew and seeming to smile.[24]

This tranquil and rich scene veils the fact that the Chinese countryside is an ideological and economic battleground, the site of the struggle between those who wish to attempt large-scale agricultural collectivization and those who prefer to make a living alone, relying on their own hard work and talent. This struggle is reflected in the vast majority of works of agricultural fiction, and while the focus is different and the emphasis varies from work to work, the central theme remains the same. All these works carry a heavy ideological emphasis. There are few frivolous tales, and no stories purport to be mere sources of amusement. The task of the post-Revolution generation is to build a socialist China, and literature faithfully reflects the execution of that task.

The People's Liberation Army in War and Peace

The People's Liberation Army (PLA) is the armed force of the Communist revolution in China, born out of guerrilla warfare against the Nationalists (KMT) and the Japanese invaders. By the time of the Japanese surrender in August 1945, the PLA had succeeded in gaining the confidence of a large portion of the population, which aided the Communist army against the Nationalist Party from 1946 to 1949. The Communist Party has always encouraged the Chinese to think of the Communist army as their own, hence, its name was changed from "Red Army" to "People's Liberation Army." Thus, the victory of the PLA is also a people's victory, and the daring and heroic exploits of the army belong to the people as well. This theme dominates many of the works depicting the activities of the PLA at war and in peace.

The number of works treating the lives of soldiers is much smaller than that of the other categories, but the impact of military tales on the population is undoubtedly great. This is because of their widespread popularity among the people, whose ideology and psychology regarding war and armed class struggle cannot help but be shaped by the militant attitudes expressed in works of this type. Moreover, the Chinese have always been fond of military fiction, as evidenced by the elevation to classic status of such works as *Romance of the Three Kingdoms* and *The Water Margin*, from which many episodes have been made into popular operas. In the past, even illiterate peasants were quite familiar with details of these works from watching the operas. In fact, the ordinary Chinese person's perception of the history of the Three Kingdoms and Sung periods, in which these classic works are set, is largely formed by the events and characterizations in these fictional tales.

One contemporary work of fiction in the military category, Ch'ü Po's novel, *Tracks in the Snowy Forest* (*Lin-hai hsüeh-yüan*, 1957), has already become a modern classic because of its high popularity and the adaptation of one of its episodes as a model revolutionary opera, *Taking Tiger Mountain by Strategy*, which has recently been discredited for its author's connections with the "Gang of Four." Ch'ü Po was a young PLA commander of an elite guerrilla unit sent in the winter of 1946 into the mountains of Northeast China to track down some Nationalist bandit-guerrilla forces who were carrying out raids from their three mountain strongholds. A career soldier with only six years of primary school education, Ch'ü Po wrote this novel as a thinly disguised autobiographical account of his wartime experiences. At the time of its publication in 1957, he was a vice-director of an industrial designing bureau. He had been severely wounded in 1950 and reassigned to a job in industry. Thus, this fine and successful novel is the work of an amateur writer who had little formal creative writing training or experience, yet it is highly regarded as an example of culture produced by a representative of the army.

The story concerns the daring exploits and clever stratagems employed by the major figures of the expedition in their successful capture of the bandit strongholds. It is, in the words of one critic, "... an adventure story ... full of scout tricks, sensational episodes and breathtaking suspense, interwoven with colorful legends and romantic myths."[25] The myths give the work an aura of fantasy resting on a foundation of revolutionary romanticism, which provides exciting and intriguing reading. In one episode, for example, the guerrillas must capture an enemy fortress in the Cave of the Nymph on Breast Mountain. An old mountaineer tells the soldiers the story behind the name of this cave: There was long ago a young woman named Iris from a mountain tribe. She was lovely, intelligent, and creative, and was betrothed to a young, courageous man aptly named Hero. One autumn Iris was kidnapped by an enemy tribesman, Fat Pig, and was taken up the mountain. Hero gave chase, battled hundreds of Fat Pig's warriors single-handedly, but was forced to retreat. That night, as Iris wept bitterly in her tent, a tremendous gust of wind swept the entire enemy camp— Hero had rounded up a band of hunters and with their help defeated the bandits completely. The lovers were reunited and made their home in a cave high on Breast Mountain, which had been transformed into a lush fairyland by four mysterious goddesses:

> There was a blinding flash and Mount Fountain began gushing water, grain sprouted on Breast Mountain, grass grew everywhere, flowers burst

into bloom and the air was filled with thousands of birds of all descriptions. Iris sang for joy, Hero tooted gaily on his flute; the two celebrated for hours. Suddenly they remembered that they ought to thank their benefactors, but the four maidens were gone. All that remained were the glorious hues of the sunset clouds.[26]

Iris had many children which she sent to childless mortals, asking for nothing in return. After living in the cave for a long period of time, the couple sailed off on a cloud, spreading happiness to people everywhere. The cave has since been known as the Cave of the Child-Bestowing Nymph.

The main elements of the myth, especially the romantic quality of the characters, contain a lyrical symbolism and an allegorical function. The events in the myth closely parallel the story of the Nymph Cave episode itself. The PLA soldiers come on the scene to rescue the poor villagers from the plundering savagery of the Nationalist bandits, just as Hero saves Iris from Fat Pig. The Communist Party, in theory, brings the hope of a bright and prosperous utopian future, asking nothing in return for its efforts, just as the altruistic fairy maidens did. The people are beneficiaries in both the myth and the PLA episode; the allegory is not lost on them. This admixture of myth and socialist realism is a good example of the so-called "combination of revolutionary realism and revolutionary romanticism." The story is a relatively sophisticated mode of writing for an amateur such as Ch'ü Po, and thus it stands as a remarkable achievement.

There are many works reflecting the lives of PLA soldiers in times of peace. Among the most famous is the novel *The Song of Ou-Yang Hai* (*Ou-Yang Hai chih ko*, 1965) by Chin Ching-mai. It fictionalizes the true story of a PLA soldier, Ou-Yang Hai, who gave his life to save others. The work is highly propagandistic because it was written in the early days of the Cultural Revolution. The author seems not to have published much after this book. During the Cultural Revolution, a large number of short stories extolling the army and its close relationship with the masses appeared. These works tend to place greater emphasis on content than on aesthetics and create a propagandistic rather than literary effect.

More representative of the good writings reflecting the role of the soldier in peacetime are the short stories of Wang Yüan-chien. Wang began his career as a correspondent and editor in the army during the War of Resistance. He began writing short stories in 1953 while still a professional soldier, and he later rose to the important post of editor of the literary publishing house of the PLA. By 1958 he had built an impressive first collection of stories and articles about army life written by an insider.

Wang's best-known story is "An Ordinary Laborer" (*P'u-t'ung lao-tung che*, 1958). The ordinary laborer is actually a high-ranking general, veteran of the wars, who has voluntarily assumed the guise of a common soldier in order to work among the men at a dam construction site (construction is one of the major tasks of the PLA in peacetime). He is physically out of shape, slow, and aging, but he works hard and is befriended by an unsuspecting young soldier who assists him on his first day. As they each shoulder an end of a carrying pole, the two quickly become friends, the young man helping the old with respect for the latter's spirit of perseverance in the harsh environment. At one point a crisis occurs: a sudden rainstorm halts the loading of dirt and gravel onto the train cars, yet some cars must be loaded. The section chief is at a staff meeting, leaving the workers disorganized. The general, with aching muscles and pain from his old war wounds, rises to the occasion without revealing his identity:

> The scene evoked a responsive chord in the general. This sort of thing oftenhappened in a unit. Everyone would know what ought to be done in a certain situation, and would be itching to do it. But because no one took the lead, an entire unit would remain immobile. At such a time, if someone said only one word the unit would immediately plunge into action. The general shook the boy's arm.
> "Come on, Young Li. Let's go to work!"[27]

Of course, it is not unusual for a general to use his command experience in any situation, but the important point in this incident is its effect on the general himself:

> His cry was like a commmand. Everyone stood up. . . . Laughing, shouting, they followed the general toward the ramp. As he ran, the general glanced behind him and felt quite excited. "How many years is it since I did this?" he asked himself.[28]

The section chief returns to the site and reveals the general's identity to the young soldier, who is understandably quite embarassed about his familiarity. But the general simply shrugs it off, calling him a "young imp," and continues to work with him. This is the spirit and behavior which the army wishes to instill in its own members, from the highest to the lowest in rank. No job and no individual is unimportant; no man is too high-ranking to do a day's work. To a large extent, this concept is responsible for the PLA's victory in the Civil War, and for the army's ability to gain the respect and admiration of a large section of the population. This story is told in a simple and nonpropagandistic way, allowing the plausibility of the situation to strike the reader without undue political preaching. Like all of Wang Yüan-chien's stories, it seems to be a slice of real life.

Storyteller's Tales and Reportage

One of the earliest forms of fiction in China was the oral tale. A storyteller would stand on a street corner, in a village square, a teahouse, or anywhere people congregated and begin to tell a story in return for monetary contributions from his listeners. As the art grew, a number of conventions developed which are peculiar to this form: serialization (to keep the listeners coming and paying each day), special phrases denoting divergence from or return to the main story line, and the interspersing of verse within the course of the narrative. Moreover, the tales were delivered in a lively, colloquial manner (in order to keep the listeners entertained), and they often contained a moral lesson. Near the time of the Sung dynasty some of these tales were transcribed *(hua-pen)* and during the Ming period they were edited in collections. The main conventions, including frequent intrusions by the narrator, were retained in the written texts to maintain the semblance of the oral tale. Both an oral and a written storyteller tradition evolved and continues to the present.

An interesting reflection of the perseverance of the storyteller tradition in contemporary China occurs in Hao Jan's story, "Jade Spring." One evening an old storyteller begins a traditional tale, a story of the old society. Jade Spring, sitting a short distance away, enters into direct competition for listeners by beginning to tell a current revolutionary story about a heroine of the War of Resistance. She succeeds in drawing the crowd away from the old storyteller, and she fires up the revolutionary spirit of her listeners, thus effectively establishing a precedent for the nightly telling of stories with a socialist content. The form of the new tales and their manner of oral presentation remain similar to the tradition, but the content is contemporary.

Although the storyteller's tale is not a major category of writing, and in fact was largely neglected during the May Fourth period, it became the center of attention during the 1950s and 1960s. It was seen to have a valuable social function, which one English translator describes as follows:

> The storyteller's art has received much attention in the 1960s as it is one of the most effective ways of bringing political and other messages to ordinary people, particularly in the villages, who are not usually in the habit of reading for pleasure. The older storytellers have been urged to drop the traditional subject matter . . . in favour of new, revolutionary themes; and youngsters are being encouraged to learn the art. The mixture of prose and verse . . . is an interesting reminder of the continuing vigour of old forms used by professional storytellers some thousand years ago.[29]

A good example of this type of story is T'ang Keng-liang's "The Paupers' Co-op" (*Ch'iung-pan-tzu pan-she*, 1965). Based on the history of a real co-op founded by poor peasants in 1952, this tale relates the trials and tribulations of a village struggling to achieve a better standard of living through collectivization. Led by Party member Wang Ku-hsing, a self-sacrificing and determined man, the paupers create a flourishing commune out of a little land and much hard work and socialist organization. As the peasants overcome obstacle after obstacle, they (and the reader or listener) learn the lesson of the story: the key to success is organization along Party lines; hard work alone is not sufficient to accomplish the job. After all, hard work has not raised the standard of living for peasants over the centuries; only collectivization, the pooling of efforts, offers the chance for the enrichment of the entire community.

This lesson is transmitted in the lively manner of traditional storytelling, just as if it were intended for oral presentation. The author utilizes many of the traditional features: lively, colloquial dialogue, intrusion by the narrator (in the form of rhetorical questions addressed to the reader), and liberal interspersing of verse at significant points in the story, as the following passage illustrates:

> The next day . . . Du Hong and his eighteen men marched off briskly to the mountains.
>
> > Were they hard pressed? Not they!
> > They coped the poor men's way.
> > Just see these men!
> > Nineteen paupers of one heart and mind
> > Plaited straw ropes and whetted their old sickles;
> > Dry rations and bedding-rolls on their backs,
> > They left their village and went into the hills.
> > Among the treacherous rocks, the towering peaks,
> > By day they cut brushwood, and they slept in an old temple at night.
> > The wind cut like a knife, snow whirled like feathers,
> > But the poor have grit and courage higher than heaven.
> > Despite their troubles they wrested treasures from the mountains,
> > And after a hard fight came home laden with spoils.
>
> In twenty days they cut more than twenty tons of brushwood, which they sold in town for 430 yuan. Was everyone pleased! These paupers had never handled so much money.[30]

The passsage reflects a revolutionary-romantic perception of the group of poor peasants, whose success in cutting brushwood is viewed as an act of heroism. Indeed, with their sickles as weapons they battle with the forces of nature, wind and mountains, and their victory is reminiscent of that of a conquering army. As in war, they bring home the spoils, which they have "wrested" from the treasure chest of nature, and their morale is high. Thus, an act of economic survival is elevated to heroic proportions, much as in works of traditional romanticism. The images are lyrical and romantic: treacherous rocks, towering peaks, an old temple at night, wind cutting like a knife. The messaage is transmitted in a context of excitement and adventure. In this manner, the storyteller achieves the dual objectives of entertainment and education.

On the opposite end from the storytelling tradition is the newest mode of writing, the form known as reportage. It is a hybrid, half truth and half fiction, which concerns itself with reporting the details of a true story with fictionalized embellishments. This form, which became popular actually as early as the 1930s, was found to be quite useful during the war period, inasmuch as it presented news and propaganda in a palatable fashion. Likewise, literary people serving as correspondents at the Korean War front (notably Pa Chin), or as travelers reporting on conditions in other countries or at home, often use this method of writing. During the Cultural Revolution, reportage was a common means of conveying policy messages to the population by presenting stories of model workers, peasants, soldiers, and political cadres. Each story presented models of behavior which the population was supposed to imitate and illustrations of the implementation of Party policy on specific issues.

A recent example of this type of writing is "The Countryside Is a University Too," an unsigned reportage article in the monthly periodical, *Chinese Literature* (April 1974). This is the semifictionalized account of the experiences of Chu Ke-chia, a high school graduate from Shanghai, who volunteered in 1969 to go to the mountains of Yunnan to help the local Tai and Aini people progress toward socialism. At the same time, his goal was to learn from them and to temper himself as a revolutionary. It is the policy of the Party to assign educated youth from the cities to a period of "tempering" and "learning from the poor and middle peasants" in the countryside. Some city youth oppose this policy, but Chu, on the contrary, decides to work in one of the most geographically distant and difficult posts among national minorities whose languages he does not speak. He is extremely dedicated and hard-working, and he finds no task too strenuous. He quickly learns the local languages, obtains a knowledge of carpentry, sewing, and mountain farming, and becomes the schoolteacher, tool repairman, and barber, among other things. At one point he is offered an opportunity to attend the university, but he refuses in order to continue to serve the people of the countryside (which is a "university" too). It is clear that the story is intended to bolster the spirit and dedication to socialism of the young people sent to the countryside by pointing out the experiences and positive attitude of one of their own as a model.

One illustration of Chu Ke-chia's dedication, and also a quaint scene, is the depiction of his first day as a schoolteacher at an Aini village:

> On the day school started, the villagers took their children, all dressed in their best, to the school. In soaring spirits Chu Ke-chia mounted the platform and began the first lesson in fluent standard Chinese. The pupils looked at each other. Some put their fingers in their mouths to prevent themselves from laughing.
> "Do you understand me?" Chu Ke-chia asked with concern. No answer came from the class.
> "Don't you understand me?" he asked again in Tai.
> "Weseigeya!" This answer, in Aini, meant: No, we don't!
> This dashed Chu Ke-chia's red-hot enthusiasm as effectively as a bucket of cold water. So the children understood no Chinese and only a smattering of Tai. He would have to teach in Aini: that was clear. But he knew very little of the dialect. . . .
>
> After months of hard work, Chu Ke-chia was able to teach in fluent Aini. He taught the children songs and told them stories, too, in their own

language. Soon they were all devoted to their teacher. And when, for the first time, his pupils wrote, "Long live Chairman Mao!" young Chu's happiness knew no bounds.[31]

This type of story tends to contain more than the average amount of pure politics, as reflected by the phrase, "Long live Chairman Mao!" Elsewhere in the narrative Chu is described as studying Marxism-Leninism and Mao Tse-tung's Thought late into the night "to arm his mind with revolutionary theory." In the end, he joins the Party and is elected an alternate member of the Central Committee of the Tenth National Party Congress. Afterward, "a new challenge confronted him: how to live up to the expectations of the Party and the people?" A true Communist, he is a dedicated and humble person, imbued with revolutionary spirit, a "socialist man" of the contemporary period. Yet, in a political sense, he is an "everyman," an ordinary high school graduate performing daily tasks, but in a rather exotic environment. The political message is clear: if Chu Ke-chia can do it, so can others, and this is the expectation for Communist youth.

Fiction and Politics in Contemporary China

All the works presented for discussion in the foregoing sections have their unique characteristics, but they possess a common element: an ideological content based upon socialist principles and Mao Tse-tung's theoretical guidelines. Each work is political in nature, treating contemporary social issues as the central focus for the structure of the plot. The characters are infused with political consciousness to varying degrees, and each is categorized (hero, villain, backward character) according to ideological criteria. Even lyrical passages describing the natural environment often contain political significance. The object of all of this politicization of fiction is to integrate literature into the mainstream of Chinese social life, to produce works of literature which both reflect and affect the development of politics and economics and the revolutionizing of the attitudes and practices of the Chinese people.

The success of each work depends on the degree to which politics is combined with artistry to produce a moral and social vision sufficiently powerful to move or persuade the reader to examine his or her ideological consciousness. This is accomplished by providing an illumination of contemporary life through characters who are convincingly motivated and situations which are "typical" (i.e., representative of the most significant conjunction of social forces). In this way a section of real life is examined, explored, and analyzed; the author thus contributes a new insight or perspective on a developing situation. The reader in turn is motivated to incorporate the central ideas expressed into his or her own social practice. The work itself has thereby attained two goals: both to reflect social life and to affect it by influencing readers.

Contemporary Chinese fiction is, therefore, an active social force, a vehicle for social change. The Communist Party, as the leading political force in the country, recognizes and encourages literature that conforms to this role just as it denigrates and disallows works of simple entertainment or purely contemplative value. While in theory it is the broad masses of the people who are the final arbiters of the social value of literary works, in practice the Party functionaries and official literary critics decide which works to publish. Thus, the works which are published and disseminated, such as those reviewed in the preceding sections, have undergone a fairly stringent political examination. Even so, times change and the political situation develops beyond the scope of works written in an earlier period. Consequently, works praised and rewarded in one political moment may fall into disrepute at a later date.

This volatile literary environment presents an insurmountable obstacle to the nonpolitical writer, not to mention the writer whose politics are in opposition to the prevailing orthodoxy. There have been short periods of time when such writers have been allowed to air their views, notably the Hundred Flowers Period (1956-1957), but their works have always been criticized heavily and sometimes even taken off the public market. Even the most orthodox Party writers find it difficult to keep abreast of the shifting political developments, as can be seen in the case of Ting Ling (mentioned above) and many others. The most telling example of this problem is the negative criticism of the veteran professional writers which occurred during the Cultural Revolution.

The Cultural Revolution (1965-1969) brought about great changes not only in culture, but also in politics. In one of the political changes, Chairman Mao's wife, Chiang Ch'ing, a former movie actress, ascended to high political power and was given responsibility for cultural matters. She utilized her power, with the aid of her close comrades, to affect the course of literary development for a decade, until the dramatic removal from power of the "Gang of Four" (of which she was a member) following Mao's death in 1976. Chiang Ch'ing had taken up the important task of revolutionizing the Peking Opera, replacing traditional themes with revolutionary ones (such as the aforementioned episode from *Tracks in the Snowy Forest*), and under her leadership the majority of the works of fiction written in the first fifteen years of the People's Republic were discredited or banned. In their place were created novels, short stories, and reportage containing highly propagandistic themes and a relatively low level of literary artistry. Thus, the political aspect of culture was overemphasized to the detriment of literary aesthetics, and the majority of the works written during and after the Cultural Revolution do not measure up to the level of revolutionary aesthetics achieved by many of the pre-Cultural Revolution novels and stories.

It is generally believed that the post-Chiang Ch'ing era of literary development will be characterized by a more liberal attitude toward aesthetics and technical achievement. Some observers speculate about a revival of flexibility in the political aspect of literary creation, resulting in some works of a less orthodox ideological content. Probably the most realistic prediction, however, is that a body of literature will emerge quite similar to that of the 1950s and early 1960s, perhaps incorporating some Western literary techniques, but of an essentially politically active and engaged nature. Whereas the policies of Chiang Ch'ing and her comrades served to stifle growth in all but one direction, the new government is now allowing some new experimentation. Under the leadership of Hua Kuo-feng and Teng Hsiao-p'ing, many significant developments have taken place. Literary works published before the Cultural Revolution, especially works of the 1920s and 1930s, have now become available and are in fact often praised. Many writers discredited during the Cultural Revolution, such as Lao She, and even those severely criticized before the Cultural Revolution, like Ting Ling, have been rehabilitated. New variations in technique and theme are allowed. For instance, love stories and works describing personal tragedies have appeared. Some veteran fiction writers, such as Pa Chin, are now actively engaged in creative writing after a lapse of more than ten years. These encouraging developments have led some observers to predict the coming of "a spring in literature and art."[32]

The Western reader, used to a different type of fiction written under dissimilar conditions, must not only gain an understanding of the principles underlying the creation of contemporary Chinese fiction, but must also determine the correct criteria for evaluating that fiction. Those who contend that there are universal aesthetic criteria by which to view such disparate works as *War and Peace* and, say, *Tracks in the Snowy Forest*, or *The Possessed* and *The Builders*, are often guilty of ignoring the dangers inherent in applying politically prejudiced and culture-bound criteria developed in the West to literature written in contemporary China. While Chinese fiction may be asked to illuminate social life, depict believable and rounded characters, and possess an ample moral and social vision, the Chinese concept of the superiority of politics over pure aesthetics as well as the necessity for "correctness" in ideological presentation must also be taken into account. Does the work serve the people by advancing their socialist consciousness?—is it faithful in depicting "typical characters under typical circumstances"?—does it combine political theory with social practice, enlightening the reader regarding the "correct" application of the two?—these are some of the questions asked by Chinese commentators and literary critics in their evaluation of the works.

At the present time, very little critical work has been done by Western scholars on this subject.[33] Therefore, it cannot be said that any acceptable criteria have been developed in the West for evaluating works of Communist fiction. Indeed, the identification of the works and discussion of them in survey fashion has barely begun.[34] The first step to be taken is the formulation of a widely accepted methodology for treating the important question of the relation between politics and literature in China so that scholars may proceed from the mere description of contemporary Chinese fiction to a thorough critical analysis and evaluation of individual works. This is one of the most important tasks for scholars of modern Chinese fiction in the coming years.[35]

NOTES

1. Mao Tse-tung, "Talks at the Yenan Forum on Literature and Art (1942)," in Mao Tse-tung, *Mao Tse-tung on Literature and Art* (Peking: Foreign Languages Press, 1967), p.22.
2. *Ibid.*, p. 16.
3. *Ibid.*, p. 21.
4. *Ibid.*, p. 30.
5. *Ibid.*, p. 19.
6. Friedrich Engels, "Letter to Margaret Harkness (1888)," in *Marxists on Literature: An Anthology*, ed. David Craig (Middlesex, England: Penguin Books, 1975), p. 269.
7. "Statutes of the Union of Soviet Writers (1934)," in *Soviet Literature Today*, ed. George Reavey (New Haven:Yale University Press, 1947), pp. 19-20.
8. Ts'ao Ming, *The Motive Force*, (*Yüan-tung li*) (Peking: Jen-min wen-hsüeh ch'u-pan-she, 1949), pp. 95-96.
9. Ai Wu, *Steeled and Tempered* (Peking: Foreign Languages Press, 1961), pp. 35-36.
10. *Ibid.*, pp. 389-390.
11. Chou Yang,*The Path of Socialist Literature and Art in China* (Peking: Foreign Languages Press, 1960), p. 14.
12. *Ibid.*, pp. 38-39.
13. Tu P'eng-ch'eng, *In Days of Peace* (Peking: Foreign Languages Press, 1962), p. 175 (A slightly modified translation.)
14. Hu Wan-ch'un, "Aging Years" (*Wan-nien*) in his *Chia-t'ing wen-ti* (*Family Problems*) (Shanghai: Writers Publishing House, 1964), p. 18.
15. Ting Ling, *The Sun Shines over the Sangkan River* (Peking: Foreign Languages Press, 1954), p. 287.
16. *Ibid.*, p. 292.
17. Chao Shu-li, Sanliwan Village (Peking: Foreign Languages Press, 1964), p. 22.
18. Liu Ch'ing, *The Builders* (Peking: Foreign Languages Press, 1964), p. 22.
19. *Ibid.*, p. 102.
20. *Ibid.*, pp. 571-572.
21. Hao Jan, "Jade Spring," in his *Bright Clouds* (Peking: Foreign Languages Press, 1974), p. 123.
22. *Ibid.*, p. 139.
23. *Ibid.*, p. 121.
24. *Ibid.*, pp. 9-10.
25. Joe C. Huang, *Heroes and Villains in Communist China* (New York: Pica Press, 1973), p. 135.
26. Ch'ü Po, *Tracks in the Snowy Forest* (Peking: Foreign Languages Press, 1965), pp. 102-103.
27. Wang Yüan-chien, *An Ordinary Laborer* (Peking: Foreign Languages Press, 1961), p. 182.
28. *Ibid.*
29. W. J. F. Jenner, *Modern Chinese Stories* (London: Oxford University Press, 1970), p. 243.
30. T'ang Keng-liang, "The Paupers' Co-op," in Jenner, *Modern Chinese Stories*, pp. 250-251.
31. "The Countryside Is a University Too," *Chinese Literature*, No. 4 (April 1974), p. 73.
32. For a discussion of some of these new developments, see Bonnie McDougall, "Research Note," *Modern Chinese Literature Newsletter*, 4, No. 1 (Spring 1978), 12-18.

33. Among the attempts at critical evaluation of post-1949 works is the collection of articles published in the *China Quarterly*, 13 (1963), and Huang, *Heroes and Villains in Communist China*, p. 135.

34. Among the best collections of post-1949 fiction, which present translations of some of the representative works, are: John Berninghausen and Ted Huters, *Revolutionary Literature in China* (White Plains, N.Y.: M. E. Sharpe, 1976); W. J. F. Jenner, *Modern Chinese Stories*; Kai-yu Hsu, *The Chinese Literary Scene* (New York: Vintage Books, 1975); and the monthly magazine *Chinese Literature*. Unfortunately, many of the translations of post-1949 fiction published in China are now out of print and unavailable in American book stores and can be found only in libraries. However, some American and Hong Kong publishers are beginning to reprint translations of the major novels. For a listing of some of these reprints, see the bibliographical section of this book.

35. For a detailed listing of post-1949 stories and novels, see Meishi Tsai, *Contemporary Chinese Novels and Short Stories, 1949-1974: An Annotated Bibliography* (Cambridge: Council on East Asian Studies, Harvard Univ., 1979). Two recent English-language anthologies of post-1949 fiction deserve attention: Winston L. Y. Yang and Nathan K. Mao, eds., *Stories of Contemporary China* (New York: Paragon Book Gallery, 1979); and Geremie Barmé and Bennett Lee, trs.' *The Wounded: New Stories of the Cultural Revolution* (Hong Kong: Joint Publishing Co., 1979). Both anthologies contain stories written since the death of Mao Tse-tung and the downfall of the Gang of Four in 1976. Kai-yu Hsu's *Literature of the People's Republic of China* (Bloomington: Indiana University Press, 1979), which is a very comprehensive collection of post-1949 literature, also contains a number of stories written since 1949. For a brief account of Chinese literature of 1979, see Winston L. Y. Yang and Nathan K. Mao, "Chinese Literature," in *1980 Britannica Book of the Year* (Chicago: Encyclopaedia Britannica, 1981), pp. 516-517.

III

Taiwan Fiction Since 1949

1. PAI HSIEN-YUNG AND OTHER ÉMIGRÉ WRITERS

Winston L.Y. Yang

Until recently, Taiwan fiction has been a neglected field of study. Since the mid-1970s, however, such scholars as C. T. Hsia, Joseph S. M. Lau, and Timothy A. Ross have contributed much to the translation and criticism of this fiction.[1] As a result of their efforts, Taiwan fiction has become better known in the West. Since a comprehensive survey of Taiwan fiction cannot be attempted within our limited space, we shall discuss only a small number of writers whose works illustrate the range of the fiction of Taiwan. This essay will first survey the development of Taiwan fiction, focusing on Pai Hsien-yung as a representative of émigré writers; in the next essay, the works of Ch'en Ying-chen will be examined as illustrative of the accomplishments of native Taiwanese writers.

The term "Taiwan fiction"[2] is used here as a matter of convenience; the same can be said of a "Taiwan writer." By Taiwan fiction we mean works authored by writers who were either born or raised in Taiwan, received their education on the island or, most important of all, have published there. Those who had emigrated to Taiwan after the Communist conquest of the mainland in 1949 and who continued their creative activities on the island are also considered Taiwan writers. Such writers as Ch'en Jo-hsi, who was born in Taiwan and is now a Canadian resident, are also regarded as Taiwan writers because they have published their major works in Taiwan despite their extended overseas stay.

The growth of literary activity in Taiwan was both slow and limited in the early years. In the first ten years or so after the Nationalist government moved to Taiwan in 1949, the main concern of the islanders was survival, and it was but natural that the government, preoccupied with the security of the island, gave scant attention to the arts and literature. The few literary magazines, mostly subsidized by the government or the Nationalist Party, were filled with stereotyped anti-Communist fiction written in a mechanical form. Little serious fiction emerged.

In part this can be attributed to the fact that in 1949 few major fiction writers had moved to Taiwan; nearly all stayed on the mainland. In the 1950s (and the early 1960s), moreover, most works of the May Fourth writers were unavailable in Taiwan. In fact, the works of such writers as Lu Hsün, Mao Tun, Pa Chin, and even Shen Ts'ung-wen, whose fiction suggests little sympathy with the Communist movement, remain banned today. This total separation from the writers of the May Fourth tradition hindered Taiwan's literary development, as did the lack of any visible interest in traditional fiction. The major classical novels, such as *Dream of the Red Chamber* and *Journey to the West,* were neither widely read nor systematically studied.[3] Western literature, too, was largely ignored; little was done in the area of translation and criticism.[4] Considering these factors, some scholars use the term "cultural desert" *(wen-hua sha-mo)* or "literary wasteland"[5] to describe the literary scene of Taiwan in those years. Of course, in discussing the literary activities of that period, we should not ignore the harsh political, social, and economic realities of the period. Lack of sufficient intellectual freedom, like the literary isolation from the major works of modern Chinese literature, was an important factor contributing to the "cultural desert." Other factors such as the "Recover the Mainland" myth have also been suggested by scholars,[6] but this myth should be viewed in perspective. Those who fled to Taiwan have always attempted to maintain their identity as legitimate representatives of China; they have viewed the Chinese Communists as an alien force and themselves as representatives of the mainstream of the Chinese tradition. In conjunction with the "Recover the Mainland" myth, they developed a sense of temporary stay in Taiwan; some even had a sense of "exile" or "rootlessness."[7] Thus, early Taiwan fiction was characterized by anti-Communism, escapism, and sentimental nostalgia for the bygone days on the mainland. For all these reasons, little serious realistic fiction revealing Taiwan life was written. In fact, no major native writers emerged until the 1960s.

It was against this background that Chiang Kuei (1908-1980), the most accomplished writer of the 1950s, gained prominence, although, ironically, he received less critical attention in Taiwan than in the West.[8] Chiang Kuei arrived in Taiwan at the age of forty in 1948. He published his first novel, *The Whirlwind (Hsüan-feng),* in 1952. Since then, he has written several other novels, including *The Rival Suns (Ch'ung-yang), The Green Sea and the Blue Sky: A Nocturne (Pi-hai ch'ing-t'ien yeh-yeh hsin), The White Horse (Pai-ma p'ien),* and *Mount Copper Cypress (T'ung-po shan).* Though devoted to anti-Communist themes, his fiction also depicts the deteriorating social, political, and economic conditions under the warlords and the Kuomintang that eventually brought success to the Communist movement. The setting of most of his novels is not Taiwan but the mainland of the early 1940s and the mid-1920s. A serious writer deeply convinced of the evils of Communism, Chiang Kuei tried to record in his fiction the history of his times as he saw it. Yet his works bear little resemblance to the stereotyped anti-Communist fiction of his contemporaries who enlarge upon Communist shortcomings while closing their eyes to the evils and failures of the Nationalists. It is little wonder that he received limited attention in Taiwan.

It was in the late 1950s that changes began to take place in every sphere of life in Taiwan. The threat of a Communist takeover gradually faded. Following the Korean War and especially after the signing of a mutual defense treaty with the United States (terminated by President Jimmy Carter in 1979), the people of Taiwan began to develop a greater sense of security. The economy showed encouraging signs of growth; the native Taiwanese began to gain economic, political, and social influence; slowly and painfully most mainlanders in Taiwan came to accept the reality of a long if not permanent stay on the island. Even though the "Recover the Mainland" myth has been dutifully maintained even until today, fewer and fewer people are still convinced of an eventual return to the mainland. And with the death of Chiang Kai-shek in 1975, the authorities finally began to draft long-range plans for developing Taiwan as a permanent home.

The literary scene began to change in the late 1950s, too. A serious journal devoted to both creative literature and literary criticism, *Literary Review (Wen-hsüeh tsa-chih)*,[9] began publication in 1956. Several other journals[10] which appeared in the late 1960s have also played an important role in promoting Taiwan literature. Toward the end of the 1950s and in the first half of the 1960s, a few writers were actively producing serious fiction. Besides Chiang Kuei, who remained active, Pai Hsien-yung (1937-) and Yü Li-hua (1931-) came into prominence. The themes of these two and others were mostly concerned with the lives of the mainlanders in Taiwan and the experiences of Chinese residents in the United States; anti-Communism was never a popular theme of the major writers of this period except Chiang Kuei.

Of the younger writers who gained prominence at this time, Pai Hsien-yung is probably the most accomplished. Departing from the hackneyed tradition of anti-Communist literature, he produced no works of propaganda, writing instead a series of short stories which realistically portray the lives of the mainland "exiles" in Taiwan and Chinese "exiles" in the United States and which reveal an in-depth understanding of their minds.

Born on the mainland, Pai Hsien-yung came to Taiwan in 1949 after twelve years in his native Kuei-lin and other places. He attended both high school and college in Taiwan. For him, life on the mainland was not much of his personal experience; he heard about it through conversations with older members and friends of his family. In contrast, Taiwan was very much a part of his immediate experience. The juxtaposition of memory of the past on the mainland and observation of life in present-day Taiwan has characterized most of his creative writing. The life of the mainlanders in Taiwan was the most important theme of his early fiction; his stories on such themes were written mostly after he came to the United States and were collected in a volume entitled *Taipei Residents (T'ai-pei jen)*[11] in 1971. His experience in America also led him to deal with another kind of Chinese exile: Chinese residents, especially students and intellectuals, in the United States.[12] All his recent and earlier stories were put together as a volume entitled *The Lonely Seventeenth Year (Chi-mo te shih-ch'i sui)*,[13] published in Taipei in 1977. During the past several years, he has published little; he is now writing a long work, *The Prodigal Sons (Nieh tzu)*, his first venture in the novel form. Pai commands a wide readership, and his new work has been attracting increasing attention since the appearance of its first installment in the literary magazine, *Modern Literature*, in 1977.[14]

Most of Pai Hsien-yung's best stories are now being translated into English.[15] Of those already available in translation, "Celestial in Mundane Exile" (*Tsê-hsien chi*), from the 1968 collection bearing the same title[16] and translated into English under the title "Li T'ung: A Chinese Girl in New York,"[17] is probably one of the best examples of Pai Hsien-yung's special gift, technique and imagination. A realistic story with a fairly simple plot, it deals with the experience of a Chinese girl stranded in New York. Li T'ung, born into a wealthy and well-educated family on the mainland, comes to the United States to attend a prestigious college, Wellesley. But before she completes her education, the Communist army takes over China. Her parents, fleeing Communist control, are drowned on a sinking ship bound for Taiwan, a tragedy which shatters her completely.[18] From then on she has to be completely on her own, financially, psychologically, and emotionally. Her life is characterized by a sense of loss and purposelessness. She is proud, self-conscious, and extremely attractive. The author gives the following account of her appearance:

> Her beauty was devastating. She literally shone in the gathering and it hurt the eye to look straight at her, as at the blinding sun that has jumped out of the sea. She had finely chiseled features and a tall, graceful figure. Her eyes, dark and flashing, were spellbinding. A riot of shining black hair, two thirds of it combed across her forehead, tumbled down on her left shoulder. On the left temple just above her ear was a hairpin, a big glistening spider made of small diamonds, its claws digging into her hair, its fat, roundish body tilted upward. She wore that day a Chinese white satin gown of silvery sheen, with a red maple leaf design. The maple leaves were each the size of a palm and flamed like balls of fire. No woman is a reliable judge of another's beauty, and I couldn't help suspecting that Hui-fen's reluctance to praise Li T'ung's looks was a form of protest. After all, standing next to Li T'ung, my bride's extreme prettiness was unmercifully overshadowed by her dazzling beauty.[19]

Such vivid descriptions of Li T'ung's physical appearance are often accompanied by subtle psychological insights. After she recovers from the tragic news, she becomes an entirely changed person. But no matter how successful she is in her career, she can never adjust herself completely to the reality of her new situation in the United States. China is where her roots are. But China is now "lost"; so are her parents. Her sense of herself as an exile is vividly evinced. For her, the glory of her family and, symbolically, that of China, are gone, yet the United States remains a strange land, despite her successful career. Unable to adjust to such realities, she tries to escape by drinking and playing mah-jongg, or by achieving greater successes in her career. Success, alcohol, gambling, and even psychological pretension, however, cannot sustain her pride and emotions. Ultimately, she ends her meaningless and drifting life. The author seems to use her as a symbol of China and to suggest that her failure is the failure of old China, which could not adjust itself to the modern world or make the changes necessary to meet the challenge from the West. But the author has injected no anti-Communist sentiments. It is through the tragedy of Li T'ung that the "tragedy" of China is revealed; the story's portrayal of a Chinese girl becomes a powerful commentary on modern China. Distinguished for its realistic technique and subtle psychological revelations, it is one of the finest Chinese stories written since the May Fourth era.

Among the "exiles" in Taiwan portrayed in Pai Hsien-yung's fiction is Yü Ch'in-lei, a professor of English literature at a local university who represents many of the émigré scholars living in both intellectually and economically reduced circumstances since their arrival from the mainland in 1948-49. In the story "Winter Nights" (*Tung-yeh*),[20] Yü, despite his early scholarly promise as an intellectual, idealistic, and revolutionary-minded student leader of the May Fourth Movement in the late 1910s, has achieved little in his specialized field. Moreover, his meager salary can hardly support his family; his difficult financial situation, nagging wife, and the lack of intellectual stimulation in Taiwan have made him lose interest in scholarly pursuits. To him, the island does not seem to offer a promising future. So he investigates the possibility of going to the United States to do research or to teach Chinese language courses in order to pay off his debts and send his promising son, a college student of science, to America. His present wife, unlike his deceased first wife, who shared his ideals and views, shows no understanding whatsoever either of the glory of his early years or of his present plight. He has found no hope for realizing the democratic ideals of the May Fourth Movement. Therefore, he would like to exile himself to America to improve his financial situation. In the story, he frankly explains what has happened to him to Wu Chu-kuo, an old friend on a brief visit to Taipei and a professor of Chinese history at the University of California at Berkeley:

> "Yes. I've not only wanted to go abroad, I have also tried to grab every opportunity to leave the country. Each year, as soon as I learned about any foreign grants to our Arts Faculty, I was always the first to apply. Five years ago, after a great deal of trouble, I finally got a Ford Foundation Fellowship for two years of research at Harvard. I was to be given almost ten thousand U.S. dollars a year. All my travel arrangements and formalities were being taken care of. The day I went to the American Consulate to have my visa signed, the Consul even shook my hand and congratulated me. But—can you imagine—as I was stepping out of the Consulate gates, a National Taiwan University student, riding past on his motor scooter, drove straight into me. The next thing I knew, I had a broken leg. . . .
>
> "Anyway, when I was in the hospital, I should have given up the fellowship immediately. Instead, I wrote to Harvard to say that my

injuries were only minor, and that I would leave for the States as soon as I was better. But I wound up staying five months, and by the time I came out, Harvard had withdrawn the fellowship...."[21]

The accident described above caused Yü permanent injuries, and he has since become lame. As a result, he has been forced to give up his plans for a visit to the United States. His hope, however, is revived by the brief return from America of Wu Chu-kuo, who, like Yü, had been an active student leader advocating democrary, science, literary reforms, and intellectual revolution during the May Fourth Movement. Instead of moving to Taiwan on the eve of the Communist takeover of the mainland in the late 1940s, Wu went to the United States and became an authority on T'ang history. Putting aside his early ideals, convictions, and concerns for China and his fellow countrymen, he has actively pursued a scholarly career. Despite his obvious success in his chosen field and a comfortable life in the United States, he tells his old friend Yü, to the latter's surprise, that he is not happy:

"Ch'in-lei, let me tell you something and you'll understand how I felt to be out of the country all these years." Wu Chu-kuo put his pipe down on the tea table, took off his silver-rimmed spectacles, and with his other hand kneaded the heavy wrinkles between his eyes. "I know what most people are thinking. They think I am having a good time visiting this country and that, giving lectures here, attending conferences there. Well, last year, I was at a convention of the Oriental History Society in San Francisco. In one session there was an American student freshly graduated from Harvard, who read a paper entitled 'A Reevaluation of the May Fourth Movement.' From the start this young fellow tore the movement to pieces. He was obviously convinced by his own eloquence. But it was his conclusion. His conclusion! These overzealous young Chinese intellectuals, he said, in an iconoclastic outburst against tradition, completely wiped out the Confucian system that had prevailed in China for over two thousand years. They were ignorant of the current condition of their country; they blindly worshipped Western culture, and had an almost superstitious belief in Western democracy and science. This created an unprecedented confusion in the Chinese intellectual climate. That is not all. As the Confucian tradition they attacked cracked up, these young people, who had grown up in a patriarchal system and lacked both independence of inquiry and the willpower to hold their own, found that they were in fact losing their only source of spiritual sustenance and, gripped by a sense of panic, they began to wander about like lost souls haunted by the spectre of a murdered father. They had overthrown Confucius, their spiritual father, and so they had to go through life carrying the burden of their crime. Thus began the long period of their spiritual exile: some threw themselves into totalitarianism; some retreated and took refuge in their tattered tradition; some fled abroad and became wise hermits concerned only with themselves. Thus what started as a revolutionary movement disintegrated and changed its nature. Then he concluded: 'Some Chinese scholars like to compare the May Fourth Movement to a Chinese Renaissance. But I consider it, at best, to be a cultural abortion.'

"By the time he finished reading the paper, there was a great deal of excitement in the room, especially among the several Chinese professors and students. Everyone turned to look at me, obviously expecting some sort of rebuttal. But I didn't say a thing, and after a while, quietly left the room. . . . To tell you the truth, Ch'in-lei, some of the youngster's conclusions wouldn't be difficult to refute. The only thing is . . . Just think, Ch'in-lei. During all these years of living abroad—they add up to several decades—what have I been really? A plain deserter. And on an occasion like that, how could I have mustered enough self-respect to stand and speak up for the May Fourth Movement? That's why, too, in all my expatriate days, I've never talked about the history of the Republican period. . . ."[22]

As for his publications, Wu Chu-kuo explains sadly: "All that stuff has been written only to fulfill the requirements of the American university system: 'publish or perish.' That's why every couple of years I would squeeze out a book. If I hadn't been required to publish, I would certainly not have written a single word."[23]

Despite Wu's revealing description of his overseas scholarly life, Yü says with a tremulous voice when Wu is about to get into a taxi:

"Chu-kuo, there's something I haven't been able to bring myself to say."
"Eh?"
"Do you think you could recommend me . . . I mean, I'd still like to go abroad to teach for a year or two, and if there is a university in the States that happens to have an opening . . ."
"Well, I'm afraid they might be reluctant to hire a Chinese to teach English literature."
"Of course, of course," Professor Yü cleared his throat "I wouldn't go to America to teach Byron—what I mean is, if there is a school which needs someone to teach Chinese or something like that . . ."
"Oh . . ." Wu Chu-kuo hesitated a moment. "Sure, I'll give it a try."[24]

These last few lines well reveal the inner thoughts of Yü Ch'in-lei. His deteriorating health, advanced age, and intellectual stagnation, as the title of the story suggests, simply mean long, cold winter nights for him. He often spends his time nostalgically recalling his youth during the era of the May Fourth Movement or reading Chinese chivalric fiction to escape from the harsh reality. His feelings of impotence and despair come out vividly.

Despite their differences in financial and professional status, both Yü and Wu, now in their sixties, can be viewed as exiles and escapists. Unable to face personal and national realities, they seek fulfillment elsewhere. While Wu seeks satisfaction or escape in scholarly success, Yü, without any future prospects, either tries to relive a life of the past which exists only in his memory or dreams of going to America to find a better economic life. In a sense, they symbolize the tragedy of twentieth-century Chinese intellectuals. Seeking to realize their ideals for a democratic and modernized China by active participation in the May Fourth Movement in their student days, both Yü and Wu have now given up their ideals and hopes. They may still retain some of their moral and patriotic concern for their own country, but it is their sense of futility and hopelessness which has distressed them most. Their plight is their inability to realize their ideals and to change the fate of China. While Yü has lost interest in serious scholarly pursuits and eventually becomes, like many other scholars in Taiwan, a symbol of intellectual stagnation, Wu, in his pursuit of academic success, has surrendered himself to the demands of the American educational system without much regard for genuine self-fulfillment. Thus, Wu views himself as a "plain deserter."[25] He specializes in T'ang history as an escape, because it is painful for him to deal with the history of modern China, whose tragedy he has witnessed personally. He has pursued a career without personal zest or moral convictions but merely to fulfill the requirements for tenure, promotion, and scholarly distinction. In his self-imposed exile in America, he exhibits, despite his success as an internationally known T'ang specialist, as much pathos as Yü does. The fates of both are not only sad but also ironic. While Wu's decision to emigrate from Peking to America may be viewed as a symbol of the desertion of China by Chinese intellectuals, Yü's ardent desire to go to the United States reveals the psychological abandonment of Taiwan by émigré scholars. Thus, "Winter Nights," as C. T. Hsia suggests, can be accepted as an elegy on "the dashed hopes of youth, of a generation of scholar-patriots who had failed to remake China according to their dreams and have to live out their lot, each according to his circumstances."[26] Through sharp contrasts between past and present, between father and son, between the China of the 1910s and 1920s and Taiwan since 1949, the author reveals the spiritual numbness and death of Chinese intellectuals.

There is little doubt that Pai Hsien-yung can be regarded as one of the most gifted and accomplished writers to have emerged from Taiwan since the late 1950s. In depicting the lives of former generals and officials exiled from the mainland to Taiwan, he has created many memorable characters in *Taipei Residents*. Their sentimental recollections, personal frustrations, and sorrowful and often tragic lives characterized by a sense of futility are vividly presented to the reader. As for the "exiled" Chinese professionals in America, he subtly unveils their dreams, problems, frustrations, and their attempts at adjustment.

Another notable writer, Yü Li-hua (1931-), like Pai Hsien-yung, has until recently shown a keen interest in the lives of the Chinese in America in her many novels and short stories. Her background is similar to that of Pai Hsien-yung. Born on the mainland but raised in Taiwan, she has been residing in the United States for more than twenty years. She has written much about Chinese students and professionals in the United States, especially about their desperate struggle for survival, their sense of hopelessness and "rootlessness," and their intellectual isolation and inability to adjust and change. Her fiction is psychologically less subtle than that of Pai Hsien-yung; some of her works show sentimental excesses and are not as tightly constructed as they should be. She has been, however, one of the most popular writers dealing with the experience of Taiwan "exiles" in the United States.[27] Moreover, her fiction covers a much broader range of such experience than Pai's does.

Toward the end of the 1960s, significant changes began to take place in almost every area of life in Taiwan. Political leaders of the older generation began to pass from the scene one after another. Even though the political succession was not completed until the death of Chiang Kai-shek in 1975, political power had long since passed into the hands of younger leaders, who were by and large realistic and pragmatic administrators and who accepted, though not officially, the notion of a long, if not permanent, stay on the island and thus moved toward rapid economic development in Taiwan. In the last several years of his life, Chiang Kai-shek, plagued by a prolonged illness, was not really in charge. His son and heir apparent, Chiang Ching-kuo, was the effective ruler of Taiwan, and he and his associates have placed major emphasis on economic development. Taiwan has since prospered as a capitalistic society. Even though political control remains rigid, some freedom and diversity have been allowed in other areas. Native Taiwanese leaders, though still a minority in the top echelons, have steadily gained power, especially in the economic field; and a new generation of writers, mostly in their thirties and forties (including many native Taiwanese), has emerged on the literary scene.

Most of these writers have few or no personal roots or experience on the mainland. Reflecting the new political trends in Taiwan, they no longer subscribe to the various political myths, and they have steadily expanded their themes and improved their techniques. Besides Pai Hsien-yung, the "second generation" Taiwan writers who have dominated the literary scene include Huang Ch'un-ming (1939-), Ch'en Jo-hsi (1938-), Ch'en Ying-chen (1936-), Lin Huai-min (1947-), Wang Wen-hsing (1939-), Wang Chen-ho (1940-), Chang Hsi-kuo (1944-), Yang Ch'ing-ch'u (1940-), Ch'i-teng Sheng (1939-), Ou-yang Tzu (1939-), and Shui Ching (1935-).[28] More than half of the writers named here are native Taiwanese. In fact, the emergence of native Taiwanese writers since the 1960s is one of the most important developments in the history of Taiwan fiction, for some of these writers have shown distinctive local flavor and native spirit and have created a new regional literature known as "native-soil literature" (*hsiang-t'u wen-hsüeh*).[29] Their fictional characters are often native Taiwanese rather than the "exiles" from the mainland or the Chinese in America. Their use of the Taiwanese dialect and emphasis on local experiences have attracted wide attention. Since the late 1960s, the literary scene in Taiwan has been quite lively, in contrast to the dearth of literary activity in the 1950s; Taiwan fiction seems to have entered a new age. Most writers show greater concern with characterization and theme; some of them have been under the heavy influence of the West, especially in technique. Although there have emerged only a few writers, such as Ch'en Ying-chen and Chang Hsi-kuo, comparable in talent to Pai Hsien-yung, a variety of achievements have been made in Taiwan fiction. The strength of this fiction has been well reflected in a number of works.

With the emergence in Taiwan of the so-called "native-soil literature" in the late 1970's, more and more Taiwan writers draw their subject matter from contemporary life in Taiwan, especially the lives of the poor and uneducated people, such as laborers, fishermen, singers, prostitutes, and dancing girls. Lately, even some sensitive political issues have been dealt with by fiction writers. "Native-soil literature" has become a controversial issue in Taiwan. It has been attacked as a movement toward the endorsement of Communist views on art and literature by critics and writers close to the government and the Nationalist Party. In contrast to the Peking government, which has initiated, since Mao Tse-tung's death in 1976, a cultural thaw, allowed a freer expression of public opinion, and paid greater attention to law and "socialist legality," the Taipei authorities seem to have adopted a more rigid policy on political and creative activities during the past several years, as reflected in the government's harsh attacks on literary magazines which have been promoting "native-soil literature" and writers and critics who advocate such literature. Other government actions include the suspension of several magazines and the arrest of a number of politically active writers and dissident native Taiwanese politicians who have become increasingly critical of the government and demanded more freedom and independence. Nevertheless, Taiwan fiction has continued to demonstrate its vitality and diversity. Even political satires have recently begun to appear. One of the best examples is Huang Fan's 1979 story, "Lai So," which satirizes not only the Communists and the Taiwan Independence Movement but also the Nationalist Government and the ruling party, the Kuomintang. The lives of Taiwan's capitalists and businessmen have become an important theme, as best represented by Chang Hsi-kuo's 1979 novel, *The Water of the Yellow River (Huang-ho chih shui)*. In 1979, another important work of the so-called "native-soil literature," Chung Chao-cheng's *The Story of the Heroes of Ma-li-k'o-wan (Ma-li-k'o-wan ti ying-hsiung ku-shih)*, which deals with the lives of the mountain tribes in Taiwan, was published.[30] In recent years, Ch'en Jo-hsi has published a number of stories that are based on her experience in China during the Cultural Revolution in the late 1960s and early 1970s. Some of these stories have been widely read in both Taiwan and the West.

On the whole, Taiwan fiction is quite different from that of the May Fourth era. Unlike the early writers, Taiwan authors, with a few exceptions, have shown less interest in social criticism or political satire until very recently. However, the sensitive political situation must have been and continues to be an important factor in their creative activity. While the early writers devoted much attention to the peasant, the poor, the uneducated, and to social and political problems, Taiwan writers, with a few recent exceptions, are essentially concerned with city residents, professionals, intellectuals, and businessmen; they are only occasionally involved in controversial social or political issues. Most early writers were interested in the creation of realistic fiction. Taiwan writers, while continuing the tradition of realism, show greater interest in psychological portraits. Compared with Communist fiction created in recent decades, especially since the Cultural Revolution, Taiwan fiction reveals a greater diversity in themes and a greater concern for technical improvement and psychological truth. A thorough appraisal of Taiwan fiction is still premature because it is difficult to view such recent literature in proper historical perspective. Nevertheless, there is no doubt that Taiwan writers have made important contributions to the history of modern Chinese fiction and that some of their works will be read for years to come.

NOTES

1. *See*, for instance, Joseph S. M. Lau, ed., *Chinese Stories from Taiwan: 1960-1970* (New York: Columbia University Press, 1976), which contains eleven stories by Taiwan writers; C. T. Hsia, ed., *Twentieth-Century Chinese Stories* (New York: Columbia University Press, 1971), which includes three Taiwan stories; Chiang Kuei, *The Whirlwind*, trans. by Timothy A. Ross (San Francisco: Chinese Materials Center, 1977); and Chi Pang-yüan et al., eds., *An Anthology of Contemporary Chinese Literature* (Taipei: National Institute for Compilation and Translation, 1975), which devotes its second volume to short stories by Taiwan writers. Recent critical studies include the following: C. T. Hsia, "The Continuing Obsession with China: Three Contemporary Writers," *Review of National Literatures*, 6 (Spring 1975), 76-99; Timothy A. Ross, *Chiang Kuei* (New York: Twayne Publishers, 1974); and Joseph S. M. Lau's two articles, " 'How Much Truth Can a Blade of Grass Carry?': Ch'en Yin-chen and the Emergence of Native Taiwanese Writers," *JAS*, 32 (1973), 623-638, and " 'Crowded Hours' Revisited: The Evocation of the Past in *Taipei jen*," *JAS*, 35 (1975), 31-48. Timothy A. Ross's article, "Taiwan Fiction: A Review of Recent Criticism," *JCLTA*, 13 (1978), 72-80, is a good summary of recent critical studies. C. T. Hsia's foreword to Joseph S. M. Lau's *Chinese Stories from Taiwan: 1960-1970*, pp. ix-xxvii, contains a good introduction to the stories included in that anthology.

2. For a brief discussion of the term "Taiwan literature," *see* C. T. Hsia, ed., *Twentieth-Century Chinese Stories*, p. xi. "Emigré writers" in this essay and the next refers to writers who were born on the mainland and emigrated to Taiwan between 1945 and 1949 (many of them later emigrated to North America), such as Pai Hsien-yung, in contrast to Taiwan-born writers, like Ch'en Ying-chen.

3. Tsi-an Hsia, "Appendix: Taiwan," in C. T. Hsia, *A History of Modern Chinese Fiction: 1917-1957* (New Haven: Yale University Press, 1961), p. 515.

4. *Ibid.*, pp. 514-515.

5. Yin Ti, for instance, used the term "literary wasteland" to describe the literary scene of Taiwan in the post-War decade. His views are cited by Timothy A. Ross, "Taiwan Fiction: A Review of Recent Criticism," p. 72.

6. *See*, for instance, Joseph S. M. Lau, " 'How Much Truth Can A Blade of Grass Carry?' " p. 624.

7. The term "rootless generation" has been used to describe some of the characters in the fiction of the woman writer Yü Li-hua. *See* C. T. Hsia, *Twentieth-Century Chinese Stories*, p. xi.

8. C. T. Hsia has a section on Chiang Kuei in his "The Continuing Obsession with China: Three Contemporary Writers," pp. 76-83, and an appendix on Chiang Kuei's *The Whirlwind* in his *A History of Modern Chinese Fiction*, 2nd ed. (New Haven: Yale

78/ESSAYS

University Press, 1971), pp. 555-562. Timothy A. Ross has published a monograph, *Chiang Kuei* (New York: Twayne Publishers, 1974). *The Whirlwind* was translated into English by Timothy A. Ross and published by Chinese Materials Center in San Francisco in 1977.

9. Founded by the late critic and scholar, T. A. Hsia (1916-1965), *Literary Review*, which had a significant impact on the development of Taiwan literature, was suspended in 1960.

10. Such as *Modern Literature (Hsien-tai wen-hsüeh), Literary Quarterly (Wen-hsüeh chi-k'an), Pure Literature (Ch'un wen-hsüeh)*, and *Chung-wai Literary Monthly (Chung-wai wen-hsüeh)*.

11. Taipei: Ch'en-chung Publishing Co., 1971.

12. His stories about Chinese residents in America were published as a volume entitled *Niu-yüeh k'o (New Yorkers)* (Hong Kong: Culture Book House, 1974).

13. Taipei: Yüan-ching Publishing House, 1977.

14. The first installment of *The Prodigal Sons* appeared in *Modern Literature (Hsien-tai wen-hsüeh)*, NS No. 1 (August 1977). Close to a quarter of a million characters in length, the novel, which deals with the gaps and conflicts between fathers and sons and other themes in the Taiwan of the 1970s, will complete its serialization in about eighteen months. This information was supplied by the author.

15. A volume of Pai Hsien-yung's short stories in English translation will be published by Indiana University Press soon.

16. Hong Kong: Cultural Book House, 1968.

17. C. T. Hsia, ed., *Twentieth-Century Chinese Stories*, pp. 220-239.

18. The sinking of the S. S. T'ai-p'ing took place in 1949 when the ship was journeying from Shanghai to Taiwan. Hundreds of wealthy and powerful families disappeared as a result and Taiwan newspapers carried extensive accounts. Pai Hsien-yung made fictional use of this event.

19. C. T. Hsia, ed., *Twentieth-Century Chinese Stories*, p. 223.

20. This story is included in Pai Hsien-yung's *Taipei Residents (T'ai-pei jen)* (Taipei: Ch'en-chung Publishing Company, 1971), pp. 197-217. An English translation of the story is in Joseph S. M. Lau, ed., *Chinese Stories from Taiwan: 1960-1970*, pp. 337-354.

21. Joseph S. M. Lau, ed., *Chinese Stories from Taiwan: 1960-1970*, p. 349.

22. *Ibid.*, pp. 345-346.

23. *Ibid.*, p. 347.

24. *Ibid.*, pp. 352-353.

25. *Ibid.*, p. 346.

26. C. T. Hsia, "The Continuing Obsession with China: Three Contemporary Writers," p. 94.

27. Widely regarded as a spokesman for the "rootless generation" in the 1960s, Yü Li-hua has published a number of novels and collections of short stories. One of her best-known novels is *Again the Palm Trees (Yu-chien tsung-lü, yu-chien tsung-lü)*, where the term "rootless generation" was first used to refer to the "exiled" Chinese students, professionals, and intellectuals in the United States. One of her finest short stories, "In Liu Village" ("*Liu-chia chuang-shang*"), first appeared in a translation by the author and C. T. Hsia in *Literature East and West*, 15, nos. 2 & 3 (1971) and was later included in Joseph S. M. Lau, ed., *Chinese Stories from Taiwan: 1960-1970*, pp. 101-142.

28. Timothy A. Ross, in a letter dated August 29, 1977, suggested that Lin Hai-yin (1919-) and Chung Li-ho (1915-1960) be added to the list of prominent Taiwan fiction writers. Lin is a popular woman writer and the editor of *Pure Literature (Ch'un wen-hsüeh)*, an important literary magazine in Taiwan; Chung might be regarded as a forerunner of Taiwan's "native-soil literature" *(hsiang-t'u wen-hsüeh)*. Yü T'ien-ts'ung, a critic in Taiwan, is an active proponent of such literature. For a discussion of Yü's views on

Taiwan fiction, see Timothy A. Ross, "Taiwan Fiction: A Review of Recent Criticism," pp. 75-76.

29. In a letter dated October 9, 1979, Timothy A. Ross proposes "nativist literature" as a translation of the term *hsiang-t'u wen-hsüeh*, whose leaders, he suggests, reject both the traditional "literati" literature and certain Western modernist influences.

30. For a brief account of Taiwan literature of 1979, see Winston L. Y. Yang and Nathan K. Mao, "Chinese Literature," *1980 Britannica Book of the Year* (Chicago: Encyclopaedia Britannica, 1981), pp. 516-517.

2. CH'EN YING-CHEN AND OTHER NATIVE WRITERS

Joseph S. M. Lau

In the preceding essay on Taiwan fiction, considerable attention has been given to émigré writers, especially Pai Hsien-yung.[1] Even though he is generally considered the most gifted of the younger émigré writers, Pai Hsien-yung did not stay in Taiwan long enough to be able to portray the life of native Taiwanes realistically.[2] In fact, his fiction deals mostly with the life of Chinese exiles from the mainland. To feel the pulses of Taiwan, therefore, we must turn to the works of the native sons, i.e., the indigenous Taiwanese writers. Until the emergence in recent years of such young local talents as Ch'en Ying-chen, Huang Ch'un-ming, Ch'i-teng Sheng, Wang Chen-ho, Shih Shu-ching, and a few others, differentiation between "indigenous Taiwanese writers" and "mainland writers" has hardly been called for.[3] This is not, of course, because Taiwan has previously produced no writers of significance;[4] rather it is because the veteran Taiwanese writers (Hsü Ti-shan, for one), like the majority of the Chinese writers of the May Fourth tradition, have no particular interest in making regionalism a part of their craft. With the young native writers, however, the case is different. Since they have never been to the mainland, regionalism—either in subject matter or in language, with the conscious use of local dialect— is for them at once a profession of artistic sensibility and an assertion of individuality. Taiwan, after all, is their Yoknapatawpha County and they are therefore most qualified to tell its truth.

In the conclusion to her essay "Literary Formosa," Lucy H. Chen (Ch'en Jo-hsi) raises a number of questions regarding the timidity of Taiwanese writers in tackling important subjects ready at hand on the island:

> Why do they not write about the changes in the cities with their new factories and the thousands of young men and women who come in from the farms to work in them? Or about the armies of government clerks in

city and provincial governments and their numb hopelessness as the cost of living climbs further out of reach of their salaries? Or about the farmers who must still stoop to push into the mud every individual shoot of rice but who now wear blue plastic raincoats from Japan instead of the old straw cloak? Or about what happens to a farm family now when it is expected that a marrying daughter take with her as her dowry, a radio, an electric fan and a sewing machine? Or about Formosa's merchants, cursing official regulations but with enough money to support a growing number of "wine-houses" with Hong Kong style furnishings and swarms of pretty 'waitresses?' Or about youth, caught up in a fierce competition for places in the universities and subject to all crosscurrents of new and old ideas?[5]

Without venturing into any of the above areas herself, she has nevertheless written a story that can be considered one of the honest attempts to portray reality in modern Taiwan fiction. "The Last Performance" (1961) is a gripping tale about a drug addict. Chin Hsi-tzu is a twenty-eight-year-old *ko-tsai-hsi* (local Taiwanese opera) actress who only ten years ago always performed to packed theaters and who is now fighting as hard to keep her voice as her audience: she has, through all the years of strenuous night life, become addicted to heroin. Worse still, because her baby Ah Pao, born out of wedlock, is breast-fed, he too has become addicted. Here is one of the pathetic scenes:

> "Auntie Ho," she closed her eyes, groaning. "Hurry! Hurry!"
> Auntie Ho filled up the feeding bottle with powdered milk.
> "Want me to add some white powder?"
> "Yes."
> Muttering, shaking her head resignedly, Auntie Ho tottered to the place where Chin Hsi-tzu had been resting a while ago, opened the drawer and took out a pack of morphine. She poured some into the bottle, covered it up with the rubber nipple, shook it for a while, and then handed it to Chin Hsi-tzu. Looking at Ah Pao sucking the nipple greedily, Chin Hsi-tzu was overwhelmed by sadness and grief. Her hatred for the child suddenly turned to a pang of guilt. My little precious. . . all your mother's sins have passed on to you through my breasts![6]

She wants to keep the child very much, and for him she is willing to sacrifice everything, including the chance to marry a tea merchant as a second wife. But what kind of a future can she offer her son? "She couldn't even imagine this. Almost every time she closed her eyes, the picture of a drug-addicted hoodlum emerged, hanging around the gambling houses. Was this my boy's future? She couldn't help shuddering at the thought of this."[7] Finally, exercising all her rational strength, she decides to let Ah Pao be adopted by one of her friends. In a language that is brisk and unsentimental, "The Last Performance" registers in the space of six pages an unforgettable note of anguish in the "lower depths" of Taiwan.

In sharp contrast to the characters in Pai Hsien-yung's work, nearly all the memorable characters created by the young Taiwanese writers are, like Chin Hsi-tzu, of humble origin. In Huang Ch'un-ming's "A Big Toy for My Son" (1968), for instance, Hsu K'un-shu, reduced to straitened circumstances, has no other choice but to accept a humiliating job as a "sandwichman" (sandwiched between two billboards) for a small town movie house. In order to attract attention, he has to daub his face with colorful makeup like a circus clown, with tufts of feathers stuck high on his top hat. Wherever he moves, children tail after him, calling him the "Sandwichman." But all this he does willingly for his forthcoming son, who would have to be given up if he had not agreed to do the commercial. "Ah Chu, let's keep the child,"[8] he tells his wife the day he gets the job. Ironically, though he is now financially able to keep his son, he has lost his identify as a father due to the nature of his work:

> Every time Ah Lung would break into tears as he watched K'un-shu leave the house for work. He would straighten his body up backwards in his mother's lap, trying to keep his father from going. Ah Chu had to say something like, "Why, Ah Lung is yours, and will still be yours when you come back," to ease his mind before he would go to work.
> *The Child likes me so much.*
> K'un-shu was filled with joy. This job enabled him to keep Ah Lung, and Ah Lung enabled him to bear its hardship.
> "You fool. So you think what Ah Lung likes is you? He only thinks there is really a thing like the way you look."
> *At that time, I thought I misunderstood Ah Chu's words,*
> "When you go out to work in the morning, either he is still sleeping, or I have already taken him out to do the laundry. While he is awake, you are wearing your makeup most of the time, and when you come back at night, he is asleep."
> *Can't be like this. But it is true that Ah Lung is getting more shy with me.*
> "Needn't I tell you that he likes the way you are dressed up, making funny faces to him? You're his big toy."
> "Ha! Ha! So I am Ah Lung's big toy. Big toy?"[9]

To Ah Lung, Hsu K'un-shu is not his father unless he is fully garbed as a sandwichman. This richly comic and affectionate scene occurs at the end when K'un-shu's employer relieves him of his humiliating job and assigns him to drive a "billboard pedicab" instead. Happy at this change, K'un-shu returns home clean-faced one night and asks Ah Chu:

> "Why aren't you in bed?"
> "Too hot inside. Ah Lung couldn't sleep."
> "Come, Ah Lung—let Papa hold you for a while."
> Ah Chu handed Ah Lung to him and went inside. Suddenly, Ah Lung burst into tears, and, no matter how hard K'un-shu tried to cradle him and tease him, the child cried only louder.
> "Naughty boy, what's wrong with Papa holding you, eh? Don't you like your father? Be good, don't cry. Don't cry."[10]

All efforts to pacify Ah Lung having failed, "K'un-shu returned the child to Ah Chu, his heart sank. He went over to Ah Chu's little dressing table, sat down, and, after some hesitation, opened the drawer from which he took out a cake of white power. He took a hard look at himself in the mirror and began to apply the powder on his face."[11]

In *A History of Modern Chinese Fiction*, C. T. Hsia sees Hui Ming (in a namesake story by Shen Ts'ung-wen) as a "perennial Chinaman abiding by the wisdom of the earth and enjoying a realistic sense of contentment."[12] In a sense, Hsu K'un-shu can also be seen as a Chinaman. Uneducated and in general uninterested in matters of the outside world that have no direct bearing on his struggle for a marginal existence, Hsu K'un-shu has become, unappealing as he seems, one of the most fulfilled characters in Taiwan fiction precisely because of his lack of any intellectual pretension. Given the sensitive political situation on Taiwan, it is very unlikely that a hero with the kind of intellectual passion and magnitude of, for example, Ch'en in *Man's Fact*, would emerge. Nor is the cultural climate hospitable enough to host a Herzog with his penchant for "a permanent question of the concepts of Man, the meaning of History and the value of Civilization."[13] For, in the eyes of the Nationalist government, the positive value of man, life, history and civilization is taken for granted. Writers and artists are therefore urged to "uphold truth, promote justice;" "oppose tyranny, control violence;" "forestall literature and the arts from turning over the subversive currents of radicalism, licentiousness and decadence."[14]

Characters with some intellectual inclination have, to be sure, appeared on the pages of Taiwan fiction from time to time. But, to borrow a famous line from Conrad's Winnie Verloc, because "things do not stand much looking into,"[15] the potential intellectual hero, whenever confronted with a hard question, either prevaricates or simply tries to be funny. One such instance is found in Lin Huai-min's novella *Cicada* (1969).

Although a native of Chia Yi, Taiwan, Lin Huai-min has written little that can be identified as the work of a regional Taiwanese writer. His language is free of local expressions and he shows no particular interest in the fate of small men from small areas. Translate it into English, substitute John and Mary for the proper names, and you still have in *Cicada* a story about the Chinese "lost generation" drinking coffee, smoking expensive cigarettes (Rothmans, to be specific), and listening to Bob Dylan at the Café Barbarian in Taipei. So Lady Brett is reincarnated in the person of Tao Tzu-ching, an equally devastating woman; and Jake Barnes finds a comfortable counterpart in Chuang Shih-huan because the latter is, in the words of Tao Tzu-ching, a "sister-boy."[16] The above remarks, it should be emphasized, are not meant to be disparaging. As a story about youthful frustration and spiritual loss, *Cicada* has managed to give us a picture of truth—however partial—precisely at the moment when it recoils from the truth.

"Let's get moving. What's the matter with you?" Tao Tzu-ching urged. "If you don't go now, your mother will be calling me soon for your whereabouts."

Reluctantly, Fan Ch'o-hsiung stood up after he had disposed of the beer bottles and cans around him.

"I was looking at that painting and was thinking. . . ."

"Thinking! You're always thinking!" Tao Tzu-ching curtly interrupted Fan Ch'o-hsiung and said: "You think too much, that's your problem. Who wants you to think? All you're supposed to do is study and study. You went through all those 'stuffing courses' in grade school so that you could pass the exams and qualify for junior high, and you did the same thing to get into high school and finally college. . . . Who asks you to think?"

"Ai! Ai!" Yang P'ei-te tugged at Tao Tzu-ching's sleeves, half smiling. "What about after college?"

"After college?" Tao Tzu-ching paused for a while, then shrugged her left shoulder and said: "To Café Barbarian."[17]

A fatuous answer for a serious question, it would seem. But what else could Tao Tzu-ching have said? If Frederic Henry was "embarrassed by the words sacred, glorious, and sacrifice," then how much more embarrassed Tao Tzu-ching must have been when all her adult life she has been fed on a regular diet of "expressions in vain" such as "Recover the Mainland" and "Preserve our Traditional Culture and Morals." The problems of students on Taiwan today are quite different from those of their May Fourth counterparts. At that time, it was quite possible for a student looking for a cause to end up with more causes than he could handle.

"Now there are only two roads to go," Li Ching-shun said to Chao Tzu-yüeh more than forty years ago in the form of advice: "Bury your head among books and after finishing your studies work for the people so as to slowly rebuild the national character and spirit, or dare your life to kill the bad ones."[18] There must be as many students on Taiwan who would like to bury their heads among books today as there were in Chao Tzu-yüeh's time. However, there is a crucial difference in purpose: students today are more concerned about winning a scholarship to study abroad (and never return) than they are about rebuilding the national character and spirit. As to the second course which Chao Tzu-yüeh proposed, there are some technical problems. "Bandit Mao and his clique" are no doubt Taiwan's archenemies, but unlike the Japanese or the evil warlords whose menace to the country was at once physical and immediate, the hated Communists are unfortunately too remote from the coffee houses of Taipei to pose an imminent threat. Ideological battles, however fiercely fought, are never as real as those actual encounters in which one may lose one's life. Perhaps this is exactly the source of the malaise of Tao Tzu-ching and her generation. They have world enough and time enough, but, with no direction, they do not know what to do with them. To Yang P'ei-te's cynical question "What after college," Tao Tzu-ching could have furnished a time-honored answer: "Get a good job and raise children." But she did not; not only because it did not conform to her cultivated rebel image, but also because such an answer would signify the end of the quest, which is the hallmark of an intellectual. And she is, though lost, supposed to be an intellectual in the making.

In the eyes of the Nationalist government in Taiwan Ch'en Ying-chen was once a "nonperson" because of his supposed antigovernment activities.[19] Yet no survey of Taiwan fiction can be complete without giving him his due attention. His importance is such that Chu Hsi-ning, in his introduction to the fiction series of *A Comprehensive Anthology of Modern Chinese Literature* (*Chung-kuo hsien-tai wen-hsüeh ta-hsi*), while excluding his work and deploring his "deviation," feels duty-bound to note parenthetically his talent and influence. Ch'en Ying-chen is a very important writer, because he is quite unique. Almost alone of his contemporaries, he addresses himself to some of the most sensitive problems of his time. "The Country Teacher" (1960), a semiautobiographical account of the consequence of disillusionment among Taiwanese intellectuals after Taiwan's restoration to China during the initial stage of Chinese rule, is one such example.

When Wu Chin-hsiang turns up quite unexpectedly one day before his family in a little Taiwan village, the Sino-Japanese War has been over for almost a year. (He was drafted for service in Borneo because the Japanese were suspicious of his nationalistic sentiments.) Though broken in spirit in the beginning as a result of his wartime memories, he begins to feel somewhat lifted by the thought that Taiwan is no longer a Japanese colony but a part of China and that, as the only educated person in the village, he is morally obligated to initiate some reforms for the betterment of his benighted countrymen. " 'Everything will be all right in the end,' he thought to himself. 'This is my country and they are my people. At least there wouldn't be any more police persecution. Indeed everything will be all right.' "[20] But in less than a year after his return something far beyond his expectation happens: the February Twenty-Eighth Incident in 1947.[21] In the light of this disaster, he sees the futility of individual efforts to redress the moral bankruptcy of a nation. How would he face his students and explain to them the fighting and killing among their countrymen? Understandably, fifty years of foreign occupation have nurtured a Taiwanese image of China that is more nostalgic than realistic, which proves tragic in the case of Wu Chin-hsiang. For idealism, unguarded by common sense, has undermined his power of reason: he fails to see that wherever madness reigns, Chinese can be as brutal as they can be human to their own kin, and that the Chinese mainlanders as a whole cannot be held responsible for the mismanagement of a warlord government. The fall from high hopes to low reality is apparently too abrupt, too painfully ironic for the country teacher to bear. As a result, his spirit takes a precipitous turn: he takes up drinking. When drunk, he cries like a baby, "for no apparent reason at all" (p.58). In the end, he takes his own life.

Wu Chin-hsiang's unhappy lot is quite typical of Ch'en Ying-chen's early autobiographical heroes: heartbroken and bewildered, they either kill themselves or waste their lives away in spiteful debauchery. Two such stories readily come to mind: "My Brother K'ang Hsiung" (*Wo-ti ti-ti K'ang Hsiung*, 1960) and "My Hometown" (*Ku Hsiang*, 1960).

"My Brother K'ang Hsiung" is nominally a story about a "rebel" and an "immoralist." The "rebel" is the unnamed elder sister[22] of the eighteen-year-old titular hero, the "immoralist" who has committed suicide before the story opens. He has left three diaries to which only his sister has access. Some of the entries are as unabashedly epigrammatic as they are childish. Examples: "Poverty itself is the biggest crime. . . . It inevitably leads one into the path of baseness and ugliness" (p. 35); "I am a nihilist without the tempestuous life of Shelly. Shelly lived on his dreams and I can only wait like a prophet. A nihilist prophet is indeed interesting" (p. 38).

But the professed nihilist and "anarchist" (p. 37) was never the undoer: he had built "in his Utopia many schools and orphanages and hospitals for the poor" (p. 38). Then what is the cause of his own undoing? To outsiders, and even to his father, K'ang Hsiung is the victim of the death wish and fantasy of nineteenth-century nihilism (p. 39). But to his sister who alone knows the secret, K'ang Hsiung was "murdered by God, anarchism, love and adolescent concupiscence" (p. 40). He lost his virginity to his "motherly landlady" (p. 38) and felt so guilty about it afterward that he spent days in self-recrimination before taking his life. His life and death are at once an irony and a paradox. As his sister comments: "There is neither sin nor God in the dictionary of a nihilist. Isn't my brother K'ang Hsiung a nihilist? A Shelley?" (p. 38). K'ang Hsiung is, in truth, a contradiction: he is a soft-hearted boy trying to look hard-boiled; a self-styled anarchist yearning for order and justice; a spiritualist with an unspoken respect for worldly gains. He confesses in his diary "I asked for fish and I got a snake; I desired food and I got a stone" (p. 39). "I have given myself to nihilism for a long time and yet I can't even free myself from the bondage of religion and morality" (p. 39).

In form and in content, "My Brother K'ang Hsiung" is as raw and sophomoric as a freshman composition could be. But, according to Yü T'ien-ts'ung, it received a sensational reception upon its publication in *Pi Hui*.[23] In our assessment of a literary work of art, its reception, whether favorable or unfavorable, has of course very little to do with our judgment. In the final analysis, "My Brother K'ang Hsiung" is not a story of characters: it is only a sketch of ideological abstractions whose meanings are not translated into immediate situations. Perhaps this accounts for its success among the discontented young men. Chuang Shih-huan, we remember, urged his friends in *Cicada* to stop complaining and do something. The answer he got from Tao Tzu-ching was a blunt one: "*For instance* ?"[24] For K'ang Hsiung and his spiritual counterparts whose understanding of the term could not be more than lexical, nihilism is of course a kind of imaginary action; somehow, they have to give a name to the nature of their suffering and identify themselves with some sort of a cause. But though it fails as a story, "My Brother K'ang Hsiung" is important in its historical context, deserving a no less significant place than Lu Hsün's "The Diary of a Madman" (1918). For "such autobiographies as yours ... so long as they are sincere ... will be of use and provide material in spite of their chaotic and fortuitous character.... They will preserve at any rate some faithful traits by which one may guess what may have lain hidden in the hearts of some raw youth of the troubled time—a knowledge not altogether valueless since from raw youth are made the generation."[25]

"My Hometown" is another story about the bleeding heart. Told in the first person narrative, it is about the spiritual descent of another unnamed semiautobiographical hero, Ko-ko (elder brother). Like Wu Chin-hsiang, the country teacher, Ko-ko is filled with reformist zeal upon return to his hometown after some years of study in Japan where, besides earning a medical degree, he also became a Christian convert. Instead of opening a private clinic as is expected, he offers his service to the local miners in the daytime and works for the church in the evening, where "his prayers sounded just like a Psalm of David" (p. 65). But in less than three years after his homecoming, his family goes bankrupt. His father dies soon afterwards. With family calamities come the personal downfall: Ko-ko is now a changed man. He gives up his practice and evangelism, opens a gambling den and takes a prostitute for a wife.

Ko-ko, for a refreshing change, does not commit suicide, and with him end the agonies of Ch'en Ying-chen's self-torturing "Promethean" heroes (p. 66). A new phase in his work has begun. His field of vision expands and his compassion, which has characterized his early stories since "The Noodle Stall" (*Mien-t'an*, 1959), becomes even more comprehensive. In the better stories of his second period, such as "A Race of Generals" (*Chiang-chün tsu*, 1964), "Poor Poor Dumb Mouths" (*Chi-ts'an-ti wu-yen-ti hsiao-tsui*, 1964), and "One Migrant Green Bird" (*I lu-se-chih hou niao*, 1964), the mainlanders, whose appearance on the island generated both excitement and frustration for the K'ang Hsiungs, begin to receive attention. Ch'en, at this point in his development, seems to have come to realize that under the present circumstances, all Chinese living in Taiwan, regardless of their origins, are alike: they are the stranded fish in Chuang Tzu's parable. To sustain life for as long as circumstances permit, they will have to moisten each other with whatever slime is left in their mouths. Thus, San-chiao-lien (triangle face), a mainlander saxophone player in "A Race of Generals," gives away all his retirement pay (NT$30,000) from the army in order to save a girl in his funeral band from being sold as a prostitute by her family. Even his good deed is futile in the end (her family sells her to a fat man all the same); but it is the gesture that counts. It signifies that blood is thicker than water, and that Taiwan, after all, is not Formosa,[26] in spite of the Kuomintang's misadministration.

In terms of his ideological development, "The Comedy of T'ang Ch'ien" (*T'ang Ch'ien ti hsi-chu*, 1967) is easily one of the most important stories Ch'en

Ying-chen has ever written. It is important as the only successful satire he has written; the other one, "The Last Summer Day" (*Tsui-hou-ti hsia-jih*, 1966), fails to make the grade. "The Comedy of T'ang Ch'ien" also amounts to a direct repudiation of all his semiautobiographical stories. After seven years of soul-searching, the country teacher finally emerges from his spiritual desolation and tilts at the intellectual poseurs of his time.

Reminiscent of some loose episodes of Ch'ien Chung-shu's *Fortress Besieged* (1947), "The Comedy of T'ang Ch'ien" is sheer fun to read. The first paragraph gives a good start:

> It was in a small, saloon-styled gathering one evening that T'ang Ch'ien had first met Lao Mo. And no sooner had she made his acquaintance than was she captivated by the expression of intellectual agony on his face. She was sitting in a corner, watching him plucking his guitar leisurely and singing "The Emerald Earth." After he had finished, a lanky teaching assistant from the geology department announced: "Lao Mo is going to give us a special talk tonight. The title is 'The Humanitarianism of Sartre' " (p. 265)

After the talk, T'ang Ch'ien, a pretty, sensuous looking girl, goes home and takes the initiative of writing to Lao Mo for an appointment to further their acquaintance. She is right in thinking that "among these intellectuals few can resist an invitation with a female signature" (p. 266). For Lao Mo, in an unmistakably Sartrean outfit, comes as directed. After some social exchange, Sartre's Chinese disciple sadly proclaims: "We are abandoned in this world, and we are doomed to die on this unhappy earth" (p. 266). T'ang Ch'ien's reaction to this enlightening observation is as swift as it is tearfully sympathetic: "Suddenly, she remembered her mother, a languorous old woman abandoned by her father. And how gloomy and unhappy her childhood had been because of this!" (pp. 266-267).

This "existential association," the linking of the abandoned human condition with "an abandoned mother," is sacrilegiously irrelevant if we are to take Lao Mo's words seriously. But satire being what it is, "the literary art of diminishing a subject by making it ridiculous and evoking toward it attitudes of amusement, contempt, or scorn,"[27] ludicrous incongruities such as this are taken for granted. What is satirized, of course, is not Sartre or existentialism per se but the given situation.

T'ang Ch'ien's comedy, to be sure, does not stop here. In fact, what is quoted above is just the beginning. But her whole history, colorful as it is, is far too long for a detailed and illustrative account. We can only give an outline. Not long after their second meeting, T'ang Ch'ien becomes Lao Mo's mistress. This represents a "Great Leap Forward" in T'ang Ch'ien's life, for now she has learned to juggle such terms as "existence," "self-transcendence," "involvement," "despair" and "fear" in her conversation without much difficulty (pp. 268-269). But philosophy and life come to a head-on crash as soon as Lao Mo discovers that T'ang Ch'ien has been pregnant for three months without his knowledge. Though philosophically an advocate of "involvement" he does not want to get involved in life. "A child will invalidate the great example we have set up for trial marriage" (p. 274); he pleads with T'ang Ch'ien not to keep the child. So T'ang Ch'ien goes for an abortion. They part soon afterward. Then something strange happens. Lao Mo, whose savage virility has at times frightened T'ang Ch'ien, suddenly becomes impotent, reportedly because of "a guilty association with infanticide" (p. 275). His own explanation is movingly humanitarian: "At the thought that the womb is but a slaughterhouse for infants, no true humanitarian can feel the sexual urge again" (p. 275).

Five months after the abortive affair, T'ang Ch'ien, now a handsomely grown woman, reemerges on the intellectual scene chaperoned by Lo Chung-ch'i, a philosophy teaching assistant and an avowed "neo-positivist" to boot. Just as she was once a reflected glory of Lao Mo's "existentialism," T'ang Ch'ien is now a fervent and sharp-tongued "neo-positivist" in battle with her ideological past. But her honeymoon with Lo Chung-ch'i does not last long. For Lao Mo, though now impotent, has left T'ang Ch'ien with an unforgettable virile memory which the positivism of Lo Chung-ch'i fails to eradicate. "He realized man in general is the kind of animal which incessantly needs to prove his own sex. And he must prove himself in bed" (p. 284), which, unfortunately, is not his forte. Hounded by fear of defeat, Lo kills himself.

For almost a year after the death of Lo Chung-ch'i, T'ang Ch'ien disappears from Taipei's intellectual society. But as can be expected of a woman of restive nature, T'ang Ch'ien's memory is too short to sustain a prolonged period of mourning for the "neo-positivist." Before long, "her flower of love bloomed for a third time" (p. 286). Her beau this time is a returned student from America by the name of Chou Hung-ta, alias George H. T. Chou, and there is nothing philosophical about him. Her conversations with him no longer center on the problems of human suffering and personal salvation, nor on the differentiation between truth and falsehood, but almost exclusively on the difference of life-styles between Taiwan and America. Duly impressed with his credentials, T'ang Ch'ien accepts the proposal of Chou Hung-ta and together they leave Taiwan for America one September. In the spring of the next year, however, news reaches Taipei that Mrs. Chou has divorced her "poor George" (p. 295) and subsequently remarried. We do not even know the name of her new husband; we only know that he holds a Ph.D. in physics and is in charge of advanced research work in a big American munitions factory. T'ang Ch'ien, as the story ends, is said to be "living a happier life than she had expected" (p. 295).

If the language used in outlining the above story seems derisive and sarcastic, it is because it is meant to do justice to the original. If satire is the reverse of self-pity, so are tangy, witty observations the logical replacements for the murky, weepy ejaculations which sprawl over a number of Ch'en Ying-chen's early tales. For Ch'en Ying-chen, this change in style is more than a technical variegation: it is a mark of his metamorphosis as a person and an artist. In an essay entitled "Modernism Rediscovered: Random Thoughts after the Performance of *Waiting for Godot*" (*Hsien-tai chu-i ti tsai-kai-fa*), he dismisses most literary expressions in Taiwan (including his own) in the name of "modernism" as "cultural masturbation."[28]

> In short, our modernistic literature has become a game of words, color, and sound that is completely divorced from the real problems of our life. Worse still, this game is played by no one other than the nitwits. Consequently, our modernistic literature can claim no exception to the following patterns: if it is not an exercise in deception, it is a puerile egoistic indulgence in sentimentalism; if it is not a show of what is most debased in modernism—degenerated nihilism, sexual perversity, senseless, linguistic and ideological obscurantism—it is the impotent gesture of someone in white gloves waving to us from the window of a moldering ivory tower (pp. 378-379).

Then what are the writers of Taiwan supposed to do in order not to be "unprecedentedly isolated from the masses?' (p. 375). He has an answer in his next important essay, "The Song of the Exiled: Random Thoughts during a Reception for Yü Li-hua" (*Liu-fang-che chih-ko*):

> In fact, the literature of a people, or a nation, should strive first to address itself to its own people; only then will it be possible to become an art for the world and the whole human race. Only those works written and loved by their people will be accepted and appreciated by other peoples. The works which are disproved and rejected by their own people are bound to be disproved and rejected by all mankind. (p. 283).

Even in translation, both the style and the message of these "random thoughts" bear an uncanny resemblance to the Maoist rhetoric. In fact, "addressing itself to one's own people" (*su-chu-yü tzu-chi-ti min-tsu*) can be loosely rendered as "in the service of one's own people" or simply "to serve the people" without losing too much in meaning. Here is an example for comparison from the writing of Mao Tse-tung: "The foreign 'eightlegged' essay, pedantry and obscurantism, must be banned; empty and abstract talk must be stopped and doctrinairism must be laid to rest to make room for the fresh and lively things of Chinese style and Chinese flavour which the common folk of China love to see and hear."[29] Of course one cannot say that Ch'en Ying-chen's views are "Maoist" simply because some isolated sentences in his essay happen to echo Maoist sentiments. And it is not the purpose of this essay to intrude upon the privacy of his political sympathy. Suffice it to say that, in point of fact, his diagnosis of the "modernistic" affectations in Taiwanese literature is mostly pertinent.

Yen Yuan-shu, for one, has similar complaints. In an article on Taiwan poetry, he has taken the modern poets to task by saying that except for their fascination with death, they do not seem to be capable of imagining another disaster.[30] That the prescription Ch'en Ying-chen gives for remedying these affectations should happen to fall, intentionally or unintentionally, in Maoist line has no direct bearing on him as a critic and a writer. A good prescription is the one that works; it makes no difference in what political style it is phrased. The same holds true for a writer, regardless of his political persuasion. Inasmuch as he has spoken the truth as he knew it, inasmuch as he dared to challenge even himself when he had suspicion about his former conviction, Ch'en Ying-chen is, as previously suggested, a unique writer as well as an honest man. By Western standards, which sometimes confuse realism with muckraking, Ch'en Ying-chen's portrayal of Taiwanese reality may seem timid. But by Taiwan standards, he has apparently taken more liberty in his writing than the governing authorities could afford. In any case, there is no doubt that he is one of the best representatives of the native Taiwanese writers.

NOTES

1. In contrast to the preceding article, this essay, reprinted with permission and revisions from the *Journal of Asian Studies*, 32 (1973), 623-638, deals with native Taiwanese writers, with Ch'en Ying-chen as their representative.

2. A native of Kweilin, Kwangsi province, Pai Hsien-yung was born in 1937. After the war, he moved with his family to Shanghai, Nanking and Hong Kong. In 1952, he settled with his family in Taipei where he received both his high school and college education. In 1963, he came to the United States for graduate studies and is at present teaching Chinese at the University of California (Santa Barbara).

3. Their representative works are discussed in my preface to Liu Shao-ming (Joseph S. M. Lau), ed., *Selected Short Stories by Native Taiwanese Writers* (*Tai-wan pen-ti tso-chia tuan-p'ien hsiao-shuo hsüan*) (Hong Kong: Hsiao-ts'ao ch'u-pan-she, 1972); hereafter, Lau, *Selected Short Stories*. See also, Joseph S. M. Lau, "The Concepts of Time and Reality in Modern Chinese Fiction," *Tamkang Review*, 4, No. 1 (1973), 1-16.

4. In 1965, Taipei's Wen-t'an ch'u-pan-she published a ten-volume anthology entitled *Works of Native Taiwanese Writers* (*Pen-sheng-chi tso-chia tso-p'in hsüan-chi*), ed. Ch'ung Chao-cheng. Mainly intended as a morale booster for Taiwanese writers, the anthology is of very uneven quality: almost anyone who has published anything is included as long as he is a native Taiwanese.

5. Lucy H. Chen, "Literary Formosa," in Mark Mancall, ed., *Formosa Today* (New York: Frederick A. Praeger, 1964), p. 140.

6. Ch'en Jo-hsi (Lucy H. Chen), "The Last Performance" (*Tsui-hou yeh-hsi*) *Hsien-tai wen-hsüeh*, No. 10 (September 1961), p. 49. This story is now included in Lau, *Selected Short Stories*. An English translation of this story is available in Joseph S. M. Lau, ed., *Chinese Stories from Taiwan: 1960-1970* (New York: Columbia University Press, 1976). Hereafter, Lau, *Chinese Stories*.

7. *Ibid.*

8. "A Big Toy for My Son" (*Erh-tzu-ti ta wan-ou*) *Wen-hsüeh chi-k'an* (Literary Quarterly), No. 6 (Taipei, February 1968), p. 41. An English version of this story is now available in Howard Goldblatt, tr., *The Drowning of an Old Cat and Other Stories by Hwang Chun-ming* (Bloomington: Indiana University Press, 1980).

9. *Ibid.*, p. 45.

10. *Ibid.*, p. 48.
11. *Ibid.*
12. C. T. Hsia, *A History of Modern Chinese Fiction*, 2nd ed. (New Haven: Yale University Press, 1971), p. 201.
13. Victor Brombert, *The Intellectual Hero: Studies in the French Novel: 1880-1955* (Chicago: University of Chicago Press, 1964), p. 18.
14. Quoted by Hsü Nan-ts'un (Ch'en Ying-chen) in "New Pointers in Kuomintang's Literary Policy" (*Hsin-ti chih-piao: Kuo-min-tang-ti wen yi chen ts'e*), *Wen-hsüeh chi-k'an*, No. 6 (February 1968), p. 87.
15. Joseph Conrad, *The Secret Agent* (Harmondsworth: Penguin Books, 1969), p. 147.
16. Lin Huai-min, *Cicada* (*Ch'an*) (Taipei: Hsien-jen-chang ch'u-pan-she, 1969), p. 102. The quotation is in the original English. An English translation of this story is included in Lau, *Chinese Stories*.
17. *Ibid.*, p. 137.
18. Lao She, *Chao Tzu-yueh* (Hong Kong: Chi P'en ch'u-pan-she, 1964), pp. 205-206. I have used C. T. Hsia's translation, which appears in his *History of Modern Chinese Fiction*, 2d ed., p. 169.
19. Because he was tried in a military court, no published account of Ch'en Ying-chen's alleged "subversive activities" has been made public by the government. The only evidence I can cite is from a secret source: a photostat copy of a classified report (dated, October 1968) issued by the Taiwan Garrison General Headquarters. According to this document, Ch'en Ying-chen, together with six others, was found guilty of "intending to overthrow the government by violence in collusion with the Communist bandits" (*i-t'u kou-chieh fei-kung, i pao-li tien-fu cheng-fu*). He was sentenced to ten years imprisonment. In August 1975, however, Ch'en and other political prisoners were granted amnesty after Chiang Kai-shek's death on 5 April of the same year.

For a biographical account of Ch'en Ying-chen's student life and his literary activities, *see* Yü T'ien-ts'ung's "Letter from Mu-cha" (*Mu-cha shu-chien*) in Appendix 2, *Selected Works of Ch'en Ying-chen* (*Ch'en Ying-chen hsüan-chi*), Liu Shao-ming (Joseph S. M. Lau), ed., (Hong Kong: Hsiao Ts'ao ch'u-pan-she, 1972), pp. 421-430.

I am indebted to Professor Yü for the valuable information provided in this letter, which has enabled me to identify some of Ch'en Ying-chen's autobiographic heroes in his early stories.

20. "The Country Teacher" (*Hsiang-ts'un chiao-shih*), *Ch'en Ying-chen hsüan-chi*, p. 54. All subsequent page references to his stories and essays will appear in parentheses after the quotations.

21. George H. Kerr has certainly given one of the most dramatic and sensational descriptions of this Incident in his *Formosa Betrayed* (London: Eyre and Spottiswoode, 1966). Here is one example: "We saw students tied together, being driven to the execution grounds, usually along the river banks and ditches about Taipei, or at the waterfront in Keelung. One foreigner counted more than thirty young bodies—bodies in student uniforms—lying along the roadside east of Taipei; they had their noses and ears slit or hacked off, and many had been castrated. Two students were beheaded near my front gate. Bodies lay unclaimed on the roadside embankment near the mission compound" (pp. 300-301).

The Chinese, however, while deploring the Kuomintang atrocity (as they would any warlord atrocities), take great exception to Kerr's "condescending" and "imperialistic" attitudes in asserting that the Taiwanese would have more welcomed the American occupation of "Formosa" than its restoration to China. *See* Liu T'ien-ts'ai, "A Taste of Freedom: A Review of P'eng Ming-min's Memoirs" (*P'ing P'eng Ming-min hui-i-lu: Tzu-yu-ti tzu-wei*) *Ming Pao Monthly* (*Ming Pao Yüeh-k'an*), No. 83 (Hong Kong, November 1972), pp. 56-66. P'eng's *A Taste of Freedom* was published in 1972 by Holt, Rinehart and Winston, New York.

22. The "unnamed hero" has been a frequent and favorite figure in the stories of the sentimental writers, such as Su Man-shu and Yü Ta-fu. In the case of Ch'en Ying-chen, however, it may not be so much a show of self-pity as it is a demonstration of personality: he might have intended his anonymous heroes to stand for the Everyman of Taiwanese *hsiao-jen-wu* (small people) whose lives would not be significant enough to deserve a full name. *San-chiao-lien* and the baton twirler girl in "A Race of Generals" are two good examples.

23. *See* Yü, *Mu-cha shu-chien*, p. 424.

24. Lin Huai-min, *Shan*, p. 177. The quotation is in original English.

25. Dostoevsky, *A Raw Youth*, quoted by Olga Lang as an epigraph to her book *Pa Chin and His Writings* (Cambridge: Harvard University Press, 1967).

26. "Formosa" was originally an innocuous Portuguese term for Taiwan. However, as it is used by the "Taiwan separatists" (*Tai-tu fen-tzu*), the term carries a political overtone. According to Liu T'ien-ts'ai, P'eng Ming-min is reported to have explained the special meaning of the term Formosa as follows: "Because Taiwan is originally a Chinese name, so we use the Portuguese term 'Formosa' in order to express our anti-Chinese sentiments." *See* "P'ing P'eng Ming-min hui-i-lu," p. 56.

27. M. H. Abrams, *A Glossary of Literary Terms* (New York: Holt, Rinhart and Winston, 1964), p. 85).

28. Yü, *Mu-cha shu-chein*, p. 428.

29. "The Role of the Chinese Communist Party in the National War," in *Selected Works of Mao Tse-tung*, (New York: International Publishers, 1954), II, 260.

30. *See* "A Few Personal Remarks on Modern Chinese Poetry", (*Tui-yü chung-kuo hsien-tai-shih ti chi-tien ch'ien-chien*) *Hsien-tai wen-hsüeh*, No. 46 (March 1972), pp. 36-43.

BIBLIOGRAPHIES

Part One:
Bibliography of Sources in Chinese Literature

Peter Li and Nathan K. Mao

I

Bibliographies and Other Reference Works

Of the various bibliographical works published in recent years a few deserve special attention. Donald A. Gibbs and Yun-chen Li's *A Bibliography of Studies and Translations of Modern Chinese Literature, 1918-1942*, and Meishi Tsai's *Contemporary Chinese Novels and Short Stories 1949-1974: An Annotated Bibliography* are useful for the study of the periods from 1918 to 1942 and 1949 to 1974 respectively. Donald A. Gibbs's *Subject and Author Index to Chinese Literature Monthly (1951-1976)* provides a good list of translations of Chinese Communist literature published between 1951 and 1976. Also useful is Hans Hinrup's *An Index to Chinese Literature*. Tien-yi Li's *Chinese Fiction: A Bibliography of Books and Articles in Chinese and English* is somewhat outdated but still useful. For current sources, including both translations and secondary studies, the annual volumes of the Association for Asian Studies's *Bibliography of Asian Studies*, the Modern Language Association's *MLA International Bibliography*, and Kyoto University's *Annual Bibliography of Oriental Studies* should be consulted. None of these bibliographies, however, is designed as a reference or critical guide, and almost all are limited in coverage.

Among other reference publications, two dictionaries of literary terms, works, and writers have been published: Jaroslav Průšek's *Dictionary of Oriental Literatures* and David Lang and D. R. Dudley's *The Penguin Companion to Classical, Oriental and African Literature*. Generally reliable, Průšek's *Dictionary* provides concise information on major works and writers; however, with only two hundred or so entries, it, too, is limited in coverage. Lang and Dudley's *Companion* is even more limited in scope and is intended for the general reader.

Two biographical dictionaries have been published: Howard L. Boorman and Richard C. Howard's *Biographical Dictionary of Republican China* and Donald Walker Klein and Anne B. Clark's *Biographic Dictionary of Chinese Communism, 1921-1965*. The former is a good source for biographical information on writers active in the first half of this century and the latter provides data on writers active in the Communist movement.

95

1   Association for Asian Studies. *Bibliography of Asian Studies.* Ann Arbor, 1956-.
    Originally known as the *Bulletin of Far Eastern Bibliography*, this is a comprehensive annual bibliography of Asian studies. It lists books, articles, and dissertations in Western languages. Studies and translations of Chinese literature are also included.

2   ———. *Cumulative Bibliography of Asian Studies, 1941-1965.* Boston: G. K. Hall, 1969-1970. 8 vols. *Cumulative Bibliography of Asian Studies, 1966-1970.* Boston: G. K. Hall, 1972-1973.
    Cumulative sets of the annual volumes of the AAS's *Bibliography of Asian Studies*. These are extensive bibliographies of Western publications on Asia.

3   BERTON, PETER and EUGENE WU. *Contemporary China: A Research Guide.* Stanford: Hoover Institution, Stanford University, 1967.
    This guide contains a listing of some sources on contemporary Chinese literature.

3a BESTERMAN, THEODORE. *A World Bibliography of Oriental Bibliographies.* Rev. and updated by J. D. Pearson. Totowa, N.J.: Rowman and Littlefield, 1975.
    The present revised edition lists more than ten thousand bibliographic titles on Asia and Oceania, including many on China.

4   BIRNBAUM, ELEAZAR. *Books on Asia from the Near East to the Far East.* Toronto: University of Toronto Press, 1971.
    A selected and annotated bibliography of books on Asia.

5   BOORMAN, HOWARD L. and RICHARD C. HOWARD, eds. *Biographical Dictionary of Republican China.* New York: Columbia University Press, 1969-1979. 5 vols.
    Includes biographies of important twentieth-century Chinese writers. Volume 4 contains an extensive bibliography, and volume 5 provides a personal name index.

6   California. University. Berkeley. East Asiatic Library. *Author-Title and Subject Catalogs.* Boston: G. K. Hall, 1968. 19 vols. First supplement, 1973. 4 vols.
    Printed catalogs of one of the best East Asian collections in the West. Very strong in Chinese literature.

7   Centre for East Asian Cultural Studies. *A Survey of Bibliographies in Western Languages Concerning East and Southeast Asian Studies.* Tokyo: Centre for East Asian Cultural Studies, 1966-1969. 2 vols.
    A guide to bibliographies in Western languages, with emphasis on the humanities and social sciences. A section on China lists a number of bibliographical guides to Chinese studies.

8   CHEN, CHARLES K. H. *A Biographical and Bibliographical Dictionary of Chinese Authors.* Hanover, N.H.: Oriental Society, 1971. Supplement, 1976.
    Arranged alphabetically, this dictionary includes several thousand entries on both ancient and modern Chinese authors.

9   CHI, CH'IU-LANG and JOHN DEENEY. *An Annotated Bibliography of English, American, & Comparative Literature for Chinese Scholars.* Taipei: Western Literature Research Institute, Tamkang College of Arts and Sciences, 1975.
    An ambitious bibiography of selected sources, mostly in English. Its listing of studies of Chinese literature, however, is limited.

10 Chicago. University. Far Eastern Library. *Catalog of the Far Eastern Library.* Boston: G. K. Hall, 1973. 18 vols.
    Printed catalogs of a well- selected collection which is strong in materials on Chinese literature.

10a CHOW, TSE-TSUNG. *Research Guide to the May Fourth Movement.*
    For annotations and bibliographic information, *see* no. 206.

11 CHU, PAO-LIANG. *Twentieth-century Chinese Writers and Their Pen Names.* Boston: G. K. Hall, 1978.
    This directory lists 7,429 pen names of 2,524 twentieth-century Chinese writers for a total of 9,953 entries, which are arranged alphabetically in one sequence, word by word, using the Wade-Giles romanization system. A very useful reference work despite some omissions and errors.

12 Columbia University. East Asian Library. *Index to Learned Chinese Periodicals.* Boston: G. K. Hall, 1962.
    An author and subject index to selected Chinese journals.

13 Contemporary China Institute. *A Bibliography of Chinese Newspapers and Periodicals in European Libraries.* Cambridge, England: Cambridge University Press, 1975.
    An extensive union list of holdings in 102 libraries in Europe, including the Soviet Union.

14 DAVIDSON, MARTHA. *A List of Published Translations from Chinese into English, French, and German.* Tentative ed. New Haven: Far Eastern Publications, Yale University, 1952 -1957. 2 parts.
    Compiled in the early 1950s, this bibliography, though outdated, is still of some use. Part II lists translations of Chinese novels and short stories.

15 EMBREE, AINSLIE T. *Asia:A Guide to Paperbacks.* Rev. ed. New York: Asia Society, 1968.
    The literature section lists, with brief annotations, a number of studies and translations of modern Chinese fiction.

16   Far Eastern Association. *Bulletin of Far Eastern Bibliography.* Washington, D.C., 1936-1940. 5 vols.
   Lists mainly English-language books and articles on the Far East.

17   ———. *Far Eastern Bibliography.* Ithaca, N.Y., 1941-1955.
   Lists mainly English-language books and articles on the Far East.

18   FRANKE, HERBERT *Sinologie.* Berlin, 1953.
   A bibliographical introduction to Sinology.

19   FRÉDÉRIC, LOUIS, ed. *Encyclopaedia of Asian Civilizations.* Cambridge: Cheng and Tsui Co., 1977-.
   A projected ten-volume encyclopedia of Asian civilizations, with a limited coverage of Chinese literature. Only one volume has been published.

20   GENTZLER, J. MASON. *Syllabus of Chinese Civilization.* New York: Columbia University Press, 1968.
   A good introductory syllabus for the study of Chinese civilization.

21   GIBBS, DONALD A. *Subject and Author Index to Chinese Literature Monthly (1951-1976).* New Haven: Far Eastern Publications, Yale University, 1978.
   A subject and author index to *Chinese Literature,* a Peking monthly which is thebest source for translations of current Chinese literature.

22   GIBBS, DONALD A. and YUN-CHEN LI. *A Bibliography of Studies and Translations of Modern Chinese Literature, 1918-1942.* Cambridge: East Asian Research Center, Harvard University, 1975.
   An extensive listing of Chinese and Western studies and English-language translations of modern Chinese literature.

23   GORDON, LEONARD H. D. and FRANK JOSEPH SHULMAN. *Doctoral Dissertations on China: A Bibliography of Studies in Western Languages, 1945-1970.* Seattle: University of Washington Press, 1972.
   An exhaustive listing of doctoral dissertations on China completed in American, European, Canadian, and Australian universities, and a few Asian institutions.

24   HALL, DAVID E. *Union Catalogue of Asian Publications.* London: Mansell, 1975.
   This author catalog of Asian titles acquired by British libraries between 1965 and 1971 covers all subjects except pure science and technology. A supplement listing publications acquired since 1971 has also been published.

25   HARTMAN, CHARLES. "Recent Publications on Chinese Literature: I. The Republic of China (Taiwan)." *CLEAR,* 1 (1979), 81-86.
   A brief bibliographic survey of important Taiwanese publications on Chinese literature, mainly premodern literature.

26 HIGHTOWER, JAMES ROBERT. *Topics in Chinese Literature: Outlines and Bibliographies.* Rev. ed. Cambridge: Harvard University Press, 1953.

This reference work, especially its bibliographies, though somewhat outdated, is still the best reference book in English on the genres and topics of Chinese literature. Includes one chapter on modern Chinese literature.

26a HINRUP, HANS J. *An Index to Chinese Literature, 1951-1976.* London: Curzon Press, 1978.

A subject index to *Chinese Literature,* the most important source for translations of current Chinese literature.

27 HORNSTEIN, LILLIAN, et al., eds. *The Reader's Companion to World Literature.* New York: New American Library, 1956.

Though essentially a reference work for the study of Western literature, this book provides some entries on Chinese literature.

28 HSU, KAI-YU. "Bibliographical Control of Modern Chinese Literature." *JCLTA,* 13 (1978), 150-152.

A brief discussion of the bibliographical control of modern Chinese literature, including a listing of important bibliographic works on modern Chinese literature.

29 HUCKER, CHARLES O. *China: A Critical Bibliography.* Tucson: University of Arizona Press, 1962.

An annotated guide to selected works in English, it is still of some use to the general reader despite its limited and somewhat outdated listing of modern Chinese fiction.

29a KELLY, JEANNE. "A Survey of Recent Soviet Studies on Chinese Literature." *CLEAR,* 2 (1980), 101-136.

A bibliographic survey of recent Soviet studies on Chinese literature.

30 KLEIN, DONALD WALKER and ANNE B. CLARK, eds. *Biographic Dictionary of Chinese Communism, 1921-1965.* Cambridge: Harvard University Press, 1971. 2 vols.

Includes short biographies of selected modern Chinese writers.

30a KUNG, WEN-KAI. *Japanese Studies of Modern Chinese Fiction.* Seattle: Far Eastern Library, University of Washington, 1972.

A list of selected Japanese studies of modern Chinese fiction.

31 Kyoto University. Zinbun Kagaku Kenkyūsyo (Jimbun Kagaku Kenkyūjo) (The Research Institute for Humanistic Studies). *Toyoshi kenkyu bunken ruimoko (Annual Bibliography of Oriental Studies).* Kyoto, 1934-.

A comprehensive annual bibliography with a section on Western-language studies of Chinese literature.

32 LANG, DAVID M., ed. *A Guide to Eastern Literatures.* New York: Frederick A. Praeger, 1971.

An ambitious guide to fifteen national literatures of Asia and the Middle East intended for the general reader. The section on Chinese literature deals very briefly with historical background, main trends, and individual writers and works, and provides a short bibliography. Contains factual errors.

33 ———— and D. R. DUDLEY, eds. *The Penguin Companion to Classical, Oriental and African Literature.* (Vol. 4 of *The Penguin Companion to World Literature*). Harmondsworth, Middlesex, England: Penguin Books, 1969.

Intended for the general reader, this companion is designed as a handy and readable "Who's Who" of the most significant writers from ancient times to the present day. The number of entries is limited and the information provided is brief. Despite some generalizations, misleading statements, and problems in the choice of material, this handy reference work should be of some use to general readers, particularly those who cannot read Chinese. The editors attempted to include authors whose works are available in translation, or whose names are likely to appear in English-language publications.

34 LEE, LEO OU-FAN. "Dissent Literature from the Cultural Revolution." *CLEAR*, 9 (1979), 59-79.

A bibliographical survey and an analysis of works by Chinese dissident writers since the Cultural Revolution (1966-1969).

35 LI, TIEN-YI. *Chinese Fiction: A Bibliography of Books and Articles in Chinese and English.* New Haven: Far Eastern Publications, Yale University, 1968.

A selective bibliographical listing of books and articles on Chinese fiction written in Chinese and English. Also included are reference works and general studies relevant to Chinese fiction. The list of English-language sources is more extensive than that of Chinese, but is by no means exhaustive. English translations of novels and short stories are included. The first Western bibliography of Chinese fiction, this list is more useful to the general reader than to the specialist because of its inclusion of many general studies in English, and because of its exclusion of Japanese and other European language sources. No annotations; somewhat outdated.

36 ————. *The History of Chinese Literature: A Selected Bibliography.* 2nd ed. New Haven: Far Eastern Publications, Yale University, 1970.

A classified and selective bibliography of studies, including books and monographs but excluding journal articles, on both classical and modern Chinese literature written in Chinese, English, French, and Japanese. Also included are translations of selected literary works, general studies, anthologies, and reference guides, such as specialized dictionaries, bibliographies, indexes, concordances, source books, and glossaries. No annotations.

37   LING, SCOTT K. *Bibliography of Chinese Humanities, 1941-1972: Studies on Chinese Philosophy, Religion, History, Geography, Biography, Art, and Language and Literature.* Taipei: Liberal Arts Press, 1975.
   Based essentially on the bibliographic data included in the *Bibliography of Asian Studies* of the Association for Asian Studies, this guide is an extensive listing of Western studies of Chinese humanities, including literature.

37a   LIU, CHUN-JO. *Controversies in Modern Chinese Intellectual History.* Cambridge: East Asian Research Center, Harvard University, 1964.
   An analytical bibliographical guide to journal articles on the May Fourth Movement and on controversies developed since the movement.

38   London. University. School of Oriental and African Studies. *Library Catalog of the School of Oriental and African Studies.* Boston: G. K. Hall, 1963. 28 vols. First supplement, 1968; second supplement, 1973.
   Printed catalogs of one of the strongest and oldest Asian and African collections in Europe.

39   LUST, JOHN. *Index Sinicus: A Catalogue of Articles Relating to China in Periodicals and Other Collective Publications, 1920-1955.* Cambridge, England: W. Heffer and Sons, 1964.
   Lists some twenty thousand articles in Western languages under broad heaings. Includes several hundred titles dealing with Chinese fiction.

40   MERHAUT, BORIS. "Bibliography of Academician Jaroslav Průšek 1958-1965." *ArOr,* 34 (1966), 574-586.
   A list of the publications of Jaroslav Průšek, who has written extensively on Chinese fiction.

41   Modern Language Association of America. *MLA International Bibliography.* New York, 1963-.
   Published annually, this is an extensive bibliographic guide to world literature; however, its coverage of Chinese literature is extremely limited.

42   NATHAN, ANDREW J. *Modern China, 1840-1972: An Introduction to Sources and Research Aids.* Ann Arbor: Center for Chinese Studies, University of Michigan, 1973.
   An introductory guide to bibliographical, biographical and other research aids and sources on late Ch'ing and twentieth-century China.

42a   National Central Library. *Directory of Contemporary Authors of the Republic of China.* Taipei: National Central Library, 1970.
   An extensive directory of Chinese writers residing in Taiwan, including some who have gone abroad.

43 New York Public Library. *Dictionary Catalog of the Oriental Collection, the Research Libraries of the New York Public Library.* Boston: G. K. Hall, 1960. 16 vols. First supplement, 1976. 8 vols.
   A printed catalog of an extensive collection of materials on Oriental subjects in bth Western and Asian languages.

44 NIENHAUSER, WILLIAM H. "Recent Publications on Chinese Literature: II. The People's Republic of China." *CLEAR*, 1 (1979), 87-95.
   A brief bibliographic survey of important Chinese publications on Chinese literature, mainly classical literature. An addendum (pp. 97-98), by W. L. Wong, lists more recent publications.

45 NUNN, G. RAYMOND. *Asia: A Selected and Annotated Guide to Reference Works.* Cambridge: M.I.T. Press, 1971.
   The section on China lists a number of reference books on Chinese literature.

46 ———. *East Asia: A Bibliography of Bibliographies.* Honolulu: East-West Center Library, University of Hawaii, 1967.
   The section on China lists a number of bibliographic works on China.

46a OKAMURA, SHIGERU. "Recent Publications on Chinese Literature: III. Japan." *CLEAR*, 2 (1980), 137-144.
   A bibliographic survey of recent Japanese publications on Chinese literature.

47 PAPER, JORDAN D. *Guide to Chinese Prose.* Boston: G. K. Hall, 1973.
   A guide to 142 English translations and studies of Chinese prose. All titles are annotated in detail. Its listing of works on Chinese fiction is limited.

48 POSNER, ARLENE and ARNE J. DE KEIJZER. *China: A Resource and Curriculum Guide.* 2nd ed. Chicago: University of Chicago Press, 1976.
   Contains a brief section on Chinese literature.

49 PRŮŠEK, JAROSLAV, ed. *Dictionary of Oriental Literatures.* London: George Allen and Unwin, 1974; New York: Basic Books, 1974. 3 vols.
   Vol. I contains some two hundred short articles on Chinese literature. Most entries provide concise information about the life and works of individual writers. Some attempts are made to evaluate works from historical and aesthetic points of view. There are also articles describing literary terms, genres, forms, schools, and movements. Emphasis on Marxist interpretation is apparent in some entries. Much space is devoted to modern literature. Entries on modern Chinese fiction are mostly by Czech scholars, including Jaroslav Průšek himself. A conveniently arranged reference work, it provides generally reliable and concise information. Though free from serious errors, it does contain significant omissions of some important writers and works. Intended for the "educated reading public" rather than for the specialist.

49a SCHULTZ, WILLIAM. "Chinese Literature and Twayne's World Author Series: A Status Report." *CLEAR*, 1 (1979), 215-217.
A report on published and forthcoming Twayne titles on Chinese authors

50 SCHYNS, JOSEPH, et al. *1500 Modern Chinese Novels and Plays*. Reprint ed. Hong Kong: Lung Men Bookstore, 1966. (Originally published in Peking in 1948.)
This work includes a listing of novels by modern Chinese writers, together with brief biographical data and plot summaries. Still a useful reference work despite errors, omissions, and obvious biases.

51 SHU, AUSTIN C. W. *Modern Chinese Authors: A List of Pseudonyms*. 2nd rev. ed. Taipei: Chinese Materials and Research Aids Service Center, 1971.
A list of the pseudonyms of modern Chinese writers.

51a SHULMAN, FRANK JOSEPH. *Doctoral Dissertations on Asia: An Annotated Bibliographical Journal of Current International Research*. Ann Arbor: Xerox University Microfilms, Winter, 1975-.
Published semiannually, it lists both completed and ongoing dissertations dealing with Asia.

52 ———. *Doctoral Dissertations on China, 1971-1975: A Bibliography of Studies in Western Languages*. Seattle: University of Washington Press, 1978.
Includes a section listing dissertations on modern and contemporary Chinese prose and fiction.

53 SKINNER, G. WILLIAM, et al. *Modern Chinese Society, 1644-1969*. Stanford: Stanford University Press, 1973. 3 vols.
A very extensive bibliography of Chinese, Japanese, and Western studies of modern Chinese society (1644-1969), this guide also lists sources useful for the study of Chinese fiction.

54 Stanford University. Hoover Institution on War, Revolution, and Peace. *Catalog of the Chinese Collection*. Boston: G. K. Hall, 1969. 13 vols. First supplement, 1972; Second supplement, 1976.
A printed catalog of the Hoover Chinese collection. Strong in the social sciences and modern Chinese literature.

55 STUCKI, CURTIS. *American Doctoral Dissertations on Asia, 1933-June, 1966*. Ithaca: Southeast Asia Program, Department of Asian Studies, Cornell University, 1968.
The most comprehensive guide to American doctoral dissertations on Asia completed before 1966.

56   TING, NAI-TUNG and LEE-HSIA HSU TING. *Chinese Folk Narratives: A Bibliographical Guide.* San Francisco: Chinese Materials Center, 1975.
        An annotated bibliography of published folk narratives, this guide consists of notes on editions and bibliographic entries of folk narratives arranged by their ethnic origins.

57   TSAI, MEISHI. *Contemporary Chinese Novels and Short Stories, 1949-1974: An Annotated Bibliography.* Cambridge: Council on East Asian Studies, Harvard University, 1979.
        A very extensive bibliographic listing of Chinese novels and stories published during the period from 1949 to 1974, excluding those by Taiwan writers. zInformation given includes some biographical data and plot summaries. There are also author, subject, and title indexes.

58   TSIEN, TSUEN-HSUIN. *China: An Annotated Bibliography of Bibliographies.* Boston: G. K. Hall, 1978.
        A comprehensive bibliography of bibliographies on China, including many entries on Chinese literature.

58a   Union Research Institute. *Hierarchies of the People's Republic of China.* Hong Kong: Union Research Institute, 1975.
        Includes brief biographical sketches of a small number of contemporary Chinese writers.

58b   ———. *Who's Who in Communist China.* Rev. ed. Hong Kong: Union Research Institute, 1969-70. 2 vols.
        Contains brief biographical information on contemporary Chinese writers.

59   U.S. Library of Congress. *Far Eastern Language Catalog.* Boston: G. K. Hall, 1972. 22 vols.
        A catalog of a very extensive collection of East Asian language materials. Strong in recent scholarly publications, it lists many English translations and about 55,000 Chinese titles.

59a   WALRAVENS, HARTMUT. "Recent Publications on Chinese Literature: IV. Europe." *CLEAR,* 2 (1980), 237-248.
        A bibliographic survey of recent European studies of Chinese literature.

59b   WU, EUGENE. *Leaders of Twentieth-century China: An Annotated Bibliography of Selected Biographical Works in the Hoover Library.* Stanford: Stanford University Press, 1956.
        A list of selected biographical works on twentieth-century Chinese leaders, including leading writers.

60   YANG, WINSTON L. Y., PETER LI, and NATHAN K. MAO. *Classical Chinese Fiction. A Guide to Its Study and Appreciation: Essays and Bibliographies.* Boston: G. K. Hall, 1978.

Although devoted to the study of classical Chinese fiction, some of the chapters in the bibliographic section, such as "Chinese-Western Comparative Studies" (IV, Part One) and "Late Ch'ing Novels" (XV, Part Two), are of use to those interested in modern Chinese fiction.

61 YU, PING-KUEN. *Chinese History: Index to Learned Articles, 1902-1962.* Hong Kong: Hong Kong East Asian Institute, 1963. *Chinese History: Index to Learned Articles, 1905-1964.* Cambridge: Harvard-Yenching Library, Harvard University, 1970.
An index to scholarly articles written in Chinese.

62 YUAN, TUNG-LI. *China in Western Literature.* New Haven: Far Eastern Publications, Yale University, 1958.
An exhaustive listing of books and monographs on China, written in English, French, and German, published between 1921 and 1957. It records, under the heading "Novels," several hundred titles, including studies and translations.

II

Journals

In recent years a large number of studies and translations of modern Chinese fiction have appeared in scholarly journals and literary magazines. Below is a selected list of such journals and magazines. The current place of publication and the year of the first issue of each journal are given. It should be noted that a few journals listed in this chapter have ceased publication or are published behind schedule. Abbreviations of frequently cited journals are given on pp. xi-xii. For a more complete listing of journals in Western languages and more detailed information on the journals listed, consult *Ulrich's International Periodicals Directory* (16th ed. New York: Bowker, 1975).

Among the journals listed below, a few merit special attention. *Renditions*, for instance, is devoted almost exclusively to translations, often with Chinese texts appended. *Chinese Literature* and *The Chinese P.E.N.* are very good sources, respectively, for translations of current Communist and Taiwan fiction. For critical articles and comparative studies of modern Chinese and Western literatures, *Chinese Literature: Essays, Articles, Reviews, Literature East and West, Tamkang Review*, and *Yearbook of Comparative and General Literature* are noteworthy. *Modern Chinese Literature Newsletter* provides useful information on modern Chinese writers and works. For selected Communist studies, *Chinese Studies in Literature* provides generally reliable translations. For East European scholarship on modern Chinese literature, *Asian and African Studies* is a very important source. Many other journals listed below, such as *China Quarterly* and *Modern China*, have also published important studies of modern and Communist literature.

63   *Acta Orientália* (Budapest, 1950-   ).
     An official publication of the Hungarian Academy of Sciences, it often publishes articles on Chinese literature. An important source of East European scholarship on China.

64   *Archiv Orientální* (Prague, 1929-   ).
     One of the most important East European journals devoted to the study of Oriental history and culture, it has published articles on modern Chinese literature.

108/ BIBLIOGRAPHIES

65   *Asia Major* (London, New Series, 1949-   ).
       An important European journal, it occasionally publishes reviews and articles on Chinese literature.

66   *Asian and African Studies* (Bratislava, 1965-   ).
       A very important East European journal for the study of modern Chinese literature.

67   *Books Abroad* (Norman, Oklahoma, 1927-   ). (New title: *World Literature Today*.)
       Has published occasional reviews of books on modern Chinese literature.

68   *Bulletin of Concerned Asian Scholars* (Charlemont, Mass., 1969-   ).
       A journal devoted to the study of Asia, especially contemporary China, and founded by a group of young, concerned Asian scholars, the *BCAS* has published studies of Chinese Communist literature.

69   *Bulletin of the School of Oriental and African Studies* (London, 1917-   ).
       The *BSOAS* and *Asia Major* are two of the most important British journals devoted to the study of Asia. Both have published reviews and articles on Chinese literature.

70   *China Quarterly* (London, 1960-   ).
       Devoted exclusively to the study of contemporary China, this British journal has published a number of articles on modern and Communist literature.

71   *Chinese Culture* (Taipei, 1957-   ).
       Occasionally publishes articles on Chinese literature.

72   *Chinese Literature* (Peking, 1951-   ).
       The most important source for translations of current Chinese literature, *Chinese Literature* has published extensive translations of works by contemporary Chinese writers. It has also published comments and articles on Communist writers and works.

73   *Chinese Literature: Essays, Articles, Reviews* (Madison, Wis., 1979-   ).
       An English-language journal, *CLEAR* regularly publishes articles, essays, and reviews of modern Chinese literature.

74   *The Chinese P.E.N.* (Taipei, 1975-   ).
       Regularly publishes translations of stories by Chinese writers residing in Taiwan and abroad. One of the best sources for translations of current Taiwan fiction.

75   *Chinese Studies in Literature* (White Plains, N.Y., 1979-   ).
       This journal publishes translations of selected Chinese Communist studies of literature with substantive introductions by their translators.

76	*CHINOPERL Papers* (Originally titled *CHINOPERL News*) (Ithaca, N.Y., 1970-).
	An annual journal, which often publishes articles on Chinese oral and performing literature.

77	*Comparative Literature* (Eugene, Ore., 1949-).
	Has published several Chinese-Western comparative literary studies.

77a	*Contemporary China* (Boulder, Colorado, 1978-).
	A journal devoted to the study of various aspects of contemporary China.

78	*Contemporary Literature in Translation* (Vancouver, B.C., 1968-).
	Has published a few translations of modern Chinese literature.

79	*Criticism* (Detroit, 1959-).
	Includes occasional reviews and studies of Chinese literature from the Western critical point of view.

80	*East-West Review* (Kyoto, 1964-).
	Presents occasional articles in English on Chinese literature.

81	*Echo* (Taipei, 1969-).
	Has published translations of works by writers residing in Taiwan.

82	*Harvard Journal of Asiatic Studies* (Cambridge, 1936-).
	Has published many specialized studies of the history, culture, institutions, and literature of traditional China and a small number of articles on modern Chinese literature.

83	*Journal of Asian Studies* (Ann Arbor, 1956-).
	Formerly known as *Far Eastern Quarterly*, the *JAS* occasionally publishes articles on modern Chinese literature.

84	*Journal Asiatique* (Paris, 1822-).
	One of the oldest journals devoted to the study of Asia, *Journal Asiatique* has published articles on Chinese literature.

85	*Journal of Oriental Literature* (Honolulu, 1964-1969).
	Published a number of short articles on both classical and modern Chinese literature in the late 1960s. Discontinued.

86	*Journal of Oriental Studies* (Hong Kong, 1954-).
	Sponsored by the University of Hong Kong, the *JOS* regularly publishes articles on Chinese literature in Chinese and in English.

87	*Journal of the American Oriental Society* (New Haven, 1843-),
	Essentially devoted to the study of ancient Middle Eastern history and culture in its early years, the *JAOS* has recently given more attention to the study of traditional China. Occasionally it publishes reviews of studies of modern Chinese literature.

88 *Journal of the Chinese Language Teachers Association* (South Orange, N.J., 1964-   ).
    Devoted in its early years to language teaching and applied linguistics, the *JCLTA* now publishes articles and reviews on modern Chinese literature.

89 *Journal of the Oriental Society of Australia* (Sydney, 1960-   ).
    Has published some articles on Chinese literature.

90 *Literature and Ideology* (Toronto, 1969-   ).
    Devoted to the study of literature and ideology, this journal is useful to those interested in the study of Chinese Communist literature.

91 *Literature East and West* (Austin, Texas, 1954-   ).
    One of the most important sources for comparative studies of Chinese and Western literatures.

92 *Modern Asian Studies* (London, 1967-   ).
    Has published several studies of modern Chinese literature.

93 *Modern China* (Beverly Hills, Calif. 1975-   ).
    An important source for articles on modern Chinese literature.

94 *Modern Chinese Literature Newsletter* (Los Angeles, 1975-1979).
    Published surveys, summaries, and reviews of studies of modern Chinese literature. Discontinued.

95 *Mondes Asiatiques* (Paris, 1975-   ).
    An important source for French studies of modern China, including its literature.

96 *New Literary History* (Charlottesville, Va., 1969-   ).
    Devoted to the study of the theory and interpretation of literature, evolution of styles, conventions and genres, reasons for literary change, interconnections between national literary histories, and so on, *New Literary History* has published occasional studies of Chinese literature.

97 *Oriens Extremus* (Wiesbaden, Germany, 1954-   ).
    An important source for German studies of Chinese literature. Some articles are published in English.

98 *Orient/West* (Tokyo, 1955-   )
    Often publishes translations of and short articles on Chinese literature.

99 *Renditions* (Hong Kong, 1973-   ).
    An important source for reliable translations of modern Chinese stories and excerpts from novels, accompanied by the original Chinese texts.

100 *Review of National Literatures* (Jamaica, N.Y., 1970-   ).
Publishes reviews of the literatures of different countries. Its Spring, 1975 issue was devoted to Chinese literature.

101 *Tamkang Review* (Taipei, 1970-   ).
The only journal devoted exclusively to the comparative study of Chinese and Western literatures, *TR* has published many comparative studies of varying quality.

102 *Tien Hsia Monthly* (Shanghai, 1935-1941).
This literary magazine published in the late 1930s contained many fine translations of Chinese fiction and poetry. Discontinued.

103 *Transactions of the International Conference of Orientalists in Japan* (Tokyo, 1960-   ).
Publishes papers in English on Chinese literature by both Japanese and Western scholars.

104 *Tsing Hua Journal of Chinese Studies* (Taipei, New Series, 1956-   ).
Has published reviews and articles in both Chinese and English on Chinese literature. Emphasis on classical literature.

105 *Yearbook of Comparative and General Literature* (Chapel Hill, N.C., 1952-   ).
One of the most important sources for Chinese-Western comparative literary studies.

106 *Yearbook of Comparative Criticism* (University Park, Penn., 1967-   ).
Occasionally publishes articles on Chinese-Western comparative criticism.

III
General Studies and Anthologies of Chinese Literature

This chapter lists selected general studies, historical surveys, and anthologies of Chinese literature; studies of Chinese literary theory and criticism and general works of Chinese history and culture are also listed. Although some of the books recorded in this chapter have a rather limited coverage of Chinese literature, they may provide the general reader with useful background information on Chinese literature and culture.

Herbert A. Giles's *History of Chinese Literature*, the first history of Chinese literature, is of course outdated. Ch'en Shou-yi's *Chinese Literature: A Historical Introduction*, a fairly comprehensive and systematic survey of Chinese literature in English, is of limited use because of extensive factual errors and problems in interpretation. Wu-chi Liu's *An Introduction to Chinese Literature*, with emphasis on major writers and works, is probably the best introduction to Chinese literature in English, though less comprehensive than Ch'en's work. James J. Y. Liu's *Essentials of Chinese Literary Art* is a good summary of the highlights of classical and modern Chinese literature.

Also, one recent collection of essays, *Chinese Approaches to Literature from Confucius to Liang Ch'i-ch'ao*, edited by Adele Rickett, contains important articles related to the study of Chinese literature.

Of the many anthologies published in recent years, Cyril Birch's two-volume *Anthology of Chinese Literature*, containing representative works of Chinese poetry, prose, fiction, and drama from early times to the present, is probably the most comprehensive and best-selected collection. There are many other anthologies, some of which are listed in this chapter.

General Studies

107   BAUER, WOLFGANG. *China and the Search for Happiness: Recurring Themes in Four Thousand Years of Chinese Cultural History*. Translated by Michael Shaw. New York: Seabury Press, 1976.
    An interpretative study of the concepts of utopia in Chinese cultural, intellectual, and literary traditions. This is a translation of the author's original work in German, *China und die Hoffnung auf Glück* (Munich: Carl Hanser Verlag, 1971).

114/BIBLIOGRAPHIES

108 BUXBAUM, DAVID C. and FREDERICK W. MOTE, eds. *Transition and Permanence: Chinese History and Culture. A Festschrift in Honor of Dr. Hsiao Kung-ch'üan.* Hong Kong: Cathay Press, 1972. (Distributed by Chinese Materials Center, San Francisco.)
A collection of essays on Chinese culture, history, and literature.

109 CEADEL, ERIC B., ed. *Literatures of the East: An Appreciation.* London: John Murray, 1953.
Chapter 6 offers a brief survey of the history of Chinese literature from its beginning to modern times.

110 CH'EN, SHIH-HSIANG. "China: Literature." In *Encyclopedia Americana.* New York: Americana Corp., 1973, Vol. VI, pp. 577-584.
A chronological account of the history of Chinese literature from the classical age to the twentieth century.

111 CH'EN, SHOU-YI. "Chinese Literature." In *Encyclopaedia Britannica.* Chicago: Encyclopaedia Britannica, 1971, Vol. V, pp. 634-640.
A chronological account, divided by major dynasties, of the history of Chinese literature.

112 ———. *Chinese Literature: A Historical Introduction.* New York: Ronald Press, 1961.
A general survey of the history of Chinese literature from its beginnings to the twentieth century, with biographical sketches of eminent writers, summaries of important works, and translations of representative works. Though voluminous, it contains many factual errors, repetitions, misprints, and problems in interpretation. Strong in historical background, it remains the only comprehensive historical survey of Chinese literature in English.

113 CLARK, RICHARD D. "Approaches to a History of Chinese Literature: Bibliographical Spectrum and Review Article." *RNL,* 6 (1975), 128-156.
This review of recent Western studies of Chinese literature is intended to give a historical perspective on the vast legacy of Chinese literature.

114 DAVIS, A. R. "Chinese Literature." In S. H. Steinberg, ed. *Cassell's Encyclopaedia of World Literature.* New York: Funk and Wagnalls, 1954, I, pp. 98-104.
A chronological survey of Chinese literature with brief comments on major novels.

115 DeBARY, WILLIAM THEODORE, WING-TSIT CHAN, and BURTON WATSON, eds. *Sources of Chinese Tradition.* New York: Columbia University Press, 1960. Paperback ed. in 2 vols.
A collection of reliable translations of important sources of the Chinese cultural tradition. As a source book, it provides a good intellectual background in Chinese literature.

General Studies and Anthologies of Chinese Literature/115

116 *Études d'histoire et de littérature chinoises offertes au Professeur Jaroslav Průšek.* Paris: Institut des Hautes Études Chinoises, 1976. (Bibliothèque de l'Institut des Hautes Études Chinoises, vol. 24).
   A collection of twenty essays on Chinese literature, including many on Chinese fiction. Most of the articles are in English.

117 FENG, YUAN-CHUN. *A Short History of Classical Chinese Literature.* Peking: Foreign Languages Press, 1958; reprint ed. Westport, Conn: Hyperion Press, 1973.
   Strongly Marxist, this short history offers a brief but readable chronological account of classical Chinese literature up to the early twentieth century.

118 FITZGERALD, C. P. *China: A Short Cultural History.* 3rd ed. New York: Frederick A. Praeger, 1961.
   A general survey of the culture and history of traditional China. Main emphasis on the major cultural achievements of each dynasty. Extensive treatment of Chinese literature.

119 FRODSHAM, J. D. *New Perspectives in Chinese Literature.* Canberra: Australian National University Press, 1970.
   The author examines Chinese lyric poetry, narrative prose, and drama from "a viewpoint which no Chinese critic has yt adopted" in order to show "how modern critical methods can be applied to the elucidation of Chinese literature."

120 GAGE, RICHARD L., ed. *The Toynbee-Ikeda Dialogue.* Tokyo: Kodansha International, 1976.
   An interesting dialogue between an eminent Western historian and a prominent Asian Buddhist leader. Elaborates Western and Asian points of view on a variety of topics, including the environment, education, literature, and the modern world, as well as the future of civilization.

121 GILES, HERBERT A. *History of Chinese Literature.* (With a supplement on the modern period by Wu-chi Liu.) New York: Frederick Ungar, 1967; Rutland, Vt.: Charles E. Tuttle, 1973.
   Originally published in 1901, this first history of Chinese literature, written by a Westerner on the basis of traditional Chinese scholarship, is outdated, but it offers the reader a glimpse of traditional Chinese views of literature. Wu-chi Liu's supplement is a good summary of twentieth-century Chinese literature.

122 GOODRICH, L. CARRINGTON. *A Short History of the Chinese People.* 3rd ed. New York: Harper and Row, 1959; paperback ed., 1963.
   One of the best surveys of Chinese history with emphasis on the material civilization of China and China's contacts with the outside world. Much less attention is given to political and intellectual history. Its coverage of literature is limited.

116/BIBLIOGRAPHIES

123   HAWKES, DAVID. "An Introductory Note [on Chinese Literature]." In Raymond Dawson, ed. *The Legacy of China*. London: Oxford University Press, 1964, pp. 80-90.
Interesting general comments on certain features of Chinese literature.

124   HIGHTOWER, JAMES R. "Chinese Literature." In *Encyclopedia International*. New York: Grolier, 1973, IV, pp. 376-378.
A brief description of major poetic forms, the evolution of drama, and prose forms.

125   ———. "Individualism in Chinese Literature." *Journal of the History of Ideas*, 22 (1961), 159-168.
A study of individualism in Chinese literature and the contrast between Confucian conformity and Taoist liberty. The author points out the pervasiveness of Confucian conformity rather than Taoist liberty in Chinese society, noting that few writers are true romantic rebels, and that still fewer have openly challenged orthodoxy. He argues that individualism is not unknown in Chinese society, but that it is appreciated and sometimes glorified only under unusual circumstances. An interesting discussion of an exciting topic.

126   HU, CHANG-TU, et al. *China: Its People, Its Society, Its Culture*. New Haven: HRAF Press, 1960.
A comprehensive topical description of China and the Chinese. Strong in its presentation of contemporary China and socio-economic aspects but weak in its discussions of traditional China and humanistic aspects. There is a chapter on art, literature, and the intellectual tradition.

127   International Federation for Modern Languages and Literatures. *Literary History and Literary Criticism*. Edited by Leon Edel. New York: New York University Press, 1965.
A collection of some one hundred papers on literary history and criticism, including a few on Chinese literature.

128   KALTENMARK-GHÉQUIER, ODILE. *Chinese Literature*. New York: Walker and Co., 1964.
A translation by Anne-Marie Geoghegan of *La littérature chinoise* (Paris: Presses Universitaires de France, 1948). Though a sketchy summary of the history of Chinese literature, this book may appeal to those with little background in the field.

129   LATOURETTE, KENNETH SCOTT. *The Chinese: Their History and Culture*. 4th ed. New York: Macmillan, 1965.
A good, lengthy survey of the history of China. Topical essays in the second half of the volume are very useful to the general reader. There are extensive comments on Chinese literature.

130 LAU, JOSEPH S. M. and LEO OU-FAN LEE, eds. *Critical Persuasions: Essays on Chinese Literature*, forthcoming.

Dedicated to the memory of T. A. Hsia (1916-1965), a prominent critic of Chinese literature, this volume includes about ten critical essays on Chinese literature.

131 LIU, JAMES J. Y. *The Chinese Knight-Errant.* Chicago: University of Chicago Press, 1967.

A comprehensive study of the tradition of knight-errantry in Chinese history and literature from the fourth century B.C. to the twentieth century. The author provides background information on knight-errantry, gives examples of historical knights, and discusses the theme of knight-errantry in poetry, drama, and fiction. Comparisons are drawn between Chinese and European knights, and between Chinese and Western chivalric literatures. Includes extensive translations.

132 ———. *Chinese Theories of Literature.* Chicago: University of Chicago Press, 1975.

The first comprehensive treatment in English of traditional Chinese theories of literature, and the first in any language to analyze these theories in a new conceptual framework. The author focuses on Chinese theories about the nature and functions of literature, mainly of poetry, making only scant references to fiction and drama.

133 ———. *Essentials of Chinese Literary Art.* North Scituate, Mass.: Duxbury Press, 1979.

A brief but well-written summary of the highlights of Chinese literature with two chapters on the modern literature.

134 ———. "Prolegomena to a Study of Traditional Chinese Theories of Literature." *LEW*, 16 (Sept. 1972), 935-949.

An analysis of the purposes of and difficulties in the author's proposed study of traditional Chinese theories of literature. This article was later revised and incorporated into the author's introduction to his *Chinese Theories of Literature* (*see* no. 132).

135 ———. "The Study of Chinese Literature in the West: Recent Developments, Current Trends, Future Prospects." *JAS*, 35 (1975), 21-30.

A general survey, without critical comments, of the study of Chinese literature (including translations and studies of classical and modern fiction) in the West between 1960 and 1975. General comments on trends and prospects. More emphasis on poetry than on fiction.

136 ———. "Worlds and Language: The Chinese Literary Tradition." In Arnold Toynbee, ed. *Half the World: The History and Culture of China and Japan.* New York: Holt, Rinehart and Winston, 1973.

A stimulating survey of the Chinese literary tradition from the *Book of Songs* (*Shih ching*) to nineteenth-century fiction. Emphasis is on poetry.

137 LIU, WU-CHI. "Chinese Literature in Translation." In Horst Frenz, ed. *Proceedings of the First Conference on Oriental-Western Literary Relations.* Chapel Hill: University of North Carolina Press, 1955, pp. 224-230.

A discussion of "the accomplishment of the Oriental scholars in their translations of the various types of Chinese literature."

138 ———. *An Introduction to Chinese Literature.* Bloomington: Indiana University Press, 1966.

Not an extensive study of Chinese literary history but a descriptive and critical account of the major accomplishments, styles, movements, writers, and works of different periods. Written for the general reader, it provides fairly reliable background information on major writers, works, and genres, accompanied by sample translations from the Chinese. Probably the best introduction to Chinese literature in English.

139 ———. "Moral and Aesthetic Values in Chinese Literature." *TR,* 1, no. 1 (April 1970), 3-13.

Mainly concerned with a historical survey of the moral and aesthetic trends in Chinese literature of the imperial period.

140 McNAIR, H. F., ed. *China.* Berkeley: University of California Press, 1946.

A collection of thirty-four articles on major aspects of Chinese history and civilization. Of use to the general reader, though somewhat outdated. There are several essays on literature.

141 MEI, Y. P. "Man and Nature in Chinese Literature." In Horst Frenz, ed. *Proceedings of the First Conference on Oriental-Western Literary Relations.* Chapel Hill: University of North Carolina Press, 1955, pp. 163-173.

A glimpse of the variety in the objectives and themes of Chinese literature.

142 *Mélanges de Sinologie offerts à Monsieur Paul Demiéville.* Paris: Presses Universitaires de France, Vol. I, 1966; Vol. II, 1974. (Bibliothèque de l'Institut des Hautes Études Chinoises, vol. 20).

Two collections of essays on Sinology, including several articles on Chinese literature. Most of the articles are in English.

143 MESKILL, JOHN T., ed. *An Introduction to Chinese Civilization.* New York: Columbia University Press, 1973; paperback ed., Lexington, Mass. D. C. Heath, 1973.

Part I is a survey of the history of China by the editor; part II consists of essays on different aspects of Chinese civilization by various specialists. A good introduction to Chinese history and civilization, this book contains informative essays on Chinese language and literature.

144 NIENHAUSER, WILLIAM H., ed. *Critical Essays on Chinese Literature.* Hong Kong: Chinese University of Hong Kong, 1976.
Dedicated to Wu-chi Liu, a prominent Western-trained Chinese scholar, this volume consists of twelve critical essays on Chinese literature, including several on fiction.

145 *Papers on China.* Cambridge: East Asian Research Center, Harvard University, 1947-.
Published irregularly, *Papers on China* consists of Harvard seminar papers on nineteenth- and twentieth-century China, including a few on literature.

146 PRŮŠEK, JAROSLAV. *Chinese History and Literature: Collection of Studies.* Dordrecht, Holland: D. Reidel Publishing Co., 1970.
This book contains essays dealing with the Chinese storytelling tradition and vernacular fiction.

147 REISCHAUER, EDWIN O., JOHN K. FAIRBANK, and ALBERT M. CRAIG. *A History of East Asian Civilization.* Boston: Houghton Mifflin, 1958-1960. Vol. I: *East Asia: The Great Tradition*; Vol. II: *East Asia: The Modern Transformation.*
A comprehensive survey of Chinese, Japanese, and Korean civilizations. The chapters on Chinese civilization are quite up-to-date in scholarship and interpretation. Strong in the history of political and social institutions, but with less emphasis on political and intellectual history. Chinese literature is treated briefly.

148 RICKETT, ADELE A., ed. *Chinese Approaches to Literature from Confucius to Liang Ch'i-ch'ao.* Princeton: Princeton University Press, 1978.
A collection of eight essays on Chinese literary history, theory, and criticism, with particular emphasis on critical terminology as applied to the various genres. Includes two essays on Chinese fiction.

149 SHADICK, HAROLD. "Chinese Literature." In *Collier's Encyclopedia.* New York: Crowell-Collier Educational Corp., 1973, VI, pp. 354-358.
A brief description of Chinese histories, philosophical writings, prose, poetry, prose fiction, and twentieth-century literature.

150 SIH, PAUL K. T., ed. *China's Literary Image.* Jamaica, N. Y.: St. John's University, 1975. (A special issue of *RNL*, 6 (1975).)
This special issue of *Review of National Literature* consists of six articles on Chinese literature, mostly on modern writers and their works.

151 WANG, CHI-CHEN. "Chinese Literature." In *Chambers's Encyclopedia.* Oxford: Pergamon Press, 1966, III, pp. 487-494.
A chronological account of the history of Chinese literature from the earliest times to the twentieth century.

152 WELLS, HENRY W. *Traditional Chinese Humor: A Study in Art and Literature*. Bloomington: Indiana University Press, 1971.

    A comprehensive analysis of traditional Chinese humor, excluding wit. The author argues that humor as comic incongruity is one of the most pervasive characteristics of Chinese literature and art; he discusses its presence in Chinese art, poetry, drama, and narrative prose. However, the term "humor" is not clearly defined, and many important works, such as *A New Account of Tales of The World* (*Shih-shuo hsin-yü*), the fifth-century collection of humorous anecdotes, are not discussed. Very few notes are provided and sources are essentially limited to English translations. Designed for the general reader.

Anthologies

153 ANDERSON, G. L., ed. *Masterpieces of the Orient*. New York: W. W. Norton, 1961; expanded ed., 1977.

    This widely used anthology of Oriental literature includes translations of excerpts from a Ming novel, *Journey to the West* (*Hsi-yu chi*); a Ch'ing novel, *The Travels of Lao Ts'an* (*Lao-ts'an yu-chi*); and three stories by a twentieth century writer, Lu Hsün.

154 BIRCH, CYRIL, ed. *Anthology of Chinese Literature*. New York: Grove Press, Vol. I, 1965; Vol. II, 1972.

    A comprehensive anthology of Chinese literature from early times to the twentieth century. Most of the works are well selected and the translations are generally accurate and readable. The general introductions and brief notes at the beginning of each section are helpful to the general reader.

155 CHAI, CH'U, and WINBERG, CHAI, trs. and eds. *A Treasury of Chinese Literature: A New Prose Anthology Including Fiction and Drama*. New York: Appleton-Century, 1965.

    Designed as an introduction to classical and modern Chinese prose literature, this anthology is divided into three parts: prose, fiction, and drama. The fiction section includes translations of stories written between the T'ang and the middle of the twentieth century as well as excerpts from the major Ming and Ch'ing novels. A fairly readable and comprehensive anthology of Chinese prose literature, it is especially suitable for those who have little background in Chinese literature.

156 LIN, YUTANG, ed. *The Wisdom of China and India*. New York: Modern Library, 1942; reprint ed., Taipei: Literature House, 1968.

    Includes extensive translations of Chinese poetry, prose, tales, anecdotes, and philosophical writings.

157 LIU, WU-CHI, et al., eds. *K'uei Hsing: A Repository of Asian Literature in Translation*. Bloomington: Indiana University Press, 1974.

    A collection of fine translations of a small number of selections from Chinese, Japanese, and Tibetan literary works, together with useful introductory notes. The emphasis is on poetry.

158   McNAUGHTON, WILLIAM, ed. *Chinese Literature: An Anthology from the Earliest Times to the Present Day.* Rutland, Vt.: Charles E. Tuttle, 1974.

This ambitious anthology attempts to cover the entire span of Chinese literature from its beginning to the present. It includes prose, fiction, poetry, and drama of different periods. The introduction and notes are useful to the general reader, even though there are extensive generalizations, misconceptions, and oversimplifications. The editor has coined innovative but misleading terms, such as "Country Music" and "The Broken Sentence." Relying heavily on existing translations, he pays only limited attention to modern literature.

159   MILLER, JAMES E., et al., eds. *Literature of the Eastern World.* Glenview, Ill.: Scott, Foresman, 1970.

Includes translations of several Chinese stories, traditional and modern. The emphasis, however, is on poetry.

160   YOHANNON, JOHN D., ed. *A Treasury of Asian Literature.* New York: New American Library, 1956.

An anthology arranged under four categories: story, drama, song, and scripture. Its introductions, chronologies, and bibliographies, though brief, are helpful. Its coverage of Chinese literature is limited.

IV

Chinese-Western Comparative Studies

In recent years comparative studies of Chinese and Western literatures have become increasingly popular. Some scholars employ Western methodologies in the study of Chinese literature; others interpret, criticize, and evaluate Chinese works on the basis of Western critical theories or critical standards, or they measure Chinese works against Western models. Despite the various approaches to comparative studies, most scholars concentrate on the similarities and differences between Chinese and Western works within the framework of different cultural and literary backgrounds and traditions. There is no doubt that such comparative studies will help the Western reader develop a better appreciation of Chinese literature. Therefore, a special effort has been made to record these studies in this chapter. (For a list of selected comparative studies of traditional Chinese fiction and classical Western fiction, see Winston L. Y. Yang, Peter Li, and Nathan Mao, *Classical Chinese Fiction* (Boston: G. K. Hall, 1978), pp. 151-159.

161 ALDRIDGE, A. OWEN. "Comparative Literature East and West: An Appraisal of the Tamkang Conference." *Yearbook of Comparative and General Literature*, no. 21 (1972), pp. 65-70.
   A report on the First International Comparative Literature Conference held in Taipei in August, 1971, and an assessment of the papers presented at the conference. The author concentrates on papers dealing exclusively with East-West relations.

162 ———. "The Second China Conference: A Recapitulation." *Yearbook of Comparative and General Literature*, no. 25 (1976), pp. 42-48. Also in *TR*, 6:2/7:1 (Oct., 1975/April, 1976), 481-492.
   A recapitulation of the Second International Comparative Literature Conference held in Taipei in 1975.

163 CARPIO, RUSTICA C. "Literary Relations between China and Other Asian Countries." *TR*, 2:2/3:1 (Oct., 1971/April, 1972), 71-79.
   General comments on literary relations between China and other Asian countries.

164 CHI, CH'IU-LANG. "The Concepts of Classicism and Romanticism: Their Application to Chinese Literature." *TR*, 3, no. 2 (Oct., 1972), 235-251.

Accepting the view that "romanticism" and "classicism" are "relativistic" concepts and "approximate" terms, the author discusses problems in applying them to the study of Chinese literature.

165 DEENEY, JOHN J., ed. *Chinese-Western Comparative Literature and Strategy.* University Press, 1980.

A collection of papers presented at the Hong East-West Comparative Literature in 1979.

166 ———. "Comparative Literature Studies in Taiwan." *TR*, 1, no. 1 (April, 1970), 119-145.

The author introduces scholars interested in comparative literature to some of the problems, questions, topics, and tasks involved in Chinese-English literary relations and surveys some of the important features of this field, such as aim, definition, scope, method, bibliography, and terminology.

167 ———. "Comparative Literature: West and/or East?" *TR*, 4, no. 2 (Oct., 1973), 157-166.

Commenting on his observations of the activities of the Seventh Congress of the International Comparative Literature Association, the author proposes several areas for further exploration, such as the limitations Chinese literature places on Chinese-Western literary relations and the contributions Chinese literature offers to the literatures of the Western world.

168 ———. "Comparativization: The Example from China." In *Proceedings of the VIIth Congress of the International Comparative Literature Association.* Budapest: Hungarian Academy of Sciences, 1979.

Using Chinese literature as an example, the author discusses "comparativization," by which he means "an attitude of mind which is habitually thinking in a comparative way and actively reading literature from a multi-dimensional point of view as well as integrating all its complex relationships."

169 ———. "New Orientations for Comparative Literature." *TR*, 8, no. 1 (April, 1977), 227-236.

Adapted from a forthcoming book in Chinese by the author under the same title, this article outlines some of the key areas in East-West literary relations and concludes with a manifesto-like call for a "Chinese School of Comparative Literature."

170 ———. "Some Reflections on the History of Comparative Literature in China." *TR*, 6:2/7:1 (Oct., 1975/April, 1976), 219-228.

General comments on comparative literature studies in Taiwan.

171 ETIEMBLE, RENE. *The Crisis in Comparative Literature.* East Lansing: Michigan State University Press, 1966.

The author, who is one of the most enthusiastic advocates of Chinese literature, suggests that the approach of comparative literature toward the Orient be changed. He urges Western comparatists to learn Asian languages, especially Chinese, which he believes should be the international working language of comparatists.

172 FOKKEMA, D. W. "Cultural Relativism and Comparative Literature." *TR*, 3 no. 2 (Oct., 1972), 59-71.

The author discusses various problems in the application of Western critical approaches to the study of Chinese literature. He raises questions about the universal features and qualities of literature, universally applicable critical criteria, and historical and cultural relativism. An interesting and provocative study.

173 ———. "Expressionism in East and West? Some Methodological Problems." *TR*, 6:2/7:1 (Oct., 1975/April, 1976), 143-157.

The author points out that "no development or phenomenon in literature can be studied in isolation, and that most so-called new literary developments or phenomena are the result of a new arrangement or organization of pre-existing elements."

173a ———. "New Strategies in the Comparative Study of Literature and Their Application to Contemporary Chinese Literature." *New Asia Academic Bulletin*, 1 (1978), 4-18.

The author proposes new strategies for the comparative study of literature and their application to contemporary Chinese literature.

174 FRENZ, HORST. "East-West Literary Relations: Outside Looking In." *TR*, 6:2/7:1 (Oct., 1975/April, 1976), 11-19.

General comments on translation and on East-West literary relations. The author traces the history of the awarding of the Nobel Prize to authors associated with Asia and tries to restore the tarnished image of Rudyard Kipling. He believes that every comparative literature program should have on its faculty those who "make East-West relations their special field of interest and research and impart their expertise to students."

175 ———, ed. *Proceedings of the First Conference on Oriental-Western Literary Relations.* Chapel Hill: University of North Carolina Press, 1955. *Asia and the Humanities: Papers Presented at the Second Conference on Oriental-Western Literary and Cultural Relations.* Bloomington: Comparative Literature Committee, Indiana University, 1959. "Proceedings of the Third Conference on Oriental-Western Literary and Cultural Relations." *Yearbook of Comparative and General Literature*, no. 11 (1962), pp. 119-236. "Proceedings of the Fourth Conference on Oriental-Western Literary and Cultural Relations." *Yearbook of Comparative and General Literature*, no. 15 (1966), pp. 157-224.

126/ BIBLIOGRAPHIES

A series of four collections of papers on Oriental-Western literary and cultural relations delivered at the four comparative literature conferences held between 1955 and 1966. Included are many papers on Chinese-Western literary relations .

176 HIGHTOWER, JAMES R. "Chinese Literature in the Context of World Literature." *Comparative Literature*, 5 (1953), 117-124.

General comments on the major achievements in Chinese literature, the place of Chinese literature in world literature, and the importance of Chinese literature for the study of world literature. The author is convinced that the study of Chinese literature will contribute greatly to the understanding of world literature.

177 International Comparative Literature Association. *Proceedings of the VIIth Congress of the International Comparative Literature Association.* Budapest: Hungarian Academy of Sciences, 1979.

Vol. I, edited by Eva Kushner and Roman Struc and entitled "Comparative Literature Today: Theory and Practice," contains papers on Chinese-Western literary relations delivered at the 1973 ICLA Congress.

178 International Federation for Modern Languages and Literatures. *Literary History and Literary Criticism.* Edited by Leon Edel. New York: New York University Press, 1965.

A collection of some one hundred papers on literary history and literary criticism, including a few on Chinese literature.

179 Korean P.E.N. Centre, ed. *Humour in Literature East and West: Proceedings [of the] XXXVII International P.E.N. Congress, June 28-July 3, 1970.* Seoul: Korean P.E.N. Centre, 1971.

A collection of papers on humor in Asian and Western literatures delivered during the 1970 P.E.N. Congress.

180 KUNST, ARTHUR. "Literature of Asia." In Newton P. Stallknecht and Horst Frenz, eds. *Comparative Literature: Method and Perspective.* Carbondale: Southern Illinois University Press, 1971, pp. 312-325.

A survey of the perplexing problems faced by comparatists interested in South and East Asian literatures, and of the benefits of their study of these literatures. Calling attention to the immensely rich but neglected Asian literatures, the author suggests that "precisely because most Asian works have no generic relation with the West, they can be used as correctives upon our parochial assumptions about the universal validity of Western literary history, theory, criticism, methodology, and technique."

181 LEFEVERE, ANDRÉ. "Western Hermeneutics and Concepts of Chinese Literary Theory." *TR*, 6:2/7:1 (Oct., 1975/April, 1976), 159-168.

A discussion of the concepts of Chinese literary theory and the application of hermeneutic thinking to the study and teaching of literature.

182   LIU, JAMES J. Y. "The Study of Chinese Literature in the West: Recent Developments, Current Trends, Future Prospects." *JAS*, 35 (1975), 21-30.
A survey of the study of Chinese literature in the West between 1960 and 1975. General comments on trends and prospects.

183   MALONE, DAVID H. "Cultural Assumptions and Western Literary Criticism." *TR*, 6:2/7:1 (Oct., 1975/April, 1976), 55-67.
Since most comparatists base their studies upon the techniques and assumptions of Western literary criticism, the author, advocating a reexamination of the existing assumptions and methodologies in the comparative study of Eastern and Western literatures, suggests that Chinese literary works be evaluated on their own terms and within their own traditions.

183a TAY, WILLIAM, ed. *China and the West: Comparative Literature Studies*. Hong Kong: Chinese University Press, 1980.
A collection of essays on comparative literature as it relates to China's literary tradition.

184   WIVELL, CHARLES. "Problems of Teaching Chinese Literature in a Comparative Literature Program." *JCLTA*, 9 (1974), 13-17.
Brief comments on the various problems in teaching Chinese literature in a comparative literature program, with emphasis on fiction.

185   YEH, CH'ING-PING. "Conservatism and Originality in Chinese Literature." *TR*, 6:2/7:1 (Oct., 1975/April, 1976), 99-108.
The author discusses conservatism and originality in Chinese literature and sketches a critical debate known as the "Quarrel of Ancients and Moderns."

186   YIP, WAI-LIM. "The Use of 'Models' in East-West Comparative Literature." *TR*, 6:2/7:1 (Oct., 1975/April, 1976), 109-126.
The author points out that it has become imperative for East-West comparatists to develop an awareness of models, "particularly when neither of the two cultural horizons has expanded itself enough to absorb and include the circumference and structuring activities of the other."

187   YU, ANTHONY C. "Problems and Prospects in Chinese-Western Literary Relations." *Yearbook of Comparative and General Literature*, no. 23 (1974), pp. 47-53.
A general discussion of major problems and prospects in the comparative study of Chinese and Western literatures.

Part Two:
Bibliography of Modern Chinese Fiction

Nathan K. Mao and Peter Li

I

General Studies and Anthologies of Modern Chinese Fiction

This chapter lists selected general studies, historical surveys, and anthologies of modern Chinese fiction; studies of modern Chinese literature, literary theory and criticism, and intellectual trends are also included. Most of the studies recorded here are general in nature and broad in coverage. However, when important items appear in major collections of essays or anthologies of stories, they are listed individually in pertinent chapters. Studies directly concerned with a specific writer are listed in the chapter devoted to him or her. Although some of the materials included have a rather limited coverage of modern Chinese literature or fiction, they may provide the general reader with useful background information on modern Chinese literature or history.

Readers are urged to pay particular attention to the following standard reference works: Tse-tsung Chow's *The May Fourth Movement: Intellectual Revolution in Modern China* and its companion *Research Guide*, C. T. Hsia's *History of Modern Chinese Fiction*, Merle Goldman's *Modern Chinese Literature in the May Fourth Era*, T. A. Hsia's *The Gate of Darkness*, and Leo Ou-fan Lee's *The Romantic Generation of Modern Chinese Writers*. Studies contributed by Cyril Birch, Paul G. Pickowicz, Milena Doleželová-Velingerová, and a few others are also useful references. For Eastern European scholarship, studies by Jaroslav Průšek, Marián Gálik, and Anna Doležalová deserve attention. Michael Gotz's analysis of modern Chinese literature studies is an informative survey of the study of modern Chinese literature in the West. For biographical information on modern Chinese writers, see Howard L. Boorman and Richard Howard's *Biographical Dictionary of Republican China* and Donald W. Klein and Anne B. Clark's *Biographic Dictionary of Chinese Communism, 1921-65*.

Many anthologies of modern Chinese literature or fiction have been published. The following deserve special attention: Volume II of Cyril Birch's *Anthology of Chinese Literature,* Chi Pang-yüan's *An Anthology of Contemporary Chinese Literature,* C. T. Hsia's *Twentieth-Century Chinese Stories,* Harold Isaacs's

Straw Sandals, Joseph S. M. Lau and Timothy Ross's *Chinese Stories from Taiwan: 1960-1970,* Walter and Ruth Meserve's *Modern Literature from China,* and Joseph S. M. Lau, Leo Ou-fan Lee, and C. T. Hsia's *Modern Chinese Stories and Novellas, 1918-1948.*

General Studies

188   BENTON, GREGOR. "The Yenan 'Literary Opposition.'" *New Left Review,* 92 (1975), 93-106.
A study of literary opposition to Communist policy on art and literature in the early 1940s.

189   BERNINGHAUSEN, JOHN and TED HUTERS, eds. *Revolutionary Literature in China.*
For annotations and bibliographic information, *see* no. 313.

190   BIRCH, CYRIL. "Change and Continuity in Chinese Fiction." In Merle Goldman, ed. *Modern Chinese Literature in the May Fourth Era.* Cambridge: Harvard University Press, 1977, pp. 385-406.
In assessing the role of the May Fourth writers in the development of Chinese literature, Birch tests their writings against those of the premodern period and those of the post-Yenan years. A comparison of three novels, Li Po-yüan's *A Brief History of Enlightenment* (1906), Mao Tun's *Midnight* (1933), and Hao Jan's *The Bright Road (Golden Highway)* (1972), Birch hopes, "will reveal not only the unique contributions of May Fourth literature to modern China but also the continuities and changes in Chinese literature between the late Qing [Ch'ing] and the People's Republic." In his analysis of the narrative mode in *A Brief History of Enlightenment,* Birch notes Li Po-yüan's use of the "simulated text" of the storyteller in addressing his audience: features such as authorial intrusion and commentary, and a continuing dialogue with the postulated reader. But in the fiction published after 1917-1919, Birch points out that the storyteller pose is dropped and the narrator becomes one with the implied author; Mao Tun's *Midnight* presents a tight overall dramatic structure as compared to the rambling *A Brief History of Enlightenment.* Birch concludes that Hao Jan in *The Bright Road* "enjoys large technical advantages: the colorful saws and symbols of the old vernacular tradition plus the more systematic narrative flow developed by the modernizers."

191   ———. "Contemporary Chinese Literature." *International P.E.N. Bulletin,* 5, no. 1 (March, 1954), 3-6.
General comments on contemporary Chinese literature.

192   ———. "Fiction of the Yenan Period." *CQ,* no. 4 (Oct./Dec., 1960), 1-11.
An analysis of fiction written by Communist writers during World War II.

193   ———, ed. *Chinese Communist Literature.*
For annotations and bibliographic information, *see* no. 701.

194 ———. "Teaching May Fourth Fiction." *MCLN*, 2, no. 1 (Spring, 1976), 1-16.

By carefully choosing readings from two recently published anthologies of modern Chinese short stories and by comparing them with Western works, Cyril Birch examines their uses of the following literary modes: the romantic-confessional, the romantic-heroic, the realistic (nineteenth-century), the psychologically realistic, the naturalistic, and the satirical. He concludes that "Chinese fiction of the period 1918-1945 presents an interesting, perhaps unique, phenomenon for the student of comparative literature, a case of sudden and temporary confluence between two highly developed but previously separate literary traditions."

195 BOORMAN, HOWARD L. *Literature and Politics in Contemporary China*. Jamaica, N.Y.: St. John's University, 1960.

A general survey of the interrelationship between literature and politics in China from 1919 to 1958.

196 ——— and RICHARD C. HOWARD, eds. *Biographical Dictionary of Republican China*. New York: Columbia University Press, 1967-1971. 5 vols.

Provides biographical information on a large number of modern Chinese writers.

197 BOROWITZ, ALBERT. *Fiction in Communist China: 1949-1953*.

For annotations and bibliographic information, *see* no. 708.

198 CH'EN, SHIH-HSIANG. "Language and Literature under Communism."

For annotations and bibliographic information, *see* no. 712.

199 CH'EN SHOU-YI. *Chinese Literature: A Historical Introduction*. New York: Ronald Press, 1961.

A comprehensive historical survey of Chinese literature in thirty-two chapters, the last two of which examine the impact of the West on modern Chinese writers, and the Literary Revolution in the late 1910s. Despite its many factual and typographical errors, it is of some use as a general reference book. For further information, *see* no. 112.

200 CHENG, CHING-MAO. "The Impact of Japanese Literary Trends on Modern Chinese Writers." In Merle Goldman, ed. *Modern Chinese Literature in the May Fourth Era*. Cambridge: Harvard University Press, 1977, pp. 63-88.

Tracing the influence of Japanese literary trends on major Chinese literary figures, such as Liang Ch'i-ch'ao, Chou Tso-jen, Lu Hsün, Mao Tun, and others, the author concludes that Japan had contributed a great deal to modern Chinese literary development, mostly as a channel for Western influence. This is particularly obvious in literary theory. Also, Japanese naturalistic fiction, especially the *watakushi-shōsetsu* autobiographical type, helped bring about the so-called 'decadent' fiction in China in the early twenties. However, its influence was rather short-lived. The only Chinese writer deeply affected by Japanese literature was Chou Tso-jen according to the author.

201   CHIN, AI-LI (SUNG). "Interdependence of Roles in Transitional China: A Structural Analysis of Attitudes in Contemporary Chinese Literature." Ph.D. Dissertation. Cambridge: Harvard University, 1951.
A study of attitudes in contemporary Chinese literature.

202   CHING, EUGENE. "The Language of Modern Chinese Literature." *RNL*, 6 (Spring, 1975), 18-38.
A discussion of the fundamental characteristics of the spoken and written Chinese language and the effects they may have on modern Chinese literature written in the vernacular.

203   CHINNERY, J. D. "Problems of Literary Reform in Modern China." Ph.D. Dissertation. London: University of London, 1955.
A study of the various problems of literary reform in China in the early decades of this century.

204   CHOU, YANG. *China's New Literature and Art.*
For annotations and bibliographic information, *see* no. 715.

205   CHOW, TSE-TSUNG. *The May Fourth Movement: Intellectual Revolution in Modern China.* Cambridge: Harvard University Press, 1960.
An important, well-documented study of the May Fourth Movement. Part I of the book gives a factual account of the development of the Movement, tracing the forces that precipitated it, its initial phase (1915-1918), the May Fourth Incident, developments following the Incident, expansion of the New Culture Movement (1919-1920), foreign attitudes toward it, the ideological and political split (1919-1921), and sociopolitical consequences (1920-1922). Part II analyzes the Literary Revolution, the new thought and the reevaluation of the Chinese tradition, and concludes with the various interpretations and evaluations of the Movement. Also included are a chronology of relevant events (1914-1923), appendices, notes, and an index. An indispensable reference guide for any student of modern China.

206   ―――. *Research Guide to the May Fourth Movement.* Cambridge: Harvard University Press, 1963.
Includes an annotated list of about 250 periodicals founded during the May Fourth period, with editors, major contributors, principles, and political background and significance, a bibliography of more than eight hundred Chinese, Japanese, and Western books and articles, and a glossary of Chinese names and terms. Much of the information is nearly impossible to obtain elsewhere, and this volume may be used independently of the author's *The May Fourth Movement* (*see* no. 205).

207 CHUNG, WEN. "National Defense Literature and Its Representative Works." *ChL*, no. 10 (Oct., 1971), 91-99.
A discussion of representative works of China's national defense literature written during World War II.

208 DAVIS, A. R. "China's Entry into World Literature." *JOSA*, 5 (Dec., 1967), 43-50.
The author devotes much attention to the years between 1900 and 1919, which he believes were the prologue to the New Literature movement.

209 ———, ed. *Search for Identity: Modern Literature and the Creative Arts in Asia.* Sydney: Angus and Robertson Publications, 1974.
A collection of papers on modern Asian literature and arts presented at the 28th International Congress of Orientalists.

210 DOLEŽALOVÁ, ANNA. "Periodization of Modern Chinese Literature." *AAS*, 14 (1978), 27-32.
The author proposes a scheme to divide the history of modern Chinese literature into six periods on the basis of "cultural-political and literary-organizational landmarks."

210a ———. "The Short Stories in *Creation Daily*." *AAS*, 9 (1973), 53-64.
An examination of seven short stories which appeared in the Creation Society's *Creation Daily*, from July 21 to November 2, 1923. These stories are representative of the literary efforts of the Society during a period of extensive activity.

211 ———. "Short Stories in the Second Volume of *Creation Quarterly*." *AAS*, 8 (1972), 33-42.
An analysis of the short stories in volume two of *Creation Quarterly*, which contained nine stories by such authors as Chang Tzu-p'ing, Yü Ta-fu, and others. These stories are marked by romanticism, subjective style, intimate themes, melancholic tone, and autobiographic elements.

212 ———. "Subject-Matters of Short Stories in the Initial Period of the Creation Society's Activities." *AAS*, 6 (1970), 131-144.
An analysis of the short stories in the first six issues of *Creation Quarterly*, the literary journal of the Creation Society.

213 DOLEŽELOVÁ-VELINGEROVÁ, MILENA. "The Origins of Modern Chinese Literature." In Merle Goldman, ed. *Modern Chinese Literature in the May Fourth Era.* Cambridge: Harvard University Press, 1977, pp. 17-36.
The author points out that modern Chinese literature, characterized by the dominance of the *pai-hua* (vernacular language), is often interpreted as a phenomenon disconnected from the Chinese literary tradition, but the author stresses that the years immediately preceding the rise of the new literature revealed substantial changes in the literary and linguistic situation in China,

which had been going on for decades and became fully realized in the late Ch'ing period. The author fully explores the close connection between language and literature in tracing the rise of the modern standard language, literature during the late Ch'ing period, and translations of foreign literature. On the basis of these linguistic, stylistic, and ideological changes, the author concludes that both historical continuity and intrinsic changes mark the origins of modern Chinese literature.

214   EBER, IRENE. "Images of Oppressed Peoples and Modern Chinese Literature." In Merle Goldman, ed. *Modern Chinese Literature in the May Fourth Era.* Cambridge: Harvard University Press, 1977, pp. 127-142.
Citing the number of translations and the nature of the works translated in China during the 1920s and '30s, the author states that Western works of the so-called small and weak peoples were of particular interest to Chinese translators and writers; that this interest in turn led them to develop similar themes, such as social injustice and oppression, national identity and emancipation, and the urban poor, in their own writings; and that eventually Chinese writers realized that each of the oppressed peoples was different and that they must write a new and distinctly Chinese literature.

215   ———. "Images of Women in Recent Chinese Fiction: Do Women Hold Up Half the Sky?".
For annotations and bibliographic information, *see* no. 717.

215a   ———. *Voices from Afar: Modern Chinese Writers on Oppressed Peoples and Their Literature.* Ann Arbor: Center for Chinese Studies, University of Michigan, 1980.
A study of the views of selected modern Chinese writers on oppressed peoples and their literature.

216   FEUERWERKER, YI-TSI. "Women as Writers in the 1920's and 1930's." In Margery Wolfe and Roxane Witke, eds. *Women in Chinese Society.* Stanford: Stanford University Press, 1975.
The author begins with a description of a new generation of women writers, namely Ting Ling, Su Hsüeh-lin, Hsieh Ping-ying, Ping Hsin, Lu Yin, Ling Shu-hua and Feng Yüan-chün, discusses some of their works at length, and concludes that what is remarkable about these women writers is "not their modest literary achievement . . . but what they managed to convey. . . . of their own condition," and that though they "lacked the balance, the mature detachment, the finality that make for great works of literature . . . their efforts to record their own autobiographies in a shifting world heighten our consciousness of the tragedy of woman's condition."

217   FOKKEMA, D. W. "Chinese Literature under the Cultural Revolution."
For annotations and bibliographic information, *see* no. 718.

218   ———. *Literary Doctrine in China and Soviet Influence, 1956-1960.*
For annotations and bibliographic information, *see* no. 719.

219 GÁLIK, MARIÁN. "The Aesthetic-Impressionistic Criticism of Küo Mo-jo." *OE*, 21 (1974), 53-66.
Traces the transition of Kuo Mo-jo's views of literature from the aesthetic-impressionistic to the expressionistic from 1920 to 1925.

220 ——. "Main Issues in the Discussion of 'National Forms' in Modern Chinese Literature." *AAS*, 10 (1974), 97-112.
A discussion of a relatively neglected period in Chinese literature from 1937 to 1942. The article analyzes some key documents of the period and relates them to the contemporary literary scene.

221 ——. "On the Influence of Foreign Ideas on Chinese Literary Criticism." *AAS*, 2 (1966), 38-48.
An examination of the beginnings of literary criticism in modern China as exemplified in the works of Liang Ch'i-ch'ao and Wang Kuo-wei. Primarily deals with their views on the novel.

221a ——. "On the Study of Modern Chinese Literature of the 1920's and 1930's: Sources, Results, Tendencies." *AAS*, 13 (1977), 99-123.
A study of important sources for the study of Chinese literature of the 1920's and 1930's and of the trends and achievements in the study of Chinese literature of that period.

222 ——. "Studies in Modern Chinese Intellectual History: I. The World and China: Cultural Impact and Response in the 20th Century." *AAS*, 11 (1975), 11-56.
Deals with China's response to the impact of Western structures and systems on China as seen through a "systemo-structural" perspective. This response is analyzed in three branches of intellectual history (literature, philosophy, and scientism).

223 ——. "Studies in Modern Chinese Literary Criticism: III. Ch'ien Hsing-ts'un and the Theory of Proletarian Realism." *AAS*, 5 (1969), 49-70
An examination of Ch'ien Hsing-ts'un, an advocate of "proletarian realism."

224 ——. "Studies in Modern Chinese Literary Criticism: VII. Liang Shih-ch'iu and New Humanism." *AAS*, 9 (1973), 29-52.
A study of Liang Shih-ch'iu's literary views during the period from 1924 to 1927 when he was most influenced by the ideas of Irving Babbitt of Harvard University with whom he studied. The article deals in detail with the question of "human nature," the basis of Liang's theory. Liang was one of the most prominent critics of the Crescent Moon Society, founded in 1928.

225 ——. "Studies in Modern Chinese Literary Criticism: IV. The Proletarian Criticism of Kuo Mo-jo." *AAS*, 6 (1970), 145-176.
Discusses Kuo Mo-jo's literary views in the late 1920s after he shifted his allegiance from the Creationists (romanticists) to the leftist writers.

226 ———. "Studies in Modern Chinese Literary Criticism: V. The Socio-Aesthetic Criticism of Ch'eng Fang-wu." *AAS*, 7 (1971), 41-78.

A study of Ch'eng Fang-wu, a literary critic and one of the founders of the Creation Society, and his theory of socioaesthetic criticism.

227 GALLA, ENDRE. "On the Reception of the So-called 'Oppressed Nations' in Modern Chinese Literature (1918-1937)." *AAS*, 6 (1970), 177-188.

A discussion of the reception, in modern Chinese literature, of the literatures of "oppressed nations," such as those of Northern, Eastern, and Southern European nations which were of special interest to Chinese writers of the May Fourth period.

228 GILES, HERBERT A. *A History of Chinese Literature*. (With a supplement on the Modern Period). New York: Frederick Unger, 1967.

This first historical survey of Chinese literature appeared in 1901. The 1967 reprint includes a new summary by Liu Wu-chi of the revolutionary changes during the fifty years following the publication of the original book and a succinct account of twentieth-century literature, including essays, poetry, and fiction. Liu mentions the works of Lu Hsün, Mao Tun, Lao She, Pa Chin, Chang T'ien-i, Ting Ling, Ai Wu, and others.

229 GOLDMAN, MERLE. "Left-Wing Criticism of the *Pai-hua* Movement." In Benjamin I. Schwartz, ed. *Reflections on the May Fourth Movement: A Symposium*. Cambridge: East Asian Research Center, Harvard University, 1972, pp. 85-94.

A study of the criticism of the colloquial or vernacular language (*pai-hua*) movement by Ch'ü Ch'iu-pai and other leftist critics and writers who considered the movement too Europeanized because it had "become dressed in European cloth and the academism of Oxford, Cambridge and Columbia," thereby losing its touch with the common people.

230 ———. *Literary Dissent in Communist China*.

For annotations and bibliographic information, *see* no. 722.

231 ———. *Modern Chinese Literature in the May Fourth Era*. Cambridge: Harvard University Press, 1977

A collection of seventeen essays, this book shows the "dynamics of change, discloses new material, and gives new interpretations" of May Fourth literature. It includes an introduction to the "extrinsic" versus the "intrinsic" approach to literature, foreign versus native Chinese influences, and the impact of May Fourth literature. Part I ("Native and Foreign impact") contains six essays on the origins of modern Chinese literature, the impact of Western literary trends, the impact of Japanese literary trends on modern Chinese writers, the impact of Russian literature on such writers as Lu Hsün and Ch'ü Ch'iu-pai, and images of oppressed peoples in modern Chinese literature. Part II ("The May Fourth Writers") consists of eight articles on the social role of the May Fourth writers, Lu Hsün's educational experience, Lu Hsün's short story "Medicine," the central contradiction in Mao Tun's earliest fiction, Mao Tun's use of political allegory, the changing relationship between literature and life, and Yü Ta-fu's role in modern Chinese literature. Part III ("Continuities and Discontinuities") has three essays on the traditional-style popular urban fiction in the 1910s and '20s, Ch'ü Ch'iu-pai's critique of the May Fourth generation, and change and continuity in Chinese fiction. All the articles, written by specialists, are critically rigorous. The book is an important contribution to the study of modern Chinese literature and should be useful to students of Chinese literature and cultural history.

232 GOTZ, MICHAEL. "The Development of Modern Chinese Literature Studies in the West: A Critical View." *Modern China*, 2 (1976), 397-416.
A perceptive survey and analysis of the attitudes and methods of four groups of Western scholars of modern Chinese literature: the anti-Communist group, the Prague school, the liberal group, and the new trend group.

233 ―――. "Images of the Worker in Contemporary Chinese Fiction (1949-64)."
For annotations and bibliographic information, *see* no. 723.

233a ―――. "Russian and Soviet Influences on Chinese Writers and Critics of the 1920s and 1930s: Three Case Studies." *Phi Theta Papers, Publication of the Oriental Students Association* (Berkeley, California), 14 (September, 1977), 70-80.
Three case studies of Russian and Soviet influences on modern Chinese literature.

234 GRIEDER, JEROME B. *Hu Shih and the Chinese Renaissance: Liberalism in the Chinese Revolution, 1917-1937*. Cambridge: Harvard University Press, 1970.
A study of Hu Shih's (1891-1962) ideas and efforts to shape China's intellectual response to the modern world. Included in this study are Hu Shih's life, analysis of his intellectual development, the implications of his ideas, and discussions of John Dewey's influence on him, Hu's elitism, and the Chinese Communist attack on Hu. An important book on the intellectual and political history of modern China.

235 GUNN, EDWARD MANSFIELD, JR. *Unwelcome Muse: Chinese Literature in Shanghai and Peking, 1937-1945*. New York: Columbia University Press, 1980.
A discussion of the developments and trends in Chinese literature in Japanese-controlled areas during World War II. Among the fiction writers discussed are Shih T'o, Su Ch'ing, Chang Ai-ling, and Ch'ien Chung-shu. The author concludes that Chinese linterature of this period is "relatively free of doctrinaire works and represents significant developments in modern Chinese literature" by pointing out its vitality and achievements.

236　　HALES, DELL R. "Social Criticism in Modern Chinese Essays and Novels." *RNL*, 6 (Spring, 1975), 39-59.
　　Discusses the close relationship between literature and society in modern China by focusing on a number of modern Chinese writers, such as Lu Hsün, Pa Chin, Lao She, and Eileen Chang.

237　　HOU, CHIEN. "Irving Babbitt and the Literary Movements in Republican China." *TR*, 4, no. 1 (April, 1973), 1-23.
　　A general account of the literary controversies in China during the 1920s. A small circle of intellectuals led by Mei Kuang-ti, Wu Mi, and Liang Shih-ch'iu, known as the Irving Babbitt group, espoused a type of classicist humanism and expressed its views in the journal *Critical Review* (*Hsüeh-heng*). Though this group was influential at one time, it eventually lost much of its influence to other groups.

238　　HSIA, C. T. *A History of Modern Chinese Fiction*. 2nd ed. New Haven: Yale University Press, 1971
　　Vast in scope, this book is a well-documented survey of modern Chinese fiction. Covering all the major and some minor authors of the period, it is divided into "The Early Period (1917-1927)," "A Decade of Growth (1928-1937)," and "The War Period and After (1937-1957)." The author sees his task as that of a literary historian: "the discovery and appraisal of excellence" in literary works; hence, he attaches little significance to the use of literary material as a mirror to reflect the politics and culture of an age. Hsia's approach to literature created an interesting controversy in the 1960s between the author and the Czech scholar, Jaroslav Průšek (*see* no. 285). The new material added to the second edition provides some information on the developments from 1958 to the end of the last decade. An important and indispensable reference work on modern Chinese fiction.

239　　――――. "On the 'Scientific' Study of Modern Chinese Literature. A Reply to Professor Průšek." *TP*, 50 (1963), 428-472.
　　In response to Jaroslav Průšek's criticism (*see* no. 285) of his *A History of Modern Chinese Fiction* (*See* no. 238), C. T. Hsia points out that Průšek has indulged in an internationalist approach to literature and upholds his own position to judge each work on its own literary merits rather than on its social significance and function. These exchanges constitute an interesting scholarly dialogue on certain serious issues in the study of modern Chinese literature.

240　　――――. "Perspectives on Chinese Literature: Obsession with China." In Alona E. Evans, et al., eds. *China in Perspective*. Wellesley, Mass.: Wellesley College, 1967, pp. 101-119. Also appears as an appendix in C. T. Hsia, *A History of Modern Chinese Fiction*. 2nd ed. New Haven: Yale University Press, 1971, pp. 533-554.
　　A stimulating analysis of the preoccupation with China's economic, political and social realities and problems as revealed in the works of modern Chinese fiction writers.

241　　――――. "Residual Femininity: Women in Chinese Communist Fiction." For annotations and bibliographic information, *see* no. 726.

242 ———. "Traditional Chinese Literature and the Modern Chinese Temper." In Cheng Chi-pao, ed. *A Symposium on Chinese Culture.* New York: China Institute in America and American Association of Teachers of Chinese Language and Culture, 1964, pp. 16-20. Also in *LEW,* 8, (Spring/Summer, 1964), 55-58.

A study of the impact of traditional Chinese literature on the modern Chinese temper.

242a ———. "Yen Fu and Liang Ch'i-ch'ao as Advocates of New Fiction." In Adele Austin Rickett, ed. *Chinese Approaches to Literature from Confucius to Liang Ch'i-ch'ao.* Princeton: Princeton University Press, 1977. pp. 221-257.

A study of the views of two prominent early twentieth-century Chinese intellectual leaders on the functions of fiction.

243 HSIA, T. A. "Ch'ü Ch'iu-po: The Making and Destruction of a Tenderhearted Communist." In T. A. Hsia, *The Gate of Darkness.* Seattle: University of Washington Press, 1968, pp. 3-54; *CQ,* no. 25 (1966), 176-212.

A revealing study of the inner thoughts of Ch'ü Ch'iu-po (Ch'ü Ch'iu-pai), an acknowledged leader of the League of Writers, and an analysis of Ch'ü's *Superfluous Words* as the last testament of a tenderhearted Communist, "soul-sick" over a life misspent in politics. Main focus is on Ch'ü's literary rather than political career.

244 ———. *Enigma of the Five Martyrs: A Study of the Leftist Literary Movement in Modern China.* Berkeley: Center for Chinese Studies, University of California, 1962. Also in T. A. Hsia. *The Gate of Darkness.* Seattle: University of Washington Press, 1968, pp. 163-234.

A biographical study of five young Communist writers executed in early 1931: Hu Yeh-p'in, Jou Shih, Feng K'eng, Yin Fu, and Li Wei-sen. The essay explores the relation between literature and politics and seeks to answer two specific questions: Why did the five become Communists? What happened to them after they became Communist?

245 ———. *The Gate of Darkness: Studies on the Leftist Literary Movement in China.* Seattle: University of Washington Press, 1968.

A penetrating "cultural criticism," fusing literary criticism with biography, history, and philosophy, of the life and times of a handful of Chinese left-wing writers in the 1920s and '30s. The author's unusual versatility, "breadth of humanity," and mastery of detail and a tremendous wealth of background information make this book of special interest not only to students of literature but also to those studying history and politics. The six essays in the volume deal mainly with literary-political figures, such as Ch'ü Ch'iu-po, Chiang Kuang-tz'u, the Five Martyrs (Hu Yeh-p'in, Jou Shih, Feng K'eng, Yin Fu, and Li Wei-sen), and Lu Hsün. Of these writers, only Lu Hsün is first rate, but the importance of the others lies not just in what they wrote but in the fact that their beliefs, actions, and self-conceptions are symptomatic of an age of revolution.

246 HSIAO, CH'IEN. *Etching of a Tormented Age*. London: George Allen and Unwin, 1942.
  A concise account of the development of modern Chinese fiction, poetry, and drama. Of particular interest is the section on the role of novelists as reformers. The author gives the reasons why modern novelists regard it as a disgrace to write merely for entertainment and why they seek to ameliorate a corrupt society; he also explains the different approaches to the study of modern Chinese fiction and discusses common themes, such as political awareness, reform of the family system, the relationship between the sexes, the portrayal of the seamy side of Republican life, and the works of Mao Tun, Yeh Shao-chün, Shen Ts'ung-wen and others.

247 HSU, KAI-YU. *The Chinese Literary Scene*.
  For annotations and bibliographic information, *see* no. 729.

248 HU, SHIH. *The Chinese Renaissance: The Haskell Lectures*. Chicago. University of Chicago Press, 1934; New York: Paragon, 1963.
  A series of six lectures delivered by Hu Shih, one of the architects of the Literary Revolution, at the University of Chicago in the summer of 1933. These are important lectures which reveal unusual insight into various aspects of China's literary, intellectual, and cultural modernization.

249 HUANG, JOE C. *Heroes and Villains in Communist China*.
  For annotations and bibliographic information, *see* no. 732.

250 ———. "Villains, Victims and Morals in Contemporary Chinese Communist Literature."
  For annotations and bibliographic information, *see* no. 733.

251 HUNTER, NEALE JAMES. "The Chinese League of Left-Wing Writers, Shanghai, 1930-1936." Ph.D. Dissertation. Canberra: Australian National University, 1973.
  A study of the activities and policies of the League of Leftist Writers in Shanghai from 1930 to 1936.

252 KALOUSKOVA, JARMILA and ZBIGNIEW SŁUPSKI. "Some Problems of Typological Analysis in Modern Chinese Fiction." In *Études d'histoire et de littérature chinoises offertes au Professeur Jaroslav Průšek*. (Paris: Institut des Hautes Études Chinoises, 1976), pp. 143-154.
  A discussion of problems of typological analysis in modern Chinese fiction.

253 KALTENMARK-GHÉQUIER, ODILE. *Chinese Literature*. New York: Walker, 1964.
  First published in France as *La littérature chinoise* in 1948, the present English version was translated by Anne-Marie Geoghegan. A very sketchy survey of Chinese literature from its beginnings to the Literary Revolution. The chapter on the Literary Revolution is brief but of some use to the general reader.

254 KLEIN, DONALD WALKER and ANNE B. CLARK, eds. *Biographic Dictionary of Chinese Communism, 1921-1965.*
For annotations and bibliographic information, *see* no. 30.

255 KUO, THOMAS C. *Ch'en Tu-hsiu (1879-1942) and the Chinese Communist Movement.* South Orange, N.J.: Seton Hall University Press, 1975.
Contains a chapter on Ch'en Tu-hsiu's views on the New Literature movement of the early twentieth century.

256 LAU, JOSEPH S. M. "The Concepts of Time and Reality in Modern Chinese Fiction." *TR*, 4, no. 1 (1973), 25-40.
An analysis of the concepts of time and reality as reflected in selected works of modern Chinese fiction.

257 ———. "Naturalism in Modern Chinese Fiction." *LEW*, 12 (1968), 149-156.
A discussion of naturalism in modern Chinese fiction.

258 LEE, LEO OU-FAN. *The Romantic Generation of Modern Chinese Writers.* Cambridge, Harvard University Press, 1973.
The purpose of the study, as stated by the author, is to examine some of the analogous influences and distinctive characteristics of the May Fourth generation of literary intellectuals. For thematic purposes, the study begins with two precursors, Lin Shu and Su Man-shu, concentrates on Yü Ta-fu, Hsü Chih-mo, Kuo Mo-jo, Chiang Kuang-tz'u and Hsiao Chün, and concludes with an analysis of the leftward drift of the new literature. Ample notes and an excellent bibliography. The author's treatment of individual writers is sympathetic, sensitive, and analytical.

259 ———. "The Romantic Temper of May Fourth Writers." In Benjamin I. Schwartz, ed. *Reflections on the May Fourth Movement: A Symposium.* Cambridge: East Asian Research Center, Harvard University, 1972, pp. 69-84.
The author points out that a predominantly romantic outlook preoccupied a segment of the literary writers in the 1920s and '30s. Their "eulogizing love, glorifying individuality, craving for rebirth," made them lose touch with reality and the "movement" came to an end.

260 LEE, PETER KING-HUNG. "Key Intellectual Issues Arising from the May Fourth Movement in China: With Particular Reference to Hu Shih, Li Ta-chao, and Liang Shu-ming." Ph.D. Dissertation. Boston: Boston University, 1974.
Deals with the views of three leading modern Chinese intellectuals: Hu Shih ("the liberal-pragmatist"), Li Ta-chao ("Marxist"), and Liang Shu-ming ("Neo-Confucianist"), and with three key issues: the new social order, science and values, and the Chinese cultural identity.

261　LI TIEN-YI. "Continuity and Change in Modern Chinese Literature." *Annals of the American Academy of Social Sciences*, no. 321 (1959), 90-99.

An account of the characteristics of modern Chinese literature contrasted with traditional literature.

262　LINK, PERRY. "Li Hsi-fan on Modern Chinese Literature." *CQ*, no. 58 (April/June, 1974), 349-356.

Based on a two-hour interview which the author had with Li Hsi-fan, a leading literary critic in China today. Li reaffirms the goal of cultivating "amateur" writers among the people and singles out Yeh Sheng-t'ao and Mao Tun as the leading writers in modern Chinese literature, in addition to Lu Hsün.

263　———. "The Rise of Modern Popular Fiction in Shanghai." Ph.D. Dissertation. Cambridge: Harvard University, 1976.

A study of the relationship between popular literature, in particular the "Mandarin Duck and Butterfly School" of writing, and urban culture. The author links the growth of popular literature to increasing urbanization. The first part of the dissertation deals with the nature of this school of literature, the second, with its dissemination and popularity.

264　———. "Traditional Style Popular Urban Fiction in the Teens and Twenties." In Merle Goldman, ed. *Modern Chinese Literature in the May Fourth Era.* Cambridge: Harvard University Press, 1977, pp. 327-350.

A study of the "Mandarin Duck and Butterfly School" type of romantic fiction which flourished in the 1910s and '20s. The author traces in detail its growth and its relationships to Westernization and to the May Fourth Movement. Discussing the question of continuity in modern Chinese literature, the author wonders if "Butterfly" fiction can be considered as an intermediary between the traditional-style fiction and contemporary mass fiction. He concludes that "Butterfly" fiction is essentially transitory, distinguished both from "what it followed and what it preceded."

265　LIU, CHÜN-JO. "The Heroes and Heroines of Modern Chinese Fiction: From Ah Q to Wu Tzu-hsü." *JAS*, 16 (Feb., 1957), 201-211.

A survey of some typical heroes in modern Chinese fiction. The works discussed are: Lu Hsün's *The True Story of Ah Q*, Pa Chin's *The Family*, Mao Tun's *Red as the Blossoms of the Second Month Are the Autumn Leaves*, Lao She's z*The Rickshaw Boy*, Shen Ts'ung-wen's *Long River*, and Feng Chih's *Wu Tzu-hsü*.

266　———. "People, Places, and Time in Five Modern Chinese Novels." In Horst Frenz, ed. *Asia and the Humanities: Papers Presented at the 2nd Conference on Oriental-Western Literary and Cultural Relations.* Bloomington: Comparative Literature Committee, Indiana University, 1959, pp. 15-25.

A study of the different ways of organizing people, places, and time in five modern Chinese novels: Pa Chin's *Autumn*, Lu Hsün's *The True Story of Ah Q*, Mao Tun's *The Eclipse*, Lao She's *Life of Niu T'ien-tz'u*, and Shen Ts'ung-wen's *The Frontier City*.

267 LIU, TS'UN-YAN. "Social and Moral Significance in Modern Chinese Fiction." *Solidarity*, 3 (Nov., 1968), 28-43.
A discussion of the social and moral significance of selected works of modern Chinese fiction.

268 LIU, WU-CHI. *An Introduction to Chinese Literature*. Bloomington: Indiana University Press, 1966.
Contains a chapter on "Contemporary Experiments and Achievements," in which the author gives an informative survey of the roles of Hu Shih, Ch'en Tu-hsiu, and Kuo Mo-jo in the Chinese Renaissance and discusses some of the works by Lu Hsün, Mao Tun, Pa Chin, Lao She, and others. For more details, *see* no. 138.

269 LU, ALEXANDER YA-LI. "Political Control of Literature in Communist China, 1949-1966."
For annotations and bibliographic information, *see* no. 736.

270 McCASKEY, MICHAEL J. "Chu Tzu-ch'ing as Essayist and Critic." Ph.D. Dissertation. New Haven: Yale University, 1965.
A study of Chu Tzu-ch'ing, the man, and his views on literature and life as a critic and essayist.

271 McDOUGALL, BONNIE S. "The Impact of Western Literary Trends." In Merle Goldman, ed. *Modern Chinese Literature in the May Fourth Era*. Cambridge: Harvard University Press, 1977, pp. 37-62.
The author points out that the Chinese intellectuals' enthusiasm for Western literature dated from the end of the Ch'ing dynasty to the outbreak of the Sino-Japanese War in 1937; that a sign of Western literary influence in China was the new respectability of the professional writer; that Western literature encouraged reformist and modernist attitudes among Chinese writers who saw themselves as prophets, reformers, and revolutionaries; and that consequently, the May Fourth writers "brought China into world literature and underlined the necessity for the new literary movement to be studied in the world context, not as an isolated phenomenon unique to China."

272 ———. *The Introduction of Western Literary Theories into Modern China, 1919-1925*. Tokyo: Centre for East Asian Cultural Studies, 1971.
The purpose of this study is "to identify and appraise some early appearances of Western literary theories" in modern China. The first chapter contains a detailed chronological account of references to Western literature and literary theories in the major magazines of the time; the second chapter discusses the reception of Western literature and theories by Chinese writers of the New Literature Movement; and in the remaining chapters, the author attempts to analyze essays written by participants in the New Literature Movement, such as Kuo Mo-jo, Shen Yen-ping (Mao Tun), and Ch'eng Fang-wu.

273 MAO, TSE-TUNG. *Mao Tse-tung on Literature and Art*.
For annotations and bibliographic information, *see* no. 737.

274 MEI, YI-TSI. "Tradition and Experiment in Modern Chinese Literature." In Horst Frenz, ed. *Proceedings of the First Conference on Oriental-Western Literary Relations*. Chapel Hill: University of North Carolina Press, 1955, pp. 107-124.
A general discussion of tradition and experiment in modern Chinese literature.

275 ODELL, LING CHUNG. "The Traditional Past in Modern Chinese Literature." *Books Abroad*, 47 (Spring, 1973), 289-294.
A brief discussion of the traditional past in modern Chinese literature.

276 *Papers on China*.
For annotations and bibliographic information *see* no. 145.

277 PHELPS, DRYDEN LINSLEY. "Letters and Arts in the War Years." In H. F. McNair, ed. *China*. Berkeley: University of California Press, 1946, pp. 406-419.
Includes brief comments on Chinese fiction written during World War II.

278 PICKOWICZ, PAUL G. "Ch'ü Ch'iu-pai and the Chinese Marxist Conception of Revolutionary Popular Literature and Art." *CQ*, (June, 1976).
An analysis of Ch'ü Ch'iu-pai's (Ch'ü Ch'iu-po's) contributions to the Chinese Marxist conception of revolutionary popular literature and art.

279 ———. "Ch'ü Ch'iu-pai and the Origins of Marxist Literary Criticism in China." Ph.D. Dissertation. Madison: University of Wisconsin, 1973.
Deals with Ch'ü Ch'iu-pai mainly as a Marxist literary critic rather than as a leader of the Communist Party. Attention is focused on the period from 1931 to 1935, on his attempts to unite the contending factions of the League of Leftist Writers, his criticism of Westernized May Fourth writers, and his close ties with Lu Hsün during those years.

280 ———. "Modern China's Artistic and Cultural Life." *Holy Cross Quarterly*, 7 (1975), 109-116.
An interesting description of artistic and cultural life in modern China.

281 ———. "On Qu Qiubai's [Ch'ü Ch'iu-pai] Critique of the May Fourth Generation: Early Chinese Marxist Literary Criticism." In Merle Goldman, ed. *Modern Chinese Literature in the May Fourth Era*. Cambridge: Harvard University Press, 1977, pp. 351-384.
According to the author, Ch'ü's 1931 critique analyzing the problems of the left-wing literary movement was the first of a typically Chinese form of Marxist literary criticism. Directing his criticism at the left-wing camp itself, Ch'ü asked to what extent the May Fourth heritage had contributed to the problems of the camp, why there had not been a clear delineation of the major

failings of the camp after the introduction of Marxist criticism in the early twenties, and whether those imported theories were suitable for Chinese conditions. Ch'ü's conclusion was that left-wing writers had "uncritically embraced foreign literary theories without having explained their relevance to the special problems of the Chinese scene." The author stresses the significance of Ch'ü's critique by pointing out that Ch'ü's concerns continued to be expressed in left-wing literary circles long after his death in 1935, and that the Communists' cases against Chou Yang and others during the Cultural Revolution of the late sixties were a continuation of arguments first made clear by Ch'ü in 1931.

282 POLLARD, DAVID E. *A Chinese Look at Literature: The Literary Values of Chou Tso-jen in Relation to the Tradition.* Berkeley: University of California Press, 1973.

This study is an examination of Chou Tso-jen's essays and lectures, and particularly of Chou's middle period when he was more absorbed in the problems of art and heritage. The author notes that Chou spoke out continually against literature being used as propaganda, that his work was written not to propose or instruct but to please himself, and that he believed that the philosophy of self-expression would bring forth the finest literary fruits. In discussing Chou's literary values, the author investigates the cases for utilitarian and expressionist theories in the history of Chinese literary criticism, thus bringing to light what leading Chinese critics have said about literature and its functions. The book includes seven chapters exploring such areas as old and new theories, individualism, "taste and tastes", "blandness" and "naturalness," secondary values ("extempore" and "impromptu," simplicity, "bitterness" and "asperity"), the essay and perspectives. Also included are two appendices on the T'ung-ch'eng and the Kung-an schools of literary criticism.

283 ———. "Chou Tso-jen and Cultivating One's Garden." *AM*, n.s. 11 (1964-1965), 180-198.

The author points out that, in contrast to his elder brother, activist Lu Hsün (Chou Shu-jen), Chou Tso-jen withdrew from the public world and moved into his own "garden." This essay traces the path of his withdrawal after 1926.

284 PRIESTLY, K. E., ed. *China's Men of Letters Yesterday and Today.* Hong Kong: Dragon Fly Books, 1963.

A collection of five essays by various authors, including Lin Yutang, Shau Wing Chan, and K. E. Priestly, who evaluate and review the Chinese literary scene during the past fifty years.

285 PRŮŠEK, JAROSLAV. "Basic Problems of the History of Modern Chinese Literature, and C. T. Hsia, *A History of Modern Chinese Fiction.*" *TP*, 49 (1962), 357-404.

Jaroslav Průšek takes C. T. Hsia to task for Hsia's "subjective approach to literature and his neglect of the social significance and function of literature" as reflected in Hsia's *A History of Modern Chinese Fiction* (*see* no. 238). He details Hsia's unjust treatment of Lu Hsün and offers his own analysis. An interesting view from a different ideological perspective.

286 ———. "A Confrontation of Traditional Oriental Literature with Modern European Literature in the Context of the Chinese Literary Revolution." *ArOr*, 32 (1964), 365-375.

An interesting study characterizing the special features of modern Chinese literature as distinguished from the traditional literature, and the effect of European literature on the Chinese literary complex. The author advocates the view of a sudden break from the past rather than gradual change in artistic structure.

287 ———, ed. *Dictionary of Oriental Literatures*.

For annotations and bibliographic information, *see* no. 49.

287a ———. *The Lyrical and the Epic: Studies of Modern Chinese Literature*. Bloomington: Indiana University Press, 1980.

Edited with an introduction by Leo Ow-fan Lee, this collection contains Průšek's selected studies of modern Chinese literature.

288 ———. "Reality and Art in Chinese Literature." *ArOr*, 32 (1964), 605-618.

A stimulating essay exploring the complex relationship between reality and artistic expression. For Průšek, successful realistic art must achieve a balance between its factual aspect (the mass of facts) and its artistic presentation. He feels that modern Chinese literature leans heavily toward the factual presentation at the expense of artistic expression.

289 ———, ed. *Studies in Modern Chinese Literature*. Berlin: Akademia-Verlag, 1964.

Contains one general essay on modern Chinese literature by Jaroslav Průšek and six studies by his students and a colleague on six writers of modern China: Kuo Mo-jo, Pa Chin, Lao She, Ping Hsin, T'ien Han, and Chao Shu-li. Most of the works examined were written between 1917 and 1937. These are detailed studies which do not deal with wide-ranging, general questions but focus on particular problems or themes.

290 ———. "Subjectivism and Individualism in Modern Chinese Literature." *ArOr*, 25 (1957), 261-286.

A study of subjectivism and individualism as reflected in modern Chinese literature.

291 ———. *Three Sketches of Chinese Literature*. Prague: Oriental Institute in Academia, 1969.

Three analytical and interpretative essays on Mao Tun, Yü Ta-fu, and Kuo Mo-jo. Readers should be aware of Průšek's view that the novel should reflect contemporary socioeconomic conditions. As a result of this view, the tormented introspective writer, Yü Ta-fu, is faulted for his inability to reflect outer reality.

292 ROY, DAVID T. *Kuo Mo-jo: The Early Years.* Cambridge: Harvard University Press, 1971.
This is a detailed study of the formative years of Kuo Mo-jo's life (1892-1924). Kuo was a most versatile twentieth-century Chinese writer and critic, having made contributions in diverse fields ranging from poetry, drama, fiction, autobiography, archaeology and paleography to literary criticism and political propaganda. The book reveals much about the process of Kuo's adoption of Marxism-Leninism and sheds light on the crucial transitional period of modern Chinese history through which Kuo lived. Kuo's early contributions to the development of modern Chinese literature are also discussed.

293 SCHULTZ, WILLIAM. "Kuo Mo-jo and the Romantic Aesthetic: 1918-1925." *JOL*, 6, no. 2 (April, 1955), 49-81.
A study of Kuo Mo-jo's early artistic development and literary views.

294 SCHWARTZ, BENJAMIN I., ed. *Reflections on the May Fourth Movement: A Symposium.* Cambridge: East Asian Research Center, Harvard University, 1973.
A collection of six essays plus an introduction by Benjamin Schwartz celebrating the fiftieth anniversary of the May Fourth Movement. These essays reassess the political, social, literary, and cultural significance of the movement. Essays by Leo Ou-fan Lee and Merle Goldman have direct bearing on the literature of the period.

295 SCOTT, A. C. *Literature and the Arts in Twentieth-Century China.* London: George Allen and Unwin, 1965.
With the general reader in mind, the author traces the developments of the last fifty years in Chinese fiction, poetry, the theater and dance, motion pictures, painting and the graphic arts, architecture, sculpture, and music. Also included is a discussion of the recent artistic achievements of Chinese living in Taiwan, Hong Kong, England and the United States.

296 SEYMOUR-SMITH, MARTIN. "Chinese Literature." In *Funk and Wagnalls Guide to Modern World Literature.* New York: Funk and Wagnalls, 1970, pp. 343-347.
A general assessment of modern Chinese literature based primarily on secondary sources. Useful to those with little background in modern Chinese literature.

297 SHIH, VINCENT Y. C. "Enthusiast and Escapist: Writers of the Older Generation."
For annotations and bibliographic information, *see* no. 742.

298 ———."Satire in Chinese Communist Literature."
For annotations and bibliographic information, *see* no. 743.

299 SIH, PAUL K. T., ed. *China's Literary Image.* Jamaica, N.Y.: St. John's University, 1975. (A special issue of *RNL*, 6 (1975).)
   This special issue of *Review of National Literatures* consists of six articles on Chinese literature, mostly on modern writers and their works.

300 SŁUPSKI, ZBIGNIEW. "Some Remarks on the First History of Modern Chinese Fiction." *ArOr*, 32 (1964), 139-152.
   A critical review of C. T. Hsia's *A History of Modern Chinese Fiction* (*see* no. 238) from the Marxist point of view.

301 SPENCE, JONATHAN. "On Chinese Revolutionary Literature." *Yale French Studies*, 39 (1967), 215-255.
   A general study of modern Chinese revolutionary literature.

302 TAGORE, AMITENDRANATH. *Literary Debates in Modern China, 1918-1937.* Tokyo: Centre for East Asian Cultural Studies, 1967.
   Depicts the complex relationship among the numerous literary societies between 1918 and 1937. Contains many translated excerpts from important documents of the period.

303 *Thirty Years of Turmoil in Asian Literature.* Taipei: The Taipei Chinese Center, International P.E.N., 1976.
   A collection of papers on modern Asian literature delivered at the Fourth Asian Writers' Conference in 1976.

304 TING, YI. *A Short History of Modern Chinese Literature.* Peking: Foreign Languages Press, 1959; reprint ed. Port Washington, N. Y.: Kennikat Press, 1970.
   Containing twelve chapters, the book traces the development of modern Chinese literature from the May Fourth period through the 1950s. The emphasis is on the importance of Communist ideology in the left-wing literary movement and the works of left-wing writers (Lu Hsün, Ch'ü Ch'iu-pai, Kuo Mo-jo, and Mao Tun among others). More noteworthy are chapters (9, 10, and 11) on the rise of reportage, production of popular literature, "street poetry," "street plays," and the reform of the folk arts. Politically oriented, the book is nonetheless an important reference book based on the Communist interpretation of modern Chinese literature.

305 TUNG, CONSTANTINE. *The Crescent Moon Society: The Minority Challenge in the Literary Movement of Modern China.* Buffalo: Council on International Studies, State University of New York, 1972.
   An account of the literary group known as the Crescent Moon Society which led an effective opposition to the leftist literary movement.

306   ———. "The Search for Order and Form: The Crescent Moon Society and the Literary Movement of Modern China, 1928-1933." Ph.D. Dissertation. Pomona: Claremont Graduate School and University Center, 1971.

An account of the Crescent Moon Society, which led a determined opposition to the leftist literary movement. The society, whose membership included Hsü Chih-mo, Wen I-to, Liang Shih-ch'iu, Yü Shang-yüan, Shen Ts'ung-wen, and Hu Shih, stood for "reason, restraint, moderation, and independence of literary creation."

307   VOGEL, EZRA. "The Unlikely Heroes: The Social Role of the May Fourth Writers." In Merle Goldman, ed. *Modern Chinese Literature in the May Fourth Era.* Cambridge: Harvard University Press, 1977, pp. 145-160.

Pointing out that the May Fourth writers, most of them trained in the Confucian classics, might have become officials, scholars, or local notables, the author states that many of them did become heroes of the following categories: the indecisive young dreamers (Yeh Sheng-t'ao, Lao She, Ch'ien Chung-shu, and Pa Chin), the moralists (Yü Ta-fu and others), the concerned elitists (Lu Hsün, Mao Tun, Ting Ling, Kuo Mo-jo, Shen Ts'ung-wen, Hao Jan, and others), and of other categories, such as the degraded moralists, the pseudoprofessionals, the celebrated intellectuals, the heroic intellectuals, and the posthumous heroes. The author concludes that the main contributions of the May Fourth writers lie in their rallying of a generation of youth to different political causes and their creation of a truly proletarian literature. To many Chinese living in China or in Taiwan today, the May Fourth writers have become "a new kind of hero, unsung because of the danger of discussing them."

308   WIDMER, ELLEN. "Qu Quibai [Ch'ü Chiu-pai] and Russian Literature." In Merle Goldman, ed. *Modern Chinese Literature in the May Fourth Era.* Cambridge: Harvard University Press, 1977, pp. 103-126.

The author points out that Ch'ü Ch'iu-pai, the critic warning his fellow intellectuals against over-involvement with foreign literature, was himself deeply interested in Russian literature and fascinated by Pushkin's prose style, Gogol's realism, Chekhov's irony, and Tolstoy's and Dostoevsky's humanism. What seems ironic to the author is that, though it was the connection with proletarian revolution that had earlier provided Ch'ü's justification for taking up Russian literature, it is literary standards that seem to prevail in his assessments. Even more interesting is Ch'ü's later stress on the utilitarian function of literature—to educate the masses. This reversal of attitude was replaced by still another after Ch'ü's capture by the Nationalists in 1935. While imprisoned, he returned to his earlier view that a literature written for intellectuals was still worth writing.

309   WOLFF, ERNST. *Chou Tso-jen.* Boston: Twayne Publishers, 1971.

Chou Tso-jen, an important figure in modern Chinese literature, was a proponent of the modern essay, of new concepts of art, and a theoretician of the function of literature, and of the nature of society and the individual in society. Besides providing a biographical account of Chou's life, the author discusses the Chinese essay, Chou's early motivation toward literature and the essay, and the stylistic elements in Chou's essays. There is also an extended analysis of Chou's essays and his period of disillusionment and literary retirement. The author concludes that Chou was not only a pioneer of the essay but also a complex man, in view of his many controversial beliefs and his collaboration with the Japanese during the Sino-Japanese War. Also included is an appendix which contains translations of several of Chou's essays.

310   WONG, SENG-TONG. "The Impact of China's Literary Movements on Malaya's Vernacular Chinese Literature from 1919 to 1941." Ph.D. Dissertation. Madison: University of Wisconsin, 1978.
　　　　A study attempting to "illustrate the relationship between Malaya's vernacular Chinese literature and China's literary movements before the Second World War."

311   YOUNG, LUNG-CHANG. "Literary Reflections of Social Change in China. 1919-1949." Ph.D. Dissertation. New York: New School for Social Research, 1964.
　　　　A study of social change in modern China as seen through the "critical lens of literature." Ten writers, including Lu Hsün, Mao Tun, and Pa Chin, and their representative works are selected and analyzed to shed light on the important question: "Under what conditions would a cultural group choose to follow a new way of life which is totally different from its tradition?"

Anthologies

312   ANDERSON, G. L., ed. *Masterpieces of the Orient.*
　　　　For annotations and bibliographic information, *see* no. 153.

313   BERNINGHAUSEN, JOHN and TED HUTERS, eds. *Revolutionary Literature in China: An Anthology.* White Plains, N. Y.: M. E. Sharpe, 1976. (Originally appeared as a special issue of *Bulletin of Concerned Asian Scholars*, no. 8 (Jan./June 1976).)
　　　　This anthology of revolutionary literature in China contains translations of theoretical essays, short stories, and a folk play by such modern writers as Mao Tun, Cheng Chen-to, Kuo Mo-jo, Ch'ü Ch'iu-pai, Ting Ling, Hao Jan, and others, dating from 1914 to 1966. The translations are by different translators, resulting in uneven quality.

314   BIRCH, CYRIL, ed. *Anthology of Chinese Literature.* New York: Grove Press, 1965-1972. 2 vols.
　　　　Volume II includes selections of Chinese literature from the fourteenth century to the present day. Noteworthy is the inclusion of Lu Hsün's "Benediction," Mao Tun's "Spring Silkworms," and Eileen Chang's "The Betrothal of Yindi." For more information, *see* no. 154.

General Studies and Anthologies of Modern Chinese Fiction/151

315   CHAI, CH'U and WINBERG CHAI, trs. and eds. *A Treasury of Chinese Literature: A New Prose Anthology Including Fiction and Drama.*
For annotations and bibliographic information, see no. 155.

316   CHI, PANG-YUAN, et al., eds. *An Anthology of Contemporary Chinese Literature: 1949-1974.*
For annotations and bibliographic information, *see* no. 868.

317   HSIA, C. T., ed. *Twentieth-Century Chinese Stories.* New York: Columbia University Press, 1971.
A well-selected anthology of nine modern Chinese stories by eight authors, chosen "for their intrinsic literary interest and their representative importance in the development of the modern Chinese short story." The authors chosen are Yü Ta-fu, Shen Ts'ung-wen, Chang T'ien-i, Wu Tsu-hsiang, Eileen Chang, Nieh Hua-ling, Shui Ching, and Pai Hsien-yung. The first five authors from Yü Ta-fu to Eileen Chang have received much attention in the editor's *A History of Modern Chinese Fiction*, while the last three are representative of Taiwan writers, who, in the editor's view, are "technically and stylistically more resourceful than their predecessors in the 1930s and '40s" and "remain characteristically Chinese in their intense awareness of their frustrations or lack of identity in Taiwan or abroad."

318   HSIAO, CH'IEN, ed. *A Harp with a Thousand Strings.* London: Pilot Press, 1944.
This interesting anthology about China is divided into six parts. Part III, "A Gallery of Portraits and Self-Portraits," consists of translations of autobiographical writings by modern Chinese writers.

319   HSU, KAI-YU. *The Chinese Literary Scene.*
For annotations and bibliographic information, *see* no. 729.

320   ISAACS, HAROLD R., ed. *Straw Sandals: Chinese Short Stories, 1918-1933.* Cambridge: M.I.T. Press, 1974.
Includes a foreword by Lu Hsün, a critical introduction by the editor, updated biographical notes on the authors, twenty-three short stories, a play, a poem, and "Notes on Chinese Left-Wing Periodicals, 1934" by Mao Tun. These works, selected to represent Chinese radical literature between 1918 and 1933, were first assembled in Peking in 1934 by the editor himself, with the advice of Lu Hsün and Mao Tun. A number of the stories were translated by George A. Kennedy and first appeared in the *China Forum*, a journal edited by Harold R. Isaacs and published in Shanghai from 1932 to 1934; the rest were translated by others and edited by Isaacs. Represented in this anthology are works of Lu Hsün, Kuo Mo-jo, Yü Ta-fu, Yeh Shao-chün, Ting Ling, Chiang Kuang-tz'u, Shih Yi, Hu Yeh-p'ing, Jou Shih, Mao Tun, Ting Chiu; Wang T'ung-chao, Cheng Nung, Ting P'ing, Ho Ku-t'ien, and Yin Fu. Thematically, the first half of the collection reflects the impact of China's modern renaissance in its rejection of traditional values and in its exploration of the relationship between the sexes, and the second half, the growing ideological conflicts and political turmoil of the 1920s and '30s.

321 JENNER, W. J. F., ed. *Modern Chinese Stories.* London: Oxford University Press, 1970.

In this twenty-piece anthology, the editor's main purpose is "to illustrate life and to enable the reader to see some Chinese views of the world." The stories, written and published in Chinese over the last fifty years, describe social protest, revolutionary action, and social construction; the authors include peasant storytellers narrating the heroic deeds of their rebel ancestors, writers whose works reflect the changing Chinese rural scene of the late 1950s and '60s, and such well-known authors as Lu Hsün, Mao Tun, Lao She, and Kuo Mo-jo. With heavy emphasis on social realism, the editor is somewhat arbitrary in stating that the stories of nearly all modern Chinese writers except Lu Hsün "have little to offer to those in search of literary novelty and brilliance." Some of the introductory notes on individual writers and works contain misleading information.

322 KAO, GEORGE, ed. *Chinese Wit and Humor.* New York: Coward-McCann, 1946; New York: Sterling Publishing Co., 1974.

The first of its kind, this anthology contains selections from both ancient and modern sources, ranging from popular jokes to Rabelaisian and picaresque humor. A section entitled "The Humor of Protest" contains selections by such modern writers as Ku Hung-ming, Lu Hsün, Lin Yutang, Lao She, Lao Hsiang, and Yao Ying.

323 LAU, JOSEPH S. M., C. T. HSIA, and LEO OU-FAN LEE, eds. *Modern Chinese Stories and Novellas, 1919-1949.* New York: Columbia University Press, forthcoming.

A comprehensive anthology of selected modern Chinese stories and novellas written between 1918 and 1948, many of which have never appeared in English elsewhere.

324 LAU, JOSEPH S. M., and TIMOTHY ROSS, eds. *Chinese Stories from Taiwan: 1960-1970.*

For annotations and bibliographic information, *see* no. 874.

325 LIN, YUTANG, tr. *Widow, Nun, and Courtesan.* New York: John Day Co., 1950; reprint ed. Westport, Conn.: Greenwood Press, 1971.

Contains three novelettes: "Widow Chuan" by the contemporary writer Lao Hsiang; "A Nun of Tai-shan" by the late Ch'ing writer Liu E, the author of *The Travels of Lao Ts'an*; and "Miss Tu," an old popular tale retold by the translator. Gives an interesting perspective on independent and strong-willed women in Chinese society.

326 LIU, WU-CH, et al., eds. *K'uei Hsing: A Repository of Asian Literature in Translation.*

For annotations and bibliographic information, *see* no. 157.

326a McDOUGALL, BONNIE S. and LEWIS S. ROBINSON, trs. *A Posthumous Son and Other Stories.* Hong Kong: Commerical Press, 1979.

A collection of three stories, including Yeh Sheng-t'ao's "A Posthumous Son" and Shen Ts'ung-wen's "Hsiao-hsiao."

General Studies and Anthologies of Modern Chinese Fiction/153

327 McNAUGHTON, WILLIAM, ed. *Chinese Literature: An Anthology from the Earliest Times to the Present Day.*
For annotations and bibliographic information, *see* no. 158.

328 MESERVE, WALTER J. and RUTH I. MESERVE, eds. *Modern Literature from China.* New York: New York University Press, 1973.
A collection of writings in various literary genres: short stories, *t'an-tz'u* (a type of popular literature), poetry, drama, essays, and speeches, and miscellaneous art forms (the folk tale, revolutionary aphorisms, reportage, and wall newspapers). The short stories section includes "The True Story of Ah Q," by Lu Hsün; "Spring Silkworms," by Mao Tun; "The Family on the Other Side of the Mountain," by Chou Li-po; and "Brother Yu Takes Office," by Lao She. All the selections are culled from other sources.

329 MILTON, D. L. and W. CLIFFORD, eds. *A Treasury of Modern Asian Stories.* New York: Mentor, 1961.
A general anthology which includes a section on Chinese literature. A few short stories and anecdotes by Lao She, Mao Tun, and Lu Hsün are included.

329a MUNRO, STANLEY R., ed. and tr. *Genesis of a Revolution: An Anthology of Modern Chinese Short Stories.* Singapore: Heinemann Educational Books (Asia), 1979.
An anthology of ten modern Chinese stories, which have not yet appeared in English elsewhere.

330 NIEH, HUA-LING, ed. *Eight Stories by Chinese Women.*
For annotations and bibliographic information, *see* no. 876.

331 SHIMER, DOROTHY BLAIR, ed. *The Mentor Book of Modern Asian Literature.* New York: New American Library, 1969.
In addition to modern poetry and drama, this volume contains excerpts from the essays of Hu Shih and Mao Tse-tung, and short stories by Lu Hsün and Mao Tun.

332 SNOW, EDGAR, ed. *Living China: Modern Chinese Short Stories.* New York: John Day Co., 1937; reprint ed. Westport, Conn.: Hyperion Press, 1973.
This anthology, one of the earliest collections of modern Chinese stories in English translation, contains a total of twenty-four stories, including five by Lu Hsün and seventeen by other authors, such as Mao Tun, Ting Ling, Pa Chin, Shen Ts'ung-wen, Yü Ta-fu, and Chang T'ien-i.

333 WANG, CHI-CHEN, tr. *Contemporary Chinese Stories.* New York: Columbia University Press, 1944; reprint ed. Westport Conn.: Greenwood Press, 1976.
A representative collection of 21 stories by 11 writers who wrote from 1918, when the Literary Revolution began, to 1937, when the Sino-Japanese War erupted. The stories were chosen for their intrinsic literary excellence, their

revelation of Chinese life and problems, and each author's established literary fame. Thematically, the stories, describing the seamy side of life (poverty, bureaucracy, war, love, and death), reflect their authors' preoccupation with their country's present and future and their desire for genuine social and political reforms. Included are five stories by Lao She, four by Chang T'ien-i, two each by Mao Tun, Lu Hsün, and Yeh Shao-chün, and one each by Lao Hsiang, Shen Ts'ung-wen, Ling Shu-hua, Yang Chen-sheng, and Feng Wen-ping. Also included are notes on the authors, a glossary, and bibliographical notes. A highly readable translation.

334 ———, ed. *Stories of China at War*. New York: Columbia University Press, 1947.
A collection of sixteen stories written between 1937 and 1942. Lao She, Mao Tun, and Kuo Mo-jo are some of the authors included.

335 WU, LUCIAN, ed. *New Chinese Stories: Twelve Short Stories by Contemporary Chinese Writers*.
For annotations and bibliographic information, *see* no. 877.

336 ———. *New Chinese Writing*.
For annotations and bibliographic information, *see* no. 878.

337 YEH, CHUN-CHAN, tr. *Three Seasons and Other Stories*. London: Staples Press, n.d. [1946?].
A collection of short stories by various modern Chinese authors, including Mao Tun and Yeh Shao-chün.

338 YUAN, CHIA-HUA and ROBERT PAYNE, trs. and eds. *Contemporary Chinese Short Stories*. London: Noel Carrington, Transatlantic Arts Co., 1946.
A good selection of modern Chinese short stories by various authors, including Mao Tun, Lu Hsün, and Chang T'ien-i.

II

Chang Ai-ling (Eileen Chang), 1920-

Born in Shanghai in 1920 and raised in an upper-class family, Chang Ai-ling, known as Eileen Chang in the West, studied at the University of Hong Kong, lived in Shanghai during the 1930s and '40s, and returned to Hong Kong in 1952. She now resides in the United States. One of the few Chinese writers proficient in both English and Chinese, she has written a number of short stories and novels, many of which have been translated into English. Some of her works are among the best in modern Chinese fiction. Especially noteworthy are "The Golden Cangue" and *The Rouge of the North*. Studies of Chang by C. T. Hsia and Stephen Cheng also deserve special attention.

Translations

339   BROWN, CAROLYN THOMPSON, tr. "Eileen Chang's 'Red Rose and White Rose.': A Translation and Afterword." Ph.D. Dissertation. Washington, D.C.: American University, 1978.

   A full translation of Chang Ai-ling's "Red Rose and White Rose," which is the story of "a young man's conflict over gratifying his personal desire for a spontaneous, passionate woman and offending social expectations, or satisfying his need for social respectability by marrying a chaste but dull woman whom he does not love." The afterword of the dissertation offers an analysis of the protagonist's character and the story's puzzling ending.

340   CHANG, EILEEN, tr. "The Betrothal of Yindi." In Cyril Birch, ed. *Anthology of Chinese Literature*. New York: Grove Press, 1965-1972, II, pp. 432-447.

   Translation of chapters 1 and 2 of *The Rouge of the North* (*Yüan nü*) (*see* no. 344).

341   ———. "The Golden Cangue." In C. T. Hsia, ed. *Twentieth-Century Chinese Stories*. New York: Columbia University Press, 1971, pp. 138-191.

   One of Eileen Chang's best works, "*Chin so chi*" is a powerful novelette on the transformation of a young, vivacious wife into a depraved, spiteful old shrew. It frankly reveals the decadence, intrigues, and cruelty within an upper-class Chinese household. A stinging indictment of the old society, it provides the reader with a mixed sense of "fascination and horror."

342 ———. *Naked Earth*. Hong Kong: Union Press, 1956.

Ch'ih-ti chih lien (*Naked Earth*) is a novel about the early years of the Communist regime, from the initial land reform through the Three-Anti Drive to the end of the Korean War in 1953. More ambitious than the *Rice-Sprout Song* in scope, it includes long expositions in the middle sections, in which the author attempts to tell all she knows about Communist China. Despite its emphasis on love, friendship, and sacrifice among the major characters, it is not a sentimental piece but a work noted especially for its purity of language and rich imagery.

343 ———. *The Rice-Sprout Song*. Hong Kong: Dragonfly Books, 1963.

Yang-ko (*The Rice-Sprout Song*) is a short novel about the land reform in China in the early 1950s; it attempts to portray the deprivations and sufferings of the villagers in China.

344 ———. *The Rouge of the North*. London: Cassell and Co., 1967.

The story of Yindi, the "Ch'i-ch'iao" of "The Golden Cangue," but considerably expanded and revised, *Yüan nü* (*The Rouge of the North*) traces the gradual depravation and degeneration of a once attractive young woman, Yindi, who is now married to a cripple. Bound to him for life, she releases her pent-up resentments on those around her, including her own children. Generally regarded as one of Chang's masterpieces.

345 ———. "Shame, Amah!" In Hua-ling Nieh, ed. *Eight Stories by Chinese Women*. Taipei: Heritage Press, 1962, pp. 92-114.

The story of a maid hired by a foreigner in Shanghai, it describes the woman's relationships with her son, her husband, and her employer, a bachelor popular with many lady friends. One of Chang's least successful stories.

346 ———. "Stale Mates." *The Reporter*, 15, no. 4 (Sept. 20, 1956), 34-38.

"*Wu-ssu i-shih*" ("Stale Mates") is a tale of matrimonial pride and malice told in a slightly lighter mode than most of Chang's longer works.

Studies

347 BOHLMEYER, JEANINE. "Eileen Chang's Bridges to China." *TR*, 5, no. 1 (April, 1974), 111-128.

A general analysis of six works by Eileen Chang. The six ("Shame, Amah!" "Stale Mates," "The Golden Cangue," *The Rouge of the North*, *The Rice-Sprout Song*, and *Naked Earth*), read together, as pointed out by the article, provide "considerable information about things Chinese."

348 BROWN, CAROLYN THOMPSON, tr. "Eileen Chang's 'Red Rose and White Rose'."

For annotations and bibliographic information, *see* no. 339.

349 CHENG, STEPHEN. "Themes and Techniques in Eileen Chang's Stories." *TR*, 8, no. 2 (Oct., 1977), 169-200.

An examination of Chang Ai-ling's "world with its assorted characters, their lives and loves," and a study of "the imagery and symbols used by Chang to depict her world and the techniques she employs to bring her world into relief."

350 FOKKEMA, D. W. "Chang Ai-ling." In Jaroslav Průšek, ed. *Dictionary of Oriental Literatures*. London: George Allen and Unwin, 1974; New York: Basic Books, 1974, I, p. 6.
A brief account of Chang's life and works.

351 HSIA, C. T. "Eileen Chang." In C. T. Hsia. *A History of Modern Chinese Fiction*. 2nd ed. New Haven: Yale University Press, 1971, pp. 389-431.
Includes a detailed analysis of "The Golden Cangue," *The Rice-Sprout Song*, *Naked Earth* (translated as *Love in Redland* by Hsia), and other short stories by Chang. Highly appreciative of Chang's talents, the author considers Chang "the best and most important writer in China today" and her short stories superior, or at least equal, in quality to the works of such modern Western women writers as Katherine Mansfield, Katherine Anne Porter, Eudora Welty, and Carson McCullers.

III

Chang T'ien-i, 1907-

Born in Nanking in 1907, Chang T'ien-i, after completing his high school education, went to Peking, where he wrote his first story, "A Dream of Three and a Half Days," in 1928. In the 1930s and '40s he published a number of stories in rapid succession and became known for his keen observation, comic exuberance, and satiric strength. After the establishment of the Communist government in Peking in 1949 he remained active for many years. He is still alive, but in poor health, reportedly paralyzed.

One of the most talented short-story writers of satire and irony, Chang T'ien-i is prolific, his works numbering some forty volumes. Translations of his short stories have appeared in various anthologies, including four in Chi-chen Wang's *Contemporary Chinese Stories*. So far there has been only one extensive study of Chang's work: a Ph.D. dissertation entitled "Zhang Tianyi's Fiction: The Beginning of Proletarian Literature in China," by Shu-ying Tsau, besides C. T. Hsia's study.

Translations

352 DURLEY, CARL B., tr. "A New Life." *Renditions*, no. 2 (Spring, 1974), pp. 31-49. Also translated by Tso Cheng. "New Life." *ChL*, no. 1 (Jan., 1955) pp. 160-180; Wang Chi-chen. "A New Life." In Chi-chen Wang, tr. *Stories of China at War*. New York: Columbia University Press, 1946, pp. 133-144.
This story ("*Hsin-sheng*") vividly dramatizes the inner conflicts of a teacher (also a writer and artist) during the Sino-Japanese War.

353 "Going to the Cinema." *People's China*, no. 12 (Dec., 1953), pp. 33-36. Reprinted in Chang T'ien-yi. *Stories of Chinese Young Pioneers*. Peking: Foreign Languages Press, 1954, pp. 1-9.
"*Ch'ü k'an tien-ying*" ("Going to the Cinema") is a short story about life in contemporary China.

354 GREGORY, MARY, tr. "Mid-Autumn Festival." *Tea Leaves,* 1, no. 1 (1965), 12-23.
"*Chung-ch'iu*" ("Mid-Autumn Festival") is a story of insult, describing how a village squire reluctantly invites his brother-in-law to a Mid-Autumn Festival dinner. Though the dishes have been prepared and on the table for some time, the host gives no indication to have anyone seated but continues to lecture his guest on the subject's ingratitude. Finally, his wife tells her brother to leave, and he faints from hunger in the courtyard. The story satirizes the sorry situation of the poor relative whose genteel upbringing has made him accept humiliation at the expense of his own pride and dignity.

355 HOU, CHIEN, tr. "Spring Breeze." In C. T. Hsia, ed. *Twentieth-Century Chinese Stories.* New York: Columbia University Press, 1971, pp. 64-89.
"*Ch'un-feng*" ("Spring Breeze") describes the shabby treatment of poor pupils by snobbish schoolteachers and well-to-do classmates out of scorn and malice toward the poor.

356 "How Lo Wen-ying Became a Young Pioneer." *ChL,* no. 3 (March, 1954), pp. 139-146. Reprinted in *Stories of Chinese Young Pioneers.* Peking: Foreign Languages Press, 1954, pp. 10-23.
This is a story about a man who decides to serve the people and the country.

357 JENNER, W. J. F., tr. "Generosity." In W. J. F. Jenner, ed. *Modern Chinese Stories.* Oxford: Oxford University Press, 1970, pp. 101-106.
"*Tu-liang*" ("Generosity") describes the life of a downtrodden rickshaw puller. Involved in an accident, he receives no pay but verbal abuse from not only his passenger but also onlookers of various social classes.

357a MAO, NATHAN K., tr. "The Bulwark." In Joseph S. M. Lau, Leo Ou-fan Lee, and C. T. Hsia, eds. *Modern Chinese Stories and Novellas, 1918-1948.* New York: Columbia University Press, forthcoming.
A scathing satire of a self-righteous Confucian prig.

358 "Mutation." In Edgar Snow, ed. *Living China; Modern Chinese Stories.* New York: John Day Co., 1937, pp. 267-288.
"*I-hsing*" ("Mutation") describes how a young woman gives up her revolutionary life to become the wife of a rich merchant.

359 SHAPIRO, SIDNEY, tr. "A Summer Night's Dream." *ChL,* no. 1 (Jan., 1962), pp. 3-39.
"*Hsia-yeh meng*" ("A Summer Night's Dream") tells the sad tale of an exploited young singer in old Shanghai and his yearning for freedom.

360 *Stories of Chinese Young Pioneers.* Peking: Foreign Languages Press, 1954.
This anthology contains three of Chang T'ien-i's short stories about life in contemporary China: "Going to the Cinema," "How Lo Wen-ying Became a Young Pioneer," and "They and We" ("*T'a-men ho wo-men*"). Also included is one of Chang's plays.

361 "They and We." *ChL,* no. 3 (March, 1954), pp. 146-151.
This story centers on commune life in contemporary China.

362 TSAU, SHU-YING, tr. "Hatred." *BCAS,* 8 (1976), 63-71.
"Ch'ou-hen tien" ("Hatred") depicts the horrors of wars among rival warlords in China during the 1920s.

363 VOCHALA, J. and I. LERVITOVA, trs. "Mr. Hua Wei." *New Orient,* 5, no. 4 (1966), 123-126. Also translated by Yeh Chun-chan. "Mr. Hua Wei." In Yeh Chun-chan, tr. *Three Seasons and Other Stories.* London: Staples Press, 1946, pp. 111-118.
One of the *Three Sketches* by Chang T'ien-i, "Mr. Hua Wei" (*"Hua Wei hsien-sheng"*) is a satiric portrait of an intellectual thriving under the confused conditions during the Sino-Japanese War.

364 WANG, CHI-CHEN, tr. *Contemporary Chinese Stories.* New York: Columbia University Press, 1944; reprinted. Westport, Conn.: Greenwood Press, 1975.
This anthology contains four stories by Chang T'ien-i: "The Inside Story," "Reunion" (*"T'uan-yüan"*), "The Road" (*"Lu"*), and "Smile" (*"Hsiao"*). All the stories reflect the cruel realities of Chinese society and are noted for the author's revelation of details in the depiction of his characters—beggars, thieves, opportunists, bureaucrats, peasants, and soldiers.

365 YANG, GLADYS, tr. *Big Lin and Little Lin.* Peking: Foreign Languages Press, 1958.
Ta Lin ho Hsiao Lin (Big Lin and Little Lin), written in 1931, is strictly a children's book which describes how two brothers encounter all sorts of talking animals and objects.

366 ———. *The Magic Gourd.* Peking: Foreign Languages Press, 1959.
Written in 1957, *Pao hu-lu ti pi-mi (The Magic Gourd)* is another children's book, describing how Wang Pao finds a magic gourd in a river.

367 YUAN, CHIA-HUA and ROBERT PAYNE, trs. "The Breasts of a Girl." In Yuan Chia-hua and Robert Payne, trs. and eds. *Contemporary Chinese Short Stories.* London: Noel Carrington, Transatlantic Arts Co., 1946, pp. 97-117.
"Pei-chi yü nai-tzu" ("The Breasts of a Girl") is a satirical tale about an old-styled Confucian gentleman and his moral pretense.

Studies

368 "Chang T'ien-i." In Howard L. Boorman and Richard C. Howard, eds. *Biographical Dictionary of Republican China* (New York: Columbia University Press, 1967-1971), I, pp. 114-115.
A brief account of Chang's life and works.

369 HSIA, C. T. "Chang T'ien-i (1907-)." In C. T. Hsia, *A History of Modern Chinese Fiction*. 2d ed. New Haven: Yale University Press, 1971, pp. 212-236.

Highly appreciative of Chang's literary talents, Hsia calls him "the most brilliant short-story writer" of the 1930s and describes him as "a Shakespearean creator who takes the predominant ideology of his age for granted and yet is able to use it as a vehicle for his superior moral intuitions."

370 LECHOWSKA, TERESA. "Chang T'ien-i." In Jaroslav Průšek, ed. *Dictionary of Oriental Literatures*. London: George Allen and Unwin, 1974; New York: Basic Books, 1974, I, pp. 7-8.

A brief account of Chang's life, major works, literary technique, and English translations of his works.

371 TSAU, SHU-YING. "Zhang Tianyi's (Chang T'ien-i) Fiction: The Beginning of Proletarian Literature in China." Ph.D. Dissertation. Toronto: University of Toronto, 1976.

A study of Chang as an exponent of proletarian literature. The author uses the structuralist method to analyze the artistic qualities of Chang's works, eighty four of which were written from 1928 to 1939.

372 YUAN, YING. "Chang Tien-yi and His Young Readers." *ChL*, no. 6 (June, 1959), pp. 137-139.

A brief introduction to Chang and his stories about children which were designed for juvenile readers.

IV

Ch'ien Chung-shu, 1910-

Ch'ien Chung-shu, the author of *Wei-ch'eng* or *Fortress Besieged* was born into a literary family in Wuhsi, Kiangsu province, in 1910. After graduating from Tsing-hua in 1933, he accepted a teaching appointment at Kuang-hua University in Shanghai. In 1935, on a Boxer Indemnity Scholarship, Ch'ien went to Oxford University and majored in English literature. After obtaining his B.Litt. degree from Oxford, he returned to China in 1937. Proficient in English, Latin, French, German, and Italian literatures, he taught at a number of institutions. After the Communist victory in 1949, he became a member of the Literary Research Institute of the Academy of Sciences. He visited the United States in April, 1979.

Ch'ien has been regarded by many as a writer distinguished for his satirical, carefully wrought works of fiction, such as *Fortress Besieged* and *Men, Beasts, and Ghosts*, both of which are noted for their "delightful portrayal of contemporary manners, comic exuberance, and tragic insight."

Some of Ch'ien's short stories were anthologized in his 1946 anthology, *Men, Beasts, and Ghosts* (*Jen, Shou, Kuei*). His most important work of fiction is *Wei-ch'eng* (*Fortress Besieged* or *The Besieged City*), published in 1947 and now available in an English translation by Jeanne Kelly and Nathan K. Mao. Critical studies by C. T. Hsia, Dennis T. Hu, and T. D. Huters are very useful for a proper appreciation of Ch'ien's works.

Translations

373   KELLY, JEANNE, tr. "The Besieged City." *Renditions*, no. 2 (Spring, 1974), pp. 65-82.

An excerpt (chapter 1) from Ch'ien Chung-shu's famous satirical novel about the alienated "returned students" in China, *The Besieged City* or *Fortress Besieged* (*Wei-ch'eng*, 1947), which is noted for its gallery of excellent comic portraits and vivid psychological analysis. The novel opens with the protagonist Fang Hung-chien's return to China from France in the summer of 1937. Chapter 1 begins on the ship *Vicomte de Bragelonne*; it introduces the protagonist and places him in a triangular relationship with Miss Pao and Miss Su, the former noted for her scanty clothing and the latter for her sophistication, and the chapter ends with Miss Pao's disembarking in Hong Kong and Fang Hung-chien's increasing familiarity with Miss Su.

374 KELLY, JEANNE and NATHAN K. MAO, trs. *Fortress Besieged.* Bloomington: Indiana University Press, 1979.

A complete translation of *Wei-ch'eng*, which has been widely acclaimed by many as one of the best modern Chinese novels. Noted for its comic exuberance, satire, and linguistic manipulation, and structured in nine chapters, the novel is a comedy of manners with much picaresque humor, as well as a scholar's novel, a satire, a commentary on courtship and marriage, and a study of one contemporary man. This translation includes a lengthy introduction to Ch'ien and his works.

375 MAO, NATHAN K. tr. "Souvenir." In Joseph S. M. Lau and Leo Ou-fan Lee, and C. T. Hsia, eds., *Modern Chinese Stories and Novellas, 1918-1948.* New York: Columbia University Press, forthcoming.

"Chi-nien," widely considered the best story in *Men, Beasts, and Ghosts* (*Jen, Shou, Kuei*), is a study of the seduction of a lonely married woman by an air force pilot during the Sino-Japanese War. The story emphasizes the heroine's feelings of guilt, fascination, and revulsion toward her extra-marital affair.

Studies

376 HSIA, C. T. "Ch'ien Chung-shu." In C. T. Hsia. *A History of Modern Chinese Fiction.* 2nd ed. New Haven: Yale University Press, 1971, pp. 432-460.

Regarding Ch'ien Chung-shu as one of the foremost modern Chinese satirists in the tradition of Wu Ching-tzu, author of the eighteenth-century satirical novel *The Scholars* (*Ju-lin wai-shih*), C. T. Hsia analyzes Ch'ien's major satirical work, *The Besieged City*, in detail and provides an English translation of a substantial part of the novel's last chapter (pp. 449-459).

377 HU, DENNIS T. "A Linguistic-Literary Approach to Ch'ien Chung-shu's Novel *Wei-ch'eng*." *JAS*, 37 (1978), 427-443.

A study of the strengths of Ch'ien's *Fortress Besieged* (*Wei-ch'eng*) as a great, carefully wrought novel from linguistic and stylistic points of view. The author shows how the use of key imageries in the novel succeeds in bringing out the main themes and how both the imagery and the skillful manipulation of language have contributed substantially to intensifying sarcasm, satire, irony, and wit. These linguistic and stylistic means have enabled Ch'ien, the author concludes, to achieve his literary end: a caricature of society. Based in part on the author's 1977 dissertation (*see* no. 378), the article cites numerous examples of Ch'ien's linguistic manipulation (for instance, personification, symbolic prefiguration, plurisignation) and of Ch'ien's semantic manipulation (verbal paradoxes, narrator intrusion).

378 ———. "A Linguistic-Literary Study of Ch'ien Chung-shu's Three Creative Works." Ph.D. Dissertation. Madison: University of Wisconsin, 1977.

Works considered in this dissertation are *Wei-ch'eng* (*Fortress Besieged*); the four short stories anthologized in *Jen Shou Kuei* (*Men, Beasts, and Ghosts*); and *Hsieh-tsai jen-sheng pien-shang* (*Marginalia of Life*), a collection of vignette-satires.

Chapter 1 introduces Ch'ien, his works and studies of him by contemporary scholars. Chapter 2 defines the theoretical basis for the critical method used in the study. Chapters 3 and 4 focus mainly on figurative language and linguistic manipulation used by Ch'ien. A set of three appendices completes the dissertation, giving summaries of *Fortress Besieged, Men, Beasts, and Ghosts*, and a listing of the essays in *Marginalia of Life*. Techniques of descriptive and interpretive linguistics are used as the tools of inquiry, leading to literary conclusions.

379 HUTERS, THEODORE DAVID. "Traditional Innovation: Qian Zhong-shu (Ch'ien Chung-shu) and Modern Chinese Letters." Ph.D. Dissertation, Stanford: Stanford University, 1977.

A dissertation divided into five chapters. The first chapter stresses Chinese literature and its cultural background; the second, the shift to iconoclasm; the third, Ch'ien Chung-shu's literary criticism; the fourth, Ch'ien's creative work, the essays and short stories; the fifth, a discussion of *Wei-ch'eng* (*Fortress Besieged*). Also included is an extensive bibliography. The most useful chapters are 3, 4, and 5.

380 SŁUPSKI, ZBIGNIEW. "Ch'ien Chung-shu." In Jaroslav Průšek, ed. *Dictionary of Oriental Literatures*. London: George Allen and Unwin 1974; New York: Basic Books, 1974, I, pp. 12-13.

A brief account of Ch'ien's life and works. The author points out that Ch'ien is primarily a satirist, and his fiction is remarkable for the gallery of excellent comic portraits he has created, reminiscent in many ways of the character-drawing of the *Ju-lin wai-shih* (The Scholars). In style, subject and philosophical outlook, Ch'ien's work has a special place in modern Chinese writing; his ironic, skeptical and even cynical attitude toward accepted values is highly unconventional.

V

Lao She (Shu Ch'ing-ch'un), 1899-1966

Born in Peking in 1899, Lao She attended Yenching University and taught Chinese at the University of London in the 1920s. Widely exposed to English fiction in London, he became extremely productive in the 1930s and '40s, having published many novels and short stories. He remained active until 1966, when he was hounded to death by the Red Guards during the Cultural Revolution. He has recently been posthumously rehabilitated.

Lao She, one of the best-known Chinese writers in the West, is noted for his *Rickshaw Boy*, a novel symbolic of China's hardships, struggles, and problems. Evan King's translation of it, though it was a 1945 Book-of-the-Month-Club selection and a best-seller, is filled with errors and the translator has even altered its original ending. A more accurate translation by Jean M. James has just been published. A number of Lao She's other novels and short stories have also been rendered into English. William A. Lyell's translation of *Cat Country*, a satirical novel on China, deserves special attention. Lao She's popular short story "Black Li and White Li" and four other stories are included in Chi-chen Wang's *Contemporary Chinese Stories*.

Two important book-length studies of Lao She have been published in recent years: Zbigniew Słupski's *The Evolution of a Modern Chinese Writer* and Ranbir Vohra's *Lao She and the Chinese Revolution*. Both are important contributions to the study of Lao She. Articles by Slupski, Vincent Y. C. Shih, Cyril Birch, and C. T. Hsia, and a book by S. R. Munro are also useful reference sources.

Translations

381 "*Camel Hsiang-tzu.*" ChL, no. 11 (Nov., 1978), pp. 3-58; no. 12 (Dec., 1978), pp. 13-72.
    An excerpt from Lao She's *Camel Hsiang-tzu* (*Rickshaw Boy*). A very faithful and fairly readable translation. For information on the novel, *see* no. 388.

382 CHAI, CH'U and WINBERG CHAI, trs. "Lao She: Lo-t'o hsiang-tzu." In Ch'u Chai and Winberg Chai, trs. and eds. *A Treasury of Chinese Literature*. New York: Appleton-Century, 1965, pp. 313-320.
    A translation of two excerpts from chapters 1 and 2 of *Rickshaw Boy*.

383 DEW, JAMES E., tr. *City of Cats.* Ann Arbor: Center for Chinese Studies, University of Michigan, 1964. (Occasional Papers, no. 3).

An abridged translation of Lao She's satirical novel, *Mao-ch'eng chi.* (The first eleven chapters of this translation are reprinted in *Renditions,* no. 10 (Autumn, 1978), pp. 21-45.)

384 HANRAHAN, GENE Z., tr. "Black Li and White Li." In Gene Z. Hanrahan, ed. *50 Great Oriental Stories.* New York: Bantam Books, 1965, pp. 81-94; Wang, Chi-chen, tr. "Black Li and White Li." In Chi-chen Wang, tr. *Contemporary Chinese Stories.* New York: Columbia University Press, 1944, pp. 25-39.

This story ("*Hei Pai Li*") describes the attitudes of two brothers toward changes in society. One becomes a radical and wrecks a number of streetcars to protect the welfare of rickshaw pullers and is finally executed, while the other moves to Shanghai and drowns himself in memory of his deceased brother.

385 *Heavensent.* London: J. M. Dent and Sons, 1951.

A translation of Lao She's novel *Niu T'ien-tz'u chuan.* An interesting novel which gives an analysis of the petit-bourgeois class as seen in the upbringing of a hero in that class. The hero is a male foundling with the name T'ien-tz'u ("Heaven Bestowed"), and the novel centers on the first twenty years of his life and demonstrates how environment shapes his character and turns him into "an ineffective middle-class intellectual." Not an accurate translation but readable.

386 JAMES, JEAN M., tr. *Rickshaw: The Novel Lo-t'o Hsiang Tzu.* Honolulu: University Press of Hawaii, 1979.

A more accurate translation than Evan King's *Rickshaw Boy* but less readable, James' book fails to adequately convey Lao She's style and flavor. (For information on King's translation, *see* no. 388).

386a JENNER, W. J. F. tr. "A Brilliant Beginning." In W. J. F. Jenner, ed. *Modern Chinese Stories.* Oxford: Oxford University Press, 1970, pp. 85-93; Lyell, William A. tr. "The Grand Opening." *EWR,* 3 (1967), 170-182; Słupski, Zbigniew and Iris Urwin, trs. "Business." *New Orient,* 2, no. 2 (1961), 17-19.

One of Lao She's prewar stories, "*K'ai-shih ta-chi*" portrays a group of uneducated people who operate an unlicensed hospital. It contains much satire on unsavory aspects of medical practice in interior China.

387 KAO, GEORGE, tr. "Dr. Mao." In George Kao, ed. *Chinese Wit and Humor.* New York: Coward-McCann, 1946; New York: Sterling Publishing Co., 1974, pp. 309-327.

An excerpt from Lao She's "*Hsi-sheng,*" a story about a Chinese scholar who holds a Ph.D. degree from Harvard and finds life in China unsatisfactory. Here Lao She's target of satire is the "returned student," who often boasts of his experience abroad and eventually finds life in his own native country unbearable.

388   KING, EVAN (ROBERT S. WARD), tr. *Rickshaw Boy*. New York: Reynal and Hitchcock, 1945.

The most popular of Lao She's novels, *Lo-t'o hsiang-tzu* (*Rickshaw Boy* or *Camel Hsiang-tzu*), tells of the bitter, futile struggles of a young, handsome rickshaw puller, Happy Boy, whose one ambition is to save enough money to buy a rickshaw of his own. Despite his sincere intentions, the social forces of Peking make him into a shiftless, mean-spirited loafer. The translator took many liberties with the original story and changed its tragic ending into a happy one without the author's consent. King's *Rickshaw Boy* was a Book-of-the-Month-Club selection in 1945 and became a "runaway" best-seller in the United States, even though it was filled with errors. The translator also added, deleted, rearranged, and rewrote passages, and even invented characters.

389   KUO, HELENA, tr. *The Drum Singers*. New York: Harcourt, Brace and Co., 1952; London: Victor Gollancz, Ltd., 1953.

This is a novel about the flight of two families of lowly drum-singers (a folk-singing group) from Hankow to Chungking in 1938 as the war against Japan worsens. The growing up of Lotus Charm, Pao Ching's young daughter, is the focus of this novel. The translation was done in collaboration with Lao She. The original Chinese version, *Ku-shu i-jen*, has never been published. (Chapters 16 and 21 of this translation appear in *Renditions*, no. 10 (Autumn 1978), pp. 53-61.)

390   ———. *The Quest for Love of Lao Lee*. New York: Reynal and Hitchcock, 1948.

A translation of Lao She's *Li-hun* (*Divorce*), a subtle, ironic novel about life in modern China. A junior official, Lao Lee, takes his unsophisticated wife and two children to Peking and soon becomes irate over the new bourgeois manners she has acquired from his colleagues' wives. The only consolation he has is his secret yearning for the discarded wife of a colleague. But the colleague and his wife soon reconcile with each other, leaving Lao Lee no one but his own wife to contend with. The main target of satire is the family man and petty official living in fear and conformity.

391   LIN, YUTANG, tr. "Talking Pictures." In George Kao, ed. *Chinese Wit and Humor*. New York: Coward-McCann, 1946; New York: Sterling Publishing Co., 1974, pp. 305-309.

"*Yu-sheng tien-ying*" ("Talking Pictures") describes the experience of seeing a movie for the first time and the many interpretations of what a movie is.

391a   LINK, PERRY, tr. "End of the Rickshaw Boy." *Renditions*, no. 10 (Autumn, 1978), pp. 78-89.

A translation of the last two chapters of Lao She's *Rickshaw Boy* (*see* no. 388).

392   LYELL, WILLIAM A., tr. *Cat Country: A Satirical Novel of China in the 1930's*. Columbus: Ohio State University Press, 1970.

A fairly accurate and readable full translation of *Mao-ch'eng chi* (*Cat Country*), a satire written in a serious vein against China's civil wars, her helplessness in the face of foreign aggression, and her opium dream of the past. A critical introduction provides much information about the author and his time.

170/ BIBLIOGRAPHIES

392a ———. "An Old and Established Name." *Renditions,* no. 10 (Autumn, 1978), pp. 62-67.
    A translation of one of Lao She's works written in the mid-1930's, this is a story about the Fortune Silk Store, an old and well-established firm.

393 ——— "Neighbors." In Wu-chi Liu, et al., eds. *K'uei Hsing: A Repository of Asian Literature in Translation.* Bloomington: Indiana University Press, 1974, pp. 81-95; Słupski, Zbigniew and Iris Urwin, trs. "Neighbors." *New Orient,* 3 (August, 1962), 123-126.
    A short but delightful story about "neighborly" quarrels and jealousies.

394 PRUITT, IDA, tr. *The Yellow Storm.* New York: Harcourt, Brace and Co., 1951.
    A readable, abridged translation of parts I and II of Lao She's trilogy *Ssu-shih t'ung-t'ang, (Four Generations under the Same Roof),* which describes how four generations live together in a family compound in Peking during the Japanese occupation. It shows the various ways in which members of the family resist the Japanese, and it may be viewed as a microcosm of occupied Peking.

395 SHAPIRO, SIDNEY, tr. "Brother Yü Takes Office." *ChL,* no. 6 (June, 1962), pp. 58-76; reprinted in Walter J. Meserve and Ruth I. Meserve, eds. *Modern Literature from China.* New York: New York University Press, 1973, pp. 94-110.
    "*Shang-jen*" ("Brother Yü Takes Office") deals with the life of a police inspector.

396 ———. "Crescent Moon." *ChL,* no. 4 (April, 1957), pp. 66-88.
    "*Yüeh-ya-erh*" ("Crescent Moon") tells the tragic tale of a destitute young girl who becomes a prostitute.

397 WANG, CHI-CHEN, tr. *Contemporary Chinese Stories.* New York: Columbia University Press, 1944, reprint ed. Westport, Conn.: Greenwood Press, 1976.
    This anthology contains the following stories by Lao She: "Black Li and White Li" ("*Hei Pai Li*"); "Liu's Court" ("*Liu-chia ta-yüan*"); "Grandma Takes Charge" ("*Pao-sun*"); "The Philanthropist" ("*Shan-jen*"); and "The Glasses" ("*Yen-ching*"). For further information on the anthology, *see* no. 333.

398 ———. "Grandma Takes Charge." In Daniel Milton and William Clifford, eds. *A Treasury of Modern Asian Stories.* New York: New American Library, 1961, pp. 166-176.
    A chilling story, "*Pao-sun*" ("Grandma Takes Charge") describes how an old, muddle-headed grandmother inadvertently kills both her new grandson and her daughter-in-law.

399 ———, ed. *Stories of China at War.* New York. Columbia University Press, 1947.

This collection contains translations of the following stories by Lao She: "The Letter from Home" ("*I-feng chia-hsin*"), tr. by Chi-chen Wang; "They Gather Heart Again" ("*Jen t'ung tz'u-hsin*"), tr. by Richard L. Jen and reprinted as "They Take Heart Again"; and "Portraits of a Traitor" ("*Ch'ieh-shuo wu-li*"), tr. by K. C. Yeh. For information on this collection, *see* no. 334.

400 YANG, GLADYS, tr. "A Vision." *ChL*, no. 6 (June, 1962), pp. 77-88.

"*Wei-shen*" ("A Vision") is a tragic tale of young love.

401 YUAN, CHIA-HUA and ROBERT PAYNE, trs. "The Last Train." In Yuan Chia-hua and Robert Payne, trs. and eds. *Contemporary Chinese Short Stories.* London: Noel Carrington, Transatlantic Arts Co., 1946, pp. 48-66; reprinted in James E. Miller, et al., eds. *Literature of the Eastern World.* Glenview, Ill.: Scott, Foresman, 1970, pp. 65-76.

"*Huo-ch'e*" ("The Last Train") describes a tragic fire which sweeps several railway cars on a New Year's Day.

Studies

402 BADY, PAUL. "Death and the Novel—On Lao She's 'Suicide' ". *Renditions*, no. 10 (Autumn, 1978), pp. 5-20.

A discussion of Lao She's "suicide" in 1966 and his posthumous rehabilitation.

402a BIRCH, CYRIL. "Lao She: The Humourist in His Humour." *CQ*, no. 8 (Oct.-Dec., 1961), 45-62.

An informative study of Lao She's life and writings emphasizing his skill as a humorist-satirist.

403 BRANDAUER, FREDERICK P. "Selected Works of Lao She and Mao Tun and Their Relevance for Christian Theology." *Ching Feng*, 11, no. 2 (1968), 25-43.

An introductory essay on Lao She and Mao Tun. The first part of the essay gives plot summaries of a number of stories included in two anthologies by Lao She and Mao Tun. The second part analyzes the most distinctive aspects of the two writers and the relevance of their selected works to Christian theology.

404 CHOU, SUI-NING PRUDENCE. "Lao She: An Intellectual's Role and Dilemma in Modern China." Ph.D. Dissertation. Berkeley: University of California, 1976.

A study of Lao She's life and selected works designed to delineate the dilemma and problems which confronted him as an intellectual in modern China.

405 DUKE, MICHAEL. "The Urban Poor in Lao She's Pre-War Short Stories." *Phi Theta Papers,* 12 (1970), 72-99. (Originally an M.A. thesis, University of California, Berkeley, 1969. A different version also appears in *JCLTA,* 13 (1978), 137-149).
  A study of the urban poor in some of Lao She's short stories written before 1937.

406 HSIA, C. T. "Lao She." In C. T. Hsia, *A History of Modern Chinese Fiction.* 2d ed. New Haven: Yale University Press, 1971, pp. 165-188, pp. 366-375.
  A critical analysis of Lao She's major novels, introduced with a brief biographical sketch. Lao She's genuine patriotism during the Sino-Japanese War, C. T. Hsia maintains, impaired Lao She's critical faculties as reflected in his post-1937 works.

406a HU, KING. "Lao She in England." *Renditions,* no. 10 (Autumn, 1978), pp. 46-52.
  An account of Lao She's life in England in 1924-1930.

406b KAO, GEORGE. "Lao She in America—Arrival and Departure." *Renditions,* no. 10 (Autumn, 1978), pp. 68-77.
  An account of Lao She's visit to the United States in 1946-49 and of the author's dealings with him.

406c ———. *Two Writers in the Cultural Revolution.* Hong Kong: Chinese University Press, 1979.
  In this study of Lao She and Ch'en Jo-hsi, the author points out their similarities: their return to China from abroad and the impact of the Cultural Revolution on them. This book also "provides a glimpse into some of Lao She's pre-1949 writings, his works of fiction in English translation not readily available elsewhere." The book also contains translations of two stories by Ch'en Jo-hsi.

407 LAO SHE. "How I Came to Write the Novel *Camel Hsiang-tzu.*" *ChL,* no. 11 (Nov., 1978), pp. 59-64.
  This is Lao She's own statement on how he came to write the novel.

408 "Lao She." In Howard L. Boorman and Richard C. Howard, eds. *Biographical Dictionary of Republican China.* New York: Columbia University Press, 1967-1971, III, pp. 132-135; IV, pp. 326-329.
  A brief account of Lao She's life and major works.

409 MUNRO, S. R. *The Function of Satire in the Works of Lao She.* Singapore: Chinese Language Centre, Nanyang University, 1977.
  A study of the function of satire in Lao She's selected works.

410 "On Lau Shaw's *City of Cat People.*" *ChL,* no. 4 (April, 1970), pp. 98-108.
  A polemical piece attacking Lao She and his *Cat Country* (*see* no. 392).

411 SHIH, VINCENT, Y. C. "Lao She, A Conformist? An Anatomy of a Wit under Constraint." In David C. Buxbaum and Frederick W. Mote, eds. *Transition and Permanence: Chinese History and Culture.* Hong Kong: Cathay Press, 1972; distributed by Chinese Materials Center, San Francisco, pp. 307-319.

This article explores the question of how a non-Communist writer can best survive under Communism. Lao She turned to his wit and humor as seen in his self-criticisms, condemnations, and other leisurely pieces. But ultimately, the author concludes, Lao She was unable to survive the attack of the Red Guards during the Cultural Revolution and died in 1966.

412 SŁUPSKI, ZBIGNIEW. *The Evolution of a Modern Chinese Writer: An Analysis of Lao She's Fiction with Biographical and Bibliographical Appendices.* Prague: Oriental Institute in Academia, 1966.

A study of Lao She and his works with special emphasis on his "subjects, the construction of his plots, his methods of characterization, the function of the environment, and so on."

413 ———. "Lao She." In Jaroslav Průšek, ed. *Dictionary of Oriental Literatures.* London: George Allen and Unwin, 1974; New York: Basic Books, 1974, I, pp. 89-90.

A brief account of Lao She's life, works, and English translations of his works.

414 ———. "The Works of Lao She during the First Phase of His Career." In Jaroslav Průšek, ed. *Studies in Modern Chinese Literature.* Berlin: Akademie-Verlag, 1964, pp. 77-95.

This essay introduces five early novels of Lao She: *The Philosophy of Old Chang (Lao Chang ti che-hsüeh), Chao Tzu-yüeh, Two of the Ma Family (Erh Ma), The Birthday of Little P'o (Hsiao-p'o ti sheng-jih),* and *Cat Country (Mao-ch'eng chi),* all written between 1924 and 1932. These novels reflect Lao She's search "for a firm philosophy of life, the right approach to his nation, and a way of writing which would best fit his personality."

415 TS'AO YU. "In Memory of Lao Sheh." *ChL,* no. 11 (Nov., 1978), pp. 65-79.

Written by the famous playwright, Ts'ao Yü, this memorial essay summarizes Lao She's life and contributions and his persecution by the Red Guards.

416 VOHRA, RANBIR. *Lao She and the Chinese Revolution.* Cambridge: East Asian Research Center, Harvard University, 1974.

Ths book, based on the author's Ph.D. dissertation (Harvard University, 1970), traces Lao She's literary and social development in terms of his major novels in the context of changes in Chinese society from 1898 to 1966. Lao She's ten novels are analyzed for their social significance. Several of his plays and short stories are also discussed. Discussions of *The Quest for Love of Lao Lee, Rickshaw Boy,* and *Biography of Niu T'ien-tz'u* are particularly illuminating.

VI
Lu Hsün (Chou Shu-jen), 1881-1936

Born into a somewhat impoverished family in Shaohsing, Chekiang in 1881, Lu Hsün studied medicine in Japan but eventually chose writing as his profession in order to serve as a "spiritual physician" to the Chinese. In the 1920s he published two volumes of short stories which established his literary reputation as a distinguished short-story writer. In his later years, especially in the last few years before his death in 1936, he wrote mostly short essays on social, literary, ideological, and political topics. Since his death, his fame has grown steadily and become almost legendary in China today. He is generally regarded as one of the greatest modern Chinese writers.

Of all the modern Chinese authors Lu Hsün is the most widely translated and studied. Practically every anthology of modern Chinese literature contains one or two stories by Lu Hsün. The most comprehensive collection of Lu Hsün's works is the four-volume *Selected Works of Lu Hsün*, translated mostly by Hsien-yi Yang and Gladys Yang. Two much shorter but more representative collections are the Yangs' *Selected Stories of Lu Hsün* and Gladys Yang's *Silent China*. Another important anthology is Chi-chen Wang's *Ah Q and Others*, which includes eleven of Lu Hsün's best short stories.

Studies of Lu Hsün are numerous. There are studies of the man, his works, his intellectual development, his role in modern Chinese history and literature, the techniques of his fiction, his psychological profile and other topics. Despite a number of doctoral dissertations on Lu Hsün, book-length studies in English are still limited. William A. Lyell's *Lu Hsün's Vision of Reality* is the most recent study of Lu Hsün's fiction; Sung-k'ang Huang's *Lu Hsün and the New Cultural Movement of Modern China* is a study of Lu Hsün's intellectual development. Among the many interesting essays are T. A. Hsia's "Aspects of the Power of Darkness in Lu Hsün's Fiction" and Leo Ou-fan Lee's several articles. Studies by Milena Doleželová-Velingerova, Douwe Fokkema, C. T. Hsia, Berta Krebsova, Jaroslav Průšek, Charles Alber, Patrick Hanan, Paul Pickowicz, William Schultz, and Harriet Mills are also useful reference sources.

Because of the large number of translations of Lu Hsün's works, the section on translations is divided into two parts. The first lists translations of individual stories under their respective Chinese titles; the second records anthologies which contain these translations.

Translations

1. Translations of Individual Stories

(1) "Ah Q cheng-chuan"

417   WANG, CHI-CHEN, tr. "Our Story of Ah Q." In Chi-chen Wang, tr. *Ah Q and Others.* New York: Columbia University Press, 1941, pp. 77-129; an excerpt entitled "Ah Q's Victories." In George Kao, ed. *Chinese Wit and Humor.* New York: Coward-McCann, 1946; New York: Sterling Publishing Co., 1974, pp. 275-282.

418   YANG, GLADYS, tr. "The True Story of Ah Q." In Gladys Yang, ed. and tr. *Silent China.* London: Oxford University Press, 1973, pp. 14-55.

419   YANG, HSIEN-YI, and GLADYS YANG, trs. "The True Story of Ah Q." In Hsien-yi Yang and Gladys Yang, trs. *Selected Stories of Lu Hsün.* Peking: Foreign Languages Press, 1960, pp. 65-112; *Selected Works of Lu Hsün.* Peking: Foreign Languages Press, 1956-1960, I, pp. 76-135; reprinted in Walter J. Meserve and Ruth I. Meserve, eds. *Modern Literature from China.* New York: New York University Press, 1973, pp.27-66.
      The best-known satirical novelette of modern China, it has created a neologism— "Ah Q-ism"—which is based on the philosophical outlook of the protagonist, Ah Q, who can always, one way or the other, rationalize his defeat into victory—a spiritual if not an actual one. This philosophy of defeatism has been blamed for much of China's backwardness, and cited as one of the serious defects of the Chinese national character in the past. In a way, the novelette is a powerful commentary on modern Chinese history.

(2) "Ch'ang-ming teng"

420   YANG, HSIEN-YI and GLADYS YANG, trs. "The Lamp That was Kept Alight." *CHL*, no. 11 (Nov., 1963), pp. 54-63.
      A tale about the inhumane treatment given to a man on the verge of madness.

(3) "Chu-fu"

421   SNOW, EDGAR and YAO HSIN-NUNG, trs. "Benediction." In Edgar Snow, ed. *Living China.* London: George G. Harrap and Co., 1936, pp. 51-74; reprinted in Cyril Birch, ed. *Anthology of Chinese Literature.* New York: Grove Press, 1965-1972, II, pp. 303-320.

422   WANG, CHI-CHEN, tr. "The Widow." In Chi-chen Wang, tr. *Ah Q and Others.* New York: Columbia University Press, 1941, pp. 184-204; reprinted in James E. Miller, et al., eds. *Literature of the Eastern World.* Glenview, Ill.: Scott, Foresman, 1970, pp. 77-89.

423 YANG, GLADYS, tr. "The New Year's Sacrifice." In W. J. F. Jenner, ed. *Modern Chinese Stories*. London: Oxford University Press, 1970, pp. 29-45.

424 YANG, HSIEN-YI and GLADYS YANG, trs. "The New Year's Sacrifice." In Hsien-yi Yang and Gladys Yang, trs. *Selected Stories of Lu Hsün*. Peking: Foreign Languages Press, 1960, pp. 125-143; and *Selected Works of Lu Hsün*. Peking: Foreign Languages Press, 1956-1960, I, pp. 150-173.

One of Lu Hsün's gloomiest tales, it is about a peasant woman, hounded to death by the evils of feudalism and superstition. The story presents a powerful attack on the evils of traditional Chinese society.

(4) "Fei-tsao"

425 WANG, CHI-CHEN, tr. "The Cake of Soap." In Chi-chen Wang, tr. *Ah Q and Others*. New York: Colunbia University Press, 1941, pp. 16-30; reprinted in George Kao, ed. *Chinese Wit and Humor*. New York: Coward-McCann, 1946; New York: Sterling Publishing Co., 1974, pp. 282-292.

426 YANG, HSIEN-YI and GLADYS YANG, trs. "Soap." In Hsien-yi Yang and Gladys Yang, trs. *Selected Stories of Lu Hsün*. Peking: Foreign Languages Press, 1960, pp. 164-177; and *Selected Works of Lu Hsün*. Peking: Foreign Languages Press, 1956-1960, I, pp. 198-211; reprinted in G. L. Anderson, ed. *Masterpieces of the Orient*. New York: W. W. Norton and Co., 1977, pp. 548-555.

A brilliant satire set in Peking where the protagonist is a Confucian moralist but a complete hypocrite, whose every gesture, speech, and thought has been thoroughly depicted by the author.

(5) "Feng-po"

427 KENNEDY, GEORGE, tr. "A Gust of Wind." In Harold R. Isaacs, ed. *Straw Sandals*. Cambridge: M.I.T. Press, 1974, pp. 33-44.

428 WANG, CHI-CHEN, tr. "Cloud over Luchen." In Chi-chen Wang, tr. *Ah Q and Others*. New York: Columbia University Press, 1941, pp. 65-76.

429 YANG, HSIEN-YI and GLADYS YANG, trs. "Storm in a Teacup." In Hsien-yi Yang and Gladys Yang, trs. *Selected Stories of Lu Hsün*, Peking: Foreign Languages Press, 1960, pp. 45-53; and *Selected Works of Lu Hsün*. Peking: Foreign Languages Press, 1956-1960, I, pp. 52-62.

430 YUAN, CHIA-HUA and ROBERT PAYNE, trs. "The Waves of the Wind." In Yuan Chia-hua and Robert Payne, eds. and trs. *Contemporary Chinese Short Stories*. London: Noel Carrington, 1946, pp. 15-25.
   A subtle satirical piece on the superficiality of the "Republican Revolution" as reflected in the comments made by humble villagers.

(6) "I-chien hsiao-shih"

431 SNOW, EDGAR and YAO HSIN-NUNG, trs. "A Little Incident." In Edgar Snow, ed. *Living China*. London: George G. Harrap and Co., 1936, pp. 41-43; reprinted in Daniel L. Milton and William Clifford, eds. *A Treasury of Modern Asian Stories*. New York: New American Library, 1961, pp. 204-205; Dorothy Blair Shimer, ed. *The Mentor Book of Modern Asian Literature*. New York: New American Library, 1969, pp. 377-379.

432 YANG, HSIEN-YI and GLADYS YANG, trs. "An Incident." In Hsien-yi Yang and Gladys Yang, trs. *Selected Stories of Lu Hsün*. Peking: Foreign Languages Press, 1960, pp. 42-44; and *Selected Works of Lu Hsün*. Peking: Foreign Languages Press, 1960, I, pp. 49-51.
   An inspiring tale about the wisdom of a common rickshaw puller over his "superiors."

(7) "Ku-hsiang"

433 WANG, CHI-CHEN, tr. "My Native Heath." In Chi-chen Wang, tr. *Ah Q and Others*. New York: Columbia University Press, 1941, pp. 3-15.

434 YANG, GLADYS, tr. "My Old Home." In W. J. F. Jenner, ed. *Modern Chinese Stories*. London: Oxford University Press, 1970, pp. 20-29.

435 YANG, HSIEN-YI and GLADYS YANG, trs. "My Old Home." In Hsien-yi Yang and Gladys Yang, trs. *Selected Stories of Lu Hsün*. Peking: Foreign Languages Press, 1960, pp. 54-64; and *Selected Works of Lu Hsün*. Peking: Foreign Languages Press, 1956-1960, I, pp. 63-75.
   A nostalgic tale exemplifying the sad truth that class distinctions are difficult to obliterate.

(8) "Ku-tu che"

436 WANG, CHI-CHEN, tr. "A Hermit at Large." In Chi-chen Wang, tr. *Ah Q and Others*. New York: Columbia University Press, 1941, pp. 130-157.

437 YANG, HSIEN-YI and GLADYS YANG, trs. "The Misanthrope." In Hsien-yi Yang and Gladys Yang, trs. *Selected Stories of Lu Hsün*. Peking: Foreign Languages Press, 1960, pp. 176-196; and *Selected Works of Lu Hsün*. Peking: Foreign Languages Press, 1956-1960, I, pp. 212-237.
A story of a disillusioned rebel who, after withdrawing from society, dies without a whimper.

(9) "K'uang-jen jih-chi"

438 KENNEDY, GEORGE A., tr. "Diary of a Madman." In Harold R. Isaacs, ed. *Straw Sandals*. Cambridge: M.I.T. Press, 1974, pp. 1-12.

439 WANG, CHI-CHEN, tr. "The Diary of a Madman." In Chi-chen Wang, tr. *Ah Q and Others*. New York: Columbia University Press, 1941, pp. 205-219.

440 YANG, GLADYS, tr. "A Madman's Diary." In Gladys Yang, tr. and ed. *Silent China*. London: Oxford University Press, 1973, pp. 3-13.

441 YANG, HSIEN-YI and GLADYS YANG, trs. "A Madman's Diary." In Hsien-yi Yang and Gladys Yang, trs. *Selected Stories of Lu Hsün*. Peking: Foreign Languages Press, 1960, pp. 7-18; and *Selected Workx of Lu Hsün*. Peking: Foreign Languages Press, 1956-1960, I, pp. 8-21; reprinted in G. L. Anderson, ed., *Masterpieces of the Orient*. New York: W. W. Norton and Co., 1977, pp. 533-540.
Lu Hsün's first short story, "A Madman's Diary," is an important document of the New Literature Movement in modern China. Written in 1918, it attacks everything inhumane, vicious, and hypocritical in old China.

(10) "K'ung I-chi"

442 KENNEDY, GEORGE A., tr. "K'ung I-chi." In Harold R. Isaacs, ed. *Straw Sandals*. Cambridge: M.I.T. Press, 1974, pp. 25-32.

443 SNOW, EDGAR and YAO HSIN-NUNG, trs. "K'ung I-chi." In Edgar Snow, ed. *Living China*. London: George G. Harrap and Co., 1936, pp. 44-50.

444 YANG, GLADYS, tr. "Kong Yiji [K'ung I-chi]." In W. J. F. Jenner. ed. *Modern Chinese Stories*. London: Oxford University Press, 1970, pp. 14-19.

445 YANG, HSIEN-YI and GLADYS YANG, trs. "Kung I-chi." In Hsien-yi Yang and Gladys Yang, trs. *Selected Stories of Lu Hsün*. Peking: Foreign Languages Press, 1960, pp. 19-24; and *Selected Works of Lu Hsün*. Peking: Foreign Languages Press, 1956-1960, I, pp. 22-28.
A touching tale about the death of a marginal member of the literati who has turned into a thief.

180/BIBLIOGRAPHIES

(11) "Li-hun"

446 SNOW, EDGAR and YAO HSIN-NUNG, trs. "Divorce." In Edgar Snow, ed. *Living China*. London: George G. Harrap and Co., 1936, pp. 85-96.

447 WANG, CHI-CHEN, tr. "The Divorce." In Chi-chen Wang, tr. *Ah Q and Others*. New York: Columbia University Press, 1941, pp. 31-44.

448 YANG, HSIEN-YI and GLADYS YANG, trs. "The Divorce." In Hsien-yi Yang and Gladys Yang, trs., *Selected Stories of Lu Hsün*. Peking: Foreign Languages Press, 1960, pp. 216-225; and *Selected Works of Lu Hsün*. Peking: Foreign Languages Press, 1956-1960, I, pp. 262-273.
   The story of a woman who, despite her distaste for her husband, tries to be reinstated in his home.

(12) "Shang-shih"

449 KENNEDY, GEORGE A., tr. "Remorse." In Harold R. Isaacs, ed. *Straw Sandals*. Cambridge: M.I.T. Press, 1974, pp. 107-128.

450 WANG, CHI-CHEN, tr. "Remorse." In Chi-chen Wang, tr. *Ah Q and Others*. New York: Columbia University Press, 1941, pp. 158-183.

451 YANG, HSIEN-YI and GLADYS YANG, trs. "Regret for the Past." In Hsien-yi Yang and Gladys Yang, trs. *Selected Stories of Lu Hsün*. Peking: Foreign Languages Press, 1960, pp. 197-215; and *Selected Works of Lu Hsün*. Peking: Foreign Languages Press, 1956-1960, I, pp. 136-149.
   A sensitive personal tale highlighting a writer's loneliness after leaving his lover.

(13) "Ti-hsiung"

452 LYELL, WILLIAM, tr. "Brothers." *Renditions*, no. 1 (Autumn, 1973), pp. 66-75.
   A fictional account of the close relationship between two brothers, similar to that between Lu Hsün and his own brother, Chou Tso-jen.

(14) "Tsai chiu-lou shang"

453 WANG, CHI-CHEN, tr. "Reunion in a Restaurant." In Chi-chen Wang, tr. *Ah Q and Others*. New York: Columbia University Press, 1941, pp. 45-58.

454 YANG, GLADYS, tr. "In the Tavern." In Gladys Yang, tr. and ed. *Silent China*. London: Oxford University Press, 1973, pp. 65-75.

455 YANG, HSIEN-YI and GLADYS YANG, trs., "In the Wineshop." In Hsien-yi Yang and Gladys Yang, trs. *Selected Stories of Lu Hsün*. Peking: Foreign Languages Press, 1960, pp. 144-155; and *Selected Works of Lu Hsün*. Peking: Foreign Languages Press, 1956-1960, I, pp. 174-187.

   A story about the confession of a once energetic youth who has lost his ideals and compromised with the demands of the old society.

(15) "Yao"

456 KENNEDY, GEORGE, tr. "Medicine." In Harold R. Isaacs, ed. *Straw Sandals*. Cambridge: M.I.T. Press, 1974, pp. 13-24.

457 SNOW, EDGAR and YAO HSIN-NUNG, trs. "Medicine." In Edgar Snow, ed. *Living China*. London: George G. Harrap and Co., 1936, pp. 29-40.

458 YANG, HSIEN-YI and GLADYS YANG, trs. "Medicine." In Hsien-yi Yang and Gladys Yang, trs. *Selected Stories of Lu Hsün*. Peking: Foreign Languages Press, 1960, pp. 25-33; and *Selected Works of Lu Hsün*. Peking: Foreign Languages Press, 1956-1960, I, pp. 29-39; reprinted in G. L. Anderson, ed. *Masterpieces of the Orient*. New York: W. W. Norton and Co., 1977, pp. 541-547.

   Through the death of two young men, Lu Hsün makes this story an exposé of folk superstition, a symbolic parable on revolutions, and a moving portrayal of the parents' sorrow over the untimely demise of their children.

2. Anthologies with Translations of Lu Hsün's Works

459 ISAACS, HAROLD R., ed. *Straw Sandals*. Cambridge: M.I.T. Press, 1974.

   This volume contains the following five short stories by Lu Hsün: "Diary of a Madman," "Medicine," "K'ung I-chi," "Gust of Wind," and "Remorse." For further information on this volume, *see* no. 320.

460 JENNER, W. J. F., ed. *Modern Chinese Stories*. London: Oxford University Press, 1970.

   Contains three stories by Lu Hsün: "Kong Yiji [K'ung I-chi]," "My Old Home," and "The New Year's Sacrifice." For further information on this anthology, *see* no. 321.

461 SNOW, EDGAR, ed. *Living China, Modern Chinese Short Stories*. New York: John Day Co. 1937; Westport, Conn.: Hyperion Press, 1973.

   Part one of this volume contains a biographical sketch of Lu Hsün and five of his stories: "Medicine," "A Little Incident," "Benediction," "Divorce," and "Kites."

462 WANG, CHI-CHEN, tr. *Ah Q and Others: Selected Stories of Lusin* [Lu Hsün]. New York: Columbia University Press, 1941; reprint ed. Westport, Conn.: Greenwood Press, 1971.
   A readable translation of eleven short stories by Lu Hsün, with an introduction by the translator.

463 ——, tr. *Contemporary Chinese Stories.* New York: Columbia University Press, 1944; reprint ed. Westport, Conn.: Greenwood Press, 1972.
   Contains two stories by Lu Hsün: "What's the Difference" and "Peking Street Scene." For further information on this anthology, *see* no. 333.

464 YANG, GLADYS, tr. and ed. *Silent China: Selected Writings of Lu Xun* [Lu Hsün]. London: Oxford University Press, 1973.
   A representative collection of Lu Hsün's works, it contains five short stories, four reminiscences, thirteen poems, and thirteen essays. The title of this volume was derived from a talk the author gave in 1927, when he pointed out the need for using the vernacular, the language of the people. A paperback edition (Oxford University Press, 1973) is readily available.

465 YANG, HSIEN-YI and GLADYS YANG, trs. *Old Tales Retold.* Peking: Foreign Languages Press, 1961, 1972.
   Contains eight stories on traditional themes retold with the purpose of satirizing contemporary subjects. Includes a preface by the author.

466 ——. *Selected Stories of Lu Hsün.* Peking: Foreign Languages Press, 1960, 1972.
   Contains eighteen stories by Lu Hsün and his preface to the first volume of his short stories entitled *Call to Arms* (*Na-han*). Arranged in chronological order. An inexpensive paperback edition (Foreign Languages Press, 1972) is also available.

467 ——, et al., trs. *Selected Works of Lu Hsün.* Peking: Foreign Languages Press, 1956-1960. 4 vols.
   This four-volume set is the most comprehensive collection of Lu Hsün's works translated into English. The first volume contains eighteen short stories, nineteen prose poems, and nine essays—Lu Hsün's best creative writings from the period between 1918 and 1927. The second volume contains seventy essays written during the same period and reflects his role as a social critic and political commentator. The third volume contains ninety-six essays written from 1928 to 1933 and shows important changes in Lu Hsün's thinking. The fourth volume contains seventy-four essays from his last years. Appended to the last volume is a chronological listing of Lu Hsün's works and their translations. Despite occasional awkwardness these translations are readable and fairly accurate. An important source for any in-depth study of Lu Hsün.

Studies

468 ALBER, CHARLES, J. "Soviet Criticism of Lu Hsün (1881-1936)." Ph.D. Dissertation. Bloomington: Indiana University, 1971.

The author points out that Soviet attitudes toward Lu Hsün from 1925 to 1968 changed from various kinds of labeling, such as "petit-bourgeois radical," "anarchist," and "Chinese Gorky," to a more realistic and mature appraisal of him as a human being beset with doubts and contradictions. Moreover, his works are evaluated in terms of their literary merits rather than as political propaganda.

469 ———. "*Wild Grass*, Symmetry and Parallelism in Lu Hsün's Prose Poems." In William H. Nienhauser, ed. *Critical Essays on Chinese Literature*. Hong Kong: Chinese University of Hong Kong, 1976, pp. 1-29.

A study of an important collection of prose poems by Lu Hsün, this essay is an exercise in creative criticism as well as an application of Gestalt psychology.

470 CHEN, PEARL HSIA. *The Social Thought of Lu Hsün*. New York: Vantage Press, 1976.

A study of Lu Hsün's social thought and his views of Chinese society as reflected in his fiction and other types of writing.

471 CHEN, PO-TA, et al. *Commemorating Lu Hsün—Our Forerunner in the Cultural Revolution*. Peking: Foreign Languages Press, 1967.

A collection of articles in memory of Lu Hsün.

472 CHINNERY, J. D. "The Influence of Western Literature on Lu Xun's [Lu Hsün] 'Diary of a Madman'." *BSOAS*, 23 (1960), 309-322.

Traces the influence of Western writers such as Gogol and Nietzsche on Lu Hsün's short story, "Diary of a Madman," a pioneering modern Chinese story and one of the most important documents of the New Literature Movement.

473 CHISOLM, LAWRENCE. "Lu Hsün and Revolution in Modern China." *Yale-French Studies*, 39 (1967), 226-241.

A general study of Lu Hsün's role as a "revolutionary" writer in China.

474 CHUA, SIEW-TEEN. "Special Features of Lu Hsün's Short Stories." *Nanyang University Journal*, 8 (1974/1975), 84-108.

Discusses the main characteristics of and analyzes a number of Lu Hsün's major short stories.

475 DOLEŽELOVÁ-VELINGEROVÁ, MILENA. "Lu Xun's [Lu Hsün] 'Medicine.'" In Merle Goldman, ed. *Modern Chinese Literature in the May Fourth Era*. Cambridge: Harvard University Press, 1977, pp. 221-232.

A detailed analysis of one of Lu Hsün's most famous short stories, "Medicine." The author claims that the story shows the traits of Lu Hsün's later work: "A subject matter derived from personal experience, a forceful (but concealed) ideological message, and a polished narrative technique."

476 FOKKEMA, DOUWE W. "Lu Xun [Lu Hsün]: The Impact of Russian Literature." In Merle Goldman, ed. *Modern Chinese Literature in the May Fourth Era*. Cambridge: Harvard University Press, 1977, pp. 89-102.

A study of the influence of Russian literature on Lu Hsün's work. The author points out that, in addition to European romanticism, Lu Hsün was influenced by Chekhov's vignettes and the symbolism of Andreyev.

477 HANAN, PATRICK. "The Technique of Lu Hsün's Fiction." *HJAS*, 34 (1974), 53-96.

An essay which demonstrates the influence of Andrew Sienkiewicz, Gogol, and Soseki on Lu Hsün's fiction (twenty eight short stories). The author argues convincingly that the power of Lu Hsün's art lies in his use of various kinds of irony and detachment which are his methods of coping with the "strong emotions which threaten to overwhelm the artist." An important contribution to the study of Lu Hsün's technique.

478 HANSON-LOWE, L. "Lu Hsün and the *True Story of Ah Q.*" *Meanjin Quarterly*, 14, no. 2 (Winter, 1955), 208-217.

A very general study of Lu Hsün and his "True Story of Ah Q."

479 HSIA, C. T. "Lu Hsün." In C. T. Hsia. *A History of Modern Chinese Fiction*. 2nd ed. New Haven: Yale University Press, 1971, pp. 28-54.

Contains a biographical sketch and an evaluation of Lu Hsün's major short stories. "Benediction," "In the Restaurant," "Soap," and "Divorce" are what Hsia considers as Lu Hsün's best stories. Hsia dismisses Lu Hsün's later years as "spiritually and intellectually shallow" when compared to his earlier productive period.

480 HSIA, T. A. "Aspects of the Power of Darkness in Lu Hsün." In T. A. Hsia. *Gate of Darkness*. Seattle: University of Washington Press, 1968, pp. 146-162. Also in *JAS*, 23 (1964), 195-207.

A powerful exploration of the dark, conflicting, and tortuous side of Lu Hsün's psyche, the aspect usually ignored by his admirers or adulators. As pointed out by Hsia, this collection of twenty four prose poems entitled *Wild Grass*—"a book of unique interest"—expresses Lu Hsün's ambivalence toward life and death, hope and despair, darkness and light, the old and the new. Lu Hsün abhors the "old China," as suggested by Hsia, yet it is the old China with all her hideousness that most attracts him; he wishes to abolish the old literary language, but it is in that medium that he achieves some of his literary successes and draws his inspiration.

481 ———. "Lu Hsün and the Dissolution of the League of Leftist Writers." In T. A. Hsia. *Gate of Darkness*. Seattle: University of Washington Press, 1968, pp. 101-145.

An essay on Lu Hsün's last years and his stormy relationship with some members of the League of Left-Wing Writers. He bitterly attacked the doctrinaire line of the National Defense League, which he considered too sectarian. He argued for "greater freedom of creation." At the time of this debate Lu Hsün was seriously ill and nearing death.

482 HSU, RAYMOND S. W. *The Style of Lu Hsün: Vocabulary and Usage.* Hong Kong: Chinese University Press, 1980.
A study of Lu Hsün's style and technique. The author shows how Lu Hsün's vocabulary reveals his training and thought.

483 HUANG, SUNG-K'ANG. *Lu Hsün and the New Culture Movement of Modern China.* Amsterdam: Djambatan, 1957; reprint ed. Westport, Conn.: Hyperion Press, 1967.
Drawing upon Lu Hsün's voluminous works, both fiction and nonfiction, the author traces his intellectual development in its complex social and political context. The emphasis of this study is on the vigorous, positive, and optimistic rather than the dark, somber, and ambivalent side of Lu Hsün. The author believes that although Lu Hsün never became a member of the Communist Party, he was a leader of the League of Left-Wing Writers and had devoted himself to the creation of a proletarian literature.

484 KREBSOVA, BERTA. "Lu Hsün and His Collection *Old Tales Retold.*" *ArOr*, 28 (1060), 225-281, 640-656; 29 (1961), 268-310.
This long article, in three installments, analyzes the eight historical stories in *Old Tales Retold* (*Ku-shih hsin-pien*). In these stories, Lu Hsün has no qualms about distorting historical facts; he attributes modern views and characteristics to his characters and uses them to criticize the evils of the present. These stories, the author concludes, are examples of the successful "mutual penetration of the past and the living present."

485 LEE, LEO OU-FAN. "Between Hope and Despair: The Metaphorical search for Meaning in Lu Hsün's *The Wild Grass.*" In Joseph S. M. Lau and Leo Ou-fan Lee, eds. *Critical Persuasions*, forthcoming.
Employing a psychoanalytic approach, the author, drawing upon examples from Lu Hsün's most self-revealing work, *The Wild Grass*, concludes that it offers a good revelation of Lu Hsün's inner conflicts.

486 ———. "Genesis of a Writer: Notes on Lu Xun's [Lu Hsün] Educational Experience, 1881-1909." In Merle Goldman, ed. *Modern Chinese Literature in the May Fourth Era.* Cambridge: Harvard University Press, 1977, pp. 161-188.
A stimulating analysis of how Lu Hsün's educational experience made him become modern China's foremost writer. The author discusses Lu Hsün's early background, his years of education in China and Japan, his changed perceptions of literature and of the writer's role, and his long mental evolution from traditional culture through science to literature.

487 ———. "Literature on the Eve of Revolution: Reflections on Lu Xun's [Lu Hsün] Leftist Years 1927-1936." *Modern China*, 2 (1976), 277-326.
A detailed analysis of Lu Hsün's perception of literature and revolution, his interest in Soviet literature, and his concern for young leftist writers. The emphasis is on Lu Hsün's agonies and contradictions as a leader of the leftist writers.

488 LIN, YUTANG, tr. "The Epigrams of Lusin [Lu Hsün]." In Lin Yutang, ed., *The Wisdom of China and India*. New York: Modern Library, 1942, pp. 1083-1090.

A collection of thirty-five short passages selected from Lu Hsün's writings. Lin's introduction is a good antidote to all the lavish praises that have been heaped upon Lu Hsün since his death. Lu Hsün himself once wrote: "By the time a great man becomes fossilized and is worshipped as great, he is already a puppet."

489 LU HSUN. *Dawn Blossoms Plucked at Dusk*. Peking: Foreign Languages Press, 1976.

A full translation of Lu Hsün's ten reminiscences and satirical essays, all critical of various aspects of the old society. Helpful for understanding his fiction.

490 LU HSUN. *Wild Grass*. Peking: Foreign Languages Press, 1974.

Translation of a collection of twenty-three of Lu Hsün's most haunting and soul-searching prose poems. Useful for understanding the darker side of Lu Hsün. A fertile ground for metaphysical and psychoanalytic critics.

491 "Lu Hsün." In Howard L. Boorman and Richard C. Howard, eds. *Biographical Dictionary of Republican China*. New York: Columbia University Press, 1967-1971, I, pp. 416-424; IV, pp. 168-171.

A brief account of Lu Hsün's life and major works.

492 LYELL, WILLIAM A. *Lu Hsün's Vision of Reality*. Berkeley: University of California Press, 1976.

An extensive study of Lu Hsün and his fiction. The first half of the book discusses Lu Hsün's life and the historical background; the second half, his short stories. The tenth chapter, entitled "A Bestiary of Lu Hsün's Fictionalized World," is a detailed analysis of Lu Hsün's fiction through the characters in his fictionalized world: intellectuals of various sorts; women; people in service occupations, such as rickshaw pullers and boatmen; rebels and madmen; and one peasant. The book is designed primarily "to introduce the author and his stories to the general public."

493 MILLS, HARRIET C. "Lu Xun [Lu Hsün]: Literature and Revolution— from Mara to Marx." In Merle Goldman, ed. *Modern Chinese Literature in the May Fourth Era*. Cambridge: Harvard University Press, 1977, pp. 189-220.

A detailed study of the evolutionary stages of Lu Hsün's thought from withdrawal to active participation in politics, as reflected in the following essays by Lu Hsün: "The Making of the Man," "The New Republic and *New Youth*," "The Road to Involvement," "Preparation for Radicalism," "The Turn to the Left," "The League of Left-Wing Writers," and "Anger and Defiance."

494 ———. "Lu Hsün: 1927-1936, The Years on the Left." Ph.D. Dissertation. New York: Columbia University, 1963.

This study focuses on Lu Hsün's later years (1927-1936). It describes his search for hope, his conversion to Marxism, and his conflict with the League of Left-Wing Writers. Also discussed are "what Lu Hsün meant to his contemporaries," and what his real impact was during those years of literary activity.

495 ———. "Lu Hsün and the Communist Party." *CQ*, no. 4 (Oct./Dec., 1960), 17-27.

An analysis of Lu Hsün's ambiguous relationship with the Communist Party in the last years of his life.

496 PICKOWICZ, PAUL G. "Lu Xun [Lu Hsün] through the Eyes of Qu Qiu-bai [Ch'ü Ch'iu-pai]: New Perspectives on Chinese Marxist Literary Polemics of the 1930's." *Modern China*, 2 (1976), 327-368.

This article sheds much light on the close relationship between Lu Hsün and Ch'ü Ch'iu-pai, the two leftist literary leaders of the 1930s. Ch'ü had compiled an anthology of Lu Hsün's essays with a long introduction in appreciation of Lu Hsün's intellectual contribution to the Chinese revolution from a Marxist point of view and in defense of Lu Hsün's "pessimism."

497 PRŮŠEK, JAROSLAV. "Lu hsün's 'Huai-chiu': A Precursor of Modern Chinese Literature." *HJAS*, 29 (1969), 169-176.

A wide-ranging discussion of the transition from "traditional" to "modern" Chinese literature. Citing Lu Hsün's short story "Remembering the Past" (*"Huai chiu"*), written in 1911 in the literary language, as a case in point the author concludes that the function of plot has been greatly weakened in modern Chinese fiction when compared to its use in traditional fiction.

498 ——— and BERTA KREBSOVA. "Lu Hsün." In Jaroslav Průšek, ed. *Dictionary of Oriental Literatures*. London: George Allen and Unwin, 1974; New York: Basic Books, 1974, I, pp. 105-107.

A succinct account of Lu Hsün's life, work and influence.

499 SCHULTZ, WILLIAM. "Lu Hsün: The Creative Years." Ph.D. Dissertation. Seattle: University of Washington, 1955

A detailed biographical study of Lu Hsün's life up to 1926 and of four collections of his literary works: two collections of short stories, *Call to Arms* (*Na-han*) and *Hesitation* (*P'ang-huang*); a collection of autobiographical sketches, *Morning Flowers Picked in the Evening* (*Chao-hua hsi-shou*); and a collection of prose poems, *Wild Grass* (*Yeh-ts'ao*). Lu Hsün's role as an innovator and a major literary influence is emphasized.

500 SEMANOV, V. I. *Lu Hsün and His Predecessors*. Tr. by Charles J. Alber. White Plains, N.Y.: M. E. Sharpe, 1980.

A study of Lu Hsün and his predecessors by a prominent Russian scholar.

501 ———. "Lu Hsün's Views on European Literature." *Asia in Soviet Studies*. Moscow: Nauka Publishing House, 1969, pp. 311-334.

An examination of Lu Hsün's evaluation of some popular European writers during the 1920s and '30s. Semanov discerns three stages in Lu Hsün's attitude toward European literature: the pre-1920 phase, the period from 1920 to 1930, and the post-1930 phase. Semanov comments that Lu Hsün well understood the "contradiction present in creative literary works."

502 SUN, SHIRLEY HSIAO-LING. "Lu Hsün and the Chinese Woodcut Movement: 1929-1936." Ph.D. Dissertation. Stanford: Stanford University, 1974.

The author stresses that Lu Hsün is known as the "Father of the Modern Chinese Woodcut Movement," that his interest in woodcuts is linked to his general aesthetic preference for folk tales and folk arts, and that his later Marxist orientation strengthened his attachment to the popular arts.

503 WANG, CHI-CHEN. "Lusin [Lu Hsün]: A Chronological Record, 1881-1936." *China Institute Bulletin*, 3 (1939), 99-125.

A detailed chronological listing of Lu Hsün's political and literary activities.

504 WEAKLAND, JOHN H. "Lusin's [Lu Hsün] 'Ah Q': A Rejected Image of Chinese Character." *Pacific Spectator*, 10 (1956), 137-146.

A discussion of Ah Q, the antihero of Lu Hsün's "The True Story of Ah Q," as representing the negative side of the Chinese character.

505 WONG, YOON-WAH. "The Influence of Western Literature on China's First Modern Story." *Nanyang University Journal*, 8/9 (1974/1975), 144-156.

Traces the influence of Gogol's "The Diary of a Madman," Garshin's "The Scarlet Flower," and Nietzsche's *Thus Spake Zarathustra* on Lu Hsün's first short story, "Diary of a Madman."

VII

Mao Tun (Shen Yen-ping), 1896-

Mao Tun, born in 1896, was a founding member of the Literary Association and the editor of *The Short Story Monthly* in the 1920s. He began writing fiction in 1927 and produced a number of well-written novels and short stories, some of which "record with documentary thoroughness the life of the student revolutionary, the plight of the native industrialist . . . and similar social and economic themes from the world between the wars." Since 1949 he has limited himself to politics and literary criticism.

To the Western reader, Mao Tun is best known for his widely anthologized short story, "Spring Silkworms." Apart from his most ambitious novel, *Midnight*, translated by Meng-hsiung Hsü, none of his other novels has been translated into English. A representative collection of his short stories is *Spring Silkworms and Other Stories*, translated by Sidney Shapiro.

The East European scholar Marián Gálik has completed several studies of Mao Tun's literary theory and criticism. Others, such as Yü-shih Chen, John Berninghausen, and Vincent Y. C. Shih, have also written important articles on this prolific writer.

Translations

506   BERNINGHAUSEN, JOHN, tr. "In Front of the Pawnshop." *BCAS*, 8 (1976), 59-62.
       A moving story about the suffering of the Chinese peasant, stressing the evils and social injustices existing in China.

507   CHAI, CH'U and WINBERG CHAI, trs. "Spring Silkworms." In Ch'u Chai and Winberg Chai, trs. and eds. *A Treasury of Chinese Literature*. New York: Appleton-Century, 1965, pp. 289-313. Shapiro, Sidney, tr. "Spring Silkworms." In Sidney Shapiro, tr. *Spring Silkworms and Other Stories*. Peking: Foreign Languages Press, 1956, pp. 9-38; reprinted with slight revisions in *ChL*, no. 7 (July, 1962), pp. 23-46. "Spring Silkworms." In Harold Isaacs, ed. *Straw Sandals*. Cambridge: M.I.T. Press, 1974, pp. 274-301. Wang, Chi-chen, tr. "Spring Silkworms." In

190/BIBLIOGRAPHIES

Chi-chen Wang, tr. *Contemporary Chinese Stories*. New York: Columbia University Press, 1944, pp. 143-158; reprinted in James E. Miller, et al., eds. *Literature of the Eastern World*. Glenview, Ill.: Scott, Foresman, 1970, pp. 90-102; reprinted in supplemented form in Cyril Birch, ed. *Anthology of Chinese Literature*. New York: Grove Press, 1965-1972, II, pp. 321-338.

The best-known and most translated of Mao Tun's short stories, "Spring Silkworms" ("*Ch'un-ts'an*"), is a moving story about the peasant Old T'ung-pao whose industry, persistence, and meticulous care in tending his silkworms are rewarded only by more hardships and mounting debts. The story "shows the bankruptcy of the peasantry under the dual pressures of imperial aggression and traditional usury."

508 HANRAHAN, GENE, tr. "The Confused Mr. Chao." In Gene Hanrahan, ed. *50 Great Oriental Stories*. New York: Bantam Books, 1965, pp. 94-102. Shapiro, Sidney, tr. "The Bewilderment of Mr. Chao." In Sidney Shapiro, tr. *Spring Silkworms and Other Stories*. Peking: Foreign Languages Press, 1956, pp. 218-227.

"The Confused Mr. Chao" ("*Chao hsien-sheng hsiang pu t'ung*") is the portrait of a Mr. Chao, a financial "operator" at the stock exchange who patiently awaits the crash of the market.

509 HSU, MENG-HSIUNG and A. C. BARNES, trs. *Midnight*. Peking: Foreign Languages Press, 1957; Washington: Center for Chinese Research Materials, Association of Research Libraries, 1970; Hong Kong: C & W Publishing Co., 1976.

Midnight (*Tzu-yeh*) is generally regarded as one of modern China's most outstanding novels because of its panoramic chronicling of the social, economic, and political events of China during the 1930s. The setting is bustling Shanghai, where Wu Sun-fu, a powerful industrialist and an advocate of national capitalism, meets his match in Chao Po-t'ao, a financier supported by foreign capital. In the final scene, the two pit their financial power against each other at the stock exchange. It is a complex novel with a welter of subplots of romance, Communist uprisings, and industrial strikes.

510 ISAACS, HAROLD R., ed. *Straw Sandals: Chinese Short Stories, 1918-1933*. Cambridge: M.I.T. Press, 1974.

Contains three short stories by Mao Tun: "Autumn Harvest," "Spring Silkworms," and "Comedy" ("*Hsi-chü*"). For further information on the book, *see* no. 320.

511 JENNER, W. J. F., tr. "On the Boat." In W. J. F. Jenner, ed. *Modern Chinese Stories*. London: Oxford University Press, 1970, pp. 75-84.

"On the Boat" ("*Ch'uan-shang*") vividly describes the atmosphere of frustration in Szechuan province, the southwestern stronghold of the Nationalist Government during World War II.

512 SHAPIRO, SIDNEY, tr. "Autumn Harvest." In Sidney Shapiro, tr. *Spring Silkworms and Other Stories*. Peking: Foreign Languages Press, 1956, pp. 39-73. "Autumn Harvest." In Harold Isaacs, ed. *Straw Sandals*. Cambridge: M.I.T. Press, 1974, pp. 302-326.

"Autumn Harvest" (*"Ch'iu-shou"*) deals with the hard life of the peasant Old T'ung-pao, whose faith in moral rectitude and hard work can no longer sustain him against mounting debts and manipulations by unethical rice merchants. The story ends with his failure and grave illness.

513 ———. *Spring Silkworms and Other Stories*. Peking: Foreign Languages Press, 1956; Washington: Center for Chinese Research Materials, Association of Research Libraries, 1970; Cambridge: Cheng and Tsui Co., 1975.

This anthology contains thirteen stories by Mao Tun, written between 1932 and 1943, on the changes in Chinese society from 1927 to 1936. "Spring Silkworms," the most famous in the collection, together with "Autumn Harvest" and "Winter Ruin" (*"Ts'an-tung"*), forms a trilogy which revolves around the weatherbeaten peasant Old T'ung-pao and his family. They meet one defeat after another until the old man is finally driven to his grave. The other ten stories ("Second Generation," "Epitome," "A True Chinese Patriot," "The Shop of the Lin Family," "Big Nose," "Great Marsh District" (also in *New Orient*, Oct., 1962, pp. 150-152), "First Morning at the Office," "Winter Ruin," "Frustration," and "Wartime") describe the impact of Japanese imperialism, a new breed of Chinese capitalists, and other pertinent social issues.

514 SNOW, EDGAR, ed. *Living China*. London: George G. Harrap and Co., 1936.

Contains two short stories by Mao Tun: "Suicide" (*"Tzu-sha"*) and "Mud" (*"Ni-ning"*). "Suicide" is also reprinted in Jörgensen (Chao Ching-shen), ed. *Contemporary Chinese Short Stories*. Shanghai: Pei-hsin shu-chü, 1946, I, pp. 32-67. For more information on Snow's *Living China*, see no. 332.

515 ——— and HSIAO CH'IEN, trs. "Mud." In Edgar Snow, ed. *Living China*. London: George G. Harrap and Co., 1936, pp. 142-151; reprinted as "War and Peace Come to the Village." In Daniel Milton zand William Clifford, eds. *A Treasury of Modern Asian Stories*. New York: New American Library, 1961, pp. 206-213.

"Mud" (*"Ni-ning"*) is a short story set in the chaotic times of the Northern Expedition of the Kuomintang (1926-1927). The comings and goings of soldiers from opposing parties in a small village cause untold suffering and confusion to the villagers.

516 WANG, CHI-CHEN, tr. *Contemporary Chinese Stories*. New York: Columbia University Press, 1944; reprint ed. Westport, Conn.: Greenwood Press, 1976.

Contains translations of two stories by Mao Tun: "Spring Silkworms" and "A True Chinese." For further information on the collection, see no. 333.

517 ———. "Heaven Has Eyes." In Chi-chen Wang, tr. *Stories of China at War.* New York: Columbia University Press, 1947, pp. 27-38. Also in *Mademoiselle* (March, 1945), 134-135, 222-227.

"Heaven Has Eyes" ("*Pao-shih*") depicts the life of a man named Chang Wen-an whose generosity brings rich rewards.

518 YEH, CHUN-CHAN, tr. *Three Seasons, and Other Stories.* London: Staples Press, n.d. [1946?].

Contains three stories by Mao Tun: "Spring Silkworms," "Autumn Harvest," and "Winter Ruin." For further information on this anthology *see* no. 337.

Studies

519 BERNARD, SUZANNE. "An interview with Mao Tun." *ChL*, no. 2 (Feb., 1979), pp. 62-79; no. 3 (March, 1979), pp. 92-95.

A summary of an interview with Mao Tun, who discussed his own works, including *Midnight*, and other subjects.

519a BERNINGHAUSEN, JOHN. "The Central Contradiction in Mao Dun's [Mao Tun] Earliest Fiction." In Merle Goldman, ed. *Modern Chinese Literature in the May Fourth Era.* Cambridge: Harvard University Press, 1977, pp. 233-259.

The author states that Mao Tun's early fictional protagonists are torn apart by their interest in "making revolution" and their search for some personal fulfillment independent of "the fate of a social class or the nation as a whole" and that this contradiction is symbolic of Mao Tun's own: the conflict between idealism and materialism.

520 ———. "Mao Dun's Fiction, 1927-1936: The Standpoint and Style of His Realism." Ph.D. Dissertation. Stanford: Stanford University, 1979.

This dissertation covers all the novels and short stories written by Mao Tun during the period from 1927 to 1936 and analyzes their literary features from a critical perspective in which literary form and structure are explored in relation to the ideological/moral vision they express.

521 BRANDAUER, FREDERICK P. "Selected Works of Lao She and Mao Tun and Their Relevance for Christian Theology." *Ching Feng*, 11, no. 2 (1968), 25-43.

A study of the relevance of the selected works of Lao She and Mao Tun for Christian theology.

522 CHEN, YU-SHIH, tr. "From Guling [Kuling] to Tokyo." *BCAS*, 8 (Jan./Mar. 1976), 38-44.

A lengthy essay (written in 1928) in which Mao Tun answers critics of his trilogy *Eclipse* (*Shih*). He provides the background of its creation and explains his own intention. At the same time, he touches on the problems of revolutionary literature. He claims that these works are only "portraits of the times" and not "revolutionary novels."

523 ———. "Mao Dun [Mao Tun] and the Use of Political Allegory in Fiction: A Case Study of His 'Autumn in Kuling.'" In Merle Goldman, ed. *Modern Chinese Literature in the May Fourth Era.* Cambridge: Harvard University Press, 1977, pp. 261-280.

The author demonstrates in her study that "Autumn in Kuling" ("*Ku-ling chih ch'iu*") is really about the Nanchang Uprising in the summer of 1927, that the story "reflects the spirit of a revolutionary epoch and is concerned with the life and destiny of more than just a few individuals," and that it "gives convincing evidence of Mao Dun's early experimentation with political allegory couched in realistic terms."

524 ———. "Mao Tun and *The Wild Roses*: A Study of the Psychology of Revolutionary Commitment." *CQ*, no. 78 (June, 1979), 291-323.

After completing his trilogy *Eclipse* in 1928, Mao Tun, physically and mentally exhausted, went to Japan, where he stayed until the spring of 1930, and wrote a collection of five stories known as *The Wild Roses*. This article is a study of the psychology of revolutionary commitment as reflected in these stories.

525 GÁLIK, MARIÁN. "A Comment on Two Collections of Mao Tun's Works." *ArOr*, 33 (1965), 614-638.

Critical comments on two important collections of Mao Tun's works published in the early 1960s: a ten-volume collection of the literary works of Mao Tun (*Mao Tun wen-chi*) published in Peking and a four-volume collection of Mao Tun's critical works (*Mao Tun p'ing-lun chi*) published in Tokyo. Mao Tun has written a total of twelve novels and approximately fifty short stories; the number of his critical and other essays is as yet untabulated.

526 ———. "A Comment on Two Studies Written on the Works of Mao Tun." *AAS*, 1 (1965), 81-103.

A lengthy critical review of two studies of Mao Tun's works.

527 ———. "From Chuang-tzu to Lenin: Mao Tun's Intellectual Development." *AAS*, 3 (1967), 98-110.

A paper delivered at the XVIIth Congress of Chinese Studies in 1965, it deals with Mao Tun's intellectual development from the time of the 1911 Revolution to his conversion to Marxist-Leninist ideology.

528 ———. *Mao Tun and Modern Chinese Literary Criticism.* Wiesbaden: Franz Steiner Verlag, 1969.

An extensive study of Mao Tun's literary and theoretical works and the development of his literary views from 1919 to 1936. As a young man of twenty-four in 1919, Mao Tun was already well versed in Western literature and had written critical articles on George Bernard Shaw and Leo Tolstoy. While writing many outstanding novels and short stories during the late 1920s and '30s, he continued his study and evaluation of Western literature. This book is a study not only of a Chinese literary critic but also of the relationship between Chinese and European literatures.

529 ———. "The Names and Pseudonyms Used by Mao Tun." *ArOr*, 31 (1968), 80-108.

A number of modern Chinese writers, for various reasons, have used many pseudonyms. (Lu Hsün, for example, used approximately 120.) The author finds that Mao Tun used approximately 60 pseudonyms at various stages during his literary career.

530 ———. "Studies in Modern Chinese Literary Criticism: I. Mao Tun, 1919-1920." *AAS*, 3 (1967), 113-140.

A study of Mao Tun's earliest attempts at literary criticism: his critical articles on George Bernard Shaw and Leo Tolstoy. It also includes an examination of Mao Tun's essay, "Tolstoy and Present-Day Russia."

531 ———. "Studies in Modern Chinese Literary Criticism: II. Mao Tun on Men of Letters, Character and Functions of Literature (1921-1922)." *AAS*, 4 (1968), 30-43.

A detailed analysis of Mao Tun's essay, "The Relationship of Literature to Man and the Old Chinese Misconception of the Writer's Position," which was written in 1921. The essay urges Chinese men of letters to assume new roles.

532 HSIA, C. T. "Mao Tun (1896-   )." In C. T. Hsia *A History of Modern Chinese Fiction*. 2nd ed. New Haven: Yale University Press, 1971, pp. 140-164, 350-359.

A critical discussion of six of Mao Tun's major novels: *Eclipse* (*Shih*), *Rainbow* (*Hung*), *The Twilight* (*Tzu-yeh*, often translated as *Midnight*), *Story of the First Stage of the War* (*Ti-i chieh-tuan ti ku-shih*), *Putrefaction* (*Fu-shih*), and *Maple Leaves as Red as February Flowers* (*Shuang-yeh hung-ssu erh-yüeh hua*), in addition to a number of short stories.

533 LAU, JOSEPH S. M. "Naturalism in Modern Chinese Fiction." *LEW*, 12 (1968), 149-158.

A critique of Mao Tun's *Midnight* (1933) from the Western perspective of naturalism even though the novel barely fits the definition.

534 McDOUGALL, BONNIE S. "The Search for Synthesis: T'ien Han and Mao Tun in 1920." In A. R. Davis, ed. *Search for Identity: Modern Literature and the Creative Arts in Asia*. Sydney: Angus and Robertson, 1974, pp. 225-254.

A study of the playwright T'ien Han and the novelist Mao Tun in 1920.

535 "Mao Tun." In Howard L. Boorman and Richard C. Howard, eds., *Biographical Dictionary of Republican China*. New York: Columbia University Press, 1967-1971, III, pp. 110-115; IV, pp. 321-323.

A brief summary of Mao Tun's life and important works.

536 "Mao Tun." In Donald Walker Klein and Anne B. Clark, eds. *Biographic Dictionary of Chinese Communism, 1921-1965.* Cambridge: Harvard University Press, 1971, II, pp. 759-764.
A short biographical account of Mao Tun together with a listing of his major works.

537 PRŮŠEK, JAROSLAV. "Mao Tun." In Jaroslav Průšek, ed. *Dictionary of Oriental Literatures.* London: George Allen and Unwin, 1974; New York: Basic Books, 1974, I, pp. 111-112.
A brief account of Mao Tun's life and works.

538 ———. *Three Sketches of Chinese Literature.*
For annotations and bibliographic information, *see* no. 291.

539 SHIH, VINCENT Y. C. "Mao Tun: The Critic." *CQ,* no. 19 (July/Sept., 1964), 84-98; no. 20 (Oct./Dec., 1964), 128-162.
An examination of the three stages in Mao Tun's career as a literary critic: as a theorist (roughly 1918-1925); as a polemicist in defense of his novels (1927-1929); as a vacillating leftist critic during 1925-1949; and as a doctrinaire Marxist critic since 1949. The author maintains that Mao Tun's role as a doctrinaire critic does not free him from the inherent conflict between Mao Tun the artist and Mao Tun the literary spokesman of the Communist Party.

540 YANG, RICHARD H. " *Midnight*: Mao Tun's Political Novel." *RNL,* 4 (Spring, 1975), 60-75.
A close reading of Mao Tun's most famous novel *Midnight*. The author discusses not only the novel's major characters and themes but also its political background.

VIII
Pa Chin (Li Fei-kan), 1904-

Born in Ch'eng-tu, Szechuan in 1904, Pa Chin was a professed anarchist in his younger years. Extremely productive, he wrote many novels and short stories in the 1930s and '40s. Criticized and purged during the Cultural Revolution, he has recently become active again on the literary scene.

Pa Chin is one of the most popular fiction writers of modern China. Among the many novels he wrote, only his *Family* and *Cold Nights* have been translated into English. There is one book-length study of Pa Chin's intellectual development by Olga Lang; another study, by Nathan Mao, emphasizing Pa Chin's achievements as a writer, has been published. Essays by C. T. Hsia, Oldrich Král, and Teresa Lechowska are also useful reference sources.

Translations

541   "*Autumn in Spring.*" *ChL,* no. 7 (July, 1979), pp. 3-37; no. 8 (Aug., 1979), pp. 31-58.
   A translation of Pa Chin's short novel, *Ch'un-t'ien li ti ch'iu-t'ien* (*Autumn in Spring*), which, written in 1932, is among his less successful works.

542   CHANG, TANG, tr. "Perseverance." *ChL,* no. 6 (June, 1963), pp. 47-62.
   "*Chien-ch'iang chan-shih*" ("Perseverance") depicts the heroic exploits of a wounded Chinese soldier in the Korean war.

543   "The Heart of a Slave." *ChL,* no. 8 (Aug., 1979), pp. 16-30.
   A translation of one of Pa Chin's less-known stories, written in 1931.

544   *Living Amongst Heroes*. Peking: Foreign Languages Press, 1954.
   Includes "A Story of Brotherly Love" ("*Ai ti ku-shih*"), a short story; essays and other pieces of reportage related to the Korean War. Most pieces are journalistic reports rather than creative fiction.

544a MAO, NATHAN K., tr. "The General." In Joseph S. M. Lau, Leo Ou-fan Lee, and C. T. Hsia, eds. *Modern Chinese Stories and Novellas, 1918-1948*. New York: Columbia University Press, forthcoming.

"*Chiang-chün*" is a story emphasizing the theme of exile. Pa Chin makes the reader feel the anguish of exile through the experience of a White Russian officer living in China, who tries not to lose his identity in a world that will always be alien to him.

545 MAO, NATHAN K. and TS'UN-YAN, LIU, trs. *Cold Nights*. Seattle: University of Washington Press, 1979; Hong Kong: Chinese University of Hong Kong Press, 1979.

One of the most mature of Pa Chin's novels, *Han-yeh* (*Cold Nights*) is about the conflicts among three protagonists in a quasitraditional household: Wang Wen-hsüan, a weak, unassertive husband; Shu-sheng, his young-looking wife who is seeking a better life; and Mrs. Wang, Wen-hsüan's mother. The traditional rivalry between the mother and the daughter-in-law forms the nucleus of the plot. The tragic story takes place in 1944, shortly before the end of the Sino-Japanese War. It is Pa Chin's best novel in "the mode of love."

546 SHAPIRO, SIDNEY, tr. *The Family*. Peking: Foreign Languages Press, 1958, 1964. Reprinted with supplements, prefaces, and an introduction by Olga Lang. Garden City, N.Y.: Doubleday, 1972.

A very popular novel of the 1930s and '40s, *Chia* (*The Family*), deals with the struggles of three Kao brothers against the oppressive Kao clan headed by an authoritarian grandfather in Ch'eng-tu. Chüeh-hsin, the oldest grandson, being good-natured, submits totally to traditional family pressures; Chüeh-min, the second grandson and a compromiser, succeeds somewhat in resisting the same family pressures; Chüeh-hui, the youngest grandson, is a rebel who eventually leaves home for further study and revolutionary work in Shanghai. Completed in 1933, *The Family* was followed by *Spring* (*Ch'un*) (1938) and *Autumn* (*Ch'iu*) (1940). The three constitute the *Turbulent Stream* (*Chi-liu*) trilogy.

547 ———. "A Moonlit Night." *ChL*, no. 5 (May, 1962), pp. 43-50.

"*Yüeh-yeh*" ("A Moonlit Night") depicts a peasant's tragic struggle against his landlord.

548 TANG, SHENG, tr. "When the Snow Melted." *ChL*, no. 5 (May, 1962), pp. 50-63.

"*Hua-hsüeh ti jih-tzu*" ("When the Snow Melted") describes the marital strife between a Chinese couple living in France and is noted for its psychological realism. One of the very best short stories by Pa Chin.

549 T'UNG, TSO, tr. "Dog." *Voice of China*, 1, no. 1 (March 15, 1938), 18-20; revised version in Edgar Snow, ed. *Living China*. London: George G. Harrap and Co., 1936, pp. 174-180.

A short piece of "biting" satire, "*Kou*" ("Dog") symbolically presents the lowly status of every Chinese living in his own country, which is controlled by foreigners. One of Pa Chin's most famous short stories, it has "the simplicity of a parable."

550   WANG, CHI-CHEN, tr. "The Puppet Dead." In Chi-chen Wang, tr. *Contemporary Chinese Stories.* New York: Columbia University Press, 1944, pp. 80-94.
   This is an excerpt from Chapter 34 of the novel *The Family*. For more information on the novel, *see* no. 333.

551   WEN, I, ed. *Short Stories by Pa Chin.* Shanghai: Chung-ying ch'u-pan she, 1941.
   This bilingual anthology includes translations of several of Pa Chin's early short stories, such as "Revenge" (*"Fu-ch'ou"*) and "First Love" (*"Ch'u-lien"*).

Studies

552   CHEN, TAN-CHEN. "Pa Chin the Novelist." *ChL,* no. 6 (1963), pp. 84-92.
   Based on an interview with Pa Chin, this essay describes his life and works before and after 1949.

553   HSIA, C. T. "Pa Chin." In C. T. Hsia, *A History of Modern Chinese Fiction.* 2nd ed. New Haven: Yale University Press, 1971, pp. 237-256, 375-388.
   The author discusses Pa Chin's theory of art, his popularity among the Chinese youth, his major novels, and a number of his short stories. He singles out *Cold Nights* and *Autumn* for praise but criticizes most of his other novels, especially their sentimental excesses.

554   KRAL, OLDŘICH. "Pa Chin's Novel *The Family*." In Jaroslav Průšek, ed. *Studies in Modern Chinese Literature.* Berlin: Akademie-Verlag, 1964, pp. 98-112.
   An examination of the "subjective sources and objective aims" of Pa Chin's *The Family,* which not only consists of many autobiographical elements but also speaks for Pa Chin's generation of youth. The novel reveals Pa Chin's attack on the old morality and the feudal family system.

555   LANG, OLGA. *Pa Chin and His Writings: Chinese Youth between Two Revolutions.* Cambridge: Harvard University Press, 1967.
   Derived from the author's dissertation (Columbia University, 1962), this sensitive biographical study of Pa Chin reveals that the source of Pa Chin's popularity is his ability to articulate the frustrations, hopes, and aspirations of the young people of his generation. The author argues that Pa Chin "wrote for youth about youth." Pa Chin's literary works, however, are treated mainly as sources for social and intellectual history, rather than as works of art. Much information on Pa Chin's early life is provided, but Pa Chin's career since 1949 is only briefly treated in the epilogue.

556   LECHOWSKA, TERESA. "In Search of a New Ideal: The Metamorphoses of Pa Chin's Model Heroes." *ArOr,* 42 (1974), 310-322.
   A study of the ideals of some of Pa Chin's heroes, whose idealism undergoes continuous change as they move from oppression to freedom.

557 ———. "Pa Chin." In Jaroslav Průšek, ed. *Dictionary of Oriental Literatures*. London: George Allen and Unwin, 1974; New York: Basic Books, 1974, I, pp. 135-136.
   A brief account of Pa Chin's life and work.

558 MAO, NATHAN K. *Pa Chin*. Boston: Twayne Publishers, 1978.
   A biographical-critical study of Pa Chin, this book consists of a biographical sketch and an analysis of his early novels and short stories, including the *Turbulent Stream (Chi-liu)* trilogy, and his works written during the war years, such as *Leisure Garden (Ch'i-yüan)* and *Cold Nights (Han-yeh)*.

559 ———. "Pa Chin's Journey in Sentiment: From Hope to Despair." *JCLTA*, 11 (May, 1976), 131-137.
   After examining Pa Chin's major works written during his most productive period, from the late 1920s to the early '40s, the author concludes that Pa Chin's journey in sentiment not only reflects the social and political changes within China during that period but also his own genuine feelings toward a people and a country that he deeply loves.

560 PA CHIN. "How I Wrote the Novel *Family*." *China Reconstructs*, 7, no. 1 (Jan., 1958), 15-17.
   A brief but interesting explanation by the author of how he wrote his novel *The Family*.

561 ———. "On *Autumn in Spring*." *ChL*, no. 7 (July, 1979), pp. 38-44.
   This article tells how Pa Chin wrote his *Autumn in Spring*.

562 "Pa Chin." In Howard L. Boorman and Richard C. Howard, eds. *Biographical Dictionary of Republican China*. New York: Columbia University Press, 1967-1971, II, pp. 297-299; IV, pp. 249-252.
   A summary of Pa Chin's life and a brief account of his major works.

563 SHIH, VINCENT Y. C. "Enthusiast and Escapist: Writers of the Older Generation."
   For annotations and bibliographic information, *see* no. 742.

564 YANG, YI. "A Man Who Conquered Fate—An Interview with Ba Jin [Pa Chin]." *ChL*, no. 8 (August, 1979), pp. 3-15.
   A summary of an interview with Pa Chin, who discusses his life, work, and views on literature.

565 YEH, SHANG-LAN MUI, tr. "To a Cousin—Preface to the 10th Edition of *Family*." *Renditions*, no. 4, (Spring, 1975), pp. 73-82.
   A previously unpublished preface by Pa Chin written in 1937. An interesting account of his creative process.

IX
Shen Ts'ung-wen, 1902-

Born in a small border town in Hunan in 1902, Shen Ts'ung-wen served in the army and received little formal education. He went to Peking at the age of twenty and began his writing career there. He taught at several universities in the 1930s and '40s. In 1949 he was forced to give up his literary career and has since been doing research at the Palace Museum in Peking.

A prolific writer, Shen has written many stories about rural and urban life, military activities, and aboriginal tribes. He is well known for his "copious imagination and dedication to his craft." Shen, an accomplished fiction writer, has published no new works of fiction since 1949.

Fifteen of Shen Ts'ung-wen's stories are collected in Ching Ti and Robert Payne's *The Chinese Earth*, which also contains a translation of his *The Border Town*. Two of Shen's best stories are included in C. T. Hsia's *Twentieth-Century Chinese Stories*. In addition to a full-length study of Shen by Nieh Hua-ling, there are several Ph.D. dissertations on him.

Translations

566   CHAI, CH'U and WINBERG CHAI, trs. "Lung Chu." In Ch'u Chai and Winberg Chai, trs. and eds. *A Treasury of Chinese Literature*. New York: Appleton-Century, 1965, pp. 321-341.

         A clumsily told love story about a handsome Miao prince, Lung Chu, and his quest for a mate. Shen's description of Lung Chu is awkward and overdone. (A translation of this story also appears in Ching Ti and Robert Payne, *The Chinese Earth*, pp. 137-151. *See* no. 567.)

567   CHING, TI and ROBERT PAYNE, trs. *The Chinese Earth*. London: George Allen and Unwin, 1947.

         This anthology contains fifteen stories by Shen Ts'ung-wen: "The Husband," "The Lovers," "Under Cover of Darkness," "The White Kid," "The Yellow Chickens," "The Rainbow," "Lung Chu," "Pai Tzu," "Three Men and a Girl," "San-san," "The Fourteenth Moon," "The Lamp," "Under Moonlight," *The Frontier City*, also known as *The Border Town*, and "Ta Wang." This is a good representative collection of Shen Ts'ung-wen's fiction but much of Shen's earthy flavor is lost in the translation.

568   LEE, YI-HSIEH, tr. "Hsiao-hsiao." *THM*, 7 (Oct., 1938), 295-309.
    The story of an orphan girl's seduction by a farm worker, her subsequent pregnancy, and the birth of their son. C. T. Hsia compares her "animal purity" to that of Lena Grove in William Faulkner's *Light in August*.

569   MACDONALD, WILLIAM L., tr. "Bandit Chief." In Cyril Birch, ed. *Anthology of Chinese Literature*. New York: Grove Press, 1965-72, II, pp. 276-285.
    An episode from Shen Ts'ung-wen's autobiography about the execution of a reformed bandit by a military commander, under whom the bandit has served as a bodyguard. (A translation of this story also appears under the title "Ta Wang" in Ching Ti and Robert Payne. *The Chinese Earth*. pp.167-176. See no. 567.)

569a McDOUGALL, BONNIE and LEWIS S. ROBINSON, trs. *A Posthumous Son and Other Stories*.
    For annotations and bibliographic information, *see* no. 326a.

570   "Pai Tzu." In Edgar Snow, ed. *Living China*. London: George G. Harrap and Co., 1936, pp. 182-187. Reprinted as "A Sailor in Port." In Daniel Milton and William Clifford, eds. *A Treasury of Modern Asian Stories*. New York: New American Library, 1961, pp. 177-181.
    This story tells the romantic exploits of a hardy sailor. (A translation of this story also appears in Ching Ti and Robert Payne. *The Chinese Earth*. pp. 15-21. See no. 567.)

571   WANG, CHI-CHEN, tr. "Night March." In Chi-chen Wang, tr. *Contemporary Chinese Stories*. New York: Columbia University Press, 1944, pp. 95-107.
    "Night March" ("*Yeh*"), which is loose in structure, presents the haunting image of an old man and the sad story of his loneliness.

572   YANG, GLADYS, tr. "The Border Town." *ChL*, no. 10 (Oct., 1962), pp. 3-45; no. 11 (Nov., 1962), pp. 38-69.
    One of Shen's best short novels about the growing up of a country girl, Ts'ui-ts'ui, who lives with her aging grandfather in an idyllic setting, *Pien-ch'eng* (*The Border Town* or *The Frontier City*) has been widely read in China. (A translation of this novel also appears in Ching Ti and Robert Payne. *The Chinese Earth*. pp. 190-289, and in *THM*, 2 (1936), 87-107, 174-196, 271-299, 360-390, under the title *Green Jade and Green Jade*, tr. by Emily Hahn and Hsin Mo-lei.)

573   YIP, WAI-LIM and C. T. HSIA, trs. "Daytime." In C. T. Hsia, ed. *Twentieth-Century Chinese Stories* (New York: Columbia University Press, 1971, pp. 47-61.
    "*Pai-jih*" ("Daytime") vividly captures one afternoon in the life of a five-year old girl—her restless energy and her adventure with her playmate.

574 ———. "Quiet." In C. T. Hsia, ed. *Twentieth-Century Chinese Stories*. New York: Columbia University Press, 1971, pp. 36-46.

"*Ching*" ("Quiet") is a poignant story about the tragedy of one refugee family as expressed through a teenage girl and her five-year-old nephew. As the two watch the comings and goings of the people in town from a terrace, an oppressive quiet reigns. Meanwhile, unknown to the girl, her father, a military officer, has died in action.

Studies

575 HSIA, C. T. "Shen Ts'ung-wen (1902-)." In C. T. Hsia. *A History of Modern Chinese Fiction* 2nd ed. New Haven: Yale University Press, 1971, pp. 189-211, 359-366.

In these pages C. T. Hsia discusses Shen Ts'ung-wen as a writer of pastoral vision. To Hsia, Shen's seemingly effortless, casual sketching of landscape as well as of human emotions has given him a unique place among China's modern writers. Shen's rich imagination, dedication to his craft, preoccupation with China's social and moral ills, and his ability to probe the minds of his characters are also noted by Hsia, who hails him as one of the most distinguished modern Chinese fiction writers.

576 HSU, KAI-YU. "Shen Cung-wen [Shen Ts'ung-wen] (1902-)." In Kai-yu Hsu. *The Chinese Literary Scene: A Writer's Visit to the People's Republic*. New York: Random House, 1975, pp. 131-139.

A summary of Kai-yu Hsu's interview with Shen in 1973. Shen talks about his life in China, his research work at the Palace Museum, and the fate of other writers, such as Ting Ling and Pa Chin.

577 KINKLEY, JEFFREY C. "Shen Ts'ung-wen's Vision of Republican China." Ph.D. Dissertation. Cambridge: Harvard University, 1978.

A study of social history through the literary works of Shen Ts'ung-wen. The author points out that social customs, symbolic significance of Shen's native region, and his military experience reveal Shen's social philosophy and his less-than-optimistic vision of Republican China.

578 MACDONALD, WILLIAM L. "Characters and Themes in Shen Ts'ung-wen's Fiction." Ph.D. Dissertation. Seattle: University of Washington, 1970.

Shen Ts'ung-wen, according to this study, seems interested in four main types of character: the young man, basically a countryboy; the virginal adolescent girl on the brink of sexual awakening; the almost Wordsworthian old man; and the mature woman. His favorite themes, as suggested by the author, are love, death, humanity, and social change, and Shen is most successful in presenting a pastoral vision of life.

579 NIEH, HUA-LING. *Shen Ts'ung-wen*. New York: Twayne Publishers, 1972.

A survey of Shen Ts'ung-wen and some of his best works. The author states that since Shen has often been regarded as a "stylist" or an "impressionist" rather than a serious writer of ficition, her study focuses on themes, style, and imagery in his fiction. While the first seven chapters are biographical, chapter 8 is a critical study of characterization in seven of his stories, and chapter 9 is a study of the themes, imagery, and style in four other stories. The book places much emphasis on Shen's symbolism, use of irony, ideal character types, psychological portrayals, and shifting moods.

580 PRINCE, ANTHONY J. "The Life and Works of Shen Ts'ung-wen." Ph.D. Dissertation. Sydney: University of Sydney, 1968.
   One of the most comprehensive studies of Shen, this dissertation includes a detailed discussion of his family background, his life as a soldier, his writing and teaching career, and his major stories.

581 PRUŠEK, JAROSLAV. "Shen Ts'ung-wen." In Jaroslav Průšek, ed. *Dictionary of Oriental Literatures*. London: George Allen and Unwin, 1974; New York: Basic Books, 1974, I, pp. 152-153.
   A brief account of Shen's life and works.

582 "Shen Ts'ung-wen." In Howard L. Boorman and Richard C. Howard, eds. *Biographical Dictionary of Republican China*. New York: Columbia University Press, 1967-1971, III, pp. 107-109; IV, pp. 318-320.
   A brief account of Shen's life and works.

583 SHIH, VINCENT Y. C. "Enthusiast and Escapist: Writers of the Older Generation."
   For annotations and bibliographic information, *see* no. 742.

X

Ting Ling (Chiang Ping-chih), 1907-

A native of Hunan province, Ting Ling studied in Shanghai, began her career as a highly personal author, and eventually became a conscientious and accomplished proletarian writer. She joined the Communist Party in 1931, but her strong and independent ideas on art and literature led to conflicts with the Party in 1942 and 1955. In 1957, both she and her second husband Ch'en Ming were severely criticized and purged by the Party for their unorthodox views on literature and for their "anti-Party" activities. Recently rehabilitated, she is best known for her 1928 short story "The Diary of Miss Sophia" (translated by A. L. Chin and Joseph S. M. Lau) and her 1952 novel *The Sun Shines over the Sangkan River* (translated by Hsien-yi and Gladys Yang), which deals with land reform in China. Of the few studies of her, Yi-tsi M. Feuerwerker's essay and Gary J. Bjorge's dissertation deserve special attention.

Translations

584   BJORGE, GARY, tr. "A Day." *BCAS*, 8 (1976), 53-56.
      "A Day" ("*I-t'ien*"), a short story written by Ting Ling in 1930, depicts the dejected mental state of a young girl in Shanghai. Her psychological condition is a reflection of social ills. Though very much disturbed by what she sees and hears, she takes no action to correct any of the wrongs in society.

585   CHIN, A. L., tr. "The Diary of Miss Sophia." In Harold R. Isaacs, ed. *Straw Sandals*. Cambridge: M.I.T. Press, 1974, pp. 129-169; Lau, Joseph S. M., tr. "Sophia's Diary." *TR*, 5, no. 1 (April, 1974), 57-96.
      "*Sha-fei nü-shih ti jih-chi*" ("Sophia's Diary") is Ting Ling's famous confessional short story in diary form about a lovesick young woman. In her diary, the woman frankly records her sexual longings and desires and reveals her loneliness and impotent fury as a warm-hearted girl. When the story was first published in 1928, it received mixed reactions from readers, many of whom condemned it for its explicit references to sex. It is one of the best stories written by Ting Ling during her first phase (1926-1929).

586 KENNEDY, GEORGE A., tr. "One Certain Night." In Harold R. Isaacs, ed. *Straw Sandals*. Cambridge: M.I.T. Press, 1974, pp. 254-260.
> This translation of "*Mou yeh*" ("One Certain Night") was originally published in *China Forum* in Shanghai in 1932. The story describes the execution of a "warm-hearted poet, faithful and hardworking;" it is based on the execution of Ting Ling's first husband, Hu Yeh-p'in, by the Kuomintang in 1931.

587 KUNG, PUSHENG, tr. *When I Was in Sha Chuan and Other Stories*. Poona, India: Kutub Publishers, 1946.
> This anthology contains translations of "When I Was in Sha Chuan" ("*Wo tsai Hsia-ts'un ti shih-hou*"), "New Faith" ("*Hsin ti hsin-nien*"), "Ping-ping" ("*Ya-sui ti hsin*"), "The Journalist and the Soldier" ("*Ju-wu*"), and "Night" ("*Yeh*").

588 MENG, TSIANG, ed. *Our Children and Others*. (Annotated by Meng Tsiang.) Shanghai: Ying-wen hsüeh-hui, 1941.
> A bilingual English-Chinese edition, it contains two of Ting Ling's short stories: "Our Children" ("*Hai-tzu men*") and "The Flood" ("*Shui*"). Also included is an essay on Ting Ling entitled "Herald of a New China" by Meng Tsiang.

589 SNOW, EDGAR, ed. *Living China*. New York: John Day Co., 1937; Westport, Conn.: Hyperion Press, 1973, pp. 154-164; 165-172.
> This book contains two stories by Ting Ling: "Flood" ("*Shui*") and "News" ("*Hsiao-hsi*").

590 VACCA, SUSAN M., tr. "In the Hospital." *Renditions*, no. 8 (Aut., 1977), pp. 123-135.
> An interesting story about Communist activities written in 1942.

591 YANG, HSIEN-I and GLADYS YANG, trs. *The Sun Shines over the Sangkan River*. Peking: Foreign Languages Press, 1954.
> *T'ai-yang chao tsai Sang-kan-ho shang* (*The Sun Shines over Sangkan River*) is Ting Ling's major novel; it won a Stalin Prize in 1951. Describing the events during the land reform in Nuanshui Village near Cholu, along the Sangkan River, the plot centers on the persecution of former landlords and the hatred of the villagers for one despotic landlord which culminates in his lynching. Mainly interested in the descriptions of land reform, Ting Ling pays little attention to psychological subtleties. Consequently, the plot is mechanical, the characters are puppetlike, and the novel is somewhat boring to read.

Studies

592 ANDERSON, COLENA M. "A Study of Two Modern Chinese Women: Ping Hsin and Ting Ling." Ph.D. Dissertation. Pomona: Claremont Graduate School and University Center, 1954.
> A comparative study of the similarities and differences in the careers of two Chinese women writers: Ping Hsin and Ting Ling.

593 BJORGE, GARY J. " 'Sophia's Diary': An Introduction." *TR*, 5, no. 1 (April, 1974), 97-110.
   A critical analysis of Ting Ling's short story "Sophia's Diary" (or "The Diary of Miss Sophia") in the context of modern Chinese literature.

594 ———. "Ting Ling's Early Years: Her Life and Literature through 1942." Ph.D. Dissertation. Madison: University of Wisconsin, 1977.
   A study of Ting Ling's early years from her birth in 1907 to the appearance of Mao Tse-tung's "Yenan Talks on Art and Literature" (*see* no. 737) in 1942. The first part of the dissertation is a biographical study of Ting Ling and the second examines her works of this early period.

594a CHANG, JUN-MEI. *Ting Ling, Her Life and Her Work*. Taipei: Institute of International Relations, 1978.
   Despite a typically political foreword, an inadequate bibliography, the lack of an updated account, and other problems, this book is of some use to the general reader.

595 FEUERWERKER, YI-TSI M. "The Changing Relationship between Literature and Life: Aspects of the Writer's Role in Ding Ling [Ting Ling]." In Merle Goldman, ed. *Modern Chinese Literature in the May Fourth Era*. Cambridge: Harvard University Press, 1977, pp. 281-307.
   This essay primarily examines the conflict within Ting Ling herself: how to reconcile "her acceptance of literature's assigned position in the overall revolutioary scheme with the need to uphold the idea of literature itself." In the 1950s, Ting Ling talked about "the transcendent possibilities of literature as a tradition, about the personal vision of life and truth communicated in an enduring form." This view was obviously contrary to the thinking of the Communist Party, which insisted that "literature should serve only the urgent needs of the present."

596 FOKKEMA, DOUWE W. "Ting Ling." In Jaroslav Průšek, ed. *Dictionary of Oriental Literatures*. London: George Allen and Unwin, 1974; New York: Basic Books, 1974, I, p. 173.
   A brief account of Ting Ling's life and her works.

597 "Ting Ling." In Howard L. Boorman and Richard C. Howard, eds. *Biographical Dictionary of Republican China*. New York: Columbia University Press, 1967-1971), III, pp. 272-276; IV, pp. 354-356.
   A biographical account of Ting Ling.

598 "Ting Ling." In Donald Walker Klein and Anne B. Clark, eds. *Biographical Dictionary of Chinese Communism, 1921-1965*. Cambridge: Harvard University Press, 1971, II, pp. 843-846.
   A biography of Ting Ling with emphasis on her later years as a Communist writer.

XI
Yü Ta-fu, 1896-1945

Born in 1896, Yü Ta-fu was educated in Japan and later founded, with others, the Creation Society. His earliest stories, including "Sinking," had an immediate impact on the contemporary audience. Their daring originality and frank revelation of sexual frustrations appealed to the younger audience but enraged the moralists, who found such revelations highly corruptive. He was executed by the Japanese police in Sumatra in 1945.

The highly introspective and subjective writings of Yü Ta-fu have attracted the attention of a few Chinese and Western scholars. His works, however, have not been extensively translated into English. Among those available in English translation are "Sinking" (translated by Joseph S. M. Lau and C. T. Hsia), and "One Intoxicating Evening of Spring Breeze" (translated by Ch'u Chai and Winberg Chai). Both well reflect his writing style. The Czech critic Anna Doležalová has done extensive work on Yü Ta-fu; her study *Yü Ta-fu: Specific Traits of His Literary Creation* is the only book-length study of Yü. Also deserving attention are studies by Leo Ou-fan Lee, Michael Egan, and Jaroslav Průšek.

Translations

599   CHAI, CH'U and WINBERG CHAI, trs. "One Intoxicating Evening of Spring Breeze." In Ch'u Chai and Winberg Chai, trs. and eds. *A Treasury of Chinese Literature*. New York: Appleton-Century, 1965, pp. 276-288; Kennedy, George A., tr. "One Spring Night." In Harold R. Isaacs, ed. *Straw Sandals*. Cambridge: M.I.T. Press, 1974, pp. 68-83; Tang, Sheng, tr. "Intoxicating Spring Nights." *ChL*, no. 3 (March, 1957), pp. 139-148.

   This story (*"Ch'un-feng ch'en-tsui ti wan-shang"*) describes a seemingly decadent hero, really a down-and-out writer, who lives in the same flat where a girl who works in a cigarette factory resides. The two soon get to know each other, but their relationship stops short of a sexual union.

600   CHANG, SU, tr. "Snowy Morning." *ChL*, no. 2 (Feb., 1962), pp. 70-84.
   "Wei-hsüeh ti tsao-ch'en" ("Snowy Morning") centers on the tragic death of a student whose personal unhappiness has caused him to become insane.

601 HUANG, SHOU-CHEN, tr. "A Humble Sacrifice." *ChL*, no. 3 (March, 1957), pp. 149-157.
   In *"Po-tien"* ("A Humble Sacrifice"), the author pays homage to a humble rickshaw puller who heroically sacrificed his own life, leaving a wife and two small children.

602 LAU, JOSEPH S. M. and C. T. HSIA, trs. "Sinking." In C. T. Hsia, ed. *Twentieth-Century Chinese Stories*. New York: Columbia University Press, 1971, pp. 3-33.
   The demoralization, degradation, and suicide of a young Chinese student in Japan are the subject of *"Ch'en-lun"* ("Sinking"). The story immediately aroused much attention when it was published in 1921 with its unabashedly autobiographical nature and its preoccupation with sexual fantasies.

603 LEE, SUE JEAN, tr. "Late-Blooming Cassia." *Voices* (formerly *Dodder*), 3, no. 1 (1971), 20-27.
   "Ch'ih kuei-hua" ("Late-Blooming Cassia") describes a decadent hero whose sexual attraction to a lovely young widow is restrained by a budding feeling of brotherly love for her.

604 McDOUGALL, BONNIE S., tr. "Smoke Shadows." *Renditions*, no. 9 (Spring, 1978), pp. 65-70.
   A translation of *"Yen-ying,"* believed to be an autobiographical tale.

605 "Wistaria and Dodder." In Edgar Snow, ed. *Living China*. London: George G. Harrap and Co. 1936, pp. 247-263.
   "Niao-lo hsing" ("Wistaria and Dodder") is a lengthy letter in which a husband confesses the tragic failure of his arranged marriage, detailing the traits of his old-fashioned wife and his wandering life in many cosmopolitan port cities.

606 YANG, GLADYS, tr. "Arbutus Cocktails." *ChL*, no. 12 (Dec., 1963), pp. 32-38.
   Satiric in tone, *"Yang-mei shao-chiu"* ("Arbutus Cocktails") depicts two former schoolmates whose ideological outlooks have changed since their last meeting a number of years ago.

607 ———061. "Flight." *ChL*, no. 12 (Dec., 1963), pp. 38-63.
   In *"Ch'u-pen"* ("Flight"), the author writes about a young revolutionary who resorts to drastic means to free himself from the entanglements of his wealthy, corrupt in-laws.

Studies

608 CHANG, RANDALL OLIVER. "Yü Ta-fu (1896-1945): The Alienated Artist in Modern Chinese Literature." Ph.D. Dissertation. Pomona: Claremont Graduate School and University Center, 1974.
   A study of Yü Ta-fu's literary career and his works written during the period between 1921 and 1935. The author maintains that since Yü's fictional protagonists are largely reflections of Yü himself, they reveal his own responses to the social and intellectual issues of the day.

609 DOLEŽALOVÁ, ANNA. "Remarks on the Life and Work of Yü Ta-fu up to 1930." *AAS*, 1 (1965), 53-80.

A survey of Yü Ta-fu's life and work up to 1930 when he joined the League of Left-wing writers. Because of the strong subjective nature of Yü's work, the author examines the relationship between his life and his work and traces Yü's inner development and his role as a writer of decadence and pessimism.

610 ———. "Two Novels of Yü Ta-fu: Two Approaches to Literary Creation." *AAS*, 4 (1968), 17-29.

A close examination of two largely neglected novels of Yü Ta-fu, *The Stray Sheep* (*Mi yang*) and *She Is a Weak Woman* (*T'a shih i-ko jo nü-tzu*) and Yü's different approaches to artistic creation.

611 ———. "Yü Ta-fu." In Jaroslav Průšek, ed. *Dictionary of Oriental Literatures*. London: George Allen and Unwin, 1974; New York: Basic Books, 1974, I, p. 214.

A brief account of Yü's life and work.

612 ———. *Yü Ta-fu: Specific Traits of His Literary Creation*. Bratislava: Publishing House of the Slovak Academy of Sciences, 1971.

A study of Yü Ta-fu's writings, focusing on: the methods of self-expression in his prose works, the quality of his creative method, and his views on the theory of literary creation. Part II of the study is on Yü's life and his literary career.

613 EGAN, MICHAEL. "Yu Da-fu [*Yü Ta-fu*] and the Transition to Modern Chinese Literature." In Merle Goldman, ed. *Modern Chinese Literature in the May Fourth Era*. Cambridge: Harvard University Press, 1977, pp. 309-324.

The author examines Yü's first two short stories, "Sinking" and "Silver-Gray Death," ("*Yin-hui se ti ssu*"), and compares them to traditional fiction, concluding that "there was indeed a transitional period between the old vernacular fiction and the 'modern' literature written after the literary revolution had produced its full effects. It can also be seen that Yü, despite his deserved reputation as an innovative writer who did much to modernize Chinese fiction, owes a debt to tradition that has perhaps been underestimated."

614 LEE, LEO OU-FAN. "Yü Ta-fu." In Leo Ou-fan Lee. *The Romantic Generation of Modern Chinese Writers*. Cambridge: Harvard University Press, 1973, pp. 81-123.

In two chapters (5 and 6), the author discusses Yü Ta-fu the man and Yü Ta-fu the writer. In "Driftings of a Loner," the author discusses Yü's childhood, student years and sex life in Japan, wanderings in China, association with the Creation Society, love of Wang Ying-hsia, and death in 1945. In "Yü Ta-fu: Visions of the Self," the author emphasizes that, for Yü, literature is autobiography; Yü chose to write in order to exorcise the demons within himself, and confession was his catharsis.

615 MELYAN, GARY G. "The Enigma of Yü Ta-fu's Death." *MS*, 29 (1970-1971), 557-588.

   An account of Yü Ta-fu's last days in Sumatra from Japanese sources. It shows that Yü was not a superpatriot, but an erratic and earnest man whose deeds were consistent with his inner beliefs.

616 PRŮŠEK, JAROSLAV. *Three Sketches of Chinese Literature.* Prague: Oriental Institute in Academia, 1969.

   In this study of three modern Chinese writers, Mao Tun, Yü Ta-fu and Kuo Mo-jo, Yü is viewed as the one who best represents the subjective tendency in literature because he paid little attention to reality.

617 "Yü Ta-fu." In Howard L. Boorman and Richard C. Howard, eds. *Biographical Dictionary of Republican China.* New York: Columbia University Press, 1967-1971, IV, pp. 70-73; 412-414.

   A brief biographical account of Yü Ta-fu.

XII
Other Modern Writers

This chapter covers other modern fiction writers, including such luminaries as Hsiao Chün, Yeh Sheng-t'ao, Hsiao Hung, and Tuan-mu Hung-liang. The reason for grouping them together is that, despite their importance, few of their works have been translated or studied in the West. Of these writers, fourteen are individually listed first, and the remaining are loosely grouped together under "Other Writers." None of the authors covered in this chapter belongs to either Taiwan or Communist writers. Taiwan and Communist writers since 1949 are respectively covered in chapters XIII and XIV.

Of the works listed in this chapter, some deserve special attention. Among them are studies of Chiang Kuang-tz'u by T. A. Hsia, Leo Ou-fan Lee, and Marián Gálik; Howard Goldblatt's translations and studies of Hsiao Hung's works; and studies and translations of Yeh Sheng-t'ao's works by David Selis, Frank B. Kelly, and A. C. Barnes. Other important contributions include translations of and articles on the fiction of Wu Tsu-hsiang by C. T. Hsia, Russell McLeod, Gladys Yang, Oldřich Král, and L. Kroutilova.

1. Chiang Kuang-tz'u (1901-1931)

A participant in the May Fourth Movement and a member of the Communist Party, Chiang Kuang-tz'u, a poet, essayist, fiction writer, and translator of Russian literature, was expelled from the Party in 1930 and died in 1931. He left behind the earliest examples of Chinese proletarian fiction.

Translations

618 "Hassan." In Harold R. Isaacs, ed. *Straw Sandals*. Cambridge: M.I.T. Press, 1974, pp. 170-173.
    This story describes the life of Hassan, a dumb Indian policeman who serves, along with Englishmen, White Russians, and Chinese, in the police force of the British-dominated International Settlement of Shanghai. This is more a sketch than a story.

Studies

619   DOLEŽALOVÁ-VLČKOVÁ, ANČA. "Chiang Kuang-tz'u." In Jaroslav Průšek, ed. *Dictionary of Oriental Literatures*. London: George Allen and Unwin, 1974; New York: Basic Books, 1974, I. p. 12.
A very brief account of Chiang's life and works.

620   GÁLIK, MARIÁN. "Studies in Modern Chinese Literary Criticism: VI. Chiang Kuang-tz'u's Concept of Revolutionary Literature." *AAS*, 8 (1972), 43-70.
For four years from 1920 to 1924, Chiang Kuang-tz'u studied in the Soviet Union. After returning to China, besides his activities as a writer of fiction, he introduced contemporary Soviet literature to China, discussed the relationship of revolution to literature, and propounded a Marxist theory of revolutionary literature. This study focuses on his concept of revolutionary literature.

621   HSIA, T. A. "The Phenomenon of Chiang Kuang-tz'u." In T. A. Hsia. *The Gate of Darkness*. Seattle: University of Washington Press, 1968, pp. 55-100.
A study of the strange case of Chiang, a self-conscious romantic revolutionary of limited talent who gave up his revolutionary life to write proletarian literature. But he died too young to see his goals fulfilled.

622   LEE, LEO OU-FAN. "Chiang Kuang-tz'u." In Leo Ou-fan Lee. *The Romantic Generation of Modern Chinese Writers*. Cambridge: Harvard University Press, 1973, pp. 201-221.
A study which stresses the romantic-tragic aspects of Chiang Kuang-tz'u's life: his less-than-successful career as a poet and writer of revolutionary literature, the death of his first wife after one month of marriage, and other personal tragedies.

2. Hsiao Ch'ien (1911-   )

Hsiao Ch'ien is an editor, scholar, and short story writer. Among his many writings are *Etchings of a Tormented Age* (in English), Chinese translations of Henry Fielding's *Jonathan Wild* and *Lamb's Tales from Shakespeare*, and a number of short stories. He visited the United States in 1979.

Translations

623   "The Conversion." In Edgar Snow ed. *Living China*. London: George G. Harrap and Co., 1936, pp. 228-246; reprinted in Daniel L. Milton and William Clifford, eds. *A Treasury of Modern Asian Stories*. New York: New American Library, 1961, pp. 185-197.
"The Conversion" ("*Kuei-i*") vividly describes one type of Chinese reaction to Christian missionaries in China.

624 HSIAO, CH'IEN, ed. and tr. *Spinners of Silk*. London: George Allen and Unwin, 1944.

    Contains eleven stories by Hsiao Ch'ien: "When Your Eaves Are Low" ("*Ai-yen*"), "The Captive" ("*Fu-lu*"), "Epidemic" ("*Hua-tzu yü Lao Huang*"), "Under the Fence of Others" ("*Li-hsia*"), "Chestnuts" ("*Li-tzu*"), "The Ramshackle Car" ("*P'o-ch'e shang*"), "Shanghai," "The Spinners of Silk" ("*Ts'an*"), "The Galloping Legs" ("*Ying-tzu ch'e ti ming-yüan*"), "The Philatelist," ("*Yu-p'iao*"), "A Rainy Evening" ("*Yü-hsi*"), and one essay, "Scenes from the Yentang Mountain" ("*Yen-tang ti hsü-mu*").

3. Hsiao Chün (Liu Chün, T'ien Chün) (1907-   )

Born in 1907 in Liaoning province to a peasant family, Hsiao Chün received little formal education and served in the army from 1925 to 1931. The husband of the woman writer Hsiao Hung and a protégé of Lu Hsün, he ran afoul of the Communist Party several times but has recently been rehabilitated.

Translations

625 "Aboard the S.S. *Dairen Maru*." In Edgar Snow, ed. *Living China*. New York: John Day and Co., 1937; Westport, Conn: Hyperion Press, 1973, pp. 207-211.

    "Aboard the S.S. *Darien Maru*" ("*Ta-lien Wan Shang*") is a factual account of the harassment of a young couple by Japanese officials aboard a ship traveling between Japan and Manchuria in the 1930s.

626 GOLDBLATT, HOWARD, tr. "Goats." *Renditions*, no. 4 (Spring, 1975), pp. 22-39.

    A powerful short story about a goat thief. Written in 1935, a period of social and political chaos in northeast China, "Goats" includes descriptions of the lives of prisoners, workers, traitors, vagabonds, and revolutionaries.

627 KING, EVAN, tr. *Village in August*. New York: Smith and Durrell, 1942; reprint ed. Westport, Conn.: Greenwood Press, 1976.

    Written in 1934, *Village in August* (*Pa-yüeh ti hsiang-ts'un*) was hailed by many as a great war novel. It is about a band of patriotic guerrilla fighters who combat the Japanese after their occupation of Manchuria in 1931. The story is complicated by a triangular love affair and the conflict between romantic love and revolutionary duty. The translation, though readable, contains extensive errors.

628 "The Third Gun." In Edgar Snow, ed. *Living China*. London: George G. Harrap and Co., 1936, pp. 212-219.

    Translation of chapter 3 of Hsiao Chün's novel *Village in August* (*see* no. 627).

Studies

629   HSIA, C. T. "Communist Fiction, I." In C. T. Hsia, *A History of Modern Chinese Fiction*. 2nd ed. New Yale University Press, 1971. pp. 257-280.
Contains extensive comments on Hsiaos Chün.

630   HSIAO, CH'IEN, tr. and ed. "Self Accounts of Two Young Writers (Chang T'ien-i and Hsiao Chün)." In Hsiao Ch'ien, ed. *A Harp with a Thousand Strings*. London: Pilot Press, 1944, pp. 294-296.
A brief self-account of Hsiao Chün, translated and edited by Hsiao Ch'ien.

631   LEE, LEO OU-FAN. "Hsiao Chün." In Leo Ou-fan Lee. *The Romantic Generation of Modern Chinese Writers*. Cambridge: Harvard University Press, 1973, pp. 222-224.
The author suggests that Hsiao Chün's life epitomizes the fate of the romantic-leftist writer. His hardy rugged individualism never seems to meet the demands of the Communist Party. His "bohemian" personal life with Hsiao Hung is also symptomatic of his individualism. After initial success with his novel *Village in August* and other works, he has been more or less silenced since the Communists came to power in 1949. (He was rehabilitated in early 1979).

4. Hsiao Hung (Chang Nai-ying) (1911-1942)

Born in Heilungkiang province, Hsiao Hung, the daughter of a wealthy landlord, was a protégé of Lu Hsün and became a popular writer in the 1930's. Once married to her fellow Manchurian writer Hsiao Chün, she died in Hong Kong in 1942.

Translations

632   GOLDBLATT, HOWARD, tr. "On the Oxcart." *ASPAC Quarterly* (Seoul, Korea), 7, no. 4 (Spring, 1976), 56-64.
A translation of one of the best pieces by Hsiao Hung, the story takes place on an oxcart going into town. During the trip, a female servant relates to the narrator, a young girl, and her carter-uncle the tragic story of her husband's execution as a military deserter years earlier.

632a   ———and ELLEN YOUNG, trs. *The Field of Life and Death* and *Tales of the Hulan River*. Bloomington: Indiana University Press, 1979.
Full translations of Hsiao Hung's two best-known works. The former realistically presents the lives of Chinese peasants, brutalized by poverty and war and bound by rigid traditions. The latter also stresses the plight of the peasant and the oppression of women in traditional China. The book also contains Lu Hsün's preface and Hu Feng's epilogue to the former and Mao Tun's preface to the latter.

633 SHAPIRO, SIDNEY, tr. "Spring in a Small Town." *ChL*, no. 8 (Aug., 1961), pp. 59-82.

One of Hsiao Hung's masterpieces, "Spring in a Small Town" ("*Hsiao ch'eng san-yüeh*") is about a young woman, Jade, who falls in love with one young man but is betrothed to another. Instead of fighting tradition, she dies of a broken heart.

634 YANG, GLADYS, tr. "Hands." *ChL*, no. 8 (Aug., 1959), pp. 36-51.

"Hands" ("*Shou*") is a moving story depicting a country girl's short-lived residence in a school and her cruel treatment by classmates and teachers because of her humble origins and her blackened hands. (Another translation, by Richard L. Jen, appears in *THM*, no. 5 (May, 1937), 498-514).

635 ———. "Harelip Feng." *ChL*, no. 2 (Feb., 1963) pp. 3-24.

An excerpt (chapter 7) from *Tales of Hulan River* (*Hu-lan ho chuan*), a book of seven chapters, each of which has its own story but is bound to the others by a common locale, a common time, and the same child-narrator. Vivid descriptions of the town of Hulan and its peasants.

Studies

636 GOLDBLATT, HOWARD. *Hsiao Hung*. Boston: Twayne Publishers, 1976.

A detailed biographical study of this talented young woman writer from northeastern China. Born in 1911, she died at the age of 30. Her works consist of four novels, numerous short stories, and some essays and poetry. Although not a prolific writer, she has earned her place among modern Chinese writers. Her sensitive character portrayals well reflect her own suffering in life.

637 MAO TUN. "Preface to *The Hulan River*." *ChL*, no. 2 (Feb., 1963), pp. 25-32.

A brief introduction to Hsiao Hung's last major work, *Tales of Hulan River* (*Hu-lan ho chuan*). A generally laudatory appraisal, it is much more favorable than those by other Communist critics.

5. Jou Shih (Chao P'ing-fu) (1901-1931)

A native of Chekiang province, Jou Shih was a close associate of Lu Hsün. He joined the Communist Party in 1930 and was executed by the Kuomintang in 1931.

Translations

638 CHANG, PEI-CHI, tr. "A Slave Mother." *ChL*, no. 1 (Jan., 1955), pp. 107-123. Jenner, W. J. F., tr. "Slave's Mother." In W. J. F. Jenner, ed. *Modern Chinese Stories*. London: Oxford University Press, 1970, pp. 47-67. Kennedy, George A. tr. "Slave Mother." In Edgar Snow, ed.

Living China. London: George G. Harrap and Co., 1936, pp. 100-126; also in Harold R. Isaacs, ed. *Straw Sandals.* Cambridge: M.I.T. Press, 1974, pp. 215-241.

The story ("*Wei nu-li ti mu-ch'in*") is a powerful tale which portrays the wretched status of women in the 1920s and '30s. A peasant woman is leased for three or four years to a man of fifty who has no son. In the end she is allowed to return to her own family.

639 SHAPIRO, SIDNEY, tr. "Threshold of Spring." *ChL,* no. 6 (June, 1963), pp. 3-42; no. 7 (July, 1963), pp. 30-64.

A short novel about a restless young intellectual and his romance with a lively and passionate girl whom he must give up as complications arise.

6. Lao Hsiang (Wang Hsiang-ch'en) (1895-   )

An essayist and short story writer, Lao Hsiang is known for writing in the Peking dialect and for his humorous style. His many satirical tales attracted much attention in the 1930s and '40s. He is known to be living in Taiwan since the end of World War II.

Translations

640 KAO, GEORGE, tr. "National Salvation through Haircut." In George Kao, ed. *Chinese Wit and Humor.* New York: Coward-McCann, 1946; New York: Sterling Publishing Co., 1974, pp. 336-339.

The story of a barber, Master An, who has developed a theory of national salvation: "China is about to perish, and the responsibility for this should be lodged . . . on the shoulders of the haircutting brotherhood."

641 LIN, YUTANG, tr. "Ah Chuan Goes to School." In George Kao, ed. *Chinese Wit and Humor.* New York: Coward-McCann, 1946; New York: Sterling Publishing Co., 1974, pp. 328-334. Wang, Chi-chen, tr. "A Country Boy Withdraws from School." In Chi-chen Wang, tr. *Contemporary Chinese Stories.* New York: Columbia University Press, 1944; reprint ed. Westport, Conn.: Greenwood Press, 1972, pp. 18-24; reprinted in Daniel L. Milton and William Clifford, eds. *A Treasury of Modern Asian Stories.* New York: New American Library, 1961, pp. 197-203.

"A Village Boy Withdraws from School" ("*Ts'un-erh ch'o-hsüeh chi*") explains a village family's reaction to its son's modern-style school.

642 ———, tr. "Widow Chuan." In Lin Yutang, tr. *Widow, Nun, and Courtesan.* New York: John Day Co., 1950; reprint ed. Westport, Conn.: Greenwood Press, 1971, pp.3-110.

"Widow Ch'üan" ("*Ch'üan-chia ts'un*"), also translated as "The Ch'üan Village," is a bawdy, rambunctious story about the return of a war hero,

Captain Ch'üan, to his home village in North China. The story is enlivened by the author's sympathetic portrayals of gamblers, cheaters, and unfettered loud women. Not an accurate translation but a readable retold version.

7. Ling Shu-hua (1901?-   )

A native of Kwangtung who lived in Peking in the 1920s, she taught in Canada and now resides in England. Also a painter, she wrote mostly on women and children and was one of the best-known women writers in the 1930s and '40s.

Translations

643   CHAN, MARIE, tr. "Embroidered Pillow." *Renditions*, no. 4 (Spring, 1975), pp. 124-127.
       The story ("*Hsiu-chen*") is about the quiet drudgery of a young genteel woman which is symbolized by a pair of pillows she has spent many months embroidering, only to have them spat and trampled upon by members of a rich family.

644   ———. "Mid-Autumn Eve." *Renditions*, no. 4 (Spring, 1975), pp. 116-123.
       The story ("*Chung-ch'iu wan*") presents a series of tragic misfortunes that occur within a modern-day family.

645   WANG, CHI-CHEN, tr. "The Helpmate." In Chi-chen Wang, tr. *Contemporary Chinese Stories*. New York: Columbia University Press, 1944; Westport, Conn.: Greenwood Press, 1975, pp. 135-142.
       "T'ai-t'ai" ("The Helpmate") is about a woman mahjong addict.

8. Lo Hua-sheng (Hsü Ti-Shan) (1893-1941)

Born in Taiwan and a member of the Literary Association, Lo Hua-sheng was a scholar, essayist, fiction writer, and expert on Buddhism and Indian philosophy.

Translations

646   SHAPIRO, SIDNEY, tr. "Big Sister Liu." *ChL*, no. 1 (Jan., 1957), pp. 79-96.
       The story of Big Sister Liu who has two husbands: one is an ex-soldier with amputated legs, and the other an apple-cider vendor's aide and scrap-paper sorter.

647   ———. "Blossoms on a Dried Poplar." *ChL*, no. 1 (Jan., 1957), pp. 63-78.
       A story of a pair of old lovers who are reunited after forty years with their love as fresh and steadfast as ever.

648   YANG, GLADYS, tr. "Director Fei's Reception Room." *ChL*, no. 1 (Jan., 1964), pp. 73-84.
      A satirical short story about a wealthy director, who is a professed philanthropist, and his many wives and concubines.

649   ———. "The Iron Fish with Gills." *ChL*, no. 1 (Jan., 1964), pp. 64-73.
      An ironic tale about a stubborn old inventor who has designed a submarine with "iron gills." When his device accidentally falls into the sea, he dives after it and drowns.

Studies

650   HSIA, C. T. "Lo Hua-sheng (1893-1941)." In C. T. Hsia. *A History of Modern Chinese Fiction*. 2nd ed. New Haven: Yale University Press, 1971, pp. 84-92.
      The author shows that Lo Hua-sheng is distinguished from other Chinese writers by his religiosity and that his stories reveal how charity, love, and patience prevail in society.

651   ROBINSON, LEWIS S. " 'Yü-kuan': The Spiritual Testament of Hsü Ti-shan." *TR*, 8, no. 2 (Oct.,1977), 147-168.
      A study of Lo Hua-sheng's story, "*Yü-kuan*," as a symbol of the author's spiritual quest.

9. Ping Hsin (Hsieh Wan-ying) (1900-   )

A native of Foochow, she is a poetess and short-story writer. Noted for her descriptions of the mother-child relationship, Ping Hsin was very popular in the 1920s and is still active in China today.

Translations

652   JEN, RICHARD L., tr. "The First Home Party." *THM*, 4 (March, 1937), 244-306.
      The story ("*Ti-i-tz'u yen-hui*") is about a home dinner party.

Studies

653   ANDERSON, COLENA M. "A Study of Two Modern Chinese Women: Ping Hsin and Ting Ling." Ph.D. Dissertation. Pomona: Claremont Graduate School and University Center, 1954.
      A critical and comparative study of two modern Chinese women writers: Ping Hsin and Ting Ling.

654   BOUSKOVÁ, MARCELA. "The Stories of Ping Hsin." In Jaroslav Průšek, *Studies in Modern Chinese Literature*. Berlin: Akademie-Verlag, 1964, pp. 114-129.
      A critical analysis of some of Ping Hsin's short stories. The author sees her as not very interested in the harsh realities of life.

655 PAO, KING-LI. "Ping Hsin: A Modern Chinese Poetess. *LEW*, 8 (Spring/Aut.,1964), 58-72.
This is a study of Ping Hsin as a poetess but it sheds some light on her works of fiction as well.

656 STOLZOVÁ, MARCELA. "Ping Hsin". In Jaroslav Průšek, ed. *Dictionary of Oriental Literatures*. London: George Allen and Unwin, 1974; New York: Basic Books, 1974, I, p. 141.
A brief account of Ping Hsin's life and works.

10. Sha T'ing (Yang T'ung-fang) (1904-   )

A native of Szechuan, he was influenced by Lu Hsün and wrote about the life of peasants. During the Sino-Japanese War he was in Yenan; after 1949 he was active in Szechuan literary circles. He is still writing fiction today.

Translations

657 "An Autumn Night." *ChL*, no. 2 (Feb.,1957), pp. 88-98; reprinted in Gene Z. Hanrahan. *50 Great Oriental Stories*. New York: Bantam Books, 1965, pp. 102-115.
The story (*"I-ke ch'iu-t'ien wan-shang"*) describes the adventures of a wandering prostitute.

658 "The Magnet." *ChL*, no. 2 (Feb.,1957), pp. 79-87.
A young boy leaving his family for Yenan is the subject of this story (*"Tz'u-li"*).

659 SHAPIRO, SIDNEY, tr. "In a Teahouse." *ChL*, no. 6 (June, 1961), pp. 112-126.
The conduct of a boisterous "loudmouth" at a local teahouse is the focus of this story (*"Tsai Ch'i-hsiang-chü ch'a-kuan li"*).

660 "Voyage Beyond the Law." In Edgar Snow. *Living China*. London: George G. Harrap and Co., 1936, pp. 320-333.
In this story (*"Hang-hsien"*), the author describes a voyage up the Yangtze River during the civil war between the Chinese Communists and the Nationalists.

661 YANG, GLADYS, tr. "The Contest." *ChL*, no. 3 (March, 1961), pp. 61-77.
Life in the commune during the Great Leap Forward period is the subject of this short tale (*"Ni chui, wo kan"*).

Studies

662   PIN, CHIH. "Sha Ting [Sha T'ing] the Novelist." *ChL*, no. 10 (Oct.,1964), pp. 97-104.

    A brief biographical account of Sha T'ing discussing his early and later works, his satiric skill, and his control of the dialect and manners of the Szechuan province.

11. Shih T'o (Wang Ch'ang-chien) (1908-   )

A novelist and short story writer, Shih T'o had little formal education. He claimed serious attention as a novelist with the publication of his *Marriage (Chieh-hun)* in 1947.

Studies

663   HSIA, C. T. "Shih T'o." In C. T. Hsia. *A History of Modern Chinese Fiction.* 2nd ed. New Haven: Yale University Press, 1971, pp. 461-468.

    The author gives a biographical sketch of Shih T'o and analyzes in detail his satirical novel *Marriage (Chieh-hun)*, which Hsia praises as a novel of genuine distinction.

664   SŁUPSKI, ZBIGNIEW. "The World of Shih T'o." *AAS*, 9 (1973), 11-28.

    The author points out that Shih T'o does not belong in the narrow limits of realism, but is an unconventional writer with his unique approach to the world of cruelty, indifference, and aimlessness.

12. Tuan-mu Hung-liang (Ts'ao Ching-p'ing) (1912-   )

A native of the Northeast, Tuan-mu Hung-liang is deeply attached to Manchuria and its people and is noted for his lyric exuberance in works such as *The Khorchin Grasslands, The Sea of Earth,* and *The Great River.* After a long period of silence, he has recently become active in Chinese literary circles again, despite illness.

Translations

665   BAUMGARTNER, MARGARET and NATHAN K. MAO, trs. "The Rapid Currents of Muddy River." In Joseph S. M. Lau, Leo Ou-fan Lee, and C. T. Hsia, eds., *Modern Chinese Stories and Novellas, 1918-1948.* New York: Columbia University Press, forthcoming.

    A story about the hunters of Manchuria and their rebellion against authority, it contains vivid descriptions of earthy and primitive characters.

665a SHAPIRO, SIDNEY, tr. "Despoiler of the Crop." *ChL*, no. 5 (May, 1963), pp. 39-56.

    About the villagers' hunt for the despoiler of their crop who turns out to be the rich peasant Pai Mao.

666 ———. "Lost." *ChL*, no. 4 (April, 1962), pp. 63-75.

    A story about the steward of the wealthy Chao family who tries to rule the peasants but loses his life during a snowstorm.

667 ———."Shadows on Egret Lake." *ChL*, no. 4 (April, 1962), pp. 54-63. Yüan, Chia-hua and Robert Payne, trs. "The Sorrows of the Lake of Egrets." In Yuan Chia-hua and Robert Payne, trs. and eds., *Contemporary Chinese Short Stories*. London: Noel Carrington, Transatlantic Arts Co., 1946, pp. 118-129; reprinted in James E. Miller, et al., eds. *Literature of the Eastern World*. Glenview, Ill.: Scott, Foresman, 1970, pp. 103-110.

    The story ("*Tz'u-lu hu ti yu-yü*") is about the hardships of the Chinese peasant. Its characters are earthy, and their actions are sometimes incomplete. Certain passages are excessively descriptive.

667a SUN, CLARA and NATHAN K. MAO, trs. "The Far-away Wind and Sand." In Joseph S. M. Lau, Leo Ou-fan Lee, and C. T. Hsia, eds., *Modern Chinese Stories and Novellas, 1918-1948*. New York: Columbia University Press, forthcoming.

    A long story about earthy heroic types who roam the mountains and ravines of Manchuria, it contains rich evocations of Manchurian scenes.

Studies

668 HSIA, C. T. "The Novels of Tuan-mu Hung-liang." In Joseph S. M. Lau and Leo Ou-fan Lee, eds. *Critical Persuasions*, forthcoming.

    A critical assessment of Tuan-mu Hung-liang, a good friend of Hsiao Hung and Hsiao Chün. The author is highly appreciative of Tuan-mu's gift as a nature lyricist.

13. Wu Tsu-hsiang (1908-   )

Writer, critic, and literary historian, Wu Tsu-hsiang wrote mostly about the gentry and peasants of his native province of Anhwei and became known for his short story collection *Hsi liu chi* (*West Willow*, 1934). Avoiding romantic-revolutionary subject matter, he adopted an unsentimental, ironic approach to rural life, as reflected in most of his short stories. Criticized during the Cultural Revolution, he has recently been rehabilitated.

Translations

669   KRÁL, OLDŘICH and L. KROUTILOVA, trs. "Medicine for the Master." *New Orient*, 6, no. 4 (Aug., 1967), 107-111.
   A powerful ironic tale, "*Kuan-kuan ti pu-p'in*" describes how a landlord's son literally lives off the milk and blood of the peasants.

670   McLEOD, RUSSELL and C. T. HSIA, trs. "Fan Village." In C. T. Hsia, ed., *Twentieth-Century Chinese Stories*. New York: Columbia University Press, 1971, pp. 102-135.
   A morbid tale of robbery, banditry, and murder, "*Fan-chia p'u*" is set in China in the 1930s. The hatred and rivalry between a mother and her daughter are its main themes.

671   YANG, GLADYS, tr. "Eighteen Hundred Piculs." *ChL*, no. 11 (Nov.,1959), pp. 61-101.
   This story ("*I-ch'ien pa-pai tan*") describes a large clan meeting, where members discuss the disposal of land and rice, while famished peasants break in and seize the rice.

Studies

672   HSIA, C. T. "Wu Tsu-hsiang." In C. T. Hsia. *A History of Modern Chinese Fiction*. 2nd ed. New Haven: Yale University Press, 1971, pp. 281-287.
   The author regards Wu Tsu-hsiang as a highly skilled writer who writes about the gentry and peasants of his native region (Anhwei province) and points out that the power of Wu's fiction lies in his keen and realistic observation of the inhumane way of life in Chinese villages in the 1930s.

673   KRÁL, OLDŘICH. "Wu Tsu-hsiang." In Jaroslav Průšek, ed. *Dictionary of Oriental Literatures*. London: George Allen and Unwin, 1974; New York: Basic Books, 1974, I, p. 205.
   A brief account of Wu's life and works.

14. Yeh Sheng-t'ao (Yeh Shao-chün) (1894-   )

A native of Kiangsu province, Yeh Sheng-t'ao for many years was a school teacher. In the early 1930s he was an editor of the K'aiming Press and wrote short stories and children's tales. Many of his stories deal with schoolchildren and teachers. Best known for his novel, *Schoolmaster Ni Huan-chih*, he has recently reappeared in public after a long period of silence.

Translations

674 BARNES, A. C., tr. *Schoolmaster Ni Huan-chih*. Peking: Foreign Languages Press, 1958.

Published in 1928, *Ni Huan-chih* documents the transformation of a young teacher, Ni Huan-chih, from an idealist into a disillusioned pessimist who dies of typhoid fever. The novel also incorporates the author's own reactions to the social issues of the time, especially educational reforms and the massacre of the Communists by the Kuomintang in 1927.

675 HOLOCH, DONALD, tr. "On the Bridge." *BCAS*, 8 (1976), 21-27.

The story (*"Ch'iao shang"*) provides a vivid portrayal of the many frustrations of a school-teacher.

675a McDOUGALL, BONNIE S. and LEWIS S. ROBINSON, trs. *A Posthumous Son and Other Stories*.

For annotations and bibliographic information, *see* no. 326a.

676 "Mr. Pan in Distress." In Harold R. Isaacs, ed. *Straw Sandals*. Cambridge: M.I.T. Press, 1974, pp. 84-106. T'ang, Sheng, tr. "How Mr. Pan Weathered the Storm." *ChL*, no. 5 (May, 1963), pp. 3-22.

The story (*"P'an hsien-sheng tsai nan-chung"*) tell the frustrating experience of a Mr. Pan and his family in Shanghai during a time of civil strife in the 1920s.

677 *The Scarecrow: A Collection of Stories for Children*. Peking: Foreign Languages Press, 1963.

Includes "The Scarecrow" (*" Tao-ts'ao jen"*) and other children's stories. Largely imitations of Andersen, most stories are extremely didactic.

678 "Three to Five Bushels More." In Harold R. Isaacs, ed. *Straw Sandals*. Cambridge: M.I.T. Press, 1974, pp. 337-347. Yang, Gladys, tr. "A Year of Good Harvest." *ChL*, no. 4 (April, 1960), pp. 37-45.

One of the few stories about peasants by Yeh, it is a realistic portrayal of the plight of the Chinese village. A number of peasants have come to town to sell their rice, only to learn that the price has drastically dropped, leaving them little money to buy their necessities.

Studies

679 HSIA, C. T. "Yeh Shao-chün." In C. T. Hsia. *A History of Modern Chinese Fiction*. 2nd ed. New Haven: Yale University Press, 1971, pp. 57-71.

The author considers Yeh a competent writer, discusses a number of Yeh's early stories which deal with school-children and teachers, comments on his dedication as a teacher, and concludes that Yeh should have been better received by his readers and critics.

680 KELLY, FRANK B. "The Writings of Yeh Sheng-t'ao." Ph.D. Dissertation. Chicago: University of Chicago, 1979.
    A literary analysis of Yeh Sheng-t'ao's writings, both fictional and nonfictional. Some of the works discussed are *Barriers* (*Ko-mo*), *In the City* (*Ch'eng-chung*), and *Ni Huan-chih*. Includes an appendix of original translations of selected works.

681 LU, CHIEN. "A Visit to Yeh Sheng-t'ao." *ChL*, no. 5 (May, 1963), pp. 88-95.
    A brief introduction to Yeh Sheng-t'ao, his short stories and children's tales.

682 PRŮŠEK, JAROSLAV. "Yeh Sheng-t'ao." In Jaroslav Průšek, ed. *Dictionary of Oriental Literatures*. London: George Allen and Unwin, 1974; New York: Basic Books, 1974, I, p. 207.
    A brief biographical account.

683 ———. "Yeh Sheng-t'ao and Anton Chekhov." *ArOr*, 38 (1970), 437-452.
    A general comparison of the works of Yeh Sheng-t'ao with those of Chekhov. Jaroslav Průšek believes that Yeh was greatly influenced by Chekhov in his direct presentation of reality.

684 SELIS, DAVID JOEL. "Yeh Shao-chün: A Critical Study of His Fiction, 1919-1944." Ph.D. Dissertation. Bloomington: Indiana University, 1975.
    A literary study of Yeh's short stories and novels written between 1919 and 1944 (his most prolific period), in terms of theme, narrative technique, plot, and characterization. The first chapter is a biographical study, and ten of Yeh's best stories are translated in the appendix.

15. Other Writers

(1) Cheng Nung (1904-   )

Cheng Nung was a native of Kianghsi and the son of a petty landlord. In 1964 he was listed as director of the Propaganda Department of the East China Bureau of the Communist Party.

685 "On the Threshing Field." In Harold R. Isaacs, ed. *Straw Sandals* Cambridge: M.I.T. Press, 1974, pp. 371-393.
    The brutal exploitation of a tenant farmer by his landlord is the main theme of this story.

(2) Chou Shou-chüan (1894-1968)

Little is known about Chou Shou-chuan, a prolific writer of popular fiction in the "Mandarin Duck and Butterfly School."

686 LINK, PERRY, tr. "We Shall Meet Again." *BCAS*, 8 (Jan./Mar.,1976), 13-19.

A typical, highly sentimental tale about love between a Chinese girl and a foreigner, written in 1914 and published in *The Saturday Magazine* (*Li-pai liu*). This and other stories of similar nature drew heavy attack by the new May Fourth writers who were determined to renovate literature and change the traditional moral values. Includes an informative introduction by the translator and an appendix (translations of two critiques of "Butterfly fiction" by Yeh Sheng-t'ao and Cheng Chen-to).

(3) Hsieh Ping-ying (1903-   )

A popular woman writer during World War II, she taught modern Chinese literature at Taiwan Normal University and is now retired.

687 LIN, ADET and ANOR LIN, trs. *Girl Rebel: The Autobiography of Hsieh Pingying*. New York: John Day Co., 1940; reprint ed. New York: Da Capo Press, 1975.

A translation of Hsieh Ping-ying's *Nü-ping tzu-chuan*, written in 1936, and selections from her *New War Diaries* (*Ts'ung-chün jih-chi*), written in 1938. This is not merely an autobiographical account, but also a story of China in an age of social upheaval and of the country's struggle for freedom and independence.

(4) Hu Yeh-p'in (1907-1931)

The husband of Ting Ling, Hu Yeh-p'in, a left-wing fiction writer, was executed by the Kuomintang in 1931. (For more information on him, *see* no. 244).

688 KENNEDY, GEORGE, tr. "Living Together." In Harold R. Isaacs, ed. *Straw Sandals*. Cambridge: M.I.T. Press 1974, pp. 207-214.

A story about life in a liberated (Communist) area, where men and women have enough to eat and behave as individuals.

689 TANG, SHENG, tr. "A Poor Man." *ChL*, no. 5 (May, 1960), pp. 37-41.

The story ("*I-ke ch'iung-jen*") is about a wretched poor man.

(5) Kuo Mo-jo (1892-1978)

A founder of the Creation Society and a pioneer of Western-style free verse in China, Kuo Mo-jo was one of the most influential literary and political figures in twentieth-century China. Primarily a poet, critic, essayist, scholar, and playwright, he wrote only a small number of short stories. (For more information on him, *see* nos. 289 and 292).

690 "Dilemma." In Edgar Snow, ed. *Living China*. London: George H. Harrap and Co., 1936), pp. 290-300.

In "Dilemma' ("*Shih-tzu chia*"), the author narrates the dilemma of a Chinese writer-doctor who must choose between going to Japan to join his

Japanese wife and two children or returning to his home in Szechuan to practice medicine. The story has definite autobiographical overtones.

691   JENNER, W. J. F., tr. "Double Performance." In W. J. F. Jenner, ed. *Modern Chinese Stories*. London: Oxford University Press, 1970, pp. 69-74.

The main episode of this story ("*Shuang huang*") takes place in Wuhan in October, 1926. The story focuses on the conflict between Christianity and revolutionary fervor among the Chinese youth of the time.

(6) Shih I (Lou Chien-nan) (1903-)

A native of Chekiang province, a member of the League of Left-Wing Writers, and a soldier, Shih I was imprisoned by the Kuomintang in 1933. After 1949 he was an important official of various cultural organizations in China.

692   "Death." In Harold R. Isaacs, ed. *Straw Sandals*. Cambridge: M.I.T. Press, 1974, pp. 426-435.

A poignant story about the torture and death of a young woman revolutionary who refuses to tell the authorities the whereabouts of her comrades.

693   "Salt." In Harold R. saacs, ed. *Straw Sandals*. Cambridge: M.I.T. Press, 1974, pp. 174-206.

A 1929 story, based on an actual incident, about organizing salt workers in the Kiangsu salt fields. Reads more like reportage than fiction.

(7) Ting Chiu (Ying Hsiu-jen) (1900-1933)

A native of Chekiang, a Communist since 1925, and a friend of Ting Ling, Ting Chiu died at the hands of the Kuomintang in 1933.

694   KENNEDY, GEORGE A., tr. "The Three Pagodas." In Harold R. Isaacs ed. *Straw Sandals*. Cambridge: M.I.T. Press, 1974, pp. 261-273.

A story about the liberation of peasants by the Communists.

(8) Tung P'ing (Ch'iu Tung-p'ing) (1901-1941)

A Communist writer, Tung P'ing was killed while fighting the Japanese in northern Kiangsu in 1941.

695   "The Courier." In Harold R. Isaacs, ed. *Straw Sandals*. Cambridge: M.I.T. Press, 1974, pp. 394-404.

A story about a messenger who, after bungling his assignment, commits suicide.

(9) Wang T'ung-chao (1898-1957)

A native of Shantung province, Wang was influenced by the May Fourth Movement and worked briefly as a teacher. He was one of the founders of the Literary Association in 1920.

696 "Fifty Dollars." In Harold R. Isaacs, ed. *Straw Sandals*. Cambridge: M.I.T. Press, 1974, pp. 348-370. Shapiro, Sidney, tr. "Fifty Yüan." *ChL*, no. 9 (Sept.,1959), pp. 99-120.

> A short story about the ruthless oppression of the peasants by the Kuomintang troops. Most of the peasants in this case are Communist guerrilla fighters.

(10) Yeh Tzu (Yü Ho-lin) (1912-1939)

A native of Hunan, Yeh Tzu, a Communist writer, wrote mainly about the peasants' resistance to oppression.

697 JENNER, W. J. F., tr. "Stealing Lotuses." In W. J. F. Jenner, ed. *Modern Chinese Stories*. London: Oxford University Press, 1970, pp. 95-100.

> The story ("*T'ou-lien*") is about a rich landlord's son who has been taught a lesson by some hardy peasant women for stealing lotuses.

698 MA, CHING-CHUN and TANG SHENG, trs. *Harvest*. Peking: Foreign Languages Press, 1960.

> *Harvest* (*Feng-shou*) contains the following six stories about the anti-rent movement in 1927: "Harvest" ("*Feng-shou*"), "Fire" ("*Huo*"), "Outside the Barbed Wire Entanglement" ("*T'ien-wang wai*"), "The Night Sentinel" ("*Yeh-shao hsien* "), "Grandpa Yang's New Year" ("*Yang kung-kung kuo-nien*") and "The Guide" ("*Hsiang-tao*").

XIII
Communist Writers Since 1949

This chapter, divided into three sections, deals with Chinese Communist fiction written since 1949. Not all the works studied were written after 1949; some were written in the late 1940s. Nonetheless, they reflect the same spirit as those written after 1949. The first section lists a number of general studies of Communist fiction, the relationship between literature and politics, the aesthetics of political writing, and the interpretation of such political literature. Among the general studies, the following deserve particular attention: *Chinese Communist Literature*, edited by Cyril Birch; *Heroes and Villains in Communist China*, by Joe C. Huang; D. W. Fokkema's "Chinese Literature under the Cultural Revolution" and *Literary Doctrine in China and Soviet Influence, 1956-1960*; Merle Goldman's *Literary Dissent in Communist China*; C. T. Hsia's "Literature and Art under Mao Tse-tung"; T. A. Hsia's "Heroes and Hero-Worship in Chinese Communist Fiction"; Kai-yu Hsu's *The Chinese Literary Scene*; and D. E. Pollard's "The Short Story in the Cultural Revolution." Three short articles, including one by Du He and two by Winston Yang and Nathan Mao, provide informative surveys of recent developments. The second section lists a number of available anthologies of Communist literature and fiction. The most comprehensive anthology is *Literature of the People's Republic of China*, edited by Kai-yu Hsu. Two anthologies of stories of the post-Mao era have become available: *Stories of Contemporary China*, edited by Winston Yang and Nathan Mao; and *The Wounded: New Stories of the Cultural Revolution, 77-78*, translated by Geremie Barmé and Bennett Lee. In the third section, translations and studies of major individual authors are listed. Only a few of these writers, such as Chao Shu-li and Hao Jan, have attracted some attention. Less-known writers, about whom little information is available, are grouped together in the last subsection of the third section. It should be pointed out that studies and translations of the post-1949 works of veteran writers who became known before 1949, such as Lao She, Pa Chin, and others, are not listed in this chapter but are recorded in the chapters devoted to them.

Since *Chinese Literature* is the best source for translations of current Chinese fiction, those interested in current Chinese stories and novels are urged to examine issues of the magazine. Of the vast number of translations of fiction published therein, only a small number have been listed in this chapter. Donald A. Gibbs's *Subject and Author Index to Chinese Literature Monthly (1951-1976)* (*see* no. 21) is a very helpful guide to these translations.

It should be further noted that the Taiwan woman author Ch'en Jo-hsi, who wrote much fiction dealing with her Taiwan experience in the 1960s, has published since 1973 a number of short stories based on her observations in China. For studies and translations of her works, see the section on her in chapter XIV.

General Studies

699   BENTON, GREGOR. "The Yenan Literary Opposition." *New Left Review*, 92 (July/Aug., 1975), 93-106.
      Translation of three essays written by Wang Shih-wei, Ting Ling, and Lo Fu in 1942. The three expose the "dark side" of life in the Yenan region, but they were silenced by Mao's talks at the Yenan Forum in May, 1942. The translations are prefaced by an informative introduction.

700   BERNINGHAUSEN, JOHN and TED HUTERS, eds. *Revolutionary Literature in China: An Anthology.*
      For annotations and bibliographic information, *see* no. 313.

701   BIRCH, CYRIL, ed. *Chinese Communist Literature.* New York: Frederick A. Praeger, 1963.
      Contains thirteen essays by eleven authors on various aspects of Chinese Communist literature. All the essays, written by specialists, deal with the literary endeavors of Chinese Communist writers in the twenty years following Mao Tse-tung's *Talks at the Yenan Forum on Literature and Art* (*see* no. 738) in 1942. The essays, focusing on topics such as war, cooperatives and communes, industrial workers, women, youth, old age, and Mao Tse-tung's poetry, critically evaluate the accomplishments and deficiencies of Chinese Communist literature. In general, the authors are critical of this body of political literature, while realizing its practical function of influencing and instilling in the reader proper political consciousness; they are also concerned with the issue of ideological control versus freedom of artistic expression in literary works.

702   ———. "Chinese Communist Literature: The Persistence of Traditional Forms." In Cyril Birch, ed. *Chinese Communist Literature.* New York: Frederick A. Praeger, 1963, pp. 74-91.
      Citing a number of examples from Chinese Communist literature, the author demonstrates the validity of Hu Shih's statement that "the stuff of which it is made is essentially the Chinese bedrock" and concludes that Chinese Communist literature is very much influenced by Chinese literary traditions.

703 ———. "Contemporary Chinese Literature." *International P.E.N. Bulletin*, 5, no. 1 (March, 1954), 3-6.
A brief survey of contemporary Chinese literature.

704 ———. "Fiction of the Yenan Period." *CQ*, no. 4 (1960), 1-11.
A general discussion of some important writers and their works that have emerged in China since Mao's Yenan talks (*see* no. 738) in 1942. The works of Chao Shu-li, Chou Li-po, and Ai Wu are mentioned and discussed.

705 BOORMAN, HOWARD L. "The Literary World of Mao Tse-tung." In Cyril Birch, ed. *Chinese Communist Literature*. New York: Frederick A. Praeger, 1963, pp. 15-38.
Surveys the "evolving political influences which have shaped Chinese imaginative writing" in a twenty-year period (1942-1962).

706 ———. *Literature and Politics in Contemporary China*.
For annotations and bibliographic information, *see* no. 195.

707 BORDEN, CAROLINE. "Characterization in Revolutionary Chinese and Reactionary American Short Stories." *Literature and Ideology*, no. 12 (1972), pp. 9-16.
An interesting comparative study.

708 BOROWITZ, ALERT. *Fiction in Communist China: 1949-1953*. Cambridge: Center for International Studies, M.I.T., 1954.
According to Mao Tun (Shen Yen-ping) in 1953, 256 novels, 159 volumes of poetry, 265 plays, and other miscellaneous works were written in China during the four-year period from 1949 to 1953. Albert Borowitz's book is an attempt to "indicate some of the trends" in Communist fiction by analyzing a number of short stories and novels.

709 BUTTERFIELD, FOX. "Literature of Dissent Rises in China." *New York Times* (Dec. 13, 1977), 1, 8.
Probably the first report on China's dissent literature in a Western language, this article provides an interesting introduction to the underground literature, some oral and some handwritten, that has emerged since the Cultural Revolution (1966-1969).

710 CHAN, S. W. "Literature in Communist China." *Problems of Communism*, 7, no. 1 (1958).
A survey of the major themes in pre-1958 Communist literature.

711 CHAO, CHUNG. *The Communist Program for Literature and Art in China*. Hong Kong: Union Research Institute, 1955.
A survey of the Communist program for art and literature in the early years of the People's Republic.

712 CH'EN, SHIH-HSIANG. "Language and Literature under Communism." In Yuan-li Wu, ed. *China: A Handbook*. New York: Frederick A. Praeger, 1973, pp. 705-736.

A summary of language reforms and literary activities in China since 1949.

713 CHIH, PIEN. " 'The Wound' Debate." *ChL*, no. 3 (March, 1979), pp. 103-105.

A discussion of the debate on Lu Hsin-hua's "The Wound," which is included in Winston L. Y. Yang and Nathan K. Mao, eds., *Stories of Contemporary China* (*see* no. 765); and Geremie Barmé and Bennett Lee, trs., *The Wounded* (*see* no. 753).

The story reveals the tragic impact of the Cultural Revolution which has become a popular literary theme since 1977.

714 CHOU, EN-LAI. "Zhou Enlai on Questions Related to Art and Literature." *ChL*, no. 6 (June, 1979), pp. 83-95.

Excerpts from Chou En-lai's 1961 speeches on art and literature.

715 CHOU, YANG. *China's New Literature and Art*. Peking: Foreign Languages Press, 1954.

Presents an official Communist view of developments in literature and art in China since 1949.

715a ———. *The Path of Socialist Literature and Art in China*. Peking: Foreign Languages Press, 1960.

A discussion of adapting traditional forms of art and literature to the needs of revolutionary ideology and of combining revolutionary romanticism with revolutionary realism.

716 DU, HE. "The Short Stories of 1978." *ChL*, no. 6 (June, 1979), pp. 113-117.

An informative survey of Chinese short stories written in 1978.

717 EBER, IRENE. "Images of Women in Recent Chinese Fiction: Do Women Hold Up Half the Sky?" *Signs: Journal of Women in Culture and Society*, 2, no. 1 (Autumn, 1976), pp. 24-34.

This essay compares the themes of female emancipation in pre-and post-1949 Chinese fiction. Citing Lu Hsün's "Regret for the Past" ("*Shang-shih*") and Mao Tun's "Suicide" ("*Tzu-sha*") as examples of the hopelessness of women's situation in the 1920s, the author points out that the literature of the 1940s no longer exudes such hopelessness. Examples include the happy ending of Chao Shu-li's "Hsiao Erh-hei's Marriage" ("*Hsiao Erh-hei chieh-hun*") and Chao's sympathies with the demands of women. Citing examples from post-1949 fiction, the author shows how land reform, participation in production, and the marriage law have positively changed the lives of women in China today.

718   FOKKEMA, D. W. "Chinese Literature under the Cultural Revolution." *LEW*, 13 (1969), 335-358.
A study of the open conflict between the demands of literature and politics during the Cultural Revolution (1966-1969). The debate in China was centered on the type of balance that should be maintained between literature and politics as well as that between literature and propaganda.

719   ———. *Literary Doctrine in China and Soviet Influence, 1956-1960.* The Hague: Mouton, 1965.
A discussion of literary doctrine in China, this study presents a picture of the literary life in the first decade under Communist rule, outlines literary events of the period, and summarizes criticisms directed at writers and artists. Also correlating literary developments in the Soviet Union with those in China, it concludes with a discussion of the Third National Congress of Writers and Artists and the Congress's condemnation of the elements of "revisionism" in literature.

719a   GIBBS, DONALD A., ed. "Dissonant Voices in Chinese Literature: Hu Feng." *Chinese Studies in Literature*, 1 (1979-1980), 3-89.
A collection of three articles (translated from the Chinese) on the anti-Hu Feng campaign of 1955, including one containing Hu's self-criticism.

720   GOLDMAN, MERLE. "The Fall of Chou Yang." *CQ*, no. 27 (July/Sept.,1966), 132-148.
A discussion of the fall of one of China's most important literary spokesmen, Chou Yang, who was purged at the beginning of the Cultural Revolution (he was rehabilitated in early 1979).

721   ———. "Hu Feng's Conflict with the Communist Literary Authorities." *CQ*, no. 12 (Oct./ Dec., 1962), 102-137.
The focus of this article is on the reaction of Hu Feng, one of the leading Marxist literary critics who allied themselves closely with the Communist Party, to changes in the government's policy regarding literary freedom.

722   ———. *Literary Dissent in Communist China.* Cambridge: Harvard University Press, 1967.
Prefaced by profiles of major revolutionary writers (Ai Ch'ing, Feng Hsüeh-feng, Ho Ch'i-fang, Hsiao Chün, Hu Feng, Ting Ling, Ch'en Po-ta, Chou Yang, Kuo Mo-jo, and others), this study in eleven chapters focuses on the conflicts between the Chinese Communist Party and Chinese writers in the 1940s and '50s. Examining such important questions as literary opposition during the Yenan period, conflicts among left-wing writers, the anti-Hu Feng campaign of 1955, the Hundred Flowers Movement, the Anti-Rightist Drive against the writers during 1957 and 1958, and the Great Leap Forward Movement, the author concludes in the last chapter ("The Significance of Literary Dissent"):"The lives of the revolutionary writers in Communist China have more importance than their literary works. Despite the party's determination to eliminate them as a distinct group and to incorporate all intellectuals into the state bureaucracy, they were an amorphous, yet indepen-

dent, island in the vast sea of the bureaucracy. . . . They remained alienated intellectuals who found themselves as alienated from the institutions and values of the new society they helped to establish as from the old ones they helped to destroy."

723   GOTZ, MICHAEL. "Images of the Worker in Contemporary Chinese Fiction (1949-1964)." Ph.D. Dissertation. Berkeley: University of California, 1977.

      The author states that in contemporary Chinese fiction the images of the Chinese worker are numerous and varied. This study centers on the fine distinctions between different types of "socialist men" or distinct character types who work in electric plants, steel mills, or other industries. In addition, the study examines the relationship between contemporary proletarian fiction and the vernacular tradition.

724   HSIA, C. T. *A History of Modern Chinese Fiction.* 2nd ed. New Haven: Yale University Press, 1971.

      Contains two chapters on Communist fiction and an appendix on Chinese Communist literature since 1958. For more information on the book, *see* no. 238.

725   ———. "Literature and Art under Mao Tse-tung." In Frank N. Trager and William Henderson, eds. *Communist China 1949-1969: A Twenty-Year Appraisal.* New York University Press, 1970, pp. 199-220.

      A critical discussion of four novels produced in the past twenty years (1949-1969): Ai Wu's *Steeled and Tempered (Pai lien ch'eng kang)*, Chou Li-po's *Great Changes in a Mountain Village (Shan-hsiang chü-pien)*, Ou-yang Shan's *The Three-Family Lane (San-chia hsiang)*, and Chin Ching-mai's *The Song of Ou-yang Hai (Ou-yang Hai chih ko)*. Also discussed are Chou Yang's literary political career and Mao's "Talks at the Yenan Forum on Literature and Art." C. T. Hsia is critical of Communist literature and pessimistic about its prospects.

726   ———. "Residual Femininity: Women in Chinese Communist Fiction." In Cyril Birch, ed. *Chinese Communist Literature.* New York: Frederick A. Praeger, 1963, pp. 158-179.

      The author makes an interesting chronological survey of the depiction of women characters in a large number of short stories from Chao Shu-li's "The Marriage of Hsiao Erh-hei" (1943) to Hsi Jung's "Corduroy" (1961). Other authors discussed include Ai Wu, Ma Feng, Shih T'o, Ai Ming-chih, Li Chun, and Liu Pin-yen.

727   HSIA, T. A. "Heroes and Hero-Worship in Chinese Communist Fiction." In Cyril Birch, ed. *Chinese Communist Literature.* New York: Frederick A. Praeger, 1963, pp. 113-138.

      The author finds in two novels, *The Song of Youth (Ch'ing-ch'un chih ko)* by Yang Mo and *Red Sun (Hung jih)* by Wu Ch'iang, "encouraging and interesting" indications of world views which do not entirely echo Party directives.

728 ———. "Twenty Years after the Yenan Forum." In Cyril Birch, ed. *Chinese Communist Literature*. New York: Frederick A. Praeger, 1963, pp. 226-253.

A critical assessment of the literary achievements in the twenty years since Mao's Yenan Forum talk (*see* no. 738) in 1942. At the Forum Mao denounced the use of realism, sentimentalism, and satire in literature and advocated ideological expression, party spirit, and national character. Communist literature in China since then has been a fulfillment of that theory with only minor deviations.

729 HSU, KAI-YU. *The Chinese Literary Scene*. New York: Vintage Books, 1975.

In the foreword, the author clearly states his attempt to include in his book "the most influential and best examples of new Chinese writing" that he found during his stay in China in 1973. A chatty introduction describes the author's meeting with many old friends, former teachers and classmates, and his exclusive interviews with some writers. The rest of the book is divided into four sections. The first contains three essays by Kuo Mo-jo and others, showing the changes "in the mood before and after the Cultural Revolution"; the second describes the changes in the Chinese theater; and the third focuses on four representative writers and their works: Hao Jan's *The Broad Road in Golden Light*, Cheng Wan-lung's short story "Springtide, Rolling Along," Yang Mo's *The Song of Youth*, and Kao Yü-pao's story "Rooster's Crow at Midnight." Also included is an interview with Shen Ts'ung-wen, the author's former teacher. The last section discusses recent developments in Chinese folk songs, ballads, and epic poetry. The book is unique in its successful combination of interviews with excerpts from literary works; it also reveals some of the attitudes toward writing in China today. Very informative and helpful for an understanding of Communist literature, especially post-Cultural Revolution writings.

730 ———. "The Bliss and the Bane: A Discussion of P.R.C. Literature." *CLEAR*, forthcoming.

A discussion of some aspects of Chinese Communist literature.

731 HUANG, JOE C. "The Elements of Nostalgia: Veteran Writers under the New Order." In Joseph S. M. Lau and Leo Ou-fan Lee, eds. *Critical Persuasions*, forthcoming.

Deals with the fate of China's "older generation" of writers—the May Fourth writers—after the establishment of the People's Republic in 1949.

732 ———. *Heroes and Villains in Communist China*. New York: Pica Press, 1973.

The author bases his discussion on his reading of twenty-four novels from the People's Republic as social documents depicting the changes in contemporary Chinese society: rural and urban life, underground struggles, guerrilla warfare, civil war, land reforms, factory workers, farmers, and soldiers in war and peace. The author also discusses the reception of recently published works, their popularity and reasons for their appeal. A good book to be read in conjunction with Cyril Birch's *Chinese Communist Literature* (*see* no. 701).

733 ———. "Villains, Victims and Morals in Contemporary Chinese Communist Literature." *CQ*, no. 46 (April/June, 1971).
   A study of the images of negative characters in contemporary Chinese Communist novels.

734 LEE, LEO OU-FAN. "Dissent Literature from the Cultural Revolution." *CLEAR*, 1 (1979), 59-79.
   An analysis of two recent works of dissent literature from China: Hsia Chih-yen's *The Coldest Winter in Peking* (*see* no. 836) and Ch'en Jo-hsi's *The Execution of Mayor Ying* (*see* no. 883), and an assessment of their significance as harbingers of a burgeoning literature of dissent that is emerging in China.

735 LI, CHI. "Communist War Stories." In Cyril Birch, ed. *Chinese Communist Literature*. New York: Frederick A. Praeger, 1963, pp. 139-157.
   An interesting survey of Chinese Communist war fiction ranging from the anti-Japanese novel *Heroes of Lü-liang* (*Lü-liang ying-hsiung chuan*, 1952) by Ma Feng and Hsi Jung, to the anti-Kuomintang novel, *Flames Ahead* (*Huo-kuang tsai ch'ien*, 1952), by Liu Pai-yü.

736 LU, ALEXANDER YA-LI. "Political Control of Literature in Communist China: 1949-1966." Ph.D. Dissertation. Bloomington: Indiana University, 1972.
   This study describes and analyzes the Communist system of literary control and evaluates its effectiveness.

737 MAO TSE-TUNG. *Mao Tse-tung on Literature and Art*. Peking: Foreign Languages Press, 1967.
   Sixteen pieces from the writings and speeches of Mao Tse-tung on various aspects of literature and art, including his most famous "Talks at the Yenan Forum on Literature and Art," delivered in May, 1942.

738 ———. "Talks at the Yenan Forum on Literature and Art." In Mao Tse-tung. *Selected Works of Mao Tse-tung*. Peking: Foreign Languages Press, 1965, III, pp. 69-97.
   The key Communist document which defines the role of literature and art in relation to politics.

738a NIEH, HUALING, ed. *Literature of the Hundred Flowers*. New York: Columbia University Press, 1981. 2 vols.
   A collection in two volumes of selected literary works and critical essays on political and artistic issues written during the 1956-57 One-Hundred Flower Campaign.

739 POLLARD, D. E. "The Short Story in the Cultural Revolution." *CQ*, no. 73 (March, 1978), 99-121.
   An analysis of the development of the short story during the Cultural Revolution (1966-1969).

740 SALISBURY, HARRISON E. "Now It's China's Cultural Thaw." *New York Times Magazine* (Dec. 4, 1977), pp. 49-128.

An interesting report on China's cultural thaw since the death of Mao Tse-tung and the fall of the "Gang of Four" in 1976. The author discusses China's new policy on art and literature, especially the relaxed control of literary and artistic activities, revival of interest in traditional art and literature, and more receptive attitudes toward Western art and literature.

741 SHIH, C. W. "Co-operatives and Communes in Chinese Communist Fiction." In Cyril Birch, ed. *Chinese Communist Literature*. New York: Frederick A. Praeger, 1963, pp. 195-211.

The author focuses attention on several novels and short stories which describe life in the communes and cooperatives: Chao Shu-li's *San-li-wan* (1955), Chou Li-po's *Great Changes in a Mountain Village* (*Shang-hsiang chü pien*, 1958), and a number of short stories by Sha T'ing and Chou Li-po. The emphasis in these works is on the struggle between the "progressive" and the "backward" forces.

742 SHIH, VINCENT Y. C. "Enthusiast and Escapist: Writers of the Older Generation." In Cyril Birch, ed. *Chinese Communist Literature*. New York: Frederick A. Praeger, 1963, pp. 92-112. Also in *CQ*, no. 13 (1963), 92-112.

A discussion of how Pa Chin and Shen Ts'ung-wen, the enthusiast and escapist respectively, have fared since the establishment of the People's Republic. Pa Chin has been enthusiastically praising the new regime while Shen Ts'ung-wen has become an escapist.

743 ———. "Satire in Chinese Communist Literature." *THJ*, n.s., 7, no. 1 (Aug.,1968), 54-70.

If it were not for the fact that "no power has been strong enough to exercise complete control over the mind of man," the author states that there would be no point in discussing satire in Communist literature. Hence, the author finds a number of examples of satire in the works of Lao She, Shen Ts'ung-wen, Mao Tun, and others.

744 SPENCE, JONATHAN. "On Chinese Revolutionary Literature."
For annotations and bibliographic information, *see* no. 301.

744a TENG, HSIAO-P'ING. "Vice-Premier Deng on Literature and Art." *Beijing Review*, no. 45 (1979), pp. 3-15.

An important speech on China's post-Mao policy on art and literature.

744b TING, YI. *A Short History of Modern Chinese Literature*.
For annotations and bibliographic information, *see* no. 304.

745 TSAI, MEI-SHI. "The Construction of Positive Types in Contemporary Chinese Fiction." Ph.D. Dissertation. Berkeley: University of California, 1975. (Part of the dissertation appears in *Criticism*, 20 (1978).

An analysis of the positive types in Communist fiction.

746 WILHELM, HELLMUT. "The Image of Youth and Age in Chinese Communist Literature." In Cyril Birch, ed. *Chinese Communist Literature*. New York: Frederick A. Praeger, 1963, pp. 180-194. Also in *CQ*, no. 13 (1963), 180-194.
   A general discussion of how youth is depicted in modern Chinese fiction in the works of Ping Hsin, Ting Ling, and Pa Chin as well as in "How Lo Wen-ying Became a Young Pioneer" by Chang T'ien-i and in the novel *The Song of Youth* by Yang Mo.

747 WITKE, ROXANE. *Comrade Chiang Ch'ing*. Boston: Little, Brown and Co., 1977.
   A biographical study of Chiang Ch'ing, the wife of Mao Tse-tung, who controlled literary and artistic developments in China from the beginning of the Cultural Revolution in 1966 until her fall in 1976. The study, based in part on the author's many interviews with Chiang Ch'ing, contains extensive references to China's policy on art and literature from 1966 to 1976.

748 ———. "A Cultural Cavalcade from Mainland China." *New York Times* (July 2, 1978), Sec. 2, 1, 20.
   Contains references to China's policy on art and literature since the fall of the "Gang of Four" (one of whom was Chiang Ch'ing) in 1976.

749 YANG, I-FAN. *The Case of Hu Feng*. Hong Kong: Union Research Institute, 1956.
   In 1955, Hu Feng, a Communist critic, was singled out for attack by the Party. This generally factual study traces in detail the literary career of Hu Feng since the 1930s and his stormy relationship with the Party. His case is significant and complicated because of Hu's long involvement and influence in Chinese literary and artistic circles.

750 YANG, RICHARD F. S. "Industrial Workers in Chinese Communist Fiction." In Cyril Birch, ed. *Chinese Communist Literature*. New York: Frederick A. Praeger, 1963, pp. 212-226.
   The author discusses three novels about the industrial worker: *Our Day of Festivity* (1952) and *Spring Comes to the Yalu River* (1954), both by Lei Chia, and *Steeled and Tempered* (1961) by Ai Wu. He fails to find the three novels inspiring.

751 YANG, WINSTON L. Y. and NATHAN K. MAO. "Literature, Chinese." In *Britannica Book of the Year*. Chicago: Encyclopaedia Britannica, Inc., 1980, pp. 516-17; 1981, pp. 520-21.
   A survey of literary developments in 1979 in China and in Taiwan.

752 ———, eds. *Stories of Contemporary China*.
   For annotations and bibliographic information, *see* no. 765A.

Anthologies

753 BARMÉ, GEREMIE and BENNETT LEE, trs. *The Wounded: New Stories of the Cultural Revolution, 77-78.* Hong Kong: Joint Publishing Co., 1979.
   A collection of eight stories (written in 1977-78) selected to serve as a representative sample of what is now known as 'new wave' literature or 'literature of the wounded', after the title story, 'The Wounded.' All of them deal with the tragic impact of the Cultural Revolution. The collection contains extensive mistranslations and grammatical, punctuation, and typographical errors.

753a BERNINGHAUSEN, JOHN and TED HUTERS, eds. *Revolutionary Literature in China: An Anthology.*
   For annotations and bibliographic information, *see* no. 313.

754 *City Cousin and Other Stories.* Peking: Foreign Languages Press, 1973.
   This collection of eight stories presents new developments in village and commune life after the Cultural Revolution: women's struggles, the training of successors, and revolutionary committees.

755 *Dawn on the River and Other Stories.* Peking: Foreign Languages Press, 1957.
   A collection of seven short stories by Chun Ching, Hai Mo, Hsi Yung, Li Wen-yüan, Lu Yang-lieh, Wang Wen-shih, and Wang Yüan-chien.

756 *Flame on High Mountain and Other Stories.* Peking: Foreign Languages Press, 1962.
   Contains twelve stories by various writers about the people's struggles for liberation from 1927 to 1937.

757 HSU, KAI-YU, ed. *Literature of the People's Republic of China: An Anthology.* Bloomington: Indiana University Press, 1979.
   The most comprehensive anthology of Chinese Communist literature, including fiction, poetry, and drama. Only new translations are included, except where the outstanding quality of an extant translation warrants inclusion. Both established authors and younger writers are featured. Among the fiction writers selected are Ting Ling, Hsiao Chün, Ou-yang Shan, Chou Li-po, Ai Wu, Chao Shu-li, Wang Chia-pin, Hu Wan-ch'un, Kao Yü-pao, and Cheng Wan-lung. Each selection is preceded by a short introduction.

758 *I Knew All Along and Other Stories.* Peking: Foreign Languages Press, 1960.
   Contains thirteen stories by various writers, including Ma Feng, Tu P'eng-ch'eng, Liu Pai-yü, and others.

759   *A New Home and Other Stories.* Peking: Foreign Languages Press, 1959.
      Eight short stories by contemporary Chinese writers about various aspects of life in China. The authors include Ai Wu, Ma Feng, Lo Pin-chi.

760   *Registration and Other Stories.* Peking: Foreign Languages Press, 1954.
      A collection of ten short stories by various writers, including Chao Shu-li and Kao Yü-pao.

761   *The Seeds and Other Stories.* Peking: Foreign Languages Press, 1972.
      A collection of fourteen stories, written by young authors during the Cultural Revolution. The stories reflect the changes that the Chinese have undergone in their "mental world and the achievements they have made in the socialist revolution and construction." Most of the authors took part in the incidents they describe; their stories are: "Red Cliff Revisited," "A Night in 'Potato' Village," "Half the Population," "Raiser of Sprouts," "Third Time to School," "The Case of the Missing Ducks," "A Detour to Dragon Village," "Raising Seedlings," "Selling Rice," "Two Ears of Rice," "Crossing Chungchou Dam," "The Seeds," "Where the Sunghua River Flows," and "The Story of Tachai."

762   *The Seven Sisters: Selected Chinese Folk Stories.* Peking: Foreign Languages Press, 1965.
      A collection of twelve folk stories from different nationalities which express "the Chinese people's longing for a free and happy life."

763   *A Snowy Day and Other Stories.* Peking: Foreign Languages Press, 1960.
      A collection of six stories by various authors on a slightly nostalgic theme.

764   *Sowing the Clouds.* Peking: Foreign Languages Press, 1961.
      A collection of ten stories by various authors, including Tu P'eng-ch'eng, Chou Li-po, and Li Chun.

765   *Wild Bull Village: Chinese Short Stories.* Peking: Foreign Languages Press, 1965.
      Contains six short stories by such contemporary writers as Ai Wu and Li Chun.

765a YANG, WINSTON L. Y. and NATHAN K. MAO, eds. *Stories of Contemporary China.* New York: Paragon Book Gallery, 1979.
      This anthology, which contains seven stories written since the death of Mao Tse-tung and the fall of the Gang of Four in 1976, is designed to reflect changes in literature in the post-Mao era and to give the reader a glimpse of life in contemporary China. Among the themes presented in these tales are love ("A Place for Love" by Liu Hsin-wu) and the tragic impact of the Cultural Revolution ("The Wound" by Lu Hsin-hua). An introduction to the book provides a brief survey of changes in literature in China since 1976.

766   *Yenan Seeds and Other Stories.* Peking: Foreign Languages Press, 1976.
      A collection of stories which deal with everyday problems of workers, peasants, and cadres in present-day China.

767 *The Young Coal-Miner and Other Stories.* Peking: Foreign Languages Press, 1958.
A collection of short stories about industrial workers.

768 *A Young Pathbreaker and Other Stories.* Peking: Foreign Languages Press, 1975.
A collection of ten stories about young people and their struggles to build a new China. The theme of industrialization in the city and the countryside is emphasized.

769 *The Young Skipper and Other Stories.* Peking: Foreign Languages Press, 1973.
A collection of stories about working men and women in their struggles to overcome difficulties after the Cultural Revolution.

Individual Writers

1. Ai Wu (T'ang Tao-keng): 1904-

Ai Wu is a native of Szechuan province. In 1931 he joined the League of Left-Wing Writers and wrote extensively during and after World War II. He remained productive after 1949. His works include several collections of short stories and a few novels, among which the most acclaimed is *Steeled and Tempered.* Purged during the Cultural Revolution, he has recently been rehabilitated.

Translations

770 HSU, RAYMOND S. W., tr. "Return by Night." *Renditions,* no. 7 (Spring, 1977), pp. 39-44.
Written in 1954, this story (*"Yeh kuei"*), one of Ai Wu's best, deals with workers and the cooperative movement.

771 JENNER, W.J.F., tr. "On the Island." In W. J. F. Jenner, ed. *Modern Chinese Stories.* London: Oxford University Press, 1970, pp. 107-119.
This story (*"Hai-tao shang"*) is set on an island in Southeast Asia. Three Chinese nationals and others are detained by the local government's epidemic control stations; they are to be disinfected before they go ashore.

772 "Mrs. Shih Ching." *ChL,* no. 3 (March, 1954), pp. 84-97.
The tale (*"Shih Ch'ing sao-tzu"*) describes the suffering of a peasant woman and her five young children who are evicted from their land and home by a ruthless landlord.

773 *Steeled and Tempered.* Peking: Foreign Languages Press, 1961.
This novel (*Pai lien ch'eng kang*) focuses on the life and work of steel workers in the Liaonan Iron and Steel Company in Liaoning province in Manchuria. The main theme, accelerated steel production, is buried among the subthemes of love, competition, jealousy, and conflict between Party cadres and technicians. The novel has been widely acclaimed.

774 SU, CHIN, tr. "Wild Bull Village." *ChL,* no. 9 (Sept., 1962), pp. 3-21; reprinted in *Wild Bull Village.* Peking: Foreign Languages Press, 1965.
   In this tale (*"Yeh-niu chai"*), the peasant girl Ah-hsiu's struggle for freedom in the old society is described along with her daughter's struggle for freedom in the new society.

775 YEH, YUNG, tr. "A New Home." In *A New Home and Other Stories.* Peking: Foreign Languages Press, 1959, pp. 54-70.
   In this story (*"Hsin ti chia"*), the joy of young newlyweds moving into their new home is emphasized.

Studies

776 FOKKEMA, D. W. "Ai Wu." In Jaroslav Průšek, ed. *Dictionary of Oriental Literatures.* London: George Allan and Unwin, 1974; New York: Basic Books, 1974, I, p. 2.
   A brief account of Ai Wu's life and work.

2. Chao Shu-li: 1906-1970

Of peasant family roots, Chao Shu-li received little formal education. He was imprisoned by the Kuomintang for the espousal of radical ideas. In the 1940s his writings were very effective in rousing the peasants against the Japanese invaders. He was severely criticized by the radical faction known as the Gang of Four during the Cultural Revolution. He died in 1970 and has been posthumously rehabilitated.

Translations

777 "Little Erhei's Marriage." *ChL,* no. 5 (May 1979), pp. 28-54.
   Written in 1943, this is the love story of Little Erhei and Little Chin, which reflects the struggles waged in the Communist countryside during World War II. It praises the new ideas of the peasants, mocks their old backward ones, and criticizes the feudal forces then existing in the countryside. Said to be based on fact, this story is among the best of Chao Shu-li's works.

778 MAO, NATHAN K. and WINSTON L. Y. YANG, trs. "The Unglovable Hands". In Kai-yu Hsu, ed., *Literature of the People's Republic of China: An Anthology.* Bloomington: Indiana University Press, 1980, pp. 494-502.
   "The Unglovable Hands" is the story of a farmer, Ch'en Ping-cheng, in which the appearance, strength, and dexterity of his hands are emphasized. Hence, they are symbolic of the old farmer himself. The story is known, as pointed out by Lao She, for its simple but thoughtful choice of diction, its accurate depiction of life in the country, and, in particular, its use of the gloves as "the thread" to link the story's many disparate elements into a coherent whole.

779 SHAPIRO, SIDNEY, tr. *The Rhymes of Li Yu-ts'ai and Other Stories*. Peking: Foreign Languages Press, 1955. First published in 1950.

Contains "The Rhymes of Li Yu-ts'ai" ("*Li Yu-ts'ai pan-hua*"), "Hsiao Erh-hei's Marriage," and two other stories. The first story uses a medieval narrative form mixed with songs to present a folksinger who sings of the suffering of the poor and the evils of corrupt landlords. The second, an extremely popular narrative, describes how a young peasant succeeds in marrying the girl he loves.

780 YANG, GLADYS, tr. *Changes in Li Village*. Peking: Foreign Languages Press, 1953.

This book (*Li-chia-chuang ti pien-ch'ien*) is a short novel about land reforms in backward Shansi province in barren North China. A peasant hero, Chang T'ieh-so, is first pitted against the opium-smoking landlords and officials. Later he becomes a Communist organizer and leads the villagers against the villainous landlords, the Japanese, and the Kuomintang troops. The novel, first published in 1949, covers the period from 1928 to 1945.

781 ———. *Sanliwan Village*. Peking: Foreign Languages Press, 1957.

Whereas his previous work *Changes in Li Village* is about land reforms, Chao's *Sanliwan Village* depicts the collectivization of land in the countryside. A former muleteer, Fan Teng-kao, who has become well-to-do as a result of land reform, is reluctant to give up his land and join the collective farm. The setting is again in Shansi province, but the novel is "ponderously descriptive" and "lacks the light touch and fast movement of his earlier works."

Studies

782 BIRCH, CYRIL. "Chao Shu-li: Creative Writing in a Communist State." *New Mexico Quarterly*, 25 (1955), 185-95.

A study of the creative art of Chao Shu-li under Mao's guidelines on literature for the masses.

783 LU, CHIEN. "Chao Shu-li and His Writing." *ChL*, no. 9 (Sept., 1964), pp. 21-26.

A brief introduction to Chao Shu-li and his work.

784 PRŮŠEK, JAROSLAV. "Chao Shu-li." In Jaroslav Průšek, ed. *Dictionary of Oriental Literatures*. London: George Allen and Unwin, 1974; New York: Basic Books, 1974, I, p. 9.

A brief account of Chao's life and work.

3. *Chin Ching-mai: 1930-*

Little is known of Chin Ching-mai. Born in Nanking, he joined the army in 1949 and was a very active fiction writer in the 1960s. His most famous work is *The Song of Ou-yang Hai*, which was hailed as a major contribution during the Cultural Revolution.

Translations

785 SHAPIRO, SIDNEY and TUNG CHEN-SHENG, trs. *The Song of Ou-yang Hai*. *ChL*, no. 7 (July, 1966), pp. 72-132; no. 8 (Aug., 1966), pp. 30-96; no. 9 (Sept., 1966), pp. 88-141; no. 10 (Oct., 1966), pp. 75-103; no. 11 (Nov., 1966), pp. 61-104. (Published in book form by Foreign Languages Press, Peking, 1966.)

   A biographical novel about a young, ambitious soldier of a poor peasant background in the People's Liberation Army. At first he is motivated by the desire to become a combat hero, but he soon learns that less-glamorous construction work is as much a part of a soldier's life as combat. He dies heroically at the age of twenty-three when, in the line of duty, he saves a train from derailment. The lesson of Ou-yang Hai shows the people how to rid themselves of ego and to become selfless in their work.

Studies

786 CHIN, CHING-MAI. "How I Conceived and Wrote *The Song of Ou-yang Hai*." *ChL*, (Nov., 1966), pp. 105-119.

   Describes the experience of the author in writing *The Song of Ou-yang Hai*.

4. Chou Li-po: 1908-1979

A native of Hunan province, Chou Li-po lived in Shanghai in the 1920s, was arrested in 1932 and released in 1934 by the Kuomintang. Later he went to Yenan and worked as a teacher at the Lu Hsün Academy. During the Cultural Revolution, he was accused of having slandered Lu Hsün and committing other offenses. He was rehabilitated in 1978 and died in 1979.

Translations

787 BRYAN, DEREK, tr. *Great Changes in a Mountain Village*. Peking: Foreign Languages Press, 1961.

   This novel (*Shan-hsiang chü-pien*) depicts the establishment of farming cooperatives following land reform. The author vividly describes life in a mountain village in Hunan and Party meetings with the villagers. For example, in his vigorous, selfless efforts to bring about the collective, Liu Yü-sheng, the head of the mutual-aid team, is divorced by his wife. This novel, written in 1958 and set in Hunan province, may be considered a sequel to his *The Hurricane* (see no. 788).

788 HSÜ, MENG-HSIUNG, tr. *The Hurricane*. Peking: Foreign Languages Press, 1955.

   A powerful novel, *The Hurricane* (*Pao-feng tsou-yü*) is about land reforms in northern Manchuria. It tells how the peasants, after their revolutionary consciousness has been raised, unleash their wrath on their landlords. Written in 1949, it won third place in the competition for the Stalin Prize for Literature in 1952.

789   HUANG, JOE, tr. "The Guest." *BCAS*, no. 8 (April/June, 1976), pp. 17-23.
       A story of a dutiful young woman who asks her prospective in-laws to postpone the wedding for the sake of the state.

Studies

790   FOKKEMA, D. W. "Chou Li-po." In Jaroslav Průšek, ed. *Dictionary of Oriental Literatures*. London: George Allen and Unwin 1974; New York: Basic Books, 1974, I, p. 19.
       A brief account of Chou's life and work.

5. Hao Jan (Liang Chin-kuang): 1932-

Born into a poor peasant family, Hao Jan published more than one hundred short stories before the Cultural Revolution and is known for his mastery of the Chinese peasants' dialect in his writings. During the Cultural Revolution he became one of the most prominent and popular Chinese writers for his several long novels. After the death of Mao Tse-tung in 1976, he was criticized for his relations with the "Gang of Four." Recently, however, he seems to have been rehabilitated.

Translations

791   *Bright Clouds*. Peking: Foreign Languages Press, 1974.
       A collection of eight stories by Hao Jan which covers a period of about ten years (1958-1968). They describe the sturdy peasants who live close to the soil and their willingness to overcome hardships. Written in the reportage style, they glorify altruism and the joy of labor.

792   "*The Bright Road*." *ChL*, no. 9 (Sept., 1975), pp. 4-66; no. 10 (Oct., 1975), pp. 4-59.
       A translation of fourteen chapters from the second volume of Hao Jan's multivolume novel *The Bright Road*, which deals with the problems of collectivization of agriculture in the early 1950s in Sweet Meadow Village in Hopei province.

793   CHANG, SU, tr. "The Vegetable Seeds." *ChL*, no. 6 (June, 1966), pp. 3-12.
       The story of Meng Chao-hsien, the leader of the vegetable team of the Production Brigade, who receives seeds, encouragement, and friendship from a neighboring community.

794   "The First Step." *ChL*, no. 1 (Jan., 1973), pp. 4-62.
       Translation of the first nine chapters of the first volume of Hao Jan's *The Bright Road*.

795 SHAPIRO, SIDNEY, tr. "Spring Rain." *ChL.*, no. 8 (Aug., 1964), pp. 3-16.
   One of Hao Jan's stories about village life written before the Cultural Revolution.

796 WONG, KAM-MING, tr. "Debut." *BCAS*, no. 8 (April/June, 1976), pp. 24-29.
   A story about a young female work-time-recorder who must not only work hard but also guard against "cheaters," those who fail to do their share.

797 YANG, GLADYS, tr. "The Eve of Her Wedding." *ChL*, no. 6 (June, 1965), pp. 20-33.
   The story of Chiu-lan, a bride-to-be who behaves quite differently from brides in the old days—she does not stop her daily work even on the eve of her wedding.

798 ———. "Sisters-in-Law." *ChL*, no. 2 (Feb., 1965), pp. 48-60.
   This story shows that even within a small family there are capitalist roaders and socialist workers.

799 YU, FAN-MING, tr."Moonlight in the Eastern Wall." *ChL*, no. 11 (Nov., 1959), pp. 47-48.
   In this story, the whole Shang family works selflessly for the Party and the community—except the mother, who is stubborn in her bourgeois ways. But even she, as shown by the author, may come to think differently.

Studies

800 CHAO, CHING. "Introducing the Writer Hao Jan." *ChL*, no. 4 (April, 1974), pp. 95-101.
   A brief introduction to Hao Jan's life and works.

801 HSU, KAI-YU. "Hao Ran [Hao Jan] (1932-)." In Kai-yu Hsu. *The Chinese Literary Scene*. New York: Vintage Books, 1975, pp. 86-114.
   Contains Hsü's interview with Hao Jan in 1973 and his translation of an excerpt from Hao's novel *The Broad Road in the Golden Light* (*Chin-kuang ta-tao*), also known as *The Bright Road*. This novel, first published in 1972, sold over four million copies in the first year.

802 HUANG, JOE C. "Hao Ran [Hao Jan]: The Peasant Novelist." *Modern China*, 2 (1976), 369-396.
   An introduction to Hao Jan and his works. The author analyzes Hao Jan's *Bright Sunny Sky* and *The Bright Road* in the context of other works of socialist realism and finds them refreshing. Also briefly sketches Hao Jan's literary career.

803   JENNER, W. J. F. "Class Struggle in a Chinese Village—A Novelist's View: Hao Ran's *Yan Yang Tian* [Yen-yang t'ien]." *Modern Asian Studies*, 1 (April, 1967), 191-206.

A detailed summary and discussion of Hao Jan's important novel *Bright Sunny Sky* (*Yen-yang t'ien*), which deals with the continuing class struggle in the cooperatives. The story takes place in 1957 in the fictional village of Tung-shan-wu. The first volume of the three-volume novel was published in 1964.

6. Kao Yü-pao: 1927-

Born into a poor peasant family in Liaoning Peninsula, fifty miles north of Port Arthur, Kao Yü-pao had a tragic childhood and joined the People's Liberation Army in 1947. The army taught him to read and to write of his own experience.

Translations

804   *My Childhood*. Peking: Foreign Languages Press, 1960. 2nd rev. ed., 1975.

An autobiographical novel about the struggles of the poverty-stricken Kao family, which was oppressed first by the landlords and later by the Japanese. The novel ends with the cruel death of Kao Yü-pao's mother at the hands of the Japanese. The novel, first published in 1955 under the title *My Childhood*, is now named after himself, *Kao Yu-pao*.

Studies

805   HSU, KAI-YU. "Gao Yu-bao [Kao Yü-pao] (1927-)." In Kai-yu Hsu. *The Chinese Literary Scene*. New York: Vintage Books, 1975, pp. 155-164.

Contains a brief account of Kao's life and the translation of an excerpt (chapter 9) from his autobiographical novel *Kao Yü-pao*.

7. Liu Ch'ing: 1916-1978

A native of Shensi province, Liu Ch'ing joined the Communist Party in 1936 and went to Yenan in 1938. He wrote a number of novels in the 1950s.

Translations

806   SHAPIRO, SIDNEY, tr. *The Builders*. Peking: Foreign Languages Press, 1964.

A novel about land reforms in the early 1950s, it is often hailed as a "landmark" in the development of socialist literature. The main character, Liang Sheng-pao, a young peasant, is the embodiment of the new "socialist man," who tries his best "to make mutual aid a success."

807   *Wall of Bronze*. Peking: Foreign Languages Press, 1954.

A novel about the Battle of Sha-chia-tien in Shensi, in August, 1947, between the People's Liberation Army and the Kuomintang forces.

Studies

808 LI, HSI-FAN. "Comments on *The Builders.*" *ChL*, no. 3 (March, 1961), pp. 131-143.

   An analysis of Liu Ch'ing's novel *The Builders* in terms of its ideological content, realistic portrayals, artistic achievement, and its depiction of the rural scene.

8. Liu Pai-yü: 1916-

A native of Hopei province, Liu Pai-yü is a novelist, war reporter, film writer, and director of a press agency. He won the 1950 Stalin Prize for his film, *Victory of the Chinese People*, and is noted for his reportage fiction, especially for works depicting the battles against the Kuomintang forces during the last stage of China's civil war. He was purged during the Cultural Revolution but has recently been rehabilitated.

Translations

809 *Flames Ahead.* Peking: Foreign Languages Press, 1954.

   This novel (*Huo-kuang tsai-ch'ien*) describes the Red Army's offensive south of the Yangtze River in 1949. The author constantly places the glorious victories against a backdrop of the previous twenty years of grievous trials and heavy losses.

810 *Six A. M. and Other Stories.* Peking: Foreign Languages Press, 1953.

   A collection of five short stories in which the author describes the courage, discipline, and determination of the masses in achieving their liberation from their oppressors.

Studies

811 PRŮŠEK, JAROSLAV. "Liu Pai-yü." In Jaroslav Průšek, ed. *Dictionary of Oriental Literatures.* London: George Allen and Unwin 1974; New York: Basic Books, 1974, I, pp. 102-103.

   A brief account of Liu Pai-yü's life and work.

9. Ma Feng (Ma Shu-ming): 1922-

Born in Hsiao-i district, Shensi province, Ma Feng is known for the lengthy novel *Lü-liang ying-hsiung chuan* (*The Heroes of Lü-liang*), authored jointly by him and Hsi Jung. This novel, modeled on the traditional Chinese novel *Shui-hu chuan* (*The Water Margin*), has many interesting narratives about the heroic deeds of the Chinese in their war against Japan.

Studies

812 PRŮŠEK, JAROSLAV. "Ma Feng." In Jaroslav Průšek, ed. *Dictionary of Oriental Literatures.* London: George Allen and Unwin, 1974; New York: Basic Books, 1974, I, p. 108.

   A brief account of Ma Feng's life and work.

10. Ou-yang Shan (Yang I): 1908-

A native of Kwangtung, Ou-yang Shan lived in Shanghai and Nanking from 1928 to 1940, joined the Communist Party in 1940, and later lived in Yenan. He was accused of revisionism and other sins by the Party in 1966, but has now been rehabilitated.

Translations

813   KUO, MEI-HUA, tr. *Uncle Kao*. Peking: Foreign Languages Press, 1957.
Written in 1946, *Uncle Kao* (*Kao Kan-ta*) is about life in a consumers' cooperative in pre-Liberation days (1941) in the Yenan region. The protagonists combat their own selfishness and prejudices of various sorts.

814   TANG, SHENG, tr. *The Bright Future*. Peking: Foreign Languages Press, 1958.
Written in 1954, *The Bright Future* (*Ch'ien-ch'eng ssu chin*) is a short, lighthearted novel about land reform and the establishment of cooperatives. The plot centers on the protagonist Shu-chien's relationship with his uncle and aunt.

815   "Three-Family Lane." *ChL*. no. 5 (May, 1961), pp. 2-71; no. 6 (June, 1961), pp. 3-68.
Translation of the first fifteen chapters of the novel *Three Family Lane* (*San chia hsiang*). The novel covers the 1920s and describes "the preparations for a Communist revolution in the historical perspective of a more general quest for humanity." The novel is also noted for its tense style and its wide range of characters.

Studies

816   FOKKEMA, D. W. "Ou-yang Shan." In Jaroslav Průšek, ed. *Dictionary of Oriental Literatures*. London: George Allen and Unwin 1974; New York: Basic Books, 1974, II, p. 135.
A brief account of Ou-yang Shan's life and work.

11. Tu P'eng-ch'eng: 1921-

A native of Shensi province born to an impoverished family, Tu P'eng-ch'eng joined the revolution and went to Yenan in 1937. He achieved fame with his 1954 novel *Defend Yenan*.

Translations

817   *In Days of Peace*. Peking: Foreign Languages Press, 1962.
This novel (*Tsai ho-p'ing ti jih-tzu li*) depicts the hardships and struggles against natural and human obstacles in constructing the three-hundred-mile-long railroad along the mountainous valley region of the Chialing River in Szechuan province. The author's realistic descriptions are based on his personal on-the-scene experience in railroad construction.

818 SHAPIRO, SIDNEY, tr. *Defend Yenan*. Peking: Foreign Languages Press, 1958.

Published in 1954, *Defend Yenan* (*Pao-wei Yen-an*) describes the six months of struggle between the People's Liberation Army (PLA) and the Kuomintang (KMT) forces in 1947. The PLA was led by P'eng Te-huai and the KMT forces by Hu Tsung-nan. The focus of attention, however, is on the company commander Chou Ta-yung and his men. Chou and his company repeatedly break out of close encirclement by the enemy and achieve the final victory.

Studies

819 TU, P'ENG-CH'ENG. "What Makes Me Write." *ChL*, no. 1 (Jan., 1960), pp. 116-123.

Describes the author's own experience in the war of liberation in the 1940s and how this experience inspired his writing.

12. Wu Ch'iang: 1910-

A native of Kiangsu province, Wu Ch'iang began his writing career in 1932 while he was a student in Shanghai. In 1937 he joined the People's Liberation Army, and during the Cultural Revolution he was accused of revisionism and other crimes.

Translations

820 BARNES, A. C. tr. *Red Sun*. Peking: Foreign Languages Press, 1964. First published in 1961.

A long novel in 72 chapters, *Red Sun* (*Hung-jih*) centers on fighting between the outnumbered People's Liberation Army and the Kuomintang forces in north China in 1946-47.

Studies

821 CHAO, LIN. "A Novel about the Liberation War." *ChL*, no. 7 (July, 1960), pp. 136-140.

An essay giving background information about Wu Ch'iang's *Red Sun*, which is based on the Battle of Lienshui in 1946-1947.

822 FOKKEMA, D. W. "Wu Ch'iang." In Jaroslav Průšek, ed, *Dictionary of Oriental Literatures*. London: George Allen and Unwin 1974; New York: Basic Books, 1974, I, p. 201.

A brief account of Wu Ch'iang's life and work.

13. Yang Mo: 1915-

Born in Hunan, Yang Mo is one of the best-known women writers in China today. Her 1958 novel, *The Song of Youth*, was criticized during the Cultural Revolution. She has recently been rehabilitated and become active again.

Translations

823   NAN, YING, tr. *The Song of Youth.* Peking: Foreign Languages Press, 1964.
       The Song of Youth (Ch'ing-ch'un chih ko) is a highly popular novel about young, idealistic students who struggle to find their place in China in the 1930s. The experience of a young woman intellectual, Lin Tao-ching, illustrates the complexities of Chinese society at the time and the clashes of personalities and beliefs among young intellectuals who fight against the Japanese invaders and the Kuomintang.

Studies

824   HSU, KAI-YU. "Yang Mo (1915-   )." In Kai-yu Hsu. *The Chinese Literary Scene.* New York: Vintage Books, 1975, pp. 139-155.
       Contains a summary of Hsu Kai-yü's interview with Yang Mo in 1973 and an excerpt from her novel *The Song of Youth (Ch'ing-ch'un chih ko)*. The novel was published in 1958, made into a movie a year later, and distributed abroad. Half a million copies of the book had been sold by 1961.

825   HUANG, CHAO-YEN. "On *The Song of Youth.*" *ChL*, no. 6 (June, 1960), pp. 138-141.
       An appreciation of the novel written by a contemporary of the author. Highly laudatory.

826   WU, YANG. "Yang Mo and Her Novel *The Song of Youth.*" *ChL*, no. 9 (Sept., 1962), pp. 111-116.
       An interview with Yang Mo, who speaks about the heroine of the novel, Lin Tao-ching, and her role as a representative of many of her contemporary fellow students of the 1920s and '30s.

14. Yao Hsüeh-yin 1910-

Little is known of Yao Hsüeh-yin, who reportedly began writing historical novels in the 1940s and taught part-time at a university before 1949. Since the fall of the "Gang of Four" in 1976, he has resumed the writing of his *Li Tzu-ch'eng—Prince Valiant*, three volumes of which have been published. This lengthy historical novel has been hailed by many as a major contribution to modern Chinese literature.

Translations

827   "Battling South of the Pass." *ChL*, no. 4 (April, 1978), pp. 10-62; no. 5 (May, 1978), pp. 29-93.
       An excerpt (chapters 7-12) from volume one of Yao Hsüeh-yin's historical novel, *Li Tzu-ch'eng - Prince Valiant*, it describes a military campaign in the southern part of Shansi.

827a "Besieged in His Palace." *ChL*, no. 6 (June, 1978), pp. 35-86; no. 7 (July, 1978), pp. 29-94; no. 8 (August, 1978), pp. 76-103.

A translation of chapters 29-33 of volume one of Yao Hsüeh-yin's *Li Tzu-ch'eng*. The excerpt reveals the complex struggle within the Ming court, its corruption, and its inevitable decline and fall.

Studies

828 MAO TUN. "An Introduction to *Li Tzu-cheng—Prince Valiant*." *ChL*, no. 6 (June, 1978), pp. 87-96.

An analysis of Yao Hsüeh-yin's *Li Tzu-ch'eng - Prince Valiant* (a projected 5-volume novel) by the veteran critic and novelist Mao Tun, who points out that Yao is the first writer to attempt to make "an analysis of the feudal society from the viewpoint of historical and dialectical materialism, and presents all these contradictions and complexities in a literary form."

15. Other Post-1949 Writers

(1) Ai Ming-chih: 1925-

829 SHAPIRO, SIDNEY and HO YU-CHIH, trs. "*Seeds of Flame.*" *ChL*, no. 4 (April, 1964), pp. 3-55; no. 5 (May, 1964), pp. 23-84.

Translation of two excerpts from the novel about Shanghai workers during the period from 1918 to 1927. The stories center on Liu Chin-sung, a young shipyard worker, and his wife who works in a tobacco factory. In the story, Liu evolves from a naive, optimistic worker into a staunch revolutionary, who is killed in the workers' uprising of 1927.

(2) Annals of Revolution

830 "*Annals of Revolution.*" *ChL*, no. 6 (June, 1975), pp. 3-75.

Translation of two chapters from the novel *Annals of Revolution*, written collectively by worker-peasant-soldier-students of Peking University. It is a chronicle of the peasant Liu Mao-ching, who struggles first against the landlords, then the Japanese, and lastly the capitalist roaders during the Cultural Revolution of 1966-1969.

(3) Ch'en Teng-k'e: 1918-

831 SHAPIRO, SIDNEY, tr. *Living Hell*. Peking: Foreign Languages Press, 1955.

A novel describing the struggle between the People's Liberation Army (PLA) and the Kuomintang forces, with emphasis on the close relationship between the people and the PLA.

(4) Chih-hsia: 1917-

832 *The Railway Guerrillas*. Peking: Foreign Languages Press, 1966.

A novel about the exploits of a unit of railway guerrillas made up of miners and railway workers during the Sino-Japanese War.

(5) Ch'in Chao-yang: 1916-

833   JAMES, JEAN, tr. "Silence." *BCAS*, no. 8 (April/June, 1976), 12-15.
      A subtle short story attacking old attitudes which should be changed in the new society.

(6) Chou Erh-fu: 1914-

834   BARNES, A. C., tr. *Morning in Shanghai*. Peking: Foreign Languages Press, 1962.
      A long novel about life in post-Liberation Shanghai. The author describes in detail the changes in thoughts, habits, and life-styles of capitalists and businessmen as they make the transformation from capitalism to socialism.

(7) Ch'ü Po: 1923-

835   SHAPIRO, SIDNEY, tr. *Tracks in the Snowy Forest*. Peking: Foreign Languages Press, 1962.
      A novel about a small detachment of the People's Liberation Army whose duty is to round up a group of Kuomintang soldiers and their leaders who are seeking refuge in the dense mountain forests of northeastern China. Several folk tales are woven into the novel.

(8) Hsia Chih-yen

836   DEE, LIANG-LAO, tr. *The Coldest Winter in Peking*. New York: Doubleday, 1978.
      A translation of a work of dissent literature, *Pei-ching tsui leng ti tung-t'ien*, by Hsia Chih-yen, which is probably the pseudonym of a former Chinese government official now living in exile in Japan. This lengthy novel has attracted much attention in the West.

(9) Hsü Kuang-yao: 1925-

837   *Little Soldier Chang Ka*. Peking: Foreign Languages Press, 1964.
      A short novel on the lively adventures of an orphan who joins the Eighth Route Army to fight against the invading Japanese Army.

838   SHAPIRO, SIDNEY, tr. *The Plains are Ablaze*. Peking: Foreign Languages Press, 1955.
      Another interesting novel on the Sino-Japanese War.

(10) Hu Wan-ch'un: 1929-

839   GOTZ, MICHAEL, tr. "Twilight Years." In Kai-yu Hsu, ed., *Literature of the People's Republic of China*. Bloomington: Indiana University Press, 1980, pp. 619-27.
      The story of the love and respect held by a group of factory apprentices for their former master worker who is now in lonely retirement. A psychological character study.

839a *Man of a Special Cut.* Peking: Foreign Languages Press, 1963.

    A collection of nine short stories written between 1955 and 1960 about various aspects of life in post-Liberation China. The author is known to be a steel worker, and the collection is generally regarded as one of the best published before the Cultural Revolution.

(11) K'ang Cho: 1920-

840 *When the Sun Comes Up.* Peking: Foreign Languages Press, 1961.

    Written between 1949 and 1958, these six short stories reflect the life and attitudes of the people during the period of transition from cooperatives to communes.

(12) Kao Yün-lan: 1910-1956

841 SHAPIRO, SIDNEY, tr. *Annals of a Provincial Town.* Peking: Foreign Languages Press, 1959.

    The author was a witness to the famous jailbreak in Amoy in 1930. After more than twenty years, at the urging of many friends, he has finally recorded his experience in a novel which tells of the imprisonment, torture, and escape of some Communist Party members from the Kuomintang prison. Although the jailbreak took place in 1930, the author places it in 1935.

(13) Li Chun: 1928-

842 *Not That Road and Other Stories.* Peking: Foreign Languages Press, 1962.

    A collection of eight short stories by Li Chun, including "Not That Road" and others.

(14) Li Liu-ju: 1887-

843 *Sixty Stirring Years.* Peking: Foreign Languages Press, 1961.

    An unusual novel which begins in 1898 during the Reform Movement led by K'ang Yu-wei and Liang Ch'i-ch'ao. This first volume of a projected three-volume series covers the period from 1898 to 1911 and describes the changes in Chinese society during those years.

(15) Liang Pin: 1914-

844 FANG, MING. "How Liang Pin Came to Write *Keep the Red Flag Flying.*" *ChL,* no. 7 (July, 1960), pp. 124-130.

    Gives the historical background to Liang Pin's novel *Keep the Red Flag Flying*

845 YANG, GLADYS, tr. *Keep the Red Flag Flying.* Peking: Foreign Languages Press, 1961.

    This novel describes the struggles of three generations of two peasant families, the Chus and the Yens, who fight against social and economic injustices in the 1920s and '30s. Their struggle in the countryside is reinforced by the Communist Party-directed student movements in the cities. A student strike in the 1930s at No. 2 Normal School in Paoting is another focal point of the novel.

846 YANG, GLADYS and KU PING-HSIN, trs. "A Tale of the Green Woods." *ChL*, no. 3 (March, 1961), pp. 97-100.
   An excerpt from Liang Pin's *The Flames Spread*, a sequel to *Keep the Red Flag Flying*. *The Flames Spread* describes the guerrilla activities of patriotic Chinese against the Kuomintang and the Japanese.

(16) Lin Yin-ju (1923?-)

847 YANG, GLADYS and CHIU SHA, trs. "In an Old City." *ChL*, no. 11 (Nov., 1965), pp. 3-68; no. 12 (Dec., 1965), pp. 36-96.
   Excerpts from the novel *In an Old City*, which describes the Chinese struggles against the Japanese during the Sino-Japanese War.

(17) Lo Kuang-pin

848 CHAO, YANG. "*The Red Crag*. A Modern Epic." *ChL*, no. 5 (May, 1965), pp. 89-97.
   Gives background information about Lo Kuang-pin's novel *The Red Crag*.

849 SHAPIRO, SIDNEY, tr. "*The Red Crag*." *ChL*, no. 5 (May, 1962), pp. 3-32; no. 6 (June, 1962), pp. 3-57; no. 7 (July, 1962), pp. 64-95.
   Translation of several parts of the novel *The Red Crag*, which tells of political prisoners captured by the Kuomintang (KMT) in Chungking during the Sino-Japanese war in the early 1940s. The story centers on the activities of two individuals, Sister Chiang and Hsu Yun-feng, who are later executed by the KMT. The novel, vast in scope, describes a large number of characters and their struggles in various parts of the country.

(18) Lu Chu-kuo: 1928-

850 CONDRON, A. M., tr. *The Battle of Sangkumryung*. Peking: Foreign Languages Press, 1961.
   A novel about the Battle of Sangkumryung in Korea fought by the Chinese People's Volunteer Army against the United States forces in 1952. The author's account is in part based on his personal experience on the Korean front, where he worked as a reporter.

(19) Ma Chia: 1910-

851 *Unfading Flowers*. Peking: Foreign Languages Press, 1961.
   An unusual novel about a group of Eighth Route Army cadres who meet with hostile forces in Inner Mongolia. Set in the windy steppes of Inner Mongolia in the spring of 1946.

(20) Pai Wei: 1911-

852 YANG, HSIEN-YI and GLADYS YANG, trs. *The Chus Reach Haven*. Peking: Foreign Languages Press, 1956. (First published in 1954.)
   A short novel about the suffering of a peasant family, the Chus, and how the agricultural reform considerably improves their situation.

(21) Shih Wen-chü

853 "A Young Hero." *ChL*, no. 8 (August, 1975), pp. 3-63.
Translation of an excerpt from the novel *Red Tassels on the Battleground*, published in 1973. It tells how a young boy gets involved with the People's Liberation Army.

(22) Wang T'ieh

854 BIRCH, CYRIL, tr. "The Smashing of the Dragon King." In Cyril Birch, ed. *Anthology of Chinese Literature.* New York: Grove Press, 1965-1972, II, pp. 402-429.
A short story about the fight against superstition which is personified in Zodiac Mah in a peasant village.

(23) Yang Shuo: 1913-1968

855 *Snowflakes.* Peking: Foreign Languages Press, 1961.
A story about a child and his mother, who searches for her missing husband during the war against Japan. The mother dies, but the boy succeeds in finding his father.

856 YUAN, KO-CHIA, tr. *A Thousand Miles of Lovely Land.* Peking: Foreign Languages Press, 1957.
Based on the author's own experiences in the Korean War, this novel sings the heroic deeds of the Chinese workers who help the Koreans maintain a key railroad.

XIV
Taiwan Writers Since 1949

Taiwan fiction, a very much neglected field until the early 1970s, refers to works dealing with Taiwan and written since 1949 by both native Taiwanese writers and those from the mainland. Ch'en Ying-chen is the best representative of the former while Pai Hsien-yung can be viewed as a good example of the latter. During the past several years a few anthologies and a number of critical studies have been published; a symposium on Taiwan fiction was held in February, 1979; its papers, to be edited by Jeannette Faurot, will be published soon.

This chapter is divided into three sections: General Studies, Anthologies, and Individual Writers (arranged in alphabetical order). Among the scholars specializing in Taiwan fiction, C. T. Hsia was the first to bring such a body of literature to the attention of the Western reader. Joseph S. M. Lau and a few others have also been promoting the study of Taiwan fiction vigorously. Three anthologies are particularly useful and important: *Twentieth-Century Chinese Stories*, edited by C. T. Hsia with the assistance of Joseph S. M. Lau; *Chinese Stories from Taiwan: 1960-1970*, edited by Joseph S. M. Lau and Timothy A. Ross; and *An Anthology of Contemporary Chinese Literature*, in two volumes, edited by Chi Pang-yuan and others. All three contain biographical information on individual authors. As for critical studies, C. T. Hsia has published a number of important works. His foreword to Joseph Lau's *Chinese Stories from Taiwan* and his other articles are important contributions. Lau's studies of Pai Hsien-yung and Ch'en Ying-chen and Timothy Ross's works on Chiang Kuei are noteworthy. (In fact, only Pai and Chiang Kuei have received much critical attention.) Ross has also published a very informative survey of recent criticism of Taiwan fiction.

General Studies

857   CHEN, LUCY H. "Literary Formosa." In Mark Mancall, ed., *Formosa Today*. New York: Frederick A. Praeger, 1964, pp. 131-141.
      A discussion of Taiwan's literary scene, the article raised a number of questions regarding the timidity of Taiwanese writers in tackling important issues.

857a CHI, PANG-YUAN. "Nostalgia as a Literary Disguise of Positive Thinking." *The Chinese P.E.N.*, (Autumn, 1978), pp. 33-42.
   A discussion of nostalgia as a literary disguise of positive thinking in Chu-Hsi-ning's "The Dawn," Ssu-ma Chung-yüan's "The Mountain," and P'eng Ko's "Mr. Candlestick."

857b FAUROT, JEANNETTE L., ed. *Chinese Fiction from Taiwan: Critical Perspectives*. Bloomington: Indiana University Press, 1980.
   A collection of eleven papers delivered at a symposium on Taiwan fiction held at the University of Texas in February, 1979.

858 HSIA, C. T. "The Continuing Obsession with China: Three Contemporary Writers." *RNL*, 6 (Spring, 1975), 76-99.
   The author examines the works of three Taiwan authors, including fiction writers Pai Hsien-yung and Chiang Kuei, and poet-essayist Yu Kuang-chung, and their obsession with the social and political issues, problems, and realities of modern and contemporary China.

859 ———. "Foreword." In Joseph S. M. Lau and Timothy A. Ross, eds. *Chinese Stories from Taiwan: 1960-1970*. New York: Columbia University Press, 1976, pp. ix-xxvii.
   An informative survey of major Taiwan fiction writers.

860 ———. *A History of Modern Chinese Fiction*.
   For annotations and bibliographic information, *see* no. 238. Discussions of several Taiwan writers are included in the appendices.

861 LAU, JOSEPH S. M. "The Concept of Time and Reality in Modern Chinese Fiction." *TR*, 4, no. 1 (1973), 25-40.
   An essay on Taiwan writers and in particular Ch'i-teng Sheng, who writes most consistently in the allegorical manner.

862 ———. "How Much Truth Can a Blade of Grass Carry: Ch'en ying-chen and the Emergence of Native Taiwanese Writers." *JAS*, 32 (Aug., 1973), 623-638.
   An essay on the works of native Taiwanese writers, especially those of Ch'en Ying-chen, a young writer arrested in 1968 for his alleged anti-government activities and not released until 1975. Alone of his contemporaries, Ch'en dares to address himself to politically sensitive issues in his fiction. Among the works discussed are Ch'en Jo-hsi's "The Last Performance" and Lin Huai-min's "Cicada" as well as Ch'en Ying-chen's "The Comedy of T'ang Ch'ien" and "The Country Teacher."

862a NATIONAL CENTRAL LIBRARY. *Directory of Contemporary Authors of the Republic of China*.
   For annotations and bibliographic information, *see* no. 42A.

863   ROSS, TIMOTHY A. "Taiwan Fiction: A Review of Recent Criticism." *JCLTA*, 13 (1978), 72-80.
    A survey of recent criticism of Taiwan fiction.

863a TUNG, CONSTANTINE P. C. "Current Literary Scene in Taiwan: An Observation." *Asian Thought and Society*, 3 (1978), 338-345.
    An observation on Taiwan's current literary scene, including the *hsiang-t'u wen-hsüeh* ("native soil literature") movement.

864   YANG, WINSTON L. Y. and NATHAN K. MAO. "Literature, Chinese."
    For annotations and bibliographic information, *see* no. 751.

865   YEN, YUAN-SHU. "The Japan Experience in Taiwanese Fiction." *TR*, 4, no. 2 (Oct., 1973), 167-188.
    An interesting article on the experience of the Taiwanese under Japanese occupation (1895-1945) as described in selected works of Taiwan fiction.

866   ———. "Social Realism in Recent Chinese Fiction in Taiwan." In *Thirty Years of Turmoil in Asian Literature*. Taipei: The Taipei Chinese Center, International P.E.N., 1976, pp. 197-231.
    A study of social realism as reflected in the works of seven Taiwan writers.

866a YIP, WAI-LIM, ed. *Chinese Arts and Literature: A Survey of Recent Trends*. Baltimore: School of Law, University of Maryland, 1977.
    A collection of survey articles on Taiwan's art and literature, including a translation of two stories by Ch'en Jo-hsi and an article on Ch'en's stories by Joseph S. M. Lau.

Anthologies

867   *Asian and Pacific Short Stories*. Rutland, Vt.: Charles E. Tuttle, 1974.
    A collection of stories from East Asian and South Pacific island countries, including those of Taiwan writers.

868   CHI, PANG-YUAN, et al., eds. *An Anthology of Contemporary Chinese Literature*. Taipei: National Institute for Compilation and Translation, 1975. 2 vols.
    These two volumes represent the most ambitious and comprehensive attempt to gather in one collection representative works of Taiwan writers from 1950 through 1975. The first volume contains 191 poems by twenty-two poets, and 32 essays by seventeen essayists. The second volume contains 23 stories by seventeen authors. Most of the essays reflect a nostalgic preoccupation with either the mainland or old Taipei. Among the 23 short stories, some are set on the mainland before 1949 and the others are concerned with Taiwan. This anthology well reflects the achievements in Taiwan literature despite the uneven quality of individual translations.

869 DAY, CLARENCE BURTON, ed. *The Candleberry Tales: Tall Tales out of the Far East.* Taipei: Chinese Materials Center, 1972.
    A collection of twelve tales from the Far East, including some by Taiwan writers.

870 HSIA, C. T., ed. *Twentieth Century Chinese Stories.*
    For annotations and bibliographic information, *see* no. 317. Contains three stories by Taiwan writers: Nieh Hua-ling, Shui Ching, and Pai Hsien-yung.

871 ING, NANCY CHANG, tr. *The Ivory Balls and Other Stories.* Taipei: Mei Ya Publications, 1970.
    Includes six stories by the following Taiwan writers: P'eng Ko, Chu Hsi-ning, Kung-sun Yen, Chung Cheng, Wang Lan, and Pan Lei.

872 ———. *New Voices: Stories and Poems by Young Chinese Writers.* 2nd ed. San Francisco: Chinese Materials Center, 1980 (First published in 1962).
    A well-selected collection of stories and poems by young authors in Taiwan, some of whom have now become major writers.

873 JOSE, F. SIONIL, ed. *Asian P.E.N. Anthology.* New York: Solidaridad, 1966.
    Contains short stories and poems from Asian countries, including the works of two Taiwan writers: Chu Hsi-ning's "Molten Iron" and Hsü Chung-pai's "Time of No Return."

874 LAU, JOSEPH S. M. and TIMOTHY A. ROSS, eds. *Chinese Stories from Taiwan: 1960-1970.* New York: Columbia University Press, 1976.
    This anthology includes, in addition to Pai Hsien-yung, ten major authors brought up and educated in Taiwan: Ch'en Jo-hsi, Wang Wen-hsing, Ch'en Ying-chen, Ch'i-teng Sheng, Wang Chen-ho, Yü Li-hua, Chang Hsi-kuo, Huang Ch'un-ming, Lin Huai-min, and Yang Ch'ing-ch'u. Either raised or educated in Taiwan, they represent the "second-generation" writers on Taiwan, and their works are thematically different from those of the émigré writers of the older generation whose nostalgic longings for their past on the mainland have kept them from focusing on their experiences in Taiwan. The stories, some written in ironic and others in humorous or straightforward styles, describe the low life in the cities, the harsh life of the peasants in the countryside, and the conflicts between Chinese and Western values, identity crisis, alienation, and drug problems. Undoubtedly the best anthology of Taiwan fiction, it also contains a foreword by C. T. Hsia, biographical sketches of the authors, and a glossary in Chinese and English.

875 LAU, JOSEPH S. M. and C. H. WANG, eds. *An Anthology of Taiwan Literature.* Bloomington: Indiana University Press, forthcoming.
    A comprehensive collection of early and recent Taiwan literature.

875a *The Muse of China*. Taipei: Chinese Women Writers' Association, 1974; Taipei: Chinese Materials Center, 1975.
> A collection of prose and fiction by women writers in Taiwan, it includes seven short stories. Among the authors included are Lin Hai-yin, Yen Yu-mei, Ai Wen, and Hsieh Ping-ying.

876 NIEH, HUA-LING, tr. and ed. *Eight Stories by Chinese Women*. Taipei: Heritage Press, 1962.
> Contains stories by eight women writers in Taiwan: Huang Chuan, P'an Jen-mu, Chen Hsiu-mei, Lin Hai-yin, Ou-yang Tzu (pen name for Hung Tse-hwei), Eileen Chang (Chang Ai-Ling), Hou Jung-sheng, and Nieh Hua-ling.

877 WU, LUCIAN, ed. *New Chinese Stories: Twelve Short Stories by Contemporary Chinese Writers*. Taipei: Heritage Press, 1961.
> A collection of twelve stories by Chinese writers in Taiwan.

878 ———. *New Chinese Writing*. Taipei: Heritage Press, 1962.
> Contains short stories by seven Taiwan writers: Pai Hsien-yung, Shih Ko, Chiang Kuei, Chiu Nan, Hung Chih-huei, Fan Tu, and Nieh Hua-ling.

878a YIP, WAI-LIM and WILLIAM TAY, eds. *Chinese Women Writers Today*. Baltimore: School of Law, University of Maryland, 1979.
> An anthology of selected stories and poems by a number of Taiwan's women writers.

Individual Writers

1. Chang Hsi-kuo: 1944-

A native of Szechuan province, Chang Hsi-kuo received his high school and college education in Taiwan and his advanced degrees in the United States. A scientist by profession, he has written a number of novels, short stories, satirical essays, and works of science fiction.

Translations

879 KWAN-TERRY, JOHN, tr. "Earth." In Joseph S. M. Lau and Timothy A. Ross, eds. *Chinese Stories from Taiwan*. New York: Columbia University Press, 1976, pp. 145-194.
> A moving story contrasting the thinking of the Taiwanese and the mainlander. The former yearns fervently to move to the city, while the latter wishes to settle down in the country to be close to the soil and develop roots.

2. Ch'en Jo-hsi (Ch'en Hsiu-mei): 1938-

Born in Taipei, Taiwan, Ch'en Jo-hsi was educated at the National Taiwan University, Mount Holyoke College, and Johns Hopkins University. In 1966 she and her husband moved to China and stayed there until 1973. She now resides in Canada. Her early stories are concerned with the life of native Taiwanese residents while her more recent works deal with Chinese life during the Cultural Revolution.

Translations

880   CH'EN, LUCY H., tr. *Spirit Calling: Tales about Taiwan.* Taipei: Heritage Press, 1962.
      Includes five of Ch'en Jo-hsi's stories originally published in *Wen-hsüeh tsa-chih* (*Literary Magazine*).

881. GOLDBLATT, HOWARD, tr. "Residency Check." *The Chinese P.E.N.* (Autumn, 1977), pp. 1-27.
      A story based on the author's observations of life in China.

882   ING, NANCY, tr."The Fish." *The Chinese P.E.N.* (Winter, 1977), pp. 1-15.
      Another story based on the author's observations of life in China.

883   ——— and Howard Goldblatt, trs. *The Execution of Mayor Yin and Other Stories from the Great Proletarian Cultural Revolution.* Bloomington: Indiana University Press, 1978.
      A collection of eight stories reflecting the author's disillusionment with the heartbreaking human waste she observed. Among her characters are peasants, intellectuals, students, and party workers. Regarded by some as the first example of "dissident literature" in English about contemporary China.

884   ———. "Short Story Tells of Professor Forced To Do Manual Labor." *New York Times* (Dec. 13, 1977), p.8.
      Contains an excerpt from "Night Duty," included in Nancy Ing and Howard Goldblatt's *The Execution of Mayor Yin and Other Stories.* (see no. 883).

884a KAO, GEORGE. *Two Writers in the Cultural Revolution.*
      For annotations and bibliographic information, *see* no. 406c.

884b McCARTHY, RICHARD M. "Chen Jo-hsi: Memories and Notes." *Renditions*, no. 10 (Autumn, 1978), pp. 90-92.
      A brief introduction to Ch'en Jo-hsi.

885   ROSS, TIMOTHY A. and JOSEPH S. M. LAU, trs. "The Last Performance." In Joseph S. M. Lau and Timothy A. Ross, *Chinese Stories from Taiwan 1960-1970.* New York: Columbia University Press, 1976, pp. 3-12.
      "The Last Performance" is the moving tragic story of an actress addicted to heroin. The story "suggests the prevalence of an underground culture destructive of rural values," and the decline in popularity of the native Taiwanese opera.

885a WANG, CHI-CHEN, tr. "Ting Yun." *Renditions*, no. 10 (Autumn, 1978), pp. 93-100.
   The story of Ting Yun, who was very idealistic during the Cultural Revolution and who has eventually been awakened to the harsh realities.

885b ———. "The Tunnel." *Renditions*, no. 10 (Autumn, 1978), pp. 101-109.
   The story of Master Hung, a worker who has retired from an electron tube factory.

885c YIP, WAI-LIM, ed. *Chinese Arts and Literature*.
   For annotations and bibliographic information, *see* no. 866a.

3. Ch'en Ying-chen (Ch'en Yung-shan): 1936-

Born and educated in Taiwan, Ch'en had been a leading figure among native Taiwan writers until his arrest by the Nationalist Government in 1968 for his alleged antigovernment activities. Released in August, 1975, he is well known for his portrayals of ordinary men and women in Taiwan.

Translations

886 CHEUNG, CHI-YIU and DENNIS T. HU, trs. "My First Case." In Joseph S. M. Lau, and Timothy A. Ross, eds. *Chinese Stories from Taiwan, 1960-1970*, pp. 29-61.
   A well-written story which depicts a rookie policeman's investigation of his "first case"—the suicide of a pessimist.

Studies

887 LAU, JOSEPH S.M. "How Much Truth Can a Blade of Grass Carry? Ch'en Ying-chen and the Emergence of Native Taiwanese Writers."
   For annotations and bibliographical information, *see* no. 862.

4. Chiang Kuei (Wang Lin-tu): 1903-1980

A native of Shantung province and a one-time propagandist and military officer in the Kuomintang Youth Bureau and army, Chiang Kuei emigrated to Taiwan in 1948 and now lives in Taichung. His works deal mostly with the deteriorating social and economic conditions of China in the 1930s and '40s which eventually led to the success of the Communist movement in China.

Translations

888 ROSS, TIMOTHY A., tr. "The Whirlwind." *Renditions*, no. 2 (Spring, 1974), pp. 118-125.
   Translation of Chapter 9 of Chiang Kuei's 1952 novel *The Whirlwind* (*Hsüan-feng*). The novel spans the two decades from the 1920s to the 1940s and tells of the vicissitudes of the Fang clan. The chapter introduces the main character Fang Pei-lan.

889 ——. *The Whirlwind.* San Francisco: Chinese Materials Center, 1977.
A complete translation of the novel which affirms "the Chinese moral and revolutionary traditions without minimizing the national conditions of decadence that have made possible the rise and triumph of Communism" in China. It contains many mistranslations.

Studies

890 HSIA, C. T. "The Continuing Obsession with China: Three Contemporary Writers."
For annotations and bibliographic information, *see* no. 858.

891 ROSS, TIMOTHY A. *Chiang Kuei.* Boston: Twayne Publishers, 1974.
Essentially a biographical study of Chiang Kuei. The first three chapters are biographical and the next four introduce four important novels: *Breaking Free* (*T'u wei*), *The Whirlwind, The Two Suns* (*Ch'ungyang*), and *Swallow Tower* (*Pi-hai ch'ing-t'ien yeh-yeh-hsin*). The book contains excessive historical material.

5. Ch'i-teng Sheng (Liu Wu-hsiung): 1939-

Educated at Taipei Normal College, Ch'i-teng Sheng is the "most consistently parabolic" among native Taiwanese writers, and many of his stories are unintelligible to the average reader.

Translations

892 ROSS, TIMOTHY A. and DENNIS T. HU., trs. "I Love Black Eyes." In Joseph S. M. Lau, and Timothy A. Ross, eds. *Chinese Stories from Taiwan 1960-1970.* New York: Columbia University Press, 1976, pp. 63-73.
A story about the strange behavior of a quiet man who is supported by his wife. Caught in a flood, he saves the life of a young prostitute, and they are trapped by the flood on top of a downtown roof. The next day, when his wife, on the roof across the street, sees him with the strange girl, he intentionally ignores his wife until, desperate, she hurls herself into the rushing flood waters.

6. Chu Hsi-ning (Chu Ch'ing-hai): 1927-

Born in Shantung province, Chu Hsi-ning, prior to coming to Taiwan and a career in the army, was a student of fine arts in Hangchow. His writing career began when he was nineteen and since then he has published four novels and nine collections of short stories. He is noted for his "finesse of craft and diction."

Translations

893 HOU, CHIEN, tr. "Dawn." In Chi Pang-yuan, et al., eds. *An Anthology of Contemporary Chinese Literature.* Taipei: National Institute for Compilation and Translation, 1975, II, pp. 115-157.
In "Dawn" the author reworks an old story which supposedly took place in late nineteenth-century China. It is about the trial of a woman accused of

adultery, the rampant miscarriage of justice, and a young bailiff's exposure to the evils of society.

894 ———. "The Wolf." In Chi Pang-yuan, et al., eds. *An Anthology of Contemporary Chinese Literature*. Taipei: National Institute for Compilation and Translation, 1975, II, pp. 77-114.

Using a symbolic and psychoanalytical approach, the author describes the sad experience of an orphan brought up in his uncle's house and the torments he receives from his vicious aunt.

895 ING, NANCY CHANG, tr. "Molten Iron." In Nancy C. Ing, tr. *The Ivory Balls and Other Stories*. Taipei: Mei Ya Publications, 1970, pp. 45-56. Also in *The Chinese P.E.N.* (Spring, 1977), pp. 22-43; and F. Sionil Jose, ed. *Asian P.E.N. Anthology*. New York: Solidaridad, 1966.

Set in a village in north China in the waning days of the Manchu regime, this is a gruesome tale of family feuds and social change.

896 KAO, GEORGE, tr. "The Men Who Smelt Gold." *Renditions*, no. 1 (Autumn, 1973), pp. 107-121.

First published in the September, 1969 issue of *Youth Literature*, this story has aroused much critical attention. With its three denouements, the story presents three or more probable outcomes to an original case of human greed and invites comparison with the Japanese film *Rashomon*.

Studies

897 CHI, PANG-YUAN. "Nostalgia as a Literary Disguise of Positive Thinking."

For annotations and bibliographic information, *see* no. 857a.

7. Chung Li-ho: 1915-60

A native of Kaohsiung, Taiwan, Chung Li-ho belongs to the first generation of native Taiwanese writers. He started his creative career painfully, often plagued by poverty, illness, and lack of education under the Japanese occupation. Noted for its realism and rich native color and spirit, his fiction brought him posthumous fame when his complete works, including eight books of novels, essays, and short stories, were published recently.

Translations

898 ROSS, TIMOTHY A., tr. "Restored to Life." *The Chinese P.E.N.* (Spring, 1977), pp. 54-70.

A story of a young father whose troubled efforts to discipline his son lead to the boy's death; later he yearns to believe that the child has been reborn.

899 ———. "The Tobacco Shed." *The Chinese P.E.N.* (Spring, 1978), pp. 91-105.

A story about the contrast between the hard life of a landless Taiwanese peasant before 1945 and the more hopeful life of his son in post-1945 Taiwan.

8. Huang Ch'un-ming: 1939-

Born in Taiwan, Huang Ch'un-ming has held a number of odd jobs, from daytime laborer to executive. Though a vagabond by nature, he deeply loves his native town, I-lan (in northeastern Taiwan), and people of humble origin.

Translations

900 GOLDBLATT, HOWARD, tr. *The Drowning of an Old Cat and Other Stories.* Bloomington: Indiana University Press, 1980.
A collection containing some of the best stories by Huang Ch'un-ming.

900a ———. ."Sayonara, Tsai Chien." *Renditions*, no. 7 (Spring, 1977), pp. 133-160. Also in *The Chinese P.E.N.* (Autumn, 1975).
A very popular story widely read in Taiwan.

901 HU, JOHN, tr. "His Son's Big Doll." In Chi Pang-yuan, et al., eds. *An Anthology of Contemporary Chinese Literature.* Taipei: National Institute for Compilation and Translation, 1975, II, pp. 321-342.
A story about the humiliations suffered by an "adman" who is garbed from head to toe in the uniform of a European military officer and carries a billboard high above his head to advertise a feature movie shown at a local theater.

902 STEELMAN, DAVID, tr. "Two Sign Painters." *The Chinese P.E.N.* (Winter, 1977) pp. 48-87.
An interesting story about two sign painters in Taiwan.

903 WIEMAN, EARL, tr. "A Flower in the Rainy Night." In Joseph S. M. Lau and Timothy A. Ross, eds. *Chinese Stories from Taiwan 1960-1970.* New York: Columbia University Press, 1976, pp. 195-241.
The original title of this story (*"Yü-yeh hua"*) is "Days for Watching the Sea" (*"K'an hai ti jih-tzu"*). A story colored by local flavor, it sings of the virtues of a prostitute-heroine who accepts life with stoicism and optimism.

9. Li Yung-p'ing: 1947-

A native of Borneo, Li Yung-p'ing was educated at the National Taiwan University and now works as an assistant in the English Department of his alma mater.

Translations

904 FU, JAMES, tr. "A La-tzu Woman." In Chi Pang-yuan et al., eds. *An Anthology of Contemporary Chinese Literature.*, Taipei: National Institute for Compilation and Translation, 1975, pp. 459-470.
This is a story of racial prejudice revealed in a Chinese family's assertion of ethnic purity and its rejection of a daughter-in-law from Borneo.

10. Lin Hai-yin: 1919-

A native of Taiwan, Lin Hai-yin was born in Japan and educated in Peking. She was a founder of the respected *Pure Literature Monthly* and has published five collections of short stories and various works of children's literature.

Translations

905   HSIAO, LIEN-REN, tr. "Gold Carp's Pleated Skirt." In Chi Pang-yuan, et al., eds. *An Anthology of Contemporary Chinese Literature.* Taipei: National Institute for Compilation and Translation, 1975, II, pp. 9-23.
     The theme of the story is concubinage, and it protests against the treatment of concubines in Chinese society.

906   ING, NANCY CHANG, tr. *Green Seaweed and Salted Eggs.* Taipei: Heritage Press, 1963.
     Includes five of Lin's short stories: "Green Seaweed and Salted Eggs," "Lan I-niang," "Do You Want a Drink of Ice Water?" "Let Us Go and See the Sea," and "Certain Sentiments." Noteworthy are "Let Us Go and See the Sea" and "Lan I-niang," stories which show the author's ability to see things from a child's point of view. She writes about children, though not for children.

907   NIEH HUA-LING, tr. "Candle." In Nieh Hua-ling, tr. and ed. *Eight Stories by Chinese Women.* Taipei: Heritage Press, 1962, pp. 53-67.
     This is a sad story of a grandmother who has outlived her usefulness. Drowned in recollections of her past, she slowly fades away and dies.

11. Lin Huai-min: 1947-

Educated in Taiwan and the United States, Lin Huai-min has an M.A. degree from the University of Iowa. He is now teaching in Taiwan and writes about introverted young men withdrawn into their own sheltered worlds. He is also the founder of a modern dance troupe.

Translations

908   LIN, HUAI-MIN, tr. "Homecoming." In Chi Pang-yuan, et al., eds. *An Anthology of Contemporary Chinese Literature.* Taipei: National Institute for Compilation and Translation, 1975, II, pp. 443-456.
     In this story, the author satirizes the changes in his once quiet hometown and the craze among young students to study abroad.

909   ROSS, TIMOTHY A. and LORRAINE S. Y. LIEU, trs. "Cicada." In Joseph S. M. Lau, and Timothy A. Ross, eds. *Chinese Stories from Taiwan.* New York: Columbia University Press, 1976, pp. 243-319.
     "Cicada" ("*Ch'an*") vividly depicts a group of young men who drink coffee, smoke cigarettes, and spend their time idly without any idea of where their future lies.

12. Nieh Hua-ling: 1926-

Born in Hupei province, Nieh Hua-ling emigrated to Taiwan after 1949 and served as the literary editor of *Free China Fortnightly* for almost eleven years. A prolific writer, she now serves as director of the International Writing Program at the University of Iowa.

Translations

910   HOU, CHIEN, tr. "The Purse." In Nieh Hua-ling, ed. *The Purse*. Taipei: Heritage Press, 1962, pp. 3-22.

   The story of a woman who once applied for a government identification card under another person's name and added eight years to her actual age. Now thirty-four, she is regarded by everyone as an old spinster. To correct her mistake, she has to tell her whole story and may be subjected to a fine and embarrassment. One day as she goes over the contents of her old purse, she reminisces about her past, especially about one man who really cared for her. In an effort to recapture her lost eight years, she decides to accept whatever embarrassment it entails to have her correct age entered on her identification card.

911   HSIA, C. T., tr. "The Several Blessings of Wang Ta-nien." In C. T. Hsia, ed. *Twentieth-Century Chinese Stories*. New York: Columbia University Press, 1971, pp. 194-201.

   A condensed version of "Dinner" ("*Wan-ts'an*") included in *The Purse* (*see* no. 912), this story describes the humble but happy life of an ordinary teacher in Taiwan.

912   NIEH, HUA-LING, ed. *The Purse*. Taipei: Heritage Press, 1962.

   Besides "The Purse," translated by Hou Chien, this collection of short stories includes three other stories translated by the author herself: "Dinner," "The Sister," and "Old Lady Kao," as well as an article entitled "Am I the Heroine?", an answer to the question of whether the author is the principal character in her novel, *The Lost Golden Bells*.

13. Ou-yang Tzu (Hung Chih-hui): 1939-

A native of Taiwan, Ou-yang Tzu now resides in the United States. Her characters are psychic forces seemingly obssessed with their search for love or identity, a search which invariably ends in bitter disappointment.

Translations

913   CHU, LIMIN, tr. "Perfect Mother." In Chi Pang-yuan, et al., eds. Taipei: National Institute for Compilation and Translation, 1975, *An Anthology of Contemporary Chinese Literature*, II, pp. 357-374.

   The author relates a nightmare of human relations experienced by a girl called Tsing-ju. Finding it difficult to accept her widow-mother's remarriage to a man she doesn't consider worthy of her "perfect mother," she schemes for her stepfather to become romantically involved with her girlfriends, only to find out from her mother that her stepfather might have been her real father.

914 ———. "Vase." In Chi Pang-yuan et al., eds. *An Anthology of Contemporary Chinese Literature*, Taipei: National Institute for Compilation and Translation, 1975, II, pp. 345-356.

In the last scene of "Vase" (*"Hua-p'ing"*), the author employs tragic irony to show how the husband of a cool, independent woman crawls on the floor before a delicate vase—his symbol of perfection. In so doing, the husband indirectly expresses his extreme frustration at his inability to command his wife's respect.

14. Pai Hsien-yung: 1937-

Born in China, the son of a prominent Nationalist general, Pai Hsien-yung was educated in Taiwan and now teaches Chinese language and literature at the University of California, Santa Barbara. He has published more than thirty stories and is known for his critically acclaimed *Taipei jen* (*Taipei Residents*), a collection of stories describing the lives of Taiwan's "exiles" from the mainland. He has often been called a "rare talent" by critics.

Translations

915 BAUMGARTNER, MARGARET, tr. "Death in Chicago," *The Chinese P.E.N.* (Autumn, 1976), pp. 1-20.

A story concerned with the struggles, financial and emotional, of a Chinese student studying in the United States.

916 CARLITZ, KATHERINE and ANTHONY C. YU, trs. "The Eternal Yin Hsüeh-yen." *Renditions*, no. 5 (Autumn, 1975), pp. 89-97.

The story of Yin Hsüeh-yen, once a famous social hostess in Shanghai, who has maintained her popularity among the elite in Taipei, Taiwan, although the time and place have changed.

916a CHENG, STEPHEN, tr. "Miss Chin's Farewell Night." *Stone Lion Review*, no. 2 (1978).

An interesting story about the life of a popular night club dancing girl.

917 CHU, LIMIN, tr. 'Jung's by the Blossom Bridge." In Chi Pang-yuan, et al., eds. *An Anthology of Contemporary Chinese Literature*. Taipei, National Institute for Compilation and Translation, 1975, II, pp. 279-294.

The story of Mr. Lu, who cannot forget his past in Kueilin, which revolved around his romance with a Miss Lo. The past constitutes his life's total meaning.

918 ———. "One Winter Evening." In Chi Pang-yuan, et al., eds. *An Anthology of Contemporary Chinese Literature*. Taipei: National Institute for Compilation and Translation, 1975, II, pp. 261-278. Kwan-Terry, John, and Stephen Lacey, trs. "Winter Nights." In Joseph S. M. Lau, and Timothy A. Ross, eds. *Chinese Stories from Taiwan*. New York: Columbia University Press, 1976, pp. 337-354.

"Winter Nights (*"Tung-yeh"*) is the story of Professor Yü, who receives his college friend, the renowned Professor Wu Chu-kuo from the United States, at his humble house in Taipei on a winter evening. Over tea and snacks, both express their disappointments in life, even though Professor Wu seems to have acquired all the outward symbols of success, such as an endowed professorship at a prestigious American institution and international fame as a historian of T'ang China. The story is known for its subtle revelation of the tragedies of modern Chinese intellectuals and for its sharp contrast between the present and the past.

919 GRANAT, DIANA, tr. "New Year's Eve." *Renditions*, no. 5 (Autumn, 1975), pp. 98-105.

A story describing the celebrations of Chinese New Year's Eve in a military dependents' quarters in Taipei, during which Major Liu and others reminisce about their glorious past on the mainland before the Communist victory in 1949.

920 ING, NANCY C., tr. "Jade Love." *The Chinese P.E.N.* (Spring, 1976), pp. 53-114. Also in Lucian Wu, ed. *New Chinese Writing*. Taipei: Heritage Press, 1962, pp. 1-63.

One of Pai Hsien-yung's best short stories, "Jade Love" (*"Yü-ch'ing sao"*) is about the love and tragedy of a pretty nursemaid, named Yü-ch'ing sao. This powerful story is told through the eyes of a boy.

921 KAO, GEORGE, HSIEN-YUNG PAI, and PATIA ISAKU, trs. *Wandering in the Garden: Waking from a Dream*. Bloomington: Indiana University Press, forthcoming.

A collection of stories about the lives of Taiwan's "exiles" from the mainland, this anthology contains some of the best stories in Taiwan literature.

921a McFADDEN, SUSAN. "Death in Chicago." *TR*, 9, no. 3 (Spring, 1979), 344-358.

A story about the life and eventual suicide of a Chinese graduate student of English literature, who has become increasingly convinced of the meaninglessness of existence.

922 PAI, HSIEN-YUNG, tr. "Hong Kong 1960." *LEW*, 9 (Dec., 1965), pp. 362-369.

A short story about the reflections of the widow of a former division commander as she is involved in an illicit relationship with her opium-smoking, blackmailing lover. Written in the stream-of-consciousness style.

923 ——— and C. T. HSIA, trs. "Li T'ung: A Chinese Girl in New York." In C. T. Hsia, ed. *Twentieth Century Chinese Stories*. New York: Columbia University Press, 1971, pp. 218-239.

A story about the degradation of a Chinese girl in New York. Having lost her motherland and her parents to the Chinese Communists, she seeks gratification through success in her professional career. The story ends with success in her professional career and with her suicide.

Studies

924 ENCARNACION, ANACLETA M. "East-West Patterns in the Fictive Worlds of Six Writers." *TR*, 7, no. 2 (Oct., 1976), 149-174.
   A comparative study of East-West patterns in the fictive worlds of six contemporary Filipino, Chinese, French, and American writers. Pai Hsien-yung's "Li T'ung: A Chinese Girl in New York" is analyzed.

924a HSIA, C. T. "The Continuing Obsession with China: Three Contemporary Writers."
   For annotations and bibliographic information, *see* no. 858.

925 LAU, JOSEPH S. M. "'Crowded Hours' Revisited: The Evocation of the Past in *Taipei jen*." *JAS*, 35 (1975), 31-47.
   A study of one of the most gifted modern Chinese writers from Taiwan whose portrayals of characters from a past generation living in Taipei have attracted much attention in recent years. The characters living in this state of "suspended animation" are best illustrated in the story "Wandering in the Garden" from the anthology *Taipei jen (Taipei Residents)*, which at once captures the nostalgic strains of the past through sound and music and the emptiness of the present. Pai Hsien-yung, a young writer in his early forties, is one of the few Western-trained Chinese writers who have not given up their Chinese cultural identity either in thought or in language.

926 LEE, MABEL. "In Lu Hsün's Footsteps ... Pai Hsien-yung, A Modern Chinese Writer." *JOSA*, 9 (1972/1973), 74-83.
   A brief analysis of a number of Pai Hsien-yung's well-known short stories.

927 McFADDEN, SUSAN. "Tradition and Talent: Western Influence in the Works of Pai Hsien-yung." *TR*, 9, no. 3 (Spring, 1979), pp. 315-358.
   An analysis of Western influences on the themes, language, and narrative technique of Pai Hsien-yung's fiction.

928 OU-YANG, TZU. "The Fictional World of Pai Hsien-yung." *Renditions*, no. 5 (Autumn, 1975), pp. 79-86.
   A detailed examination of fourteen short stories in *Taipei Resident*, discussing Pai's acute contrast between "now" and "then," his three types of characters, his presentation of the war between the soul and the flesh, and his revelation of the riddle of life and death. This article was originally written in Chinese and translated by Cynthia Liu.

15. P'an Jen-mu: 1920-

Born in Manchuria and educated in Chungking, P'an Jen-mu is now the chief editor of the Children's Reading Program sponsored by the Ministry of Education in Taiwan.

Translations

929   HOU, CHIEN, tr. "Little World of Joys and Sorrows." In Chi Pang-yuan, et al., eds. *An Anthology of Contemporary Chinese Literature.* Taipei: National Institute for Compilation and Translation, 1975, II, pp. 41-53.
    This story portrays a teacher's happy adjustments to his teaching life in a small town in Taiwan.

16. P'eng Ko (Yao P'eng): 1926-

A native of Hopei province, P'eng Ko is a prominent newspaper editor and a prolific writer.

Translations

930   HSIAO, LIEN-REN, tr. "Mr. Candlestick." In Chi Pang-yuan, et al., eds. *An Anthology of Contemporary Chinese Literature*, Taipei: National Institute for Compilation and Translation, 1975, II, pp. 57-74.
    A nostalgic piece in which the narrator reminisces about a tall, lanky military officer called "Mr. Candlestick," who died valiantly in one of the battles against the Chinese Communists.

Studies

931   CHI, PANG-YUAN. "Nostalgia as a Literary Disguise of Positive Thinking."
    For annotations and bibliographic information, *see* no. 857a.

17. Shih Sung: 1946-

Born in Shanghai, Shih Sung, an artist by profession, in recreating the "No-cha" myth, has encouraged "many other young writers to dig for themes in the rich heritage of Chinese classics" and folklore.

Translations

932   CHI, PANG-YUAN, tr. "No Cha in *The Investiture of the Gods.*" In Chi Pang-yuan et al., eds. *An Anthology of Contemporary Chinese Literature.* Taipei: National Institute for Compilation and Translation, 1975, II, pp. 423-439. Hegel, Robert E. tr. "No-cha: *The Investiture of the Gods.*" *Echo*, 2, no. 3 (March, 1972), 47-52; 2, no. 4 (April, 1972), 40-44.
    A modern version of No Cha's sojourn on earth. No Cha is a colorful mythical figure in the sixteenth-century novel *Investiture of the Gods.*

18. Shih Shu-ch'ing: 1945-

A native of Taiwan and married to an American, Shih Shu-ch'ing now teaches drama at National Chengchi University in Taiwan.

Translations

933 McLELLAN, JOHN, tr. "The Oldtimer." In Chi Pang-yuan, et al., eds. *An Anthology of Contemporary Chinese Literature.* Taipei: National Institute for Compilation and Translation, 1935, II, pp. 377-400.

  A story of an old carpenter who reveals the loneliness and frustration of his life in the tales he tells to a younger man.

934 ———. "The Upside-Down Ladder to Heaven." In Chi Pang-yuan, et al., eds. *An Anthology of Contemporary Chinese Literature.* Taipei: National Institute for Compilation and Translation, 1975, II, pp. 401-420.

  This story of a mental patient is divided into several sections, beginning with "A Medical Conference," "The Intern's Fantasy: Number 1 A Myth," "The Intern's Fantasy: Number 2 Monologue of P'an Ti-lin, The First Day," and followed by "The Second Day" and "The Third Day." The story reveals much about the patient's as well as the intern's own abnormality.

935 SHIH, SHU-CH'ING, tr. *The Barren Years and Other Short Stories and Plays.* San Francisco: Chinese Materials Center, 1975.

  An anthology of five stories and two plays by Shih Shu-ch'ing, which "evidence[s] a certain fascination with what is strange or even a bit bizarre in human nature" and deals mostly with aspects of the author's childhood in central Taiwan and her experiences in New York.

19. Shui Ching (Yang I): 1935-

A native of Kiangsu province and a graduate of the National Taiwan University, Shui Ching is a serious writer who seeks to assimilate the techniques of Western masters into his own work.

Translations

936 SHUI CHING and C. T. HSIA, trs. "Hi Lili Hi Li . . ." In C. T. Hsia, ed. *Twentieth-Century Chinese Stories.* New York: Columbia University Press, 1971, pp. 204-217.

  In this story based on the author's experience in Borneo, the protagonist awakes to the sudden political changes which threaten his way of life. After repeated attempts to establish human contact in his nightmarish wanderings, he finds the jungle tempting and succumbs to the spell of his former girlfriend who beckons him to seek solace in the primeval forest.

20. Ssu-ma Chung-yüan (Wu Yen-mei): 1933-

A one-time professional soldier, Ssu-ma Chung-yüan came to Taiwan in 1949 and has now become a prolific writer of stories and novels.

Translations

937 CHI, PANG-YUAN, tr. "The Mountain." In Chi Pang-yuan, et al., eds. *An Anthology of Contemporary Chinese Literature.* Taipei: National Institute for Compilation and Translation, 1975, II, pp. 207-231.

  A story of how a heroic old man miraculously saves a town from pillaging by bandits.

938 ———. "The Red Phoenix." In Chi Pang-yuan, et al., eds. *An Anthology of Contemporary Chinese Literature*. Taipei: National Institute for Compilation and Translation, 1975, II, pp. 177-205.
    This story reveals much about pawnshop business in China and describes the deeds of one legendary connoisseur of antiques.

939 McLELLAN, JOHN, tr. " Toad Well." *The Chinese P.E.N.* (Winter, 1976), pp. 68-95.
    A story about the war between two feuding communities over Toad Well, a spring known for its magical power to cure scabbies.

Studies

940 CHI, PANG-YUAN. "Nostalgia as a Literary Disguise of Positive Thinking."
    For annotations and bibliographic information, *see* no. 857a.

21. Tuan Ts'ai-hua: 1933-

A native of Kiangsu province, Tuan served for many years in the armed forces. In his collections of short stories, he is noted for masculine themes and the creation of many larger-than-life heroes.

Translations

941 YEN YUAN-SHU, tr. "The Feast of 'Flower Pattern' Wine." In Chi Pang-yuan, et al., eds., *An Anthology of Contemporary Chinese Literature*. Taipei: National Institute for Compilation and Translation, 1975, II, pp. 235-247.
    Written in the early days of the author's career, this story takes place near the Peach Blossom Creek where the villagers are celebrating their landlord's daughter's wedding in a garden of 3,600 peach trees. The wedding proceeds well until a white horse runs wild. As the horse frightens and scatters the guests and swerves toward the bride, a wandering monk throws a cup at the horse and prevents the bride from being hurt.

22. Wang Chen-ho: 1940-

A native of Taiwan, Wang Chen-ho was educated at the National Taiwan University and was a visiting artist at the University of Iowa's International Writing Program (1972-1973). After achieving fame with his story "An Oxcart for Dowry," he has been writing plays, one of which, entitled "Hoping You Will Return Soon" ("*Wang ni tsao kuei*"), was published in 1973.

Translations

942 WANG CHEN-HO and JON JACKSON, trs. "An Oxcart for Dowry." In Joseph S. M. Lau and Timothy A. Ross, eds. *Chinese Stories from Taiwan: 1960-1970*. New York: Columbia University Press, 1976, pp. 75-99.

"An Oxcart for Dowry" ("*Chia-chuang i-niu-ch'e*") is not only an immensely funny tale written in a local dialect largely created by the author himself to achieve a comic effect, but also an allegory in its depiction of a middle-aged deaf man who allows himself to be cuckolded for economic gain. He, in the words of C. T. Hsia, is a "Chinese Job almost."

23. Wang Shang-i: 1936-1962.

A native of Honan province, Wang grew up in Taiwan and died of cancer in 1962. During his student days at the National Taiwan University, he wrote a number of short stories and essays which have been popular among young readers.

Translations

943   DEENEY, JOHN J., tr. "Chant of Great Grief." In Chi Pang-yuan, et al., eds. *An Anthology of Contemporary Chinese Literature*. Taipei: National Institute for Compilation and Translation, 1975, II, pp. 251-253.
   A story about the death and burial of a once-prominent government official and the career of his son, which make the narrator wonder about the ultimate meaning of life itself.

24. Wang Ting-chün: 1925-

Born in Shantung in 1925, Wang Ting-chün is one of the most productive and versatile writers in Taiwan today. He is also a critic, essayist, and playwright.

Translations

944   CHAU, SIMON, S. C., tr. "The Wailing Chamber." *Renditions*, no. 8 (Autumn, 1977), pp: 137-146.
   A widely read story written in 1974.

945   CHEN, UNA Y. T., tr. "The Soil." *The Chinese P.E.N.* (Summer, 1978), pp. 57-78.
   Another popular story widely read in Taiwan.

25. Wang Wen-hsing: 1939-

Born in Fukien province, Wang began his writing career when he was a student at the National Taiwan University. He was a cofounder of *Modern Literature* and now teaches at his alma mater. He is best known for his recent novel *Change in the Family* (*Chia-pien*).

Translations

946   CH'EN, CHU-YÜN, tr. "Flaw." In Joseph S. M. Lau, and Timothy A. Ross, eds. *Chinese Stories from Taiwan: 1960-1970*. New York: Columbia University Press, 1976, pp. 15-27.
   "Flaw" ("*Ch'ien-ch'üeh*") centers on a boy's awakening to his sexual needs and the perfidies of the adult world.

947 SHEN, LI-FEN, tr. "The Two Women." *The Chinese P.E.N.* (Summer, 1978), pp. 79-90.
   An interesting story about the life of a possessive woman married to a man in Taiwan who has left his former wife behind in Hong Kong.

948 ——. "Line of Fate." In Chi Pang-yuan, et al., eds. *An Anthology of Contemporary Chinese Literature.* Taipei: National Institute for Compilation and Translation, 1975, II, pp. 297-308.
   A story of an ugly fifth-grade child who reads the palms of his classmates, including that of a sickly child called Kao. The self-proclaimed fortuneteller predicts that Kao will live only to the age of thirty because his "life line" is very short. Deeply upset, Kao uses a razor to extend his "line of life." After a week in a hospital, he has an indelible scar on his left palm which looks exactly like a "life line."

949 ——. "The Man in Black." In Chi Pang-yuan, et al., eds. *An Anthology of Contemporary Chinese Literature.* Taipei: National Institute for Compilation and Translation, 1975, II, pp. 309-318.
   A story of a man wearing a black gown at a family banquet, which is designed to show the dark side of human nature. He has successfully advanced his own career through his clever schemes, and he unnecessarily frightens a young child by the faces he makes at her.

Studies

949a SHU, JAMES C. T. "Iconoclasm in Taiwan Literature: *A Change in the Family.*" *CLEAR,* (1980), 73-86.
   A critical study designed to demonstrate that the central theme of *Change in the Family (Chia-pien)* is iconoclasm on the most comprehensive level. The author concludes that the novel attacks not only the Chinese family system, but also Chinese ethics, Taiwan society, and human relations in a claustrophobic milieu.

26. Yang Ch'ing-ch'u: 1940-

Born in Tainan, Taiwan, Yang Ch'ing-ch'u publishes regularly in literary supplements to newspapers. Though he has been quite popular with his readers, few critics have taken his work seriously.

Translations

950 KELLY, JEANNE and JOSEPH S. M. LAU, trs. "Enemies." In Joseph S. M. Lau and Timothy A. Ross, eds. *Chinese Stories from Taiwan.* New York: Columbia University Press, 1976, pp. 321-335.
   A grim tale set during the Japanese occupation of Taiwan, "Enemies" ("*Yüan-chia*") describes how the Japanese police, in the name of Confucian morality, line up village girls and squeeze their breasts to see which one of them has abandoned a newborn infant in a public privy.

27. *Yü Li-hua: 1931-*

Born in Shanghai and educated at the National Taiwan University, she now teaches at the State University of New York in Albany. The author of a number of popular novels, she is regarded as the spokesperson for the "rootless generation," the exiled Chinese residing in the United States.

Translations

951 HSIAO, LIEN-REN, tr. "Glass Marbles Scattered All over the Ground." In Chi Pang-yuan, et al., eds. *An Anthology of Contemporary Chinese Literature.* Taipei: National Institute for Compilation and Translation, 1975, II, pp. 161-173.

The story of a woman who seeks to possess her brother permanently, and of his rebellion and final independence from her influence.

952 YÜ LI-HUA and C. T. HSIA, trs. "In Liu Village." In Joseph S. M. Lau and Timothy A. Ross, eds. *Chinese Stories from Taiwan: 1960-1970.* New York: Columbia University Press, 1976, pp. 101-142.

"In Liu Village" ("*Liu-chia chuang-shang*") is a tragic story which takes place in a village under Japanese occupation in Chekiang. The heroine, Ts'ui-o, after having been sexually assaulted by the village head, faces not only the enmity of her husband but also that of her stubborn and nasty mother-in-law, who nearly succeeds in ruining her life.

A Note on the Contributors

WINSTON L. Y. YANG, who received his Ph.D. in Chinese from Stanford University, is a fellow of the Royal Asiatic Society of Great Britain and Ireland and Professor of Chinese at Seton Hall University. He is the author or editor of the following books: *Classical Chinese Fiction* (G. K. Hall, 1978), *Modern Chinese Fiction* (G. K. Hall, 1981), *Critical Essays on Chinese Fiction* (Chinese University of Hong Kong Press, 1980), *Stories of Contemporary China* (Paragon Book Gallery, 1979), *Mao Tsung-kang* (Twayne Publishers, forthcoming), and *Studies in Traditional Chinese Fiction* (forthcoming). He is also a contributor to *Dictionary of Ming Biography* (Columbia University Press, 1976); *Encyclopaedia Britannica Yearbook*, (Chicago, 1978-80); *Chine Ancienne* (Paris: L'Asiathèque, 1977); *Proceedings of the 7th Congress of the International Comparative Literature Association* (Hungarian Academy of Sciences, 1979); and *Literature of the People's Republic of China* (Indiana University Press, 1980).

NATHAN K. MAO was educated at New Asia College (Hong Kong), Yale, and the University of Wisconsin (Ph.D., 1966). He is the translator of Li Yü's *Twelve Towers* (1975), Pa Chin's *Cold Nights* (1978), and Ch'ien Chung-shu's *Fortress Besieged* (1979); the co-author of *Classical Chinese Fiction* (1978); the co-editor of *Modern Chinese Fiction* (1981) and *Stories of Contemporary China* (1979). He is now Professor of English at Shippensburg State College, Shippensburg, Pennsylvania.

JOSEPH S. M. LAU received his B.A. in English from National Taiwan University and his Ph.D. in Comparative Literature from Indiana University in 1966. He has taught at Miami University (Ohio), the University of Hawaii, the Chinese University of Hong Kong and the University of Singapore. He is now Professor of Chinese at the University of Wisconsin, Madison. His English publications include *Ts'ao Yü: The Reluctant Disciple of Chekhov and O'Neill* (Hong Kong University Press, 1970); *Chinese Stories from Taiwan: 1960-1970* (Columbia University Press, 1976); *Traditional Chinese Stories: Themes and Variations* (Columbia University Press, 1978) and *Modern Chinese Stories and Novellas: 1919-1949* (Columbia University Press, forthcoming). He is now a co-editor of the Chinese Translation Series for Indiana University Press.

A Note on the Contributors

HOWARD GOLDBLATT, who received his Ph.D. in Chinese Literature from Indiana University, is Associate Professor of Chinese at San Francisco State University. His publications include many articles, translations, and book reviews. He is the author of *Hsiao Hung* (Twayne Publishers, 1976) and translator of *The Execution of Mayor Yin and Other Stories from the Great Proletarian Cultural Revolution* (Indiana University Press, 1978) and *The Field of Life and Death and Tales of Hulan River* (Indiana University Press, 1979).

MICHAEL GOTZ is a specialist in Chinese Communist Literature. He was trained at the University of California at Berkeley (Ph.D., 1977) and has taught Chinese literature at the University of California in Los Angeles. He is the founder and editor of *Modern Chinese Literature Newsletter*, which has published many articles and reports on modern Chinese literature. He is the author of several articles and book reviews, including "The Development of Modern Chinese Literature Studies in the West: A Critical View" (*Modern China*, July, 1976).

PETER LI received his B.A. from the University of Washington and his Ph.D. in Chinese Literature from the University of Chicago. At present an Associate Professor of Chinese at Rutgers University, he is a contributor to *Chinese Narrative* (Princeton University Press, 1977), *Traditional Chinese Stories* (Columbia University Press, 1978), and *The Chinese Novel at the Turn of the Century* (University of Toronto, 1980); the author of *Tseng P'u* (Twayne Publishers, 1980), and the co-author of *Classical Chinese Fiction* (G. K. Hall, 1978).

INDEX

A

"Aboard the S.S. Dairen Maru," 625
Acta Orientalia, 63
Alber, Charles J., 468, 469, 550
Aldridge, A. Owen, 161, 162
Anderson, Colena M., 592, 653
Anderson, G. L., 153, 312, 441, 458
Annals of Revolution, 830
Archiv Orientální, 64
Asia Major, 65
Asian and African Studies, 66
Association for Asian Studies, 1, 2
"*Autumn in Spring,*" 541
"An Autumn Night," 657

B

Bady, Paul, 402
Barmé, Geremie, 753
Barnes, A. C., 509, 674, 820, 834
"Battling South of the Pass," 827
Bauer, Wolfgang, 107
Baumgartner, Margaret, 665, 915
Benton, Gregor, 188, 699
Bernard, Suzanne, 519
Berninghausen, John, 189, 313, 506, 519a, 520, 700, 753a
Berton, Peter, 3
"Besieged in His Palace," 827a
Besterman, Theodore, 3a
Birch, Cyril, 154, 190, 191, 192, 193, 194, 314, 340, 402a, 507, 701, 702, 703, 704, 726, 727, 735, 741, 742, 750, 782, 854
Birnbaum, Eleazar, 4
Bjorge, Gary J., 584, 593, 594
Bohlmeyer, Jeanine, 347
Books Abroad, see *World Literature Today*
Boorman, Howard L., 5, 195, 196, 368, 491, 535, 562, 582, 597, 617, 705, 706
Borden, Caroline, 707
Borowitz, Albert, 197, 708
Boušková, Marcela, 654
Brandauer, Frederick P., 403, 521

Bright Clouds, 791
"*The Bright Road,*" 792
Brown, Carolyn Thompson, 339, 348
Bryan, Derek, 787
Bulletin of Concerned Asian Scholars, 68
Bulletin of the School of Oriental and African Studies, 69
Butterfield, Fox, 709
Buxbaum, David C., 108, 411

C

California, University. Berkeley. East Asiatic Library, 6
"*Camel Hsiang-tsu,*" 381
Carlitz, Katherine, 916
Carpio, Rustica C., 163
Ceadel, Eric B., 109
Centre for East Asian Cultural Studies, 7
Chai, Ch'u, 155, 315, 382, 507, 566, 599
Chai, Winberg, 155, 315, 382, 507, 566, 599
Chan, Marie, 643, 644
Chan, S. W., 710
Chan, Wing-tsit, 115
Chang, Eileen, 340, 341, 342, 343, 344, 345, 346
Chang, Jun-mei, 594a
Chang, Pei-chi, 638
Chang, Randall Oliver, 608
Chang, Su, 600, 793
Chang, Tang, 542
"Chang T'ien-i," 368
Chao, Ching, 800
Chao, Chung, 711
Chao, Lin, 821
Chao, Yang, 848
Chau, Simon, S. C., 944
Chen Charles K. H., 8
Ch'en, Chu-yün, 946
Ch'en, Li-fan, 947, 948
Ch'en, Lucy H., 857, 800
Chen, Pearl Hsia, 470
Chen, Po-ta, 471
Ch'en, Shih-hsiang, 110, 198, 712

Ch'en Shou-yi, 111, 112, 199
Chen, Tan-chen, 552
Chen, Una Y. T., 945
Chen, Yu-shih, 522, 523, 524
Cheng, Ching-mao, 200
Cheng, Stephen, 349, 916a
Cheung, Chi-yiu, 886
Chi, Ch'iu-lang, 9, 164
Chi, Pang-yuan, 316, 857a, 868, 893, 897, 901, 905, 908, 914, 917, 918, 929, 931, 932, 933, 934, 937, 938, 940, 941, 943, 948, 949, 951
Chiang, Ping-chih, see Ting Ling
Chicago University. Far Eastern Library, 10
Chih, Pien, 713
Chin, Ai-li (Sung), 201, 585
Chin, Ching-mai, 786
China Quarterly, 70
Chinese Culture, 71
Chinese Literature, 72
Chinese Literature: Essays, Articles, Reviews, 73
The Chinese P. E. N., 74
Chinese Studies in Literature, 75
Ching, Eugene, 202
Ching Ti, 567
Chinnery, J. D., 203, 472
CHINOPERL Papers, 76
Chisolm, Lawrence, 473
Chiu Sha, 847
Chou, En-lai, 714
Chou' Shu-jen, see Lu Hsün
Chou, Sui-ning Prudence, 404
Chou, Yang, 204, 715, 715a
Chow, Tse-tsung, 10a, 205, 206
Chu, Limin, 913, 914, 917, 918
Chu, Pao-liang, 11
Chua, Siew-teen, 474
Chung, Wen, 207
City Cousin and Other Stories, 754
Clark, Anne, B., 30, 254, 598
Clark, Richard D., 113
Clifford, William, 329, 431, 623
Columbia University. East Asian Library, 12
Comparative Literature, 77
Condron, A. M., 850
Contemporary China, 77a
Contemporary China Institute, 13
Contemporary Literature in Translaation, 78
"The Courier," 695
Craig, Albert M., 147
Criticism, 79

D

Davidson, Martha, 14
Davis, A. R., 114, 208, 209, 534
Dawn on the River and Other Stories, 755
Dawson, Raymond, 123
Day, Clarence Burton, 869

"Death," 692
De Bary, William Theodore, 115
Dee, Liang-lao, 836
Deeney, John J., 9, 165, 166, 167, 168, 169, 170, 943
De Keijzer, Arne J., 48
Dew, James E., 383
"Dilemma," 690
Doležalová, Anna, 210, 210a, 211, 212, 609, 610, 611, 612
Doležalová-Vlčkova, Anča, 619
Doleželová-Velingerová, Milena, 213, 475
Du, He, 716
Dudley, D. R., 33
Duke, Michael, 405
Durley, Carl B., 352

E

East-West Review, 80
Eber, Irene, 214, 215, 215a, 717
Echo, 81
Egan, Michael, 613
Embree, Ainslie T., 15
Encarnacion, Anacleta M., 924
Etiemble, René, 171
Etudes d'histoire et de littérature chinoises offertes au Professeur Jaroslav Průšek, 262

F

Fairbank, John K., 147
Fang, Ming, 884
Far Eastern Association, 16, 17
Faurot, Jeannette L., 857a
Feng, Yuan-chun, 117
Feuerwerker, Yi-tsi M., 216, 595
"Fifty Dollars," 696
"The First Step," 794
Fitzgerald, C. P., 118
Flame on High Mountain and Other Stories, 756
Flames Ahead, 809
Fokkema, D. W., 172, 173, 173a, 217, 218, 350, 476, 596, 718, 719, 776, 790, 816, 822
Franke, Herbert, 18
Frédéric, Louis, 19
Frenz, Horst, 137, 141, 174, 175, 180, 266, 274
Frodsham, J. D., 119
Fu, James, 904

G

Gage, Richard L., 120
Gálik, Marián, 219, 220, 221, 221a, 222, 223, 224, 225, 226, 525, 526, 527, 528, 529, 530, 531, 620
Gentzler, J. Mason, 20
Geoghegan, Anne-Marie, 128

Gibbs, Donald A., 21, 22, 719a
Giles, Herbert A., 121, 228
"Going to Cinema," 353
Goldblatt, Howard, 632, 632a, 626, 636, 881, 883, 884, 900, 900a
Goldman, Merle, 190, 200, 213, 214, 229, 230, 231, 264, 271, 281, 307, 308, 475, 476, 486, 494, 519a, 523, 595, 614, 622, 720, 721, 722
Goodrich, L. Carrington, 122
Gordon, Leonard H. D., 23
Gotz, Michael, 232, 233, 233a, 723, 839
Granat, Diana, 919
Gregory, Mary, 354
Grieder, Jerome B., 234
Gunn, Edward Mansfield, Jr., 235

H

Hales, Dell R., 236
Hall, David E., 24
Hanan, Patrick, 477
Hanrahan, Gene Z., 384, 508, 657
Hanson-Lowe, L., 478
Hartman, Charles, 25
Harvard Journal of Asiatic Studies, 82
Hawkes, David, 123
"The Heart of a Slave," 543
Heavensent, 385
Hegel, Robert, E., 932
Henderson, William, 725
Hightower, James R., 26, 124, 125, 176
Hinrup, Hans J., 26a
Ho, Yu-chih, 829
Holoch, Donald, 675
Hornstein, Lillian, 27
Hou, Chien, 237, 355, 893, 894, 910, 929
"How Lo Wen-ying Became a Young Pioneer," 356
Howard, Richard C., 5, 196, 368, 491, 535, 562, 582, 597, 617
Hsia, C. T., 238, 239, 240, 241, 242, 242a, 317, 341, 351, 355, 369, 376, 406, 479, 532, 553, 573, 574, 575, 602, 629, 650, 663, 668, 670, 672, 679, 724, 725, 726, 858, 859, 860, 870, 890, 911, 923, 936, 952
Hsia, T. A. 243, 244, 245, 480, 481, 621, 727, 728
Hsiao, Ch'ien, 246, 318, 624, 630
Hsiao, Lien-ren, 905, 930, 951
Hsü, Kai-yu, 28, 247, 319, 576, 729, 730, 757, 801, 805, 824
Hsü, Meng-hsiung, 509, 788
Hsü, Raymong S. W., 482, 770
Hu, Chang-tu, 126
Hu, Dennis T., 377, 378, 886, 892
Hu, John, 901
Hu, King, 406a
Hu, Shih, 248
Huang, Chao-yen, 825
Huang, Joe C., 249, 250, 731, 732, 733, 789, 802
Huang, Shou-chen, 601
Huang, Sung-k,ang, 483
Hucker, Charles O., 29
Hunter, Neale James, 251
Huters, Theodore David, 189, 313, 379, 700, 753a

I

I Knew All Along and Other Stories, 758
In Days of Peace, 817
Ing, Nancy Chang, 871, 872, 882, 883, 884, 895, 906, 920
International Comparative Literature Association, 177
International Federation for Modern Languages & Literatures, 127, 178
Isaacs, Harold R., 320, 427, 438, 442, 456, 459, 507, 510, 586, 599, 618, 638, 676, 685, 688, 692, 693, 694, 695, 696
Isaku, Patia, 921

J

Jackson, Jon, 942
James, Jean M., 386, 833
Jen, Richard L., 652
Jenner, W. J. F., 321, 357, 386a, 423, 434, 444, 460, 511, 638, 691, 697, 771, 803
Jose, F. Sionil, 873, 895
Journal Asiatique, 84
Journal of Asian Studies, 83
Journal of Oriental Literature, 85
Journal of Oriental Studies, 86
Journal of the American Oriental Society, 87
Journal of the Chinese Teachers Association, 88
Journal of the Oriental Society of Australia, 89

K

Kalouskova, Jarmila, 252
Kaltenmark-Ghéquier, Odile, 128, 253
Kao, George, 322, 387, 406b, 406c, 425, 640, 884a, 896, 921
Kelly, Frank B., 680
Kelly, Jeanne, 29a, 373, 374, 950
Kennedy, George, 427, 438, 442, 449, 456, 586, 589, 638, 688, 694
King, Evan (Robert S. Ward), 388, 627,
Kinkley, Jeffrey C., 577
Klein, Donald Walker, 30, 254, 598
Korean P.E.N. Centre, 179
Král, Oldřich, 554, 669, 673
Krebsova, Berta, 484, 498
Kroutilova, L., 669
Ku, Ping-hsin, 846
Kung, Pusheng, 587

Kung, Wen-kai, 30a
Kunst, Arthur, 180
Kuo, Helena, 389, 390
Kuo, Hei-hua, 813
Kuo, Thomas C., 255
Kwan-Terry, John, 879, 918
Kyoto University. Zinbun Kagaku Ken kyu-syo, 31

L

Lacey, Stephen, 918
Lang, David M., 32, 33
Lang, Olga, 555
Lao She, 407
"Lao She," 408
Latourette, Kenneth Scott, 129
Lau, Joseph S. M., 130, 256, 257, 323, 324, 533, 602, 668, 859, 861, 862, 874, 875, 879, 885, 886, 887, 892, 903, 909, 918, 925, 942, 946, 950, 952
Lechowska, Teresa, 370, 556, 557
Lee Bennett, 753
Lee, Leo Ou-fan, 34, 130, 258, 259, 323, 485, 486, 487, 614, 622, 631, 668, 734
Lee, Mabel, 926
Lee, Peter King-hung, 260
Lee, Sue Jean, 603
Lee, Yi-hsieh, 568
Lefevere, André, 181
Lervitova, I., 363
Li Chi, 735
Li, Fei-kan, *see* Pa Chin
Li, Hsi-fan, 808
Li, Peter, 60
Li, Tien-yi, 35, 36, 261
Li, Yun-chen, 22
Lieu, Lorraine S. Y., 909
Lin, Adet, 687
Lin, Anor, 687
Lin, Huai-min, 908
Lin, Yutang, 156, 325, 391, 488, 641, 642, 848
Ling, Scott K., 37
Link, Perry, 262, 263, 264, 391a, 686
Literature and Ideology, 90
Literature East and West, 91
"Little Erhei's Marriage," 777
Little Soldier Chang Ka, 837
Liu, Chün-jo, 37a, 265, 266
Liu, James J.Y., 131, 132, 133, 134, 135, 136, 182
Liu, Ts'un-yan, 267, 545
Liu, Wu-chi, 121, 137, 138, 139, 157, 268, 326
Living Amongst Heroes, 544
London. University. School of Oriental and African Studies, 38
Lu, Alexander Ya-li, 269, 736
Lu, Chien, 681, 783
Lu Hsün, 489, 490

"Lu Hsün," 491
Lust, John, 39
Lyell, William A., 392, 392a, 393, 452, 492

M

Ma, Ching-chun, 698
McCarthy, Richard M., 884b
McCaskey, Michael J., 270
MacDonald, William L., 327, 569, 578
McDougall, Bonnie S., 271, 272, 326a, 534, 569a, 604, 675a
McFadden, Susan, 927
McLellan, John, 933, 934, 939
McLeod, Russell, 670
McNair, H. F., 140
McNaughton, William, 158, 327
"The Magnet," 658
Malone, David H., 183
Man of a Special Cut, 839a
Mao, Nathan K., 60, 374, 357a, 375, 544a, 545, 558, 559, 665, 667a, 751, 752, 765a, 778, 864
Mao, Tse-tung, 273, 737, 738
Mao Tun, 637, 828
"Mao Tun," 535, 536
Mei, Yi-tsi, 274
Mei, Y. P., 141
Mélanges de Sinologie offerts à Monsieur Paul Demiéville, 142
Melyna, Gary G., 615
Meng, Tsiang, 588
Merhaut, Boris, 40
Meserve, Ruth I., 328
Meserve, Walter J., 328
Meskill, John T., 143
Miller, James E., 159, 401, 422, 507
Mills, Harriet, C., 493, 494, 495
Milton, Daniel L., 329, 431, 623
Modern Asian Studies, 92
Modern China, 93
Modern Chinese Literature Newsletter, 94
Modern Language Association of America, 41
Mondes Asiatiques, 95
Mote, Frederick W., 108, 411
"Mr. Pan in Distress," 676
"Mrs. Shih Ching," 772
Munro, Stanley R., 329a, 409
The Muse of China, 875a
"Mutation," 358
My Childhood, 804

N

Nan, Ying, 823
Nathan, Andrew J., 42
National Central Library (Taipei), 42a, 862a
A New Home and Other Stories, 759
New Literary History, 96

New York Public Library, 43
Nieh, Hua-ling, 330, 345, 579, 738a, 876, 907, 910, 912
Nienhauser, William H., 44, 144
Not That Road and Other Stories, 842
Nunn, G. Raymond, 45, 46

O

Odell, Ling Chung, 275
Okamura, Shigeru, 46a
"On Lau Shaw's *City of Cat People*," 410
"On the Threshing Field," 685
Oriens Extremus, 97
Orient/West, 98
Ou-yang, Tzu, 928

P

Pa Chin, 560, 561
"Pa Chin," 562
Pai, Hsien-yung, 921, 922, 923
"Pai Tzu," 570
Pao, King-li, 655
Paper, Jordan D., 47
Papers on China, 145, 276
Payne, Robert, 338, 367, 401, 430, 567
Phelps, Dryden Linsley, 277
Pickowicz, Paul G., 278, 279, 280, 281, 796
Pin, Chih, 662
Pollard, David E., 282, 283, 739
Posner, Arlene, 48
Priestly, K. E., 284
Prince, Anthony, J., 580
Pruitt, Ida, 394
Průšek, Jaroslav, 49, 146, 285, 286, 287, 287a, 288, 289, 290, 291, 414, 496, 497, 498, 537, 538, 554, 557, 580, 596, 611, 616, 619, 656, 673, 682, 683, 776, 784, 790, 811, 812, 816

R

The Railway Guerrillas, 832
Registration and Other Stories, 760
Reischauer, Edwin O., 147
Renditions, 99
Review of National Literature, 100
Rickett, Adele A., 148
Robinson, Lewis S., 326a, 569a, 651, 675a
Ross, Timothy A., 324, 859, 863, 874, 879, 885, 886, 888, 889, 891, 892, 898, 899, 903, 909, 918, 942, 946, 950, 952
Roy, David T., 292

S

Salisbury, Harrison E., 740
"Salt," 693
The Scarecrow: A Collection of Stories for Children, 677

Schultz, William, 49a, 293, 499
Schwartz, Benjamin I., 294
Schyns, Joseph, 50
Scott, A. C., 295
The Seeds and Other Stories, 761
Selis, David Joel, 684
Semanov, V. I., 500, 501
The Seven Sisters, 762
Seymour-Smith, Martin, 296
Shadick, Harold, 149
Shapiro, Sidney, 359, 395, 396, 507, 508, 512, 513, 546, 547' 633, 639, 646, 647, 659, 665a, 666, 667, 779, 785, 795, 806, 807, 818, 829, 831, 835, 838, 841, 849
"Shen Ts'ung-wen," 582
Shen, Yen-Ping, *see* Mao Tun
Shih, C. W., 741
Shih, Shu-ch'ing, 935
Shih, Vincent Y. C., 297, 298, 411, 539, 563, 583, 742, 743
Shimer, Dorothy Blair, 331, 431
Shu, Austin C. W., 51
Shu, Ch'ing-chun, *see* Lao She
Shu, James C. T., 949a
Shui, Ching, 936
Shulman, Frank Joseph, 23, 51a, 52
Sih, Paul K. T., 150, 299
Six A.M. and Other Stories, 810
Sixty Stirring Years, 843
Skinner, G. William, 53
Slupski, Zbigniew, 252, 300, 380, 412, 413, 414, 664
Snow, Edgar, 332, 421, 431, 443, 446, 457, 461, 514, 515, 549, 570, 589, 623, 625, 628, 638, 660, 690
Snowflakes, 855
A Snowy Day and Other Stories, 763
Sowing the Clouds, 764
Spence, Jonathan, 301, 744
Stallknecht, Newton P., 180
Stanford University. Hoover Institution on War, Revolution, and Peace, 54
Steeled and Tempered, 773
Steelman, David, 902
Stolzová, Marcela, 656
Stories of Chinese Young Pioneers, 356, 360
Stucki, Curtis, 55
Su, Chin, 774
Sun, Clara, 667a
Sun, Shirley Hsiao-ling, 502

T

Tagore, Amitendranath, 302
Tamkang Review, 101
Tang, Sheng, 548, 599, 689, 698, 814
Tay, William, 183a
Teng, Hsiao-p'ing, 744a
"They and We," 361

"The Third Gun," 628
Thirty Years of Turmoil in Asian Literature, 303
"Three to Five Bushels More," 678
"Three-Family Lane," 815
Tien Hsia Monthly, 102
Ting, Lee-Hsia Hsu, 56
"Ting Ling," 597, 598
Ting, Nai-tung, 56
Ting, Yi, 304, 744b
Toynbee, Arnold, 136
Trager, Frank N., 725
Transactions of the International Conference of Orientalists in Japan, 103
Tsai, Mei-shi, 57, 745
Tsao, Yu, 415
Tsau, Shu-ying, 362, 371
Tsien, Tsuen-hsuin, 58
Tsing Hua Journal of Chinese Studies, 104
Tso, Cheng, 352
Tu, Peng-cheng, 819
Tung, Chen-sheng, 785
Tung, Constantine, 305, 306
T'ung, Tso, 549

U

Unfading Flowers, 851
Union Research Institute, 58a, 58b
U.S. Library of Congress, 59

V

Vacca, Susan M., 590
Vochala, J., 363
Vogel, Ezra, 307
Vohra, Ranbir, 416
Voyage Beyond the Law," 660

W

Walravens, Hartmut, 59a
Wang, Chi-chen, 151, 333, 334, 352, 364, 384, 397, 398, 399, 417, 422, 425, 428, 433, 436, 439, 447, 450, 453, 462, 463, 503, 507, 516, 517, 541, 550, 645, 885a, 885b
Wang, C. H., 875
Wang, Chen-ho, 942
Watson, Burton, 115
Weakland, John H., 504
Wells, Henry W., 152
Wen I., 551
When the Sun Comes Up, 840
Widmer, Ellen, 308
Wieman, Earl, 903
Wild Bull Village, 774, 765

Wilhelm, Hellmut, 746
"Wistaria and Dodder," 605
Witke, Roxane, 216, 747, 748
Wivell, Charles, 184
Wolfe, Margery, 216
Wolff, Ernst, 309
Wong, Kam-ming, 796
Wong, Seng-tong, 310
Wong, Yoon-wah, 505
World Literature Today, 67
Wu, Eugene, 3, 59b
Wu, Lucian, 335, 336, 877, 878, 920
Wy Yang, 826

Y

Yang, Gladys, 365, 366, 400, 418, 419, 420, 423, 424, 426, 429, 432, 434, 435, 437, 440, 441, 444, 445, 448, 451, 454, 455, 458, 464, 465, 466, 467, 572, 591, 606, 607, 634, 635, 648, 649, 661, 671, 780, 781, 797, 798, 845, 846, 852, 887
Yang, Hsien-yi, 419, 420, 424, 426, 429, 432, 435, 437, 441, 445, 448, 451, 455, 458, 465, 466, 467, 591, 852
Yang, I-fan, 749
Yang, Richard F. S., 750
Yang, Richard H., 540
Yang, Winston L. Y., 60, 751, 752, 765a, 778, 864
Yang, Yi, 564
Yao, Hsin-nung, 421, 431, 443, 446, 457
Yearbook of Comparative and General Literature, 105
Yearbook of Comparative Criticism, 106
Yeh, Ch'ing-ping, 185
Yeh, Chun-chan, 337, 363, 518
Yeh, Shang-lan Mui, 565
Yen, Yuan-shu, 865, 866,941
Yeh, Yung, 775
Yenan Seeds and Other Stories, 766
Yeung, Ellen, 632a
Yip, Wai-lim, 186, 573, 574, 866a, 885e
Yohannan, John D., 160
Young, Lung-chang, 311
The Young Coal-Miner and Other Stories, 767
"A Young Hero," 853
A Young Pathbreaker and Other Stories, 768
The Young Skipper and Other Stories, 769
Yu, Anthony C., 187, 916
Yu, Fan-ming, 799
Yu, Li-hua, 952
Yu, Ping-Kuen, 61
"Yü Ta-fu," 617
Yuan, Chia-hua, 338, 367, 372, 401, 430, 856
Yung, Tung-li, 62

INDEXED IN Balay #BE1562
and
MLA Bib.

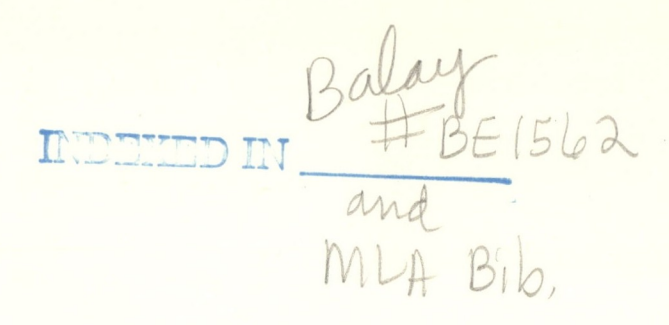

R0144014253 HUM R
                  895.
      45.00   S 109
                  YA1

YANG, WINSTON L.Y.
      MODERN CHINESE
FICTION

Houston Public Libraries
FOR LIBRARY USE ONLY